Born in Brighton and brought up in Suffolk, EMILY HAUSER studied Classics at Cambridge, where she was taught by Mary Beard. She attended Harvard as a Fulbright Scholar before going on to Yale to complete her PhD. She has now returned to Harvard as a Junior Fellow. *For the Most Beautiful* – the first book in the Golden Apple trilogy – was her debut novel and retells the story of the siege of Troy. Her second, *For the Winner*, is a brilliant reimagining of the myth of Atalanta and the legend of Jason, the Argonauts and the search for the Golden Fleece. *For the Immortal* brings the trilogy to a thrilling close.

To find out more, visit www.emilyhauser.com

Also by Emily Hauser

FOR THE MOST BEAUTIFUL
FOR THE WINNER

and published by Black Swan

For the Immortal

Emily Hauser

BLACK SWAN

TRANSWORLD PUBLISHERS
61–63 Uxbridge Road, London W5 5SA
www.penguin.co.uk

Transworld is part of the Penguin Random House group of companies
whose addresses can be found at global.penguinrandomhouse.com

First published in Great Britain in 2017 by Doubleday
an imprint of Transworld Publishers
Black Swan edition published 2018

A CIP catalogue record for this book
is available from the British Library.

ISBN
9781784160685

Typeset in 11/15pt Adobe Caslon by Jouve (UK), Milton Keynes.
Printed and bound in Great Britain by Clays Ltd, Elcograf S.p.A.

Penguin Random House is committed to a sustainable
future for our business, our readers and our planet. This book
is made from Forest Stewardship Council® certified paper.

1 3 5 7 9 10 8 6 4 2

For Athina, Natalia and Arabella, who started it all
and for Oliver, always

ὣς οἵ γ' ἀμφίεπον τάφον Ἕκτορος· ἦλθε δ' Ἀμαζών,
Ἄρηος θυγάτηρ μεγαλήτορος ἀνδροφόνοιο . . .

And so they buried Hector; and then came the Amazon,
the daughter of Ares, the great-hearted man-slayer . . .

Iliad 24, lines 804f.
According to an early manuscript of Homer's *Iliad*

Contents

Acknowledgements

At the close of the Golden Apple trilogy, I want to start by thanking my brilliant editor, Simon Taylor, and all the wonderful team at Transworld, who made all this possible in the first place. I will always be so grateful to you, Simon, not only for the chance you gave me to write and your conviction in the trilogy, but for your unfailing enthusiasm and your expert help and advice in making the books what they are. The same goes to the wonderful Tash Barsby: *For the Immortal* owes so much to your insight and comments – Hippolyta wouldn't be the same without you. A huge debt of thanks is also due to my fantastic agent, Roger Field, master of the re-shelve, whose firm belief in the trilogy, expertise in Mycenaean weaponry, and advice and support over the years have been indispensable. And I'm so grateful to all the team at Transworld who have brought my books alive so beautifully: my publicist, Hannah Bright, for her amazing ability to organize across multiple time zones; Becky Glibbery, Sarah Whittaker and the rest of the art department, who did such a fantastic job in designing the covers for the trilogy; my wonderful copy-editor, Hazel Orme; as well as Viv Thompson, Phil Lord and Candy Ikwuwunna. You are all a part of the Golden Apple trilogy, and I'm so grateful for everything you do and have done to help bring the ancient world to vivid life.

This book required perhaps more research than any other I have written, given the sheer quantity (and time span) of ancient sources traversed, the historical research required to get to grips with the Amazons, and the fact that – as a classicist – I have rarely ventured beyond the confines of Greco-Roman culture and language. I am therefore hugely indebted to several scholars for their generous time and expertise: Professors Prods Oktor Skjaervo and Jeremy Rau at Harvard University for their assistance with Scythian; as well as Sam Blankenship for her help with Old Persian and Avestan. I would also like to give particular mention to Adrienne Mayor's *The Amazons: Lives and Legends of Warrior Women across the Ancient World* (2014): Mayor's detailed and incisive history was what enabled me to move past stereotyped Amazon images to envision a living culture, and I am indebted to her. I am also grateful to Stratis and Elena who welcomed us so hospitably on our visit to Skyros, and to Caleb Dean and Emily Kanter at Cambridge Naturals for sharing their expertise in herbs and being tolerant enough to answer my questions about lemon balm.

As always, it has been my colleagues, friends and family who have supported me and given me the time, space and encouragement to enable the books to flourish. I am particularly grateful both to Yale University and to Harvard University for the supportive environments and outstanding resources from which I was lucky enough to benefit during the writing of the books, as well as the continuing advice and support of my inspirational mentors, Emily Greenwood,

Acknowledgements

Greg Nagy, Laura Slatkin, Diana Kleiner and many others. And, as before, I owe a great deal to the wonderful people of The Biscuit in Somerville, who always cheered me on from the sidelines, brightened my day with their conversation and laughter, and witnessed both the start and the finish of this book: Hannah, Ilona, Dava, the two Emilys, Ryan, Bryan, Andrew, Choo, Greta and all the others. And my family have been an incredible source of support, as always, helping me get the symptoms of malaria right, as well as listening with endless patience as I read passages aloud (always with voices).

My wonderful friends – Farzana, Alice, Zoe and Iyad, and everyone else – have been the backbone of these books from their very inception. This last of the Golden Apple trilogy is therefore dedicated to three dear friends in particular, Athina, Natalia and Arabella, who I met in Greece on our very own Greek Odyssey ten years ago this summer. I'm so very grateful to have the three of you in my life, and can't wait for more years of aubergines (and Classics) ahead. Finally, this book is dedicated, as always, to my incredible husband Oliver, whose support, love, encouragement and unfailing belief in me from the very first has made these past eight years both an adventure and a joy every day.

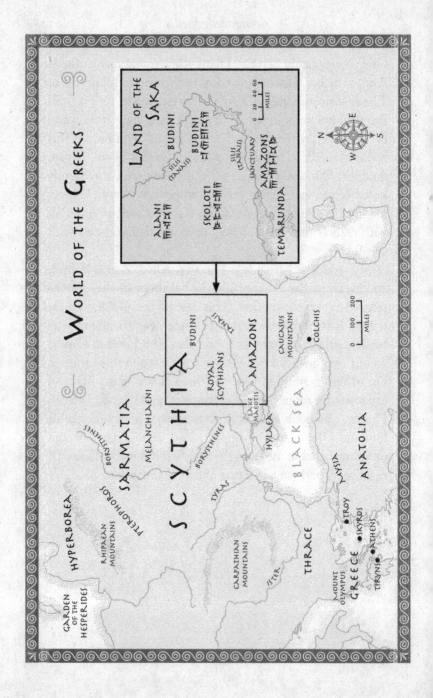

Prologue

The sky above Delphi is dark. All is quiet. The birds do not yet sing in this sacred place. The only movement is a torch bobbing, like a firefly, through the darkened underbrush, as a man walks along the winding path to the slopes of Mount Parnassus, where the oracle of the gods has her home. Here, in the fissure of rock where the gods' prophet dwells, is where boundaries blur, where the division between mortal and immortal is broken, rent in two, like a cut veil, and the words of the gods blow through the rift to men. Here all is slanted, strange. A mortal woman speaks the divine tongue. Steam, rancorous and bitter, billows up from the Underworld, breaking through cracks in the earth. And a cave, where a lone priestess crouches muttering over the holy smoke, will become the greatest sanctuary of all, summoning pilgrims from across the world, commanding gifts of gold and marble monuments to the prophet. In years to come, kings will crawl on their knees to hear the gods' commands, build their fate on the words of a mad priestess, while empires rise and fall to the will of the divine.

Here, in the crucible of the gods, destiny itself will be forged.
And the first prophecy is about to be made.
The figure emerges from the wooded path, his torch's light

sweeping the cavern into a gash of darkness, his boots trampling the sage-sprigs scattered on the ground. He crouches to enter the darkness of the cave, his eyes smarting and nostrils burning at the sulphurous smoke that fills it. As his vision adjusts he sees her: a woman hunched over the embers of a fire, her hair loose over her shoulders, her eyes wide, unblinking as she stares at him.

'You have come, then,' is all she says, and her voice is thick, as if it is a long time since she has spoken.

'You are Pythia?' he asks.

'And you are Alcides.' It is not a question.

He hesitates, thrown by her confidence, then masters himself. 'I am Alcides, son of Zeus and Alcmene, descendant of Alcaeus.'

'And,' she says, leaning towards him over the embers, 'you have something to ask of me.'

He does not answer, but props his torch against the rock where it turns the smoke drifting through the cavern into streams of orange-gold, and kneels before her. 'Yes.'

She pauses, apparently waiting, then says, 'You had better ask it.' She pokes at the ash with a stick. 'You have travelled far from Thebes to do so.'

He swallows, and uncertainty crosses his face, making him seem much younger all of a sudden: a boy, asking where he belongs, why he is here. Why his father did not want him.

'I want to know,' he says, his voice louder than usual, 'how I may join the gods.'

The priestess takes a deep, shuddering breath, a gasp that rattles through the cavern, extinguishing the torch so that the only light is the red glow of the embers. Smoke begins to swirl thick around her, and her eyes roll back in her head, white veined with scarlet.

'Pythia?' The man starts forward, as if to reach for her, but

her voice snaps him back, low, harsh, resounding through the darkness, as if the spirits of the Underworld are grating an echo to her words in the caverns of Tartarus beneath:

> 'Destined by Zeus to rule the race of the heroes of Greece,
> son of a god and leader of men, yet the anger of Hera
> stands in your way – and she, unappeased, shall cause you
> to fail. Zeus betrayed her, his wife, years before when he
> lay with Alcmene and begot you, a falseness and grief to
> the queen of the gods. Hera rages at you and all that you
> are, the proof and the object of her envy.'

She takes a rasping breath, ribs shuddering, her head lolling, as if the force of the gods that ploughs through her is too much for her mortal frame.

> 'If to appease her still is your wish and you seek to dwell on
> Olympus, hear my warning and heed it well. Twelve
> labours must you perform, twelve perilous tasks as no man
> before or after shall do, with fierce beasts to slay and lions
> to tame, then birds of bronze beaks and fire-breathing
> bulls, such as befit the first and greatest hero of Greece. For
> Eurystheus, king of Tiryns, shall you perform them and
> with his sons and daughter for ten years shall live till the
> tasks are done.
>   'Two fates therefore stand before you; two paths
> towards the end of death which you alone can choose. If
> you leave and take on the labours, never again shall you
> see your home, Thebes, but Zeus has sworn by his decree
> you shall become a god, and mortals across the earth for
> eternity shall worship you, son of a god with glory

*undying; and Hera has ruled that, if you complete them,
she shall accept you, and you shall be known as Hercules.*

*'But if you fail, or the labours reject, then she will
ensure you nameless shall vanish, unsung and obscure,
unknown and unspoken, immortal no more.'*

*She falls silent, slumped forwards, her chin on her chest. The eerie
light ebbs, the echoes of Tartarus are still, and the cavern is dark
once more. The man who will be known as Hercules watches her,
waiting for more.*

*'I have a choice?' he says at once, when she raises her head, her
eyes blurred in the blackness and smoke. A scowl darkens his features. 'I came to you, priestess, for answers. I came to know my
destiny, to learn the dictates of the Fates, to know what I should do.'*

'That depends on what you want.'

*He leans towards her, the answer coming quick as a breath of
wind skimming over water. 'Immortality.'*

*She considers him for a moment, and the sulphur smoke drifts
between them: the priestess weak, her breathing slurred, her gaze
fixed on the man, eager, desperate, fervent.*

'Then it seems, son of Zeus, you have made your choice already.'

*On Mount Olympus, one of the Muses stirs from her seat within
the Hall of the Fates. Concealed behind a pillar at the colonnade's
edge, so she may see and not be seen, she has been keeping vigil
through the night, gazing through the open portico, which affords
a view of the peoples on earth. The rosy fingertips of dawn are
creeping over the horizon, bathing the land below in soft light
and shading the birds flying across the shore into ink-like blots. To
the mortals in their dwellings in the valleys, as they wake and
prepare to cut their meadows with the scythe or pluck the grapes*

from the vines, it is simply another new day; but in the shadows of the night, an age has passed. A new era has begun. The Muse gets to her feet, draws her cloak around her and pulls her hood to shield her face.

At last, it is time.

She walks, her footsteps hushed and her figure shadowed in the near-darkness, towards an alcove hidden in the far corner where, when she slides back the screen painted to resemble the marble that surrounds it, a cedar chest is revealed, dark-stained with age and fitted with a bronze lock. The hall is lit only by a few oil-lamps, which are guttering to the very ends of their wicks, but Calliope, eldest of the Muses, does not need light to find her way. She looks around her, eyes darting between each of the scroll-laden shelves and the desks littered with papyrus and ink-stands, searching for intruders, for spies. The hall is empty, and there are no shadows or whispers to warn her she is being watched. She draws a key from the folds of her cloak and fits it with ease into the lock. There is a moment's silence, and then a click. The lid swings open.

And there they are: the three golden apples she and Hermes stole, all those years ago, when Hera and Zeus were newly wed and the earth-goddess herself fashioned an apple tree of molten gold to bless the marriage. For a moment, as the scent of cedar, mixed with centuries of dust, washes over her, she allows herself to be transported in memory. She remembers how, at Zeus and Hera's wedding-feast, when the gods were deep in their cups, she had whispered to Hermes, god of thieving, what she wanted to do; how, together, as night drew its dark veil over the banqueting hall, they had crept to the golden-apple tree and, as Hermes kept watch, she had plucked its fruit. She smiles to think how the earth beneath them had quivered and shaken at their perfidy, and they had run over the heaving ground, three apples clutched to her chest; how next day, climbing from her marriage-bed and setting the oak-crown on her head for the first time, Hera had discovered the apples were missing and raged at her loss, though she knew not who had stolen them. How she had set the three daughters of Atlas to guard the tree, one for each of the apples lost, and placed it in a garden at the world's end, so that none could steal again from the queen of the gods.

Calliope traces the curves of the apples with the tip of her fore-finger, one by one, as a mother would caress the cheek of her newborn child. Three spheres, smooth and round and gleaming in the low light of the lamps, their stalks like golden filaments, their surfaces polished. Each side by side within the box, encircled with engraved patterns of gold carved into the wood.

Three, she thinks.

One for each of them.

She glances over her shoulder, bright-eyed, knowing, as her gaze falls on the shelves and writing implements, that after what she is about to do she may never see Olympus again.

Knowing that she is risking everything on the greatest gamble she will ever take.

She snaps the coffer shut and tucks it under one arm. Turning to walk across the hall, her pace quickening now, her cape flying out behind her, she thinks only of where she will hide herself and her three prizes. She needs to be at hand, among the mortals, to wait to spring at the correct moment. It will be a delicate balance, to remain hidden from Hera, and yet to hold back until she is absolutely sure – and her choice of hiding-place will be of utmost importance. There are many places for concealment within the mortal world, but she has planned this day for thousands of years, purposeful and resolute as the Muse of Epic should be, and she has already made her decision. She will go to the vast forests at the world's edge, where the eagles soar, alone, brushing the tree-tops with their wings.

A moment later, she reaches the colonnade again at the edge of Olympus, and the expanse of sky that stretches from the mountain's brink to the horizon. She closes her eyes, standing between two lofty columns, the rock falling steeply away beneath her, to feel the warmth of the sun upon her face: the first light of a new age.

The last time she may ever see the sun from Olympus' peak.

She clutches the casket more tightly to her chest.

And then she sweeps her cloak around her and leaps, graceful as a swallow, into the emptiness of the morning air.

The age of heroes has begun.

AMAZON

Fifteen years before the Trojan War

*Hippolyta had a war-belt, a symbol of her prowess above
all the other Amazons; and Hercules was sent to fetch it,
because Admete, daughter of Eurystheus, desired it.*

Apollodorus, *Library* 2.5.9

Fatal Wounds

Hippolyta

Amazons, Land of the Saka

The Thirty-ninth Day after the Day of Storms in the Season of Tar, 1265 BC

The frost bit at my lips and stung my eyes as I vaulted onto the back of my horse Kati, heart pounding hard with the mixed fear and blood-lust that was my inheritance, and my duty as queen.

'*Go, go!*' I shouted, kicking at her flanks and pulling at the reins. She reared, her breath pouring from her nostrils like smoke, her eyes white, as the first riders galloped towards our camp, ploughing up clouds of snow from their hoofs, screaming battle-cries.

'Melanippe!' I shouted, and I circled her tent, ice crystals forming on my eyelashes. 'Melanippe!'

She emerged, tying her war-belt around her waist and carrying two spears. She tossed one to me, and I caught it left-handed, thrusting it into the straps of the baldric over my back. 'Budini?' she asked, glancing at the rust-red hair beneath the riders' stiff caps.

I nodded. 'They must know Orithyia has taken our troops

13

to Hialea. They mean us to surrender without a battle, else they would not keep their distance.'

She snorted. 'Without a battle? Then they do not know the Amazons.' She vaulted onto the back of her horse, a high-necked black with a white mark upon his forehead. She was about to ride out when I reached forwards and placed my hand upon her arm, my gaze searching her face. 'The children of the tribe – Teuspa remains to protect them, as before?'

Her eyes rested briefly upon mine. 'Teuspa stays, along with his guard.'

I nodded my approval, and she galloped off towards the other tents. I pulled Kati around and circled back, eyes scanning the camp, picking out the figure of the councillor, Agar; Ioxeia, the aged and skilful priest of the tribe, wearing her wolf-pelt over her shoulders; Toxis, tightening her war-belt and fastening her daughter Polemusa's baldric, readying herself for battle. Many of the Amazons were already throwing felt rugs over their horses' backs and mounting, leather boots crusted with snow, iron daggers glinting in the low evening light, bows and quivers hanging from their belts, shields slung over their shoulders on straps.

Though the wind was howling across the plain, slicing at the exposed skin on my face and whistling in my ears, so that I could hardly hear the cries of the invaders, I rode out before all my warriors, determined to give them a sight of their queen before we joined battle. They brought their horses into line as I passed, the band of my twelve finest warrior-women first, then the young girls just ripening to womanhood, Polemusa among them, men with greying beards flecked with snow and boys with the slim limbs of youth. They bowed their heads to their horses' necks, and my deer-hide cloak flew behind me as I rode, nodding to each in turn, my throat tight and my breathing sharp, as it always was before battle. I reached the end of the line and held my bow to the lowering skies, the general of this ice-hardened army.

'*Oiorpata!*' I cried.

'*Oiorpata!*' The Amazons returned the *uran*, the battle-cry.

Melanippe rode forwards, and I nodded to her, once. At my signal, my warrior-guard peeled off from the rest of the troops, their horses cantering behind Melanippe away through the camp, smooth as ripples on water, shields bouncing against their backs.

'*Oiorpata!*' I cried again, to the rest of the warriors, and I wheeled around, then galloped towards the camp's edge where the Budini were still circling, whirling their pointed bronze *sagaris*-axes around their heads and yelling their cries of battle. I urged my horse on, head bent against the wind, and behind me I heard the beat of many hundred hoofs against the snow and the swish of arrows past my ears as the Amazons sent a deadly hail upon the invaders. I let go of the reins, guiding Kati with my knees as my mother had taught me when I was young, and Kati a spindle-legged foal. I drew four red-striped shafts from my quiver and set them to my bow, drew back the string with my thumb and fired the first, then the second, third and fourth in rapid succession as I galloped on, easeful as a sharp-keeled ship cutting through the waves. I saw each hit their target, three Budini warriors toppling from their mounts with a dull *thud* and a scream of pain, and gritted my teeth; the fourth clutched at his arm as blood poured through his tunic and spread upon the ground with a dark red stain.

Ahead, the Budini regrouped, falling back into a single mass of armoured warriors, pointed *sagaris* held weighted in their hands, horses stamping nervously at the ground. I smiled grimly and drew my spear to my shoulder, my other hand resting upon Kati's neck, and hurled it, straight and graceful as a flying bird. There was a shriek of agony and a *thump* as a Budini slumped forwards, the spear shaft buried in his chest. His horse bucked and reared and he slid off into the snow, legs stuck out beneath him. The Budini howled, raised their battle-axes and hammered them upon their shields, then charged towards us, yelling and whirling their *sagaris* around and around their heads.

It was time – the hammering of my heart in my chest was telling me so. Melanippe and my guard would have reached the riverbank.

The Budini would see, now, why we were the most skilled warriors among the people of the Saka.

'Retreat!' I cried. 'Retreat!'

I barely touched the reins for Kati to turn, and around me the masses of Amazon troops were wheeling back, stamping down the snow, manes flying out in the wind as we galloped faster than circling birds, racing away from the camp towards the frozen expanse of the Silis river and the hunched snow-covered trees. Behind us the Budini whooped and hissed and clattered their battle-axes upon their shields. I glanced over my shoulder, saw them following, shrieking, teeth white in the gathering dusk. *Only a moment longer*, I told myself as my hips thudded into my horse's back and the glimmer of the campfires retreated into the darkness. *It has to be a moment longer . . .*

And then we were upon the snow-laden skeletons of the trees, and Melanippe and my warrior-guard were screeching out of the cover at the Budini's left flank, bows raised, hailing arrows and glittering with iron.

'Now!'

It was the fire of my anger that guided me as I turned upon my horse, drew my bow and, with the ferocity of a wolf-mother protecting her cubs, flung five arrows, one upon another, among the unsuspecting Budini. The twang of bowstrings around me and the darts slicing through the air told me that others of my warriors had done the same. Cries and screams of agony from the Budini, trapped between the frozen river-ice and the looming trees, flew towards us upon the wind, but I shut my ears to them and drew again, determined not to lose sight of the tents in the distance through the snow lashed up by our horses' hoofs and the shrieking winds of the plains.

'Again!' My cry whipped past my warriors, and once more I sent my arrows hissing towards the enemy who had dared to attack my people, until the howls of injured Budini pierced the air, like the shrieks of eagles on the hunt.

'Now – around!' I called. I pulled on the reins to bring Kati to the right and lowered my head, urging her on. Around me the Amazons were wheeling back towards the camp, horses snorting, arrow after arrow slicing through the winter air in a cloud of bronze and iron. And then I felt a sudden stab of horror in my stomach as the blizzard parted for a moment to reveal, dimly through the snowstorm, a group of Budini who had separated from the main force, attacking the tents, looting them, and cutting free the horses we had left behind.

'*No!*'

I leant forwards, my throat tight, my heart pounding against my ribs, and with all the training born of a lifetime spent on the plains, I urged Kati forward, her coat slippery with sweat beneath my hands. Behind me the Amazons were galloping so fast that the earth shuddered beneath us. Still I pushed Kati harder, the breath screaming in my lungs, her flanks heaving beneath me – my whole body focused on reaching my camp, my home, my people.

There were eight or ten Budini, fighting hand to hand with the guard I had left behind, though I could not make out Teuspa among them. One by one, as I came nearer, the intruders spotted us approaching, and I could see them vaulting back onto their horses, calling out to each other to flee. My arrows sliced at the air, rage and fury so powerful within me that I felt as if I were a beacon of fire blazing to the heavens. My heart was burning, and I longed for nothing but to keep them away for as long as I lived. But as Kati stormed into the camp, billowing steam into the air, the last were already galloping towards the frosted flat surface of the river to the north, following the retreating remainder of their army, five looted horses held by the reins and cantering beside them. I let out a yell of frustration and buried my hand in my quiver, drew four arrows and, one after another, sent them after the intruders with all the strength I had. The blurring clouds of snow and the growing darkness creeping over the horizon obscured my vision, and my arrows plunged to the ground.

I slapped my hand hard against my thigh, the corners of my eyes encrusted with ice.

Melanippe rode up beside me. 'They are gone, sister. They're gone.'

I ignored her, tugging at the reins to bring Kati around and leaping down into the snow, pushing my way to the nearest dwelling.

'Teres?' I cried, my voice shaking. 'Ainippe?'

Two children, not yet ten years old, peered out through the tent's flap, their heads shrouded with fur caps, their dark eyes round. I let out a breath that misted the air before me and ran on through the camp, determined to see all those who had stayed behind. I checked each of the tents where I knew a child dwelt, and clasped them tight to me as, one by one, I found them safe. I watched, my heart rent with pain and relief, as snow-sodden mothers embraced them, and ordered Ioxeia to tend those of the warriors who had been wounded. At last I reached Melanippe's tent, a patchwork of felt and deer-hides.

'Teuspa?' I called.

There was a moment of silence. Then Melanippe's husband emerged from the tent, one hand covered with blood.

My breath caught in my chest.

'Cayster,' was all he said.

Ἀδμήτη

Admete

Tiryns, Greece

The Eighth Day of the Month of Zeus, 1265 BC

I closed my eyes as I entered the herbary, as I always did, to fill my senses with it. Of course, it was the herbs I always smelt first: the nutty warmth of powdered cumin; the autumn must of chaste-berries; mint-sweet lemon balm; lily-of-the-valley, delicate as a spring morning. But then, after the scents and the rush of names, properties and preparations through my mind, something more. *Safety. Certainty.* I loved the way the plants followed the rhythm of the seasons: how you could always be sure that the poppies would bloom scarlet over the meadows in spring, the grapes darken at summer's end. I loved the stoppered jars lining the shelves of the preparation-room, each painted by my hand with the name of the herb it contained, ordered, predictable. The satisfaction of identifying a complaint, finding the appropriate herbs, and applying them to heal the body – all with a quiet certainty of their efficacy – was beyond any I had ever known.

I smiled as I opened my eyes to take in the familiar scene.

To my right, the longest of the trestle tables where I prepared my herbs, mottled where it was stained with their juices; to my left, the water-jars filled to the brim as I had directed and propped against the wall; and before me the hearth, flames bathing my skin with warmth and drying the bunches of herbs and garlic bulbs I had gathered that hung from the rafters. The room was dark, as herbs prefer it, lit only by the golden wash of the flames and the lamp I had set by the weighing-scales. I set down the jar of oil I had gone to the kitchens to retrieve, and drew my stool towards the table to begin my work again.

'You will wear your eyes out if you labour late, with so little light to see by.'

One of the priest-healers, Laodamas, had entered from the store-room, his belly preceding him, his robes wafting the scent of firesmoke and incense towards me. I looked up from the dried thyme sprigs I was plucking. 'It is hardly late, Laodamas. The owl does not yet sing.'

He rapped my knuckles with the wooden spoon I had used earlier to mix an infusion of camomile. 'It is the aching of your temples you should observe, not the hooting of birds,' he said, placing both hands on the table and frowning down at me. 'No amount of eyebright will bring back your sight once it is lost.'

I sighed. 'That is true.' I bowed my head and picked a few more leaves. 'But this thyme is quite dried out, and I would set it to store before it becomes too brittle.'

'And then?' he asked. 'What else needs to be done, Admete? Will you not invent another task – the bandages to be cleaned, the tiles to be scrubbed and washed, the creams and ointments in the store-room to be checked to ascertain that they have not soured, though you checked them only yesterday?' He laid a hand over mine, the skin slippery in the heat of the fire. 'You work too hard, my dear. The running of the palace of Tiryns is not your concern alone, and it will continue quite as well without you labouring yourself into the grave. You should learn to accept help, to reconcile yourself to the fact that you are a mere mortal, who needs meat and good wine and sleep like the rest of us.'

'I do not claim otherwise,' I said, withdrawing my hand from his and patting his fingers briefly. I sighed. 'I thank you for your care of me, Laodamas, truly I do. But I am afraid – I do not say it lightly – that Tiryns has grave need of help now that Alexander is gone. I am glad to do what little I can.'

'But surely your younger brothers—'

'My brothers know nothing of kingship except its title, as you yourself are well aware.'

'My lord Alexander –' he ventured.

'– is away from home at present in Egypt and . . .' I bit my lip, thinking of Iphimedon, my elder by two years and the next in line to the throne, how heavily his many lost bets at dice and drunken routs in the taverns of the city weighed on my father's mind. 'We are all the more in need of aid without him. I am quite happy to be here, and to help the healers as I can.' I smiled at him as I took up the thyme again, though I knew that I spoke only part of the truth, and that if I met his gaze my eyes would be my undoing. 'I beg you to go to the evening feast, and to let my father know that I shall be there presently.'

I sighed again as he left, raising a hand to rub my face. At least it was quiet now, with only the spitting logs for company.

It was dark as the deepest hours of night beyond the window that opened onto the court, and my fingers were sore from rubbing thyme stems, when the door opened again.

'Alcides!' I dropped the herb and pushed back my stool to welcome him, brushing my palms on my apron.

He chuckled as he strode towards me, boots still fresh with mud from the roads, and pulled me into his embrace. 'You know I allow none other but you to call me that now,' he said, ruffling my hair and standing back with a glint in his eye, a smirk at one corner of his mouth. 'I am almost done with my labours. They all call me Hercules, these days.'

'I know that,' I said, grinning at him. I poked a finger at his chest. 'I am your friend, and so you shall always be Alcides to me. And in any case,' my eyes swivelled towards him, 'as you said – you are not done with your labours. The prophecy is not yet fulfilled.'

The laugh he gave was less exuberant, not his usual deep belly-roar, and there was a slight crease between his brows, but I hardly cared. 'And Iberia?' I pressed him, sliding back to sit on the edge of the table and swinging my legs, filled with pleasure to have him returned. I took him in, smiling to see him unchanged: the gleaming eyes and firm, sensitive mouth; the curling brown hair falling to his beard, light at the jaw as it was dark on his head; the tightly bound torso, longer than his legs, which were thick and stout; his squat way of standing with feet planted wide and arms crossed over his chest. 'Was it frightful? Did you subdue the cattle of Geryon?'

'I not only subdued them,' he said, 'but the entire peninsula of Iberia, and drove them back through the lands of the Celts as an offering to your father.'

'By the gods,' I said, touching him lightly with the toe of my sandal, 'that is a labour well done! And you have . . . ?'

'Two tasks remaining,' he said.

He let out a breath and leant back against the doorpost, his eyes unfocused.

I stilled myself and placed my elbows on my thighs, inclining towards him. 'What is it?' I asked, not smiling now, watching the shadows of the flames on his face.

He shook his head.

'Alcides.' I pushed myself from the table and walked over to take his hand, feeling the rough skin beneath the fingers where he handled his sword. 'You can confide in me.'

'I know that,' he said.

'Then?'

He turned to me, though his eyes still flicked back and forth. 'It is hard to admit.'

I waited, allowing him time to formulate his thoughts, listening to the dried stems rustling on the table as the draught from beneath the door blew them.

'Eight years I have lived here,' he said at last. 'What happens if I do not succeed in completing the labours? How could I return to Thebes, to Amphitryon, more alone even than I was before, and a proven failure at that?'

'You know the answer,' I said, pressing his hand. 'You can stay here. My father would welcome you and gladly.'

'And then,' he turned his eyes to me, doubt and uncertainty written on his face, 'what if I complete them?'

'Then you will receive everything you have wished for since you came to this court with the words of the oracle still echoing in your ears.'

'Yes, but . . .' He dropped my hand and began to pace, his

24

shadow long over the opposite wall. His voice was anguished, barely a whisper, as he said, 'What if my father – what if Zeus – what if he—' He shook his head, his throat working. 'I cannot even say it.'

I moved towards him and folded him in my arms, took his head on my shoulder, as I would an infant suffering from the whooping cough. 'I know what it is you fear,' I said, my voice low in his ear. 'But trust me, Alcides. I have known you these eight years. I know the loyalty and the courage that lie within you. You will be enough for him.'

He raised his head at once. 'I should not have mentioned it – your mother – I did not wish to pain you, Admete.' He was talking quickly, and it was he, now, who took my hand. 'I am sorry for it.'

'For what?' I tried to keep my voice carefree, pulling myself from his grip and walking over to the jar of thyme on the trestle table, as if I had just recalled it. 'It was many years ago, and a wound that is long healed.'

He had opened his mouth to respond when the door from the court slammed against the wall, bringing with it a sharp blast of winter wind. I looked up, startled.

'My lady Admete.' A figure tumbled into the room, a torch in her hand and her breath coming short and fast.

'Elais – what is it?'

She tried to catch her breath, her cheeks bright with cold. 'It is your brother, my lady, the eldest and heir to the throne of Tiryns.'

'Alexander?' I asked, feeling the blood drain from my face. 'Oh, gods, what of him?'

'He is returned – from Egypt,' she said.

'What?' I turned to Alcides, frowning, still taking in her

words, as if asking him to correct her. 'Can this be true? In the midst of these tempests, this season of winter sea-storms?'

'I know as little of this as you,' he said, spreading his hands, but Elais interrupted him.

'It is even so, my lady,' she said. Her eyes were wide with fright and red-rimmed as I turned to her. 'He is sweating with a fever the like of which neither I nor any other of the priests has ever seen. None of the healers in Egypt could cure him. His men tell me they determined at last to bring him back to Tiryns, despite it not being the season for sailing, to see if you might aid him. Oh, I beg you, my lady, come quick, for he is near to fainting after the voyage, and raves all kinds of madness.'

My skin prickled with fear, but I felt my training as a healer overtake it as I had taught myself. With all the death and pain I had seen over many years of tending spotted plagues and infections, breech births and suppurating wounds, my spirit would have broken if I could not trust in my skill to the very last. 'Very well,' I said, running to the store-room and grasping a handful of feverfew from its jar. 'This will do until I can bring him here and prepare more. Alcides,' I strode back into the room, and he was at my side in a moment, 'will you carry a jar of water for me?' I pointed to them. 'Elais, take these linens.'

I snatched up the lamp from the table, glowing dimly now but enough to see us to the harbour, and faced the door, bare-armed against the biting wind, my heart blazing like the hearth behind me. 'Take me to him.'

𒀭𒀭𒀭𒀭𒀭𒀭𒀭

Hippolyta

Amazons, Land of the Saka

The Thirty-ninth Day after the Day of Storms in the Season of Tar, 1265 BC

I pushed past Teuspa into the tent, a veil of darkness over-taking my vision. Through the dim light I saw Cayster lying inside on a bed of pelts, Melanippe stroking his hair and murmuring to him, pale-faced, as she held up a lamp, illuminating a gash running the length of his thigh that was oozing blood. He was whimpering, tears streaming down his cheeks, his dark eyes wide and frightened. I put a hand upon the tent-post.

'Melanippe,' I said, trying to keep my voice from shaking, 'fetch Ioxeia.'

She bent to kiss the boy, lingering over him and pressing his hand in hers, then handed me the lamp, her fingers trembling, and swept from the tent.

I moved around the hearth and laid the back of my hand against his forehead. His skin was warmed by the fire but not flaming with fever. *Thank the gods for that.* I took his

27

hand in mine and held it tight, feeling the fingers enclosed within my own and a burning pain within my chest.

'It is natural for you to feel concern for him, my queen,' a voice said. My hand slipped – I had thought I was alone. 'But he will be well.'

I looked around. Teuspa had entered and was squatting by the fire, stoking it and sending sparks shooting up into the air. I dropped Cayster's hand.

'You were unharmed?'

'Nothing of consequence. And I took one of the Budini for it. But there were too many for me to protect Cayster, and by then they were hot with blood-lust as well as looting.'

He lapsed into silence. I sat on Cayster's bed and twisted my fingers in my lap, trying to trust that all would be well, to act as if the howling of the wind outside and the sound of the snow blowing in against the animal hides of the tent distracted me from his whimpers of pain.

At last the opening to the tent parted, with a freezing blast and a swirl of snow, and I leapt to my feet, heart hammering at my throat. 'Ioxeia? Are you there?'

Melanippe entered, and after her the priest and healer of the Amazons, an elderly woman of more than sixty years, one eye blinded in battle, her wolf's-pelt cloak glittering with snow and her white hair frosted. She was carrying a pitcher, several cloths, and pouches of herbs thrown over her arm. She poured a little water from the pitcher into the cauldron set over the fire before kneeling down by Cayster. Melanippe glanced at me, her face drawn, and I nodded my thanks, tight-lipped.

Ioxeia was now pressing Cayster's wound gently with her

fingers. I felt the gall rise in my belly, and longed to command her to cease, but she was inspecting the rest of his leg now, checking for other wounds, then feeling with her fingers along the bones.

'It is but a surface wound,' she said finally, turning to Melanippe and Teuspa. Melanippe let out a half-sob and closed her eyes, and Teuspa drew her to him, taking deep, steadying breaths, his gaze over-bright. *The gods be thanked*, I thought, bringing a hand to my forehead and turning away. 'I have drawn as much of the illness from him as I can. Rest, plenty of *koumiss*, and the mercy of Tar the storm-god should heal him in time. For now,' I heard the sound of a cloth being dipped into water and wrung out again, 'keep this soaked with water and press it to the wound until the stars appear in the sky. I shall return then and bind his leg myself.'

I turned to Melanippe as Ioxeia left the tent. 'I am so relieved for you, sister,' I said, my hands on her forearms, gripping into the skin. 'But I must see to the others of our tribe.' She nodded, biting her lip to stop it trembling. 'Will you and Teuspa manage alone?'

'Of course.'

'Then – I will leave you.'

As I pushed open the tent-flap I glanced back at Cayster, his eyes closed now, tears gathered on the lashes, as the warmed cloth soothed him. His father was singing to him, and I saw Cayster's eyelids flutter; and I felt a hollow tug of sadness at their closeness. I bent my head and left, stepping out into the snow.

The sun was but a thin orange line upon the horizon. I started to unbuckle my war-belt, the symbol of the ruler of the tribe, given to us by the storm-god Tar and handed down from my mother, the queen before me. It was wide enough to cover me from hips to navel, leather plated with gold plaques and equipped with straps from which my battle-axe, bow-case and sword hung. My fingers brushed the eagle pendant on its thong by my quiver, the amulet and *tamga* of our clan. It was the most sacred and precious sign to the Amazons, and as I touched it, I thought of all the queens who had gone before me, whose thumbs had rubbed the eagle after victory: some small comfort in the aftermath of the battle, surrounded by the warriors I had led to risk their lives. Men and women busied around me, dragging the bodies of the dead Budini beyond the camp to bury in the snowdrifts, throwing blankets of felt over their horses' backs to keep them warm. I stopped to let a pair of men pass me, their swords still gore-crusted from the battle. As I turned aside, for a moment, just a moment, it was as if a warm breeze blew over my face – a breeze scented with rosemary and thyme and bay leaves.

I closed my eyes and took a deep breath.

Wind whips over the water, turning it white. The sea laps against the shore, and foam swirls over the pebbles, splashing around my ankles as I hold up my robes, trying not to wet them. He laughs at me, pulls me down, and I fall into the water, laughing too, my hair streaming down my back . . .

There was a clang of metal, and I opened my eyes. A group of Amazons were stripping one of the Budini of his armour and tossing it in a pile onto the blood-soaked snow, the shield clattering against the breastplate, the sword thrown on top, the broken spear shaft set aside for firewood. I looked back to Melanippe's tent. She was standing before it, watching me, her arms crossed and her face creased in a frown.

She knows what I am thinking. I felt a flicker of shame creep up my neck and blaze upon my cheeks.

I turned, bowed my head against the freezing wind, and made my way through the snow across the Amazon camp.

Ἀδμήτη

Admete

Tiryns, Greece

The Eighth Day of the Month of Zeus, 1265 BC

We ran through the corridors that adjoined the inner court, down the steps and across the yard. Rain was slanting through the black air upon the paving slabs, and I had to hold a hand over my oil-lamp to prevent it going out. The guards at the tower nodded to me as I passed and swung the gates forwards so that we could clatter, slipping in our sandals, down the stone steps towards the postern gate. Elais' torch sputtered ahead of me as I slid past her through the door and beyond the outer walls, my heart rattling in my chest, my eyes squinting against the rain, to the harbour where a cluster of torches bloomed in the darkness.

And then a light bobbed towards us: a slave, laden with clothes tied into bundles with twine, his face gleaming with rain. 'My lady Admete!'

'Rhoecus!' I lost my footing as I tried to stop, and flung a hand to the wall to steady myself, scraping my skin on the stone. 'Alexander – where is he?'

'Taken to his chambers already, my lady,' he said. 'They wanted to lay him down. He's in a bad way.'

Without hesitation I turned back, colliding with Alcides and almost causing Elais to drop her torch.

'He's in his chambers,' I called, as I gathered my skirts in one hand and ran up the steps.

Back across the yard, up the staircase and into the lowering darkness of the palace, along the corridor that skirted the Great Hall, past the empty queen's rooms and to the double doors that led to Alexander's chambers. As they swung back, pushed open by the guards, I felt the heat of the room assail me, the air stifling – they had lit a fire, at least. A crowd of men and slaves thronged around Alexander's bed: I saw at once my father, my brothers Iphimedon and Eurybius, and the twins Mentor and Perimedes, all of them fair as my father had been, though the king's hair was streaked now with grey and coarse with age. They would have to go, of course. At once I set down my oil-lamp on a side-table and turned to Alcides, all activity and business.

'Set a cauldron to boil on the fire,' I threw at him. 'Elais, the linens – over by the bed.'

My father heard my voice and turned. In two breaths he was across the room and by my side, his hand gripping my shoulder, his brow creased. 'Can you heal him?' He rubbed his forehead with his fingers as he spoke, chafing the skin, as if by doing so he could somehow avert the danger that threatened his eldest son.

'I will have to see him before I can tell. But I will do all I can – I swear it.'

He stooped and pressed a swift kiss to my head. 'Go, then.'

I pushed past Mentor and waved away the slave who was

bent over Alexander, fussing at him with a cloth. At last I saw him. I recoiled, horrified to see how far the fever had gone. He lay twitching and convulsing on the sheets, the blankets tossed back and his under-tunic stained dark with sweat. There was a sickly pallor to his skin where the fire-light gleamed over it, and his hair was slicked to his head; his eyes were closed, the whites just showing, rolling back and forth. I pressed my hand to his forehead. *Oh, gods.* Hot as a stone in the sun at the height of summer. I felt the first tremor of fear. Yet there were no blisters, no pockmarks on his skin, as far as I could see. *No plague, then.*

'He needs rest,' I said to the gathered crowd. 'You have served him well,' I told his slaves. 'You too, father, brothers. You did well to bring him here.' I bowed to them. 'But now he needs my care. The ministration of herbs and the peace of sleep will be the best cure.'

The guards swung open the doors, and first the slaves, then Alcides and Elais left the chamber, treading over the tiles like shadows.

Eurybius reached out for my hand as he passed. 'You – you will be able to cure him, sister, will you not?'

I pressed his fingers to my lips, then to my forehead, summoning my strength for the long night at Alexander's bedside. 'I will do my best, Eurybius.'

His gaze wavered. 'Our mother would have—'

'We have managed long enough without her.' My father had approached, and waved Eurybius away; he melted into the darkness with my younger brothers and Iphimedon.

There was a moment's silence in which the fire in the hearth spat and sparked, and Alexander moaned, muttering beneath his breath.

'Work hard for him, Admete.' My father's voice was strained. Our eyes met, speaking words we need not utter: the years he had spent on Alexander, grooming him to be king; the mastery of Egyptian and Hittite; the training in diplomacy; the knowledge of trade, palace accounts, the methods of dealing justice – all the heir of Tiryns would need. All that Iphimedon, boisterous, carefree, selfish, did not know. 'It is more important,' my father swallowed, 'more important than anything else that he is cured.'

A last grip of my shoulder, painfully tight, and then he, too, was gone.

I turned back to the bed as the door clicked shut, with nothing but the harsh rattle of Alexander's feverish whispers to accompany me. With a deep breath, I moved towards the cauldron Alcides had set over the fire and ladled the bubbling water into Alexander's goblet, my hands shaking as I dropped in the feverfew. I gripped the cup, readying myself for the long, hard battle ahead.

For, though I would not admit it to anyone, I had known the first instant I saw him that Alexander was closer to Charon's boat and a passage to the Underworld than he had ever been.

The Last Labours

𒀸𒉌𒍑𒄿𒆠𒈠𒅔

Hippolyta

Amazons, Land of the Saka

The Fortieth Day after the Day of Storms in the Season of Tar, 1265 BC

The sound of hoofbeats echoed across the camp. I dropped the sword I had been sharpening to the ground and it clattered upon the whetstone as I left my tent. Brilliant sunlight and an expanse of blue sky forced their way upon my senses, and at the edge of the camp a stampede of high-necked horses . . .

'Orithyia!' I ran towards her, boots crunching on the ice.

She leapt from her mount and embraced me briefly. 'Sister.'

'You look tired,' I said, drawing back and examining her. Her eyes were creased and her cheeks whipped by the wind, the hilt of the sword at her waist crusted with old blood and the shoulder of her tunic ripped, showing a slowly healing gash slashed through the inked image of a soaring eagle on her skin.

'The work of a Hialean?' I asked.

She nodded. 'But I sent him to the gods for it,' she said, and grinned at me, revealing white teeth.

I gave a half-smile. Orithyia's blood-lust was famed even among the Amazons. 'It is good to have you back, sister. We have missed you.'

She bent to pick up the reins of her horse and we walked towards the camp, feet sinking into the snow.

'And the raid on Hialea?' I asked, glancing back towards the crowd of warriors behind us, now dismounting with a clatter of swords, patting their horses, reuniting with husbands and wives who ran from the camp carrying woven rugs and pouches of warmed *koumiss*. I felt my voice tighten as I asked, 'Did we lose any?'

'Not as many as the Hialeans,' she said. 'And we took twenty steeds before we left. But yes, we lost Toxaris and Artimpata. And I had to leave Areto. She would not have survived the journey back across the Silis river in any case.'

I nodded, my fists clenched tight so that the knuckles whitened, and my thumb went again to the eagle on my belt. *You are the queen*, I thought. *You cannot mourn every loss. And without those horses your people would not survive the winter.*

'And you?' Orithyia asked, cutting across my thoughts as we turned into the clearing at the camp's centre. Her horse whinnied, knowing his home, and she patted his rump where the *tamga* had been branded and let go of the reins. I watched him canter to a group of horses feeding from a trough filled with dried grass from the summer plains. A couple of children laughed as he tossed his head with joy to feed again.

'A raid from the Budini,' I said. 'We expect another, for they did not capture many horses. Melanippe and I have been in need of your counsel.'

'You? The queen of the Amazons, who excels above us all in battle? Requiring counsel from me?'

I bowed my head. 'I am queen as the eldest of the daughters of Marpesia – you know that, sister.'

She clapped me on the shoulder. 'You are queen because you are the wisest and strongest of us all,' she said. 'The gods would not have made it otherwise. But before I give you war-counsel, I must change my clothes. I have not been fully dry for several days, and my feet are cold as ice from the ride.'

The council took place in my tent, crowded, as it always was, the heat from the fire mixing with that of the bodies pressed against each other on stools. These were my advisers and guides, who gave counsel to the queen and upheld her decisions among the people. Six were warriors, advanced in years, who had excelled in battle and preserved their lives longest on the plain; the other six were members of my guard, fleet of foot and swift horse-riders, chosen for their skill with the *sagaris* and the spear. Tent-holders like Teuspa, who raised the Amazons' children, were not admitted – yet the council was not devoid of men, just as not all women rode to war. All among our people trained to fight from the first, all growing up side by side, young men and women alike. The first time they fought in war they rode to battle together, killed an enemy side by side, tasted the slice of the iron in the air and felt the sting of blood upon the sword; and that night, when they returned, sacrificed to the gods and, while the stars swam in the sky, selected a partner to mate. The next dawn, as the sun rose over the plain and the priests blessed them as Amazons, the men and the women declared their choice – to be a tent-holder and care for

Amazons to come, or ride out again as a warrior to protect our tribe. Only one had no choice. Only one had the task of her life's work allotted to her by birth, not by preference. For me, daughter of the queen in a line of women stretching back to the first founders, there was – there had always been – no other way. *And*, I thought with warmth, as I gazed around the faces of my council in the flickering half-light, *I lay my life at my people's feet with pride*.

Aella, my swiftest horsewoman, broad-cheeked and slim as a bird, was handing to Ioxeia, the healer, a pouch of *koumiss*, then spearing fish from the fire and mare's-milk cheese. Orithyia stood beside the entrance, her dark hair plaited down her back and swinging from side to side as she gestured in argument with the councillor Agar. Melanippe sat, one knee curled into her chest, at Orithyia's feet, throwing another salted fish into the sizzling pan of butter on the fire. The youngest of the three daughters of Marpesia, Melanippe had been the most carefree of us all, riding for hours upon the plains on her beloved mount Akhal, a beautiful dark horse with the spirit of a wild deer, until he had been killed in battle, speared by one of the Tisgita and cut up for his meat. Without Akhal, Melanippe had lost herself, turned inwards, become quiet and sometimes sullen, and wild with vengeance in battle. It was as if the playful girl who had galloped through the meadows was gone for ever.

I took up a lamp and stood, my breathing coming faster and a rushing through my fingers, even though for years I had had to stand before the council and plan our battles, our movements over the plain. I glanced at my war-belt, draped over a low table, the plates of gold gleaming in the firelight, the golden scales decorating the quiver shimmering like stars. *So it must always be, for my mother, my sisters, my people.* I straightened my back, feeling my strength come from the belt as if from a draught of the gods.

'As you see,' I said, and as I spoke the elders of the group fell silent, 'Orithyia is returned, with victory in the raid over the Hialeans and horses to supply our meat for the winter.' A few of my Amazon guard nodded, or turned to each other to talk, and I saw Aella reach over to grasp Orithyia by the hand. None of the elders spoke or moved. Battle was not a contest to be won between the tribes of the open grassland: it was a struggle for existence, as bare and as primal as a starving wolf stalking its prey, and victory meant merely to survive a little longer. The elders knew it as well as I; my band of fighters would learn it soon enough. 'But, as far as we know, the Budini to the north are running low on their supplies. The Silis river has been frozen many months, and they lost several fighters in their raid. They will be growing desperate. I believe we should expect another attack.'

'Then we attack them first!' Orithyia was on her feet, her hand at the hilt of the sword hanging from the war-belt at her waist. The light from the fire cast dancing shadows across her face, darkening the hollows of her eyes and the ridge of her cheekbones. 'We are warriors, are we not? Have we not been taught to ride and to fight from our earliest days in order to best the peoples of the plain and to blazon the name of the Amazons across the land?'

'We were taught to fight,' Ioxeia said, licking her lips and leaning forwards, her voice harsh-edged with age, 'to protect our people. We move in search of better herding-places. We raid for meat and weapons when we must. We fight to protect what we have. No more.'

Orithyia slammed a hand into the tent-post, and I felt the hides overhead shake upon their frame. The smoke of the fire curled to one side as a breeze blew through the tent and snaked across my cheek. 'And if we do that, what then? Do we sit idly and wait for the Budini to attack?'

'Daughter of Marpesia,' Agar said, his voice snapping, 'recall yourself. You are speaking to the representative of the gods.'

'It is the gods I am thinking of!' she retorted. 'Does Tar, lord of war, find honour in defeat? Does Tabiti, lady of the fire, seek the shadows of the forest?'

I could see my Amazons muttering to each other, Aella's expression half hesitant, half hopeful, Xanthippe beside her, one hand already upon the hilt of her iron sword.

'That is enough!' My voice rang out more strongly than I had meant it to, and all the council turned towards me, their chatter silenced. 'Orithyia, I thank you for your words, but you forget that I am queen of this tribe.' My impatience with her bit at me, urging me on. Melanippe and I had wished for her return and her counsel . . . *And yet*, I thought, *we should have known on which side she would fall. With Orithyia it is always war.* 'You did well in Hialea. But I prefer not to attack. We are a tribe of horse-riders and worshippers of the gods, living close to the black earth and the winged eagle and the deer, and though we fight with pride and honour we are not seekers of battle. You speak of blazoning our name across the land of the Saka tribes. Yet I would rather have us spoken of for our skill with our proud-stepping horses than as man-killers, would you not?'

'You told me you wished for my counsel,' she said, arms folded across her chest, her sword swinging at her side and catching the light of the flames, her mouth now set in a grim line with no trace of her earlier smile. 'That is my advice.'

I forced myself not to take her challenge. 'Councillors?' I said, taking refuge in movement and getting to my feet, looking around the circle, meeting each by eye: the elders Agar, Iphito and Ioxeia, my fighters Aella and Xanthippe. Their faces were half shadowed in the darkness of the tent, and I could see the scars outlined, like silver threads, on their cheeks and jaws, each of them taken in battle for the Amazons. 'Do we choose war against the Budini, or do we wait here to defend ourselves? Those for battle,' a few shoulders shrugged, a couple of dark eyes glanced my way, 'and those for—'

'For the queen.' Ioxeia finished my sentence for me. She stood and gave me her hand, and I felt the skin, tough as hide and ridged with scars, beneath my fingers. One after another, the elders, then many of my war-band stood and placed their hands in mine, though Xanthippe and Aella moved to Orithyia.

'A decision, then,' I said, my eyes fixed on Orithyia's, as though daring her to defy me. I could almost feel the heat of the anger radiating from her stance – feet planted apart, arms folded. But I would not allow her to sway me. 'We wait,' I said, 'and if the Budini come for our horses, we defend ourselves – but no more.'

Ἀδμήτη

Admete

Tiryns, Greece
The Twelfth Day of the Month of
Sweet Wine, 1265 BC

I knelt in the dirt, the skin of my hands chafing as I tried to uproot a tenacious weed. Two months had passed since Alexander's ship had arrived from Egypt, and the herb-garden in the outer court beyond the herbary was blossoming with the first signs of spring. The mayweed had already unfurled into bright daisy-like flowers, and bees were buzzing over the blossoms of the rosemary bush; the mandrake's petals were still green, though tinged each passing day with white, and the flowers of the borage were open to reveal their dark purple hearts.

Yet I could take no joy in it. For Alexander sweated and groaned with fever, and though – thank the gods – he lived, I was exercising every skill and all the herb lore I possessed, and still, I could only lessen his suffering, not end it.

I tugged harder, venting my frustration, my fatigue. Days and days I had spent stripping willow-bark and boiling it to a pulp, straining it till my fingernails were stained brown; I had endured so many nights when I barely slept for sponging Alexander's forehead and tipping infusions between his dry lips. Though I hated to admit it even to myself, it was a relief to be in the open air, outside the stifling closeness of his chamber where the fire continually blazed and the dusty scent of willow and bitter feverfew hung on the air. I pulled again, fingers knotted around the stem, and at last it gave way, roots tearing up from the black soil. I threw it into the basket beside me and reached for another.

What sickness can it be? My mind wandered again to my brother, even as my hands performed the routine task, asking the question, the riddle that had taunted and plagued me ever since his return. What illness could fell such a man at the peak of his health, when he had survived all the sweats and poxes of childhood? What disease could form such a strange distinctive pattern, such as neither I nor any of the priests had seen before?

The image of the clay tablets stacked on shelves in the herbary, arranged by illness as I had observed them and dotted over with the impress of my stylus, rose before me.

Regular as the change of the seasons, the fever builds to its height every ninth day before releasing its grip, only to return again. The single beneficial thing that can be said of it is that it seems the decline is very gradual, since it is a cyclical fever and not continuous, and the sufferer – though growing always weaker – has a few days each cycle to recover strength. At its worst, it produces sweating, uncontainable shivering and chills, weakness and pallor, nausea, vomiting, even delirium. A decoction of white willow-bark alleviates discomfort, while fresh feverfew leaves lessen the heat in the body when chewed. No cure as yet.

No cure as yet. I bit my lip. They were like a curse, those words, taunting me to try harder, to search further. *There is a herb. There has to be a herb – somewhere.*

Unthinking, my mind still raking through the plants that might serve, I pulled up the sleeves of my tunic, streaking my forearm with dirt. Sweat prickled beneath my arms and beads of moisture clung to my temples. Though the morning was cool and the dew still on the rose-leaves, I had been in the garden for several hours, pruning and weeding, and it was hot work.

And then, as I reached for the spade, I caught a glimpse – black, like my own shadow – of the *tamga* branded into my inner arm.

I sank back on my heels, staring at the pattern inked into the skin, the lines mottled where they ran across the veins, my thoughts drifting over it.

When had I first realized my mother was an Amazon? It had come slowly, I think: little pieces of evidence disclosing themselves. The way she had plaited her hair, so differently from the other women. The days she would spend alone, riding over the Argive hills, returning to the hall for the evening meal with her cheeks bright, when my father would call her his *wild one*. The songs she used to sing to me, filled with tales of horses galloping across the plain beneath an unending sky. The *tamga* branded on her arm.

There were many times, when I was younger, that I wished it was not there, this mark of my heritage. I had lain in my cot at night after the nurse had put us all to bed, trying to rub it off with my thumb till the skin blazed red and itched. Later I had been proud to show it, treasuring my mother's only legacy to me. I had thought it made me special, placed me above my brothers, who bore no *tamga* to show their birthright. And now I hid the mark beneath long linen sleeves, and though I still plaited my hair down my back for her, I walked with my arm pressed to my side, my fingers clenched around the cuff.

For I had learnt, in ways I did not want to remember – blurred memories of insults, vicious hands tugging at my plait, accusations, refusals to allow a *barbarian* to heal their ills – that it was not easy to be – I felt warmth spread through my chest, in spite of it – *the daughter of an Amazon in Greece.*

And then, all at once, with the suddenness and force of a lightning bolt shivering through the veined trunk of an ash tree, I knew, with a mix of fear and joy, where I might find a cure.

'Admete!'

A voice rang across the court, breaking into my thoughts. I started and dropped the spade. Hastily, I pulled down my sleeves and got to my feet.

'Oh, it's you,' I said, as Alcides came into view, climbing over the low wall of the portico. He walked through the shaded yard into the slant of sunlight that lit the herb-garden. I saw that he was dressed for the hunt: a sword-belt over his tunic, two spears and a shield on his back, a javelin in one hand.

'You go ahead,' he called, over his shoulder, to someone I could not see. 'I will follow you shortly.'

'You are going on a hunt with my brothers?' I asked, as he approached, shielding his eyes against the sun.

'Yes, indeed – with Eurybius, Mentor and Perimedes. Iphimedon still sleeps.'

I picked up the spade again and pushed the sole of my foot against it, driving it into the earth.

'I have not seen you for several days.'

'Yes, well,' I grunted, as I lifted soil and dropped it into the basket with the weeds, 'I have been attending to Alexander.'

I felt his eyes on me as I thrust the spade back into the rosebed.

'You do not look well,' he said.

I took a deep breath, ready to retort that I hardly had the hours to look to myself, that perhaps some assistance from him and my brothers would not go amiss, but the words faded on my lips as weariness overtook me. 'I do not know what more I can do,' I said, pushing the spade into the earth so that it stood upright. I drew a hand across my aching eyes.

He hovered where he stood by the mandrakes. 'Surely the priest-healers . . . You do not have to heal him alone.'

'My father has dedicated more votives to the hill-sanctuary of Apollo Paeon than any has before,' I said. 'The priests believe in magic, curses and evil spirits. They have exorcized the spirits from my brother's body with sacrifices and incantations, and still he is no better. I do not doubt the gods – to you, of all people, I need not justify that.' I smiled faintly at him. 'But to believe that they send sickness as a mark of their displeasure is to think it the stigma of sin, and that I will not credit.'

'I know your theory,' he said, and he was rubbing with his

thumb at the shaft of his javelin, following it with his eyes as he spoke, 'that disease comes from the body, that since the body is made of earth and returns to dust when we die, it may be healed by the plants of the earth. You have told me of this. But if the herbs are not effective . . .'

His voice trailed into silence. I knew he did not wish to criticize me, but his less frequent visits to Alexander's chambers, his quick-changing moods, his inability to stand still or leave his hands unoccupied, even when he had come to the herbary, and his habit of going out hunting almost daily were enough to tell me what he left unspoken. He had been held in the palace all winter without a task to distract him while my father worried over Alexander, and he found life at Tiryns stultifying. He was not a man who could sit in silence in a sick chamber for an hour, let alone days at a time.

Yet the journey to fetch the cure would free him – and you would be doing it for Alexander.

'I – I have a thought,' I said slowly.

'Yes?' The fingers of his left hand were tapping against his thigh, and I knew he was regretting his decision to talk to me, longing to be gone.

'I think perhaps my mother . . .' I said, my voice very quiet.

The tapping of his fingers ceased. 'What of her?' he asked, his eyebrows lifted, eyes now fully focused on me.

'She was – she is a healer,' I said. 'She taught me all I know before she left. And she spoke often of herbs in the land of the Amazons, potent beyond those we have here in Greece. I think . . .' I hesitated '. . . it is not that herbs do not work, or that the disease is incurable, but that we need to search for the correct plant, and the knowledge to go with it.'

I looked up to see him dash his javelin to the ground, his eyes bright, expression transformed. 'But, Admete, that is it! You should make a task of it! Have your father send me on my eleventh labour to the Amazons – he would deny you nothing, if it will be of help to Alexander – and I can bring back to you whichever herb you need.'

'Yes.' I rubbed my hands together, the dirt crumbling over the skin, feeling uneasy. 'But how would you know which it was when even I do not? You have no skill with herbs.'

I was nearing the only conclusion, yet I drew back from it, as a colt shies from thunder in a storm. I could see comprehension dawning on his face, the words forming.

'But, then, you should come with me! Who else, in Zeus' name, knows as much of herbs as you, and speaks Scythian too?'

His energy was contagious – I could feel it rising within me. And yet . . . and yet . . .

I bit my lip. 'Alcides, I do not know.'

'Know what?' He clapped me on the shoulder, and the bees above the periwinkles swirled around me, buzzing, as I stumbled. 'The course of action is clear, is it not? The eleventh labour shall be to the realm of the Amazons – a step towards my immortality, a cure for Alexander, and the prospect that you should be reunited with your mother.'

So much for his doubts, I thought. *I wish I could dismiss mine as easily.* 'But, Alcides, you will not hear me. What if . . .' I broke off one of the dark winter stems of the rose bush beside me, playing with it between my fingers '. . . what if I am misguided, and I only suggest this because I wish to see her again?'

'What does it matter?'

I stared at him, the bees humming in the background. 'It matters because I must find a cure for Alexander.'

He let out a breath through his teeth. 'Very well,' he said, bending to pick up his javelin and leaning close to whisper in my ear. 'Then what of this? If you can cure Alexander within the next three days, we shall not mention the Amazons again.' He cocked a smile at the dark plait tossed over my shoulder, as if to nod to the fact that I was, and would always be, half an Amazon, whether we spoke of it or not. 'But if you cannot, then we will take this plan to your father, the king, and he will make the decision as to what is best for Alexander. Then it will be at his judgement, not yours, that we journey together to the east.'

'But—'

'Three days,' he said, overruling me. 'And now I must leave. But in three days,' he placed his hands around my waist, lifting me up into the air so that I gasped, his eyes gleaming and all trace of irritation gone, 'we will speak again.'

He let me to the ground and strode away, waving a hand and grinning broadly. I dropped my hands to my sides and let out a breath. My eyes roved over the herb-garden before me, the thyme and the sage, the borage and valerian – the garden she and I had planted together, all those years before, when I had skipped beside her as she worked, and measured my height by the growth of the rosemary bush.

I turned aside and hugged my arms to my chest, allowing myself, for the first time in many years, to hope.

Perhaps I would see my mother again after all.

𒀭𒆠𒉺𒀭𒈬𒈠

Hippolyta

Amazons, Land of the Saka

The Sixteenth Day before the Day of Earth
in the Season of Apia, 1265 BC

The months passed, and as the first green tips of grass poked through the snow and the breeze blew warmer from the south, melting the Silis into floating ice-floes, the raids from the Budini lessened – though whether they were satisfied for the winter or merely biding their time I did not know. Cayster's wound had healed, the scar knotting neatly in the skin, and for many days Agar could be found on the plain training the boy to ride his colt with the other young Amazons, while I oversaw the preparations for the festival of the earth-goddess Apia. It was fulfilling work – there was much to do, and I was eager it should be done well. We built the temple to the goddess ourselves, as tradition demanded, a pile of brushwood to which we added each day, foraging among the trees by the Silis river as soon as the ferns and leaves of the undergrowth were visible again. I oversaw the blacksmiths, who forged the swords that would be planted in the temple – a symbol of the iron the earth-goddess gave forth for our use – and left them, my face flushed with the heat of their fires and the ringing of hammer on anvil in my ears. I spoke with the horse-master, who assured me that the steeds to be sacrificed to the goddess were healthy and fattening well on the spring flowers.

As the day ended, and the sun flared pink-tinged on the horizon, I met with Agar leading Cayster, Teres and Ainippe into the camp, each mounted on a young colt.

'You sit well,' I said to them, nodding my approval. Cayster's mount shifted and he raised his arms to balance, letting the reins splay out to the side.

'No, no,' I said. 'Keep your hands down, like this.' I guided them to his hips. 'Feel the horse,' I said, putting my hands on either side of his belly and letting him sway with the animal's movement; I felt his sturdy legs gripping hard, and a wave of affection for him overtook me. *A little Amazon already.* 'There, that's it. Softer, softer now.'

Ahead of us, Melanippe emerged from her tent, holding a lamp and smiling. 'Cayster, you are a true horseman!'

'See, mother!' he called. 'I am riding alone, without Agar to guide me!'

'Indeed, I see you,' she laughed, 'but your father,' I turned aside, my hand slipping to the reins, 'is famished and eager for his dinner, so you had better come in, with your horse or without him.'

Agar hooked his hands beneath the boy's shoulders and lifted him to the ground.

I moved to turn away. And then I felt the trembling of the earth beneath my feet – so slight that the grass tips barely quivered. So faint, that none but an Amazon born onto the soil of the plains would feel it, and among them only their queen.

I stared up at the sky. The grass stretched gold-green to the pink smudge of the sun. And then there, to the north, pinpricks of black, like an inked tattoo—

'Budini!'

My heart hammered in time with the thundering of their hoofs beneath my feet. Agar was staring at me, Melanippe had whirled around to look out to the horizon.

'Budini?' Agar called. 'After so long?'

I did not reply. The fear and rage of war flared to life within me as I turned, my mind sharp, like the edge of a sword. I almost threw Cayster back onto his colt and took the reins of his mount with Teres and Ainippe's. 'Mela-nippe,' I called. 'I want you to lead the charge. Sound the war-cry, and get the tent-holders out to fight, too – anyone you can spare. I wager the Budini have come in force. We should do the same.'

Her eyes narrowed as Agar ran past, shouting orders to those nearby and checking his bow-case upon his belt. 'And what will you do?'

'Stay here,' I said. 'Guard the camp. They came too close last time.'

'Alone? Your sword-arm is the strongest we have, sister, but to fight them off alone—'

I forestalled her. 'There is no time, Melanippe! I need to do this. *Go!*'

The Budini were racing towards us over the plain, shrieks piercing the air, like the cries of eagles. As I strode through the camp with the reins of the children's horses in one hand, calling out the war-cry, my troops were readying themselves, arming with swords, shields and battle-axes, throwing blankets on their horses' backs, leaping to mount. As soon as we reached my tent I lifted down Teres, Ainippe and Cayster, who darted within, eyes wide and whimpering at the sword I was drawing, with a soft singing sound, from the gold-studded sheath on my war-belt.

'Orithyia!' I caught her arm as she passed. She turned towards me, her hands already on her horse's back. 'Protect our people.'

She nodded, then swung herself up to mount. I felt all the sinews of my body tense with apprehension, but I knew what I had to do. I could not risk leaving the young Amazons to Teuspa's care. Not after what had happened when I had last left the camp in the charge of the rearguard. *What almost happened*, I corrected myself.

'*Oiorpata!*' I yelled, stretching my sword-point up to the sky, and the Amazons on their snorting, stamping horses throughout the camp bellowed back the cry. Melanippe galloped towards us, her hair streaming behind her. Then, turning her horse so she could see every one of the Amazons, she shook the shaft of her spear. The blade whirled and flashed. '*Oiorpata!*'

'*Oiorpata!*' the troops responded.

Melanippe squeezed her thighs into her horse's sides and pulled on the reins so that he reared, tossing his black mane.

'Now – *go!*'

I slapped Ippa's hindquarters, Orithyia yelled the war-cry once more and, with a clatter of shields and stamping of hoofs, the Amazons were gone.

I took up my shield from within my tent, slotted my left arm through the strap and ran across the deserted camp. Here and there the dark eyes of a child peered out at me through the tent-flaps. I held my sword out before me, whirling this way and that so that my footprints in the grass looked like those of a dancer at the festivals of the gods. The sounds of bronze crashing on bronze drifted towards me from the open plain, battle-cries, screams, the whinnying of horses. Coming to rest at the edge of the camp nearest the Budini, not far from my own felt-covered tent, I planted my feet on the ground and held up my sword before me, ready for any sign of an outrider.

It happened in a swirl of hoofs and a swish of *sagaris* above my head: two Budini had broken free and were charging my left side. Heart pounding, I ducked to the ground out of range of the *sagaris* and sliced at the legs of the front rider's horse with my sword, then whirled around, still crouching low, and did the same to the second. The warriors tumbled to the ground, as their horses shrieked and fell, writhing and kicking. The two men stumbled to their feet, their rust-red beards crusted with mud, hands slippery with sweat on their *sagaris*.

'Leave now,' I said, my voice low with threat, my sword held steady in my hand, 'and I will allow you to go unharmed. Attempt to attack, and you will wish that your mother had never borne you to die such an inglorious death.'

One warrior snarled, lips pulled back over his teeth, and raised his *sagaris* to his shoulder. The other started forwards, swinging his own. I watched him, eyes narrowed, blood rushing in my ears, knowing that my safety lay in waiting for the attack, waiting, though every nerve screamed at me to rush him, to drive him off.

And then he darted forwards from my left side, raising his axe and bringing the point down in a skull-splitting blow. I blocked it with my shield, then whirled around to parry the second warrior, who sliced at me from the right. He drew his sword with a shriek of metal and we began to duel, the throbbing echoes of blade against blade making the muscles of my forearm shake with the force, and all the time I was beating off the attacks of the first assailant with my shield as he panted and spat with effort. I was as focused as a falcon hovering above its prey, my gaze as narrow as the edge of my blade. *Parry, block, attack*, my feet whirling over the grass, my whole body tensed as I *thrust—*

One of my boots slipped in a track of mud left by one of the horses' hoofs, and I lost my balance. My sword veered off course and my opponent's blade slid across my right forearm, the iron gashing through my tunic and ripping open the skin. I gasped as the pain shimmered up my arm. At once, not allowing myself to cease, not even for a moment, I dropped my shield and took my sword into my left hand. Then, with a grunt, I raised it to block the *sagaris'* blow. I could feel the battle-rage mounting within me, gritted my teeth and allowed the searing pain to turn to anger, to fill my body with fire.

I leapt forwards, screaming, sword swirling and flashing like a flame. Blades shrieked and hissed. The Budini were beginning to give ground – I could sense them weakening as I pushed them further and further from my tent towards where their wounded horses were still screaming and kicking, trying to stand. Summoning all my anger and the shreds of my strength, as one warrior attacked I lunged forwards, brought my blade to his and, quick as a flickering flame, circled it around and down, knocking it from his hand. I picked it up as the other attacker started towards me, then turned and parried his blow with both blades, my wounded arm lacerated with pain. Then, turning the hilt of the sword towards him, I thrust it into his face as hard as I could. It made contact with his jaw. I felt the bones splinter and heard his howl as he dropped to his knees, clutching his face.

'Do you wish for another warning?' I roared, holding my sword high above his head.

The first warrior was already running for the plain, his tunic clinging to his knees in the winds blowing from the sea. My victim staggered to his feet, eyes reeling with pain, then ran too, staunching the blood from his chin with one hand and leaving a trail of scarlet ribboning behind him.

That night, after the battle was done, I was lying alone in my tent, my arm bathed and wrapped in linen, the embers of the fire glowing with the last of their warmth. The Amazons had driven off the Budini without any losses to our side. I had protected our tribe. I had done what I intended to do. I should have been at ease but, as always after battle, I was heartsore and agitated, and it had little to do with my wound.

I tried to turn upon my bed, feeling the wolf-pelts shift beneath my naked skin, but there was no relief. I lay there, longing for sleep, with nothing to distract me from the wind over the plain and the whirling of my thoughts.

When at last I fell asleep, I dreamt again of the Greek.

Ἀδμήτη

Admete

Tiryns, Greece

The Fifteenth Day of the Month
of Sweet Wine, 1265 BC

The days passed with no improvement in Alexander but, determined to try everything, I essayed every cure I could imagine. Infusions of yarrow. Tinctures of wormwood and gentian, imported from Thrace. Thyme, lemon balm, elderflower heated in water. Onion, baked over the fire, and the juice drunk with honey.

Yet the sun had risen and fallen over the walls of Tiryns twice, and saw me standing now with Alcides before my father's throne in the Great Hall, exhausted, hopeful, ashamed – wrung with emotion like a dried-out cloth. It was late in the day and pine torches crackled in the brackets, their flames dancing up the walls and casting long blue and gold shadows. A single ray of evening sunlight poured through the opening in the hall's roof, turning the flames of the round central hearth pale by comparison, and bathing the lapis-blue walls in colour so that the figures painted over them – the dogs chasing the boar at the hunt; the dancer leaping over the bull's horns – seemed truly to move.

'Daughter?'

I felt colour rise to my cheeks as I realized I had allowed my attention to wander – with the little rest I had taken these past months, it was becoming more and more common. I turned to my father, seated on the stone-carved throne with its serpentine base, his cloak swept over the side: the throne of Tiryns, on which Alexander was destined to sit. I saw at once, looking into my father's face in the half-light, that Alexander's illness did not weigh heavily on me alone. His beard was thin, skin showing through on the jaw, and untrimmed; his eyes were creased and reddened, suggesting that he, too, had not slept much, and he was twisting the rings on his fingers.

'You have come with news of Alexander?'

Alcides shifted by my side, eager to speak; but I was determined to have my say first. I needed my father to know how desperate I was, how miserable that I could not cure Alexander, how intent on finding the herb that would heal him.

'He is no better, father,' I said, hating the words as I spoke them. 'I have exhausted all my cures. I wish I could do more.'

He stopped circling his rings and shook his head. 'No, no, Admete. You have done more for your brothers than I could ever have hoped. You have been mother and sister to them. There is no more I can ask of you.'

He reached forwards and tilted my face up to his, fingers beneath my chin, and let out a sigh. 'Your looks are so like hers.' He plucked at the dark plait and swung it over my shoulder. 'So very like hers. Of all my children . . .'

I bit my lip and slid a sideways glance at Alcides.

My father sat back in his throne and leant his head on his hands, fingers massaging the temples.

'Indeed, it is of that,' I ventured into the silence, 'which we have come to speak to you.'

He said nothing, and Alcides gave me a vigorous nod, then gestured to me that I should go on. 'I was uneasy at first,' I said, 'when the thought first came to me, so I beg you not to judge it too hastily. But I have no cures left in my store that I have not tried, and without a different herb – different knowledge – Alexander will not heal. I believe,' I swallowed and plunged on, my throat dry, for I had not spoken of them to him in many years, 'that the Amazons, versed in healing as they are, with plants and herbs from across the eastern world such as we do not have in Greece, may have the cure.'

Blue smoke from the hearth swirled around the hall and spiralled up towards the sky. Slowly, my father looked up, frowning, his eyes barely open, hooded with tiredness. 'You wish to journey to the Amazons?'

'I believe I am the only one in Tiryns with the knowledge of herbs to recognize which may aid him,' I said carefully, 'and the only one to speak Scythian.'

'No,' he said, 'no, no – it is too dangerous.' His gaze was searching back and forth now, his mouth drawn. It was the same lost look he had worn for many years, after the day that he and I had woken to find my mother had slipped away from the palace and out onto the goat-trodden hills of the Argolid, vanishing as swiftly as the morning mists. 'You cannot leave – I cannot lose you, too.'

I moved forwards and laid my hand over his, stilling the trembling of his fingers. 'I would never leave you, father, as you know,' I said, the memory of the pain and grief we had suffered aching within me, fresh as it had been fifteen years before. 'But we know, both of us, that Iphimedon will not be the heir to Tiryns that Alexander is. We must find a cure. And you said yourself, that my mother was a healer without compare. I have thought of this often these past days, and I believe it is the only way.'

'But how would we fare without you?' he asked. 'Who would care for Alexander? Your brothers?'

'Mentor and Perimedes are sixteen years of age,' I said. 'They are not the infants I raised but men grown, and I will have Elais take on the care of Alexander. With a little under-standing, the treatment of willow-bark is easy to apply. There is nothing I can do for him at present that she cannot.'

There was a moment as my father took me in. Then he waved his hand. 'But the kingdom! If the other kings – Atreus in Mycenae, Laertes in Ithaca, Peleus in Phthia – if they hear that I am sending my only daughter across the world for fear of my son's demise, they will deem Tiryns weak, without an heir, trusting in Alexander's death. You know nothing of diplomacy, daughter, but a king must seem strong, always, to his enemies and his allies, or both may besiege him. Then we would be ruined indeed.'

Alcides moved beside me, and I saw he was red-faced with the desire to speak, his eyes gleaming. 'But, my lord, do you not see? That is why I am here!' It seemed he could hold himself back no longer. 'If you will only send me to the Ama-zons as my next task then I may accompany her. To the kings of Greece it will seem merely another labour to perform, yet I may ensure she encounters no danger, and at the same time fulfil my obligation to you and the queen of the gods.'

'Our concern is with Alexander, Alcides, not your

immortality,' I said, throwing him a look, though inside I felt a twinge of guilt. *And what of your concerns, Admete?* a voice asked within my head. *Are you so disinterested? Do you not also seek the Amazons for yourself, as well as Alexander?* But I forced myself to press back the doubts, as I had done many times since Alcides and I had spoken in the garden. *I have tried all my skills*, I reasoned, weighing the arguments against myself, like a healer at the scales balancing herbs. *And I heard my mother speak of herbs with great powers traded with the Amazons from the east. Though I am not disinterested, yet still I know it is our only hope.* 'My suggestion, father,' I said aloud, 'is that we send Alcides on a quest to the Amazons that the gods will consider worthy. To wrest the war-belt from Hippolyta, the famed Amazon queen, perhaps. That would be a fine labour, and more than an adequate front for the true cause of our expedition.'

I held his gaze as the shadows of the torches passed over his face. 'You know I am always truthful with you, father,' I said, lowering my voice. 'I have considered it. And I do believe,' I nodded, as if to confirm it, 'that this is the only way to save Alexander.'

He let out a breath, his eyes moving from me to Alcides. Then he spread his hands wide till the ring-gems, carnelian, red jasper and agate, glimmered like embers in the firelight.

'Very well, then. You must go.'

Alcides knelt to kiss my father's hand, and when he stood I saw his eyes were burning, kindled by the prospect of a quest and glory. 'I will perform the labour as I have the others,' he said. 'I will not fail.'

My father seemed not to hear him. 'But if the Amazons do not have the herbs you seek, daughter,' he said, his gaze concentrated on me, the fixed stare of a general marshalling his troops, 'then I pray Alcides seeks them out as the final labour of the twelve – whatever he has to do. You may say, Alcides, I gave the task to you before you left. I do not wish anyone to know the true reason for your journey, lest the news of Alexander's illness be used against us.'

I bowed my head, even as Alcides beside me tensed – thinking, always, of his glory. I could almost hear his thoughts: *The end of my labours.* 'Of course, father. As you say.'

'And, Admete.' He held out his hand and drew me towards him. Close to, he looked wearier and older than ever, his eyebrows threaded with grey and the skin around his eyes creased in many folds. 'I cannot prevent you seeking your mother. You are of the age now that she was when I wedded her, old enough to guide your own actions – but I give you this warning.' He lowered his voice beneath the sound of the fire spitting on the hearth, though I doubted whether Alcides, deep in contemplation of his labours, would hear him. 'She left Greece because she did not belong here, because she could not tame her Amazon spirit. Do not think that you will find yourself in her.'

I nodded, not a little startled by his bluntness. Then I stepped back.

'And so – do we prepare the voyage?' Alcides was almost bounding on his toes beside me.

My father pressed himself to stand, hands braced on the arms of the throne. 'Yes,' he said, stepping from the dais and placing an arm around my shoulders, holding me to him. I felt myself ache at the prospect of leaving him, yet – at the same time – thrill to be gone. 'We prepare the voyage at once.'

King and Queen of the Gods

Mount Olympus

The afternoon sunlight slants into Hera's chamber, gilding the cedarwood chests and stools, as the queen of the gods gathers her cloak and fastens it around her neck. Iris is sitting on the edge of her bed, swinging her legs and frowning. 'Remind me again why you are so certain that Calliope stole the apples.'

Hera's fingers fumble at the clasp. 'Since when do you take such an interest?'

Iris shrugs, picking at the woollen coverlet. 'I am your messenger, am I not?' She looks up at Hera with a veiled expression and a twist to her mouth that might be sardonic. 'I have to take an interest in all your affairs.'

Hera glares at her, as if to determine whether or not Iris is trying to provoke her. Seeming to decide in her favour, she moves to the bronze mirror propped on her dressing-table and, bending to fasten the cloak properly, she says, 'Because she left Olympus.'

'And surely no god would leave Olympus except for some devious purpose,' Iris says.

'Exactly.' Hera chooses to ignore the irony in Iris's voice. 'She has been gone for four months – four! The other Muses – Melpomene, Erato, Clio and the rest,' she tuts, 'they have such forgettable names – all say they have no idea where she is, or why she is gone.' She straightens and pats her hair, which is twisted on

69

her head beneath her oak-wreath crown. 'I swear that no Muse would flee Olympus if it were not for some scheme. They are crafty tricksters, all of them, with their fine words and their story-telling and the way they make truth out of lies.' She wrinkles her nose, and picks up a hairpin, twisting a loose curl around her finger and sliding it neatly into her bun.

'And this is sufficient reason to follow her?'

'Not entirely,' Hera says, and as she turns to Iris she is smiling, her hands spread wide, like an orator making an unassailable point. 'You see, Hermes told me she has the golden apples.'

'What?' Iris stops picking at the coverlet and gives Hera her full attention at last. She narrows her eyes. 'And you trust Hermes?'

Hera shrugs. 'His story is convincing. He says he saw Calliope at the tree, pulling three of them from the branches on the night that Zeus and I were married.'

'Why would he tell you? You do not suspect him of sending you on a false trail?'

'No,' Hera says, peering in the mirror as she places another pin. 'You see, Hermes is such a trickster that I think he fully anticipated I wouldn't believe him and, on the off-chance that I did, I imagine he thought it would be a good laugh to set me after Calliope. Loyalty,' she fixes the pin into her hair and straightens up, 'is not Hermes' strong suit.'

Iris cocks her head to one side, considering. 'You have a point.'

Silence falls between them as Hera ties her girdle around her waist, and all that can be heard is the cooing of the doves in the trees beyond the window and the humming cicadas.

'And if Calliope has the apples, you want them because . . . ?'

'Because no one steals from the queen of the gods,' Hera says, rounding on Iris, her eyes flashing and her tone suddenly sharp.

'No one. Every golden apple was a gift of Earth and belongs to me and me alone –'

'You mean, you and Zeus.' Iris corrects her, eyebrows arched.

'– and I will not have it said that I will put up with petty theft!'

Iris holds up her hands as she slips off the bed and walks over to Hera, then helps to draw her hood over her head. 'I simply thought you would be more occupied with Hercules. Given that he's Zeus' son.'

Hera waves her away. 'Hercules will set up his own sword to fall upon,' she says, walking towards the door and opening it, so that a chink of golden sunlight slices across the marble floor. 'He is set on a voyage for the Amazons and,' a smile glimmers on her lips, 'if they do not deal with him themselves, I have a plan to sort him out.'

Iris holds the door for her and, with a brief nod, Hera steps out into the corridor, her cloak tucked around her and her ankles flashing as she makes her way to the edge of Olympus, after Calliope.

Iris lingers, watching her retreating back, one arm twisted around the doorpost. 'Oh, I do not doubt that you have.'

The king of the gods turns to his messenger, where they are both crouching hidden in a box hedge in Hera's garden, watching her pass.

'So,' Zeus whispers, 'you found a way to distract her?'

Hermes nods, sending a shower of scented leaves over them both. 'Told her about Calliope and the golden apples,' he mutters. 'It was the only thing I could come up with.'

'You don't think Calliope will—'

'Mind?' Hermes scratches his chin. 'I doubt it. I mean, she expected Hera to come after her some time – that no-one-steals-from-the-queen-of-the-gods nonsense. Calliope knew it was only

For the Immortal

a matter of time. And it's the perfect distraction, anyway. Hera's been obsessed with her authority ever since you made her queen of the gods. I reckon it's the only thing she cares about as much as . . . well,' his eyes slide sideways to Zeus, 'your marriage.'

Zeus flicks a spider from the branch before him. It sails into the air on a silver string. 'You know,' he says, turning to Hermes, 'I don't understand it. It's only one affair. And, yes, I suppose Alcmene was my first, other than Hera, but what about the others, after Alcmene? I don't know why she's so upset.'

Hermes winks. 'Maybe it's because she doesn't know about the others.'

'Well, I was wise to hide them, wasn't I,' says Zeus, 'if this is how she reacts? Going after my son, preventing his immortality – what does she mean by it?'

'I'd say,' Hermes replies, in a mock-serious tone, 'that she probably means to stop you lying with other women. But,' he nudges Zeus with his elbow, dislodging a few more leaves, 'what does it matter? We have her out of the way so we can give Hercules a little help. No problem, is there?'

But Zeus' cheeks are flushed. 'It's just that – well, I don't like to admit it, Hermes—' He stutters into silence. 'I miss Hera,' he says.

'Oh.' Hermes is taken aback. This is not his area of expertise. 'Well, maybe you should try Aphrodite . . .'

'It's just . . .' Zeus says, leaning against a nearby bough and curling his beard around one finger, a wistful expression on his face '. . . it's not that Alcmene and the others weren't fun, but nobody likes change. And,' the red flush creeps up his forehead, 'she hasn't – you know – we haven't . . . since she found out Hercules is mine. Since she heard the oracle at Delphi.'

Hermes gives a low whistle. 'That's a long time.'

72

'But,' Zeus sighs, 'it's also too much fun provoking her to stop.'

'Now, that I do understand. Honestly,' Hermes holds up his hands, 'nothing on Olympus – nothing – matches Hera's indignant fury for comedy value.'

He makes to back out of the hedge, still chuckling, but Zeus catches him by the wrist, and not a moment too soon. Iris has just emerged from Hera's chambers and is walking along the portico that runs the length of the garden, her expression thoughtful.

The two gods wait in silence for her to pass, hardly moving, and an insect buzzes between the branches, enjoying the warm spring afternoon.

At last, the echoing slap of her sandals recedes into the distance. Zeus lets out the breath he has been holding. 'You don't think she heard?'

Hermes shakes his head. 'But we'd better be careful,' he says quietly. 'Look, we'll deal with your marital problems another time. It's about Hercules now, isn't it?'

Zeus purses his lips. 'Yes. Hercules.'

'So?' Hermes lets the question hang between them. 'You asked for a distraction for Hera.' He waves a hand through the branches towards the portico where the queen of the gods and her messenger disappeared moments before. 'What's the plan?'

'The eleventh labour,' Zeus says, seeming to come to himself. 'It's a voyage to the Amazons.'

'Ah,' Hermes says, his interest caught. 'The Amazons. I once had something of a dalliance with—'

'We'll need to ensure a fair voyage for him – make sure the journey is as smooth as possible,' Zeus mutters, ignoring him. 'I was thinking—'

'Poseidon?'

Hermes and Zeus exchange looks of understanding. Any god

wishing to control the winds for a favoured mortal always makes Poseidon, god of the sea, their first port of call.

'Not to worry. It's done.'

Zeus grasps his hand as they back out of the box bush and onto the grass of Hera's garden, picking twigs and leaves from their hair.

'Good lad,' he says, setting his oak-leaf crown straight as Hermes brushes a beetle from his shoulder. 'We'll need a strong south-westerly to get Hercules to Scythia before Hera notices anything.'

On Land and Sea

Ἀδμήτη

Admete

The moment had come. After a few days of rushed
preparation – in which I had given Elais instructions in the
herbs to be used for Alexander, and Alcides had gathered
companions for our voyage – we were setting off, as I had
barely allowed myself to hope we would.

To the Amazons.

To my mother.

I was seated in the ship Alcides had commissioned for the
voyage, a good-sized vessel with fifteen rowing-benches and a
sail that billowed in the wind, like a swallow's wing. I twisted
around on the thwart – close to the back of the ship, so I would
be out of the rowers' way, though at present the wind was
strong enough that we had no need of oars – and felt the breeze
blow into my face, salt-filled and fresh. Tiryns rose behind me,
with its high-built walls and gate-tower, the flanks of the hill
beneath it covered with yellow-flowering broom. I hugged my
knees to my chest, excitement and trepidation filling me in

equal measure. *My home*. I felt an ache in my heart to lose it: the warm scents of the herbary, the humming of the bees in the herb-garden, all those places that had been the measure of my days, the boundary of my world. A lurch of fear clutched me as the image of Alexander, panting and writhing on his bed, rose before me. With a wave of sickness, I thought of cures I might have forgotten to try, preparations I had failed to impart to Elais, and for a moment I wished for nothing more than to turn the ship around and head back to the harbour where my youngest brothers were still gathered – I could make out the sandy fairness of Mentor's hair as Perimedes ran after him, pelting him with pebbles.

'Admete.'

Alcides swung a leg over the rowing-bench before me. His hair was ruffled in the wind. 'What? Such a melancholy expression!' he exclaimed, bending to catch my hands, but I drew them away.

'Don't,' I said, chewing my lip.

There was a moment's silence, as the ropes slapped in the wind and the waves smacked the hull. 'Oh, Alcides,' I burst out, my gaze still on the walls of Tiryns, 'have I made a terrible mistake?'

He laid a hand on my shoulder, as if he knew that, given the chance, I would throw myself into the sea and swim for home to rid myself of this wretched feeling. 'No,' he said, and he grinned at me, cocksure as a sparrow. 'Come, cease your doubting, Admete. This will be a great adventure, one of which they will speak for hundreds of years.' He nudged me with an elbow. 'You should learn not to be so cautious – surely your mother was not so!'

'Surely not.' I swallowed and blinked to clear the blurring

of my eyes. 'I have been thinking the same. Perhaps I am not courageous enough to follow her. Perhaps I should have stayed in Tiryns, where I belong. Perhaps there is too much Greek in me, after all.'

He laughed, tilting his head back, his teeth white. 'You think Greeks cannot be courageous? Have I not told you of my labours?'

'Why, yes, you have,' I said, sliding my eyes sideways at him and smiling a little in spite of myself. 'Some hundred times, I believe. But – no – I mean,' I bit my lip again, 'I never told you, did I, why she left?'

A wave burst into the hull, spraying us both with salt water as he frowned at me. 'I thought it was because she and your father disagreed,' he said. 'You heard them quarrelling, did you not? You heard him telling her it was not proper for a queen of the Greeks to ride out all the day long. Was it not simply a marriage ill-made?'

I shook my head. My throat constricted, such that I could not speak.

'I think,' I said at last, struggling to keep my voice even, my eyes fixed on the waves as they broke against the ship, 'I think it was – I think she left because of me.'

Another silence. A tern flew chattering overhead, an early visitor to the Greek skies and first herald of the summer months.

'You know that is absurd.'

I rounded on him, stung. 'As absurd as doubting that the king of the gods will accept his own son?'

A tinge flushed his cheeks to match the russet of his beard. He braced both hands against the thwart, and I watched the knuckles whiten. 'You know it cannot be true.'

'She chided me,' I said. There was no one else in the world to whom I had told this, not even my father, and though my trust in Alcides was as fathom-deep as the waters over which we now sped, I found I could not meet his eyes for the shame of it, for the fear that I had left Greece when I should not. Fear that I might find her among the Amazons, and hear her confirm it: that I had not been enough to keep her. 'The day before she left . . .' my voice faltered '. . . she came upon me in my chambers, where my maid was putting up my hair in the Greek style. My father had ordered it so, for an envoy had been sent to visit him from Sparta, and he wished me to be well presented. She sent the maid away, took out all the pins and ribbons and combed out the curls. Then she plaited it again, and told me that –' I turned away, swallowing the sob that was threatening to break forth '– that I should be proud to be an Amazon. That she had not given up her own freedom to see me decked out in the chains of Greek finery. And then,' I blinked hard, 'when I awoke the next day, and found her gone, I ran all through the palace and over the hills of Argos looking for her, screaming for her, telling her how sorry I was and that I would wear my hair plaited always for her.' I squeezed my eyes shut, my fingers curling around my hair. 'Every day after that I ran down to the postern gate in the city walls and waited there for her, in case she returned, my breath catching in my chest at every ship coming into harbour – because perhaps this would be the one that brought her. But she never came.'

I turned my gaze to Alcides, and saw that – thank the gods – he was not laughing at me. 'And now,' I said, my voice thin, 'I fear that she was right.'

He leant forwards and covered my hand with his own.

'You have more courage than she ever did,' he said, his eyes burning as they fixed on mine with a kind of quiet rage. 'I swear it. You should have told me.'

I shrugged, though the comfort of his words and his hand warmed me more than I could say. 'I told you the most part.'

'Admete,' he said, 'look at me. I will tell you a truth, and you must remember it. Though I have travelled far from Tiryns these past years, you are truly the most selfless person I have met.' He waved away my rebuttal. 'No, I am not trying to be kind. I speak the truth, and it comes but rarely so you should listen well.' A smile twisted his lips. 'If your mother left, it was for her reasons and hers alone, and none of your doing.' He pressed my fingers between his own, then slid his hand into mine and pulled me to stand. 'You will accompany me on this voyage,' he said, gesturing with our clasped hands to the sail that flapped behind us. 'You will find a cure for Alexander. You will see your mother and you will recognize, as I do, as your father has always done, that, Amazon or no, she was not a mother enough for you.'

I shook my head, overwhelmed by his words, but he let my hand go and took my chin between his thumb and forefinger. 'You bow to no one,' he said, raising my head higher. 'No one.'

I smiled up at him, the corners of my mouth trembling, and in that moment I felt a rush of joy, as if a weight had been lifted from the scales of my judgement. With the balance redressed, I could take the measure of myself once more.

'Yes,' I said, anticipation rising within me. 'Yes,' I repeated. 'I will find a cure for Alexander. I will see my mother.'

'You will.'

He grinned at me, and then, with a nod, he reached up for one of the sail-ropes and swung himself away towards the lords gathered by the bow. I looked out to sea, at the retreating green-grey line of the land, leaning on the ship's side and repeating his words, like an oath.

I will find a cure for Alexander.

I will see my mother again.

I pressed my lips together, filled with determination. *I will.*

𒀭𒉿𒍝𒀪𒆷𒈝

Hippolyta

Amazons, Land of the Saka
The Seventeenth Day after the Day of Earth
in the Season of Apia, 1265 BC

I thrust a leather bag of *koumiss* into my pouch along with a hunk of cheese and some fried fish. My quiver was already filled and strapped to my war-belt, my *sagaris* ready at my hip, my cape over my shoulders and my felt cap on my head when Melanippe ducked into the tent.

'Kati is tied up outside,' she said. 'Are you ready?'

I nodded.

'You are doing the right thing,' Melanippe said. 'It has been long enough – you know that. You do not want to end as Antimache did.'

I nodded again. 'I know.'

I picked up a ewer of water and poured it over the fire, which sputtered and steamed, then went out with a thick billow of smoke. The only light now was the lamp in Melanippe's hand and the rays of the moon glowing like pearls on the damp grass outside. I walked past her and out into the night air, fresh and clear as a mountain spring. The moon was a round globe hanging in the sky, and I felt her influence on me, calming, placating – perhaps even hopeful.

Pray the goddess this may be over soon, I thought. *Pray the goddess I may be free of this torment.*

I leapt up to mount, taking the reins in one hand and wheeling Kati around to face upriver. Melanippe's eyes were large in the moonlight as she stroked Kati's nose. 'May the goddess protect you,' she said.

I tried to smile at her but could not. My heart was too full, with the eddying whirl of exhaustion and fear that had plagued me for so long. Instead I nodded once more. Then I spurred Kati out of the camp, her hoofs scattering clods of black earth, without looking back.

The journey to the goddess's sanctuary took me towards the river. The plain was silent except for the beat of the horse's hoofs and the occasional distant howl of the wolves, piercing my heart, like the barb of an arrow, with their plaintive cry. Now that I had decided, after five years' torment, to be free of the Greek, I found that the memories were coming more insistently than ever, struggling like a captive animal at the end of the chase. With nothing to distract me but the rubbing of the rug against my thighs and the bite of the air upon my lips, I let myself give into them once more – *one last time.*

We are sitting on a rock near the island's shore amid the grey-green shrub; the sea glitters below us in shades of turquoise and blue. My feet are bare – his too – and scorched by the sun as he winds his arms around me. I feel my body shiver, like the feathers of a bird in flight, at his touch.

'*Like this,*' *he says, and guides my fingers to the strings of the lyre. Together we pluck the notes, fingers intertwined, and I start to sing, moving my lips to the tune.*

'Leave the singing to the poets,' he says, and closes my mouth with his.

Hot tears rolled down my cheeks and fell one by one upon my lap.

Night surrounds us as we run towards the grove, hand in hand and breathless, laughing. Nearby, bathed in moonlight, the choirs celebrate the festival of the god, dancing and clashing the cymbals. He catches me and pulls me into the shadows of the pines, presses me hard against a tree and, without waiting, he takes me in the thick darkness of the night. The stars whirl above us and the moon blushes red as I cry out in pleasure, my broken voice mixing with the chants of the worshippers as they dance, and he tells me there is no other life for him than this.

I closed my eyes, fingers shaking on the reins, angered at the thought of the promises he had no right to make, how far he had failed me. And from the bitterness of my resentment I allowed the last vision to rise.

I am standing on the bare outcrop of rock where we played the lyre together, but this time I am alone. I am leaning forwards, my eyes red and rimmed with tears, yet straining to follow a speck of white on the blue ocean as it fades to the horizon. I crouch, my mouth open in a silent cry. The wind blows through my loose hair, the tears run onto my lips, and I allow myself to feel fully the terrible ache of loss and betrayal.

He has left me.

He has left me.

Ἀδμήτη

Admete

Court of Lycus, Mysia

The Eighteenth Day of the Month
of Sailing, 1265 BC

For one who had never travelled further than the boundaries
of the Argolid, and whose only knowledge of distant lands
was the shallow-bottomed barges that came in carrying
herbs and spices for my stores, the journey was filled with
wonders enough to distract me from my cares, plagued as
I was by worry for my brother and anxious to return home. I
learnt more of my companions as we travelled. Theseus, lord
of Athens, spoke little with me, though Alcides seemed
much engaged with him. When I overheard their conversations, on the nights we stopped at the islands dotting the
sea, they seemed to be mostly on Theseus' side, tales of
his exploits. The three brothers and nobles of his court in
Athens I liked better: Solois, in particular, had a keen eye
for the birds that flocked over the islands on their spring
passage north, following our course. Occasionally, when
he tired of the conversation of the lords, we would walk
together from the shore over the meadow pastures and up

the flanks of the grassy island hills, looking for their nesting-grounds. Telemus of Salamis was a man of few words, but Argive Timiades would talk with me from time to time, recalling the vine-dotted plains of our home. And on the isle of Paros, Alcides had claimed two more for our voyage, the brothers Perses and Sthenelus.

But though the company of Alcides – when Theseus could spare him – Solois, and the recollections of Timiades pleased me, what truly filled me with hope were the plants. There were so many different varieties, and I could not help but think that one among them might be the cure for Alexander's illness. On Paros I found a type of fennel that clung close to the rocks by the coast, with a salt-like taste; when picked and eaten fresh, it proved a useful aid to digestion. On Icaria, the villagers near the bay showed me an infusion of sage, garlic and honey, which they drank as a cure-all. I had brought my stylus with me from the herbary, tied to my girdle, and Solois taught me to shape clay from river-mud into tablets – the slaves in Tiryns had always done it for me – so that I could record the new plants and their properties. When we put in at Troy, whose ramparts marked the entrance to the churning waters of the Hellespont, King Priam welcomed us to his halls, and the queen led me to her store-room so that I could document the herbs I found there. That night, the king sacrificed a pair of black-fleeced rams to the gods in our honour, and we drank and feasted with the Trojans – the men with the nobles in the hall, and I with the queen and her daughter Cassandra, a pretty child of five years, in her chambers.

Now, having crossed the Hellespont to the Propontis, the crew brought the ship onto the beach of a river delta, red clay and sand interspersed with tufts of marsh-green. The sun was casting long shadows over the hills ahead as I took Alcides' hand and leapt onto the shore. A messenger was already waiting to greet us – our ship had been sighted, no doubt, as it neared the bay – and hailed Alcides and Theseus, his cloak flapping in the breeze blowing off the sea.

'Lycus, king of the Mariandyni, welcomes you to his shores!' The herald gave a short bow. 'You are Greeks?'

'Hercules, son of Zeus,' Alcides said, inclining his head. 'And these are Theseus, son of Aegeus,' he pointed to each as he spoke, 'Telemus of Salamis, Timiades of Argos, Thoas, Solois and Euneos of Athens, then Perses and Sthenelus, of Paros.'

I bowed my head, preparing to hear my name, but Alcides said no more. I made as if to brush the folds of my skirt to cover the movement, but felt a flare of irritation at his arrogance. I was there, too, was I not? And though I might not be a hero of Greece, was I not still the daughter of Eurystheus, king of Tiryns? Was it not I who had suggested the task of the war-belt of Hippolyta? I glared at him, but he appeared not to notice.

'King Lycus is in need of your assistance,' the messenger said. 'He offers in return gifts, and his guest-friendship, for as long as you should need to stay in our lands.'

'What manner of assistance?' I called, from where I stood towards the back of the gathered Greek nobles. 'We are already bound upon a quest in aid of my brother.'

The herald acted as if he had not heard me. From what little I could see of his face, through the men standing shoulder to shoulder before me, his eyes did not even flick towards me. 'The king is at present engaged in a battle with Amycus, lord of the Bebryces. Your fame has preceded you, son of Zeus. Tales of your great deeds have reached us, even here.' I saw Alcides flush with pleasure. 'King Lycus requests your aid, and the aid of your fighting companions, against the Bebryces – so that he may put this war to rest at last and earn back the lands that are rightfully his.'

'You have it,' Alcides said at once, and held out his hand to clasp the herald's. 'I would consider it an honour to assist your king.'

I frowned at him and tried to push past Timiades and Telemus, who stood before me, to tell him that we were not come to make war but to find a cure for Alexander – that every day we lingered my brother might be closer to death – but the messenger had already turned aside, leading Alcides along the path from the shore.

'Alcides!' I shouted after him. 'Alcides!'

But he did not hear me over the clattering of bronze as the slaves began to unload the weapons from the ship.

Hippolyta

River Silis, Land of the Saka

The Nineteenth Day after the Day of Earth in the Season of Apia, 1265 BC

I lay down to sleep, spreading my wolf-pelt cloak on the damp grass and cocooning myself in it. I still wore my fur-lined boots, and my hands were warm in my felt and hide gloves; it was a fair, cloudless night, and the air was fresh on my skin.

I felt drained, my eyes heavy with fatigue. I had arrived at the sanctuary two days before and hardly slept since. The fire-goddess Tabiti required worship at every rising of the sun and the moon, but most of all when the moon was full and golden, so I had spent that night praying aloud on my knees before the sacred black stone, carved with its ancient images of leaping deer, proud-stepping horses and carved bows, the symbols of our people. The next day I had hunted over the plain – on foot, for stealth was the only way to catch an eagle – and pierced a bird with my arrow as it settled to feed on a carcass. I had built a fire to sacrifice to the goddess, then flayed and roasted the meat, offered the best parts to

Tabiti and partaken of the rest myself. I had sung to the sun as it lit the sky at dawn, and danced beneath the circle of the moon as it floated above.

I ran my fingers over my war-belt, which I had unbuckled and laid beside me, stroking the ridges and hollows of the embossed plates and the stitching that bound and attached them all like the customs of our tribe. I checked my bow and arrows, fastening the lid on the quiver, saw that my *sagaris* lay beside me newly sharpened, then glanced at my horse. I had hobbled her with a length of rope, then covered her with a blanket against the night's chill, and she was cropping the grass nearby. The sky overhead beyond the moon's glow was scattered with stars, and I felt the tight band of resentment and grief around my chest loosen a little as I remembered how my mother had told me that the spirits of our ancestors lived in the stars and looked down upon us. There was Targitaus, first king of the Saka, son of the river Silis, gleaming to the north, and those three stars, set in line, glittering side by side, were his three sons, Leipoxais, Arpoxais and Colaxais, and beside them his daughter Opoea, founders of the many Saka tribes.

May you look down on me tonight, ancestors, and grant me peace.

I had done everything the goddess required. Now all I had to do was wait for her to lift this fire from my heart.

I lay very still and closed my eyes. Had the mothergoddess taken my pain? In my mind I saw sea-foam swirling around my ankles, and the shape of a winged sail, leaving me.

My eyes flew open and I turned over, gritting my teeth and staring across the moon-flooded grass.

I will overcome this, I thought. *I will.*
I must.

And it was as I repeated these words to myself that the goddess threw the blessed veil of sleep over me, and for that night at least I was free of him.

Ἀδμήτη

Admete

Six days later, the battle between the Mariandyni and the
Bebryces still raged. Pent up in the palace of Lycus, and
having long checked the herb-store for remedies – there
were none of which I did not already know, and certainly
none that would be of any use to Alexander – I was furious
with Alcides. As the sun dropped to the west, Lycus and the
Greeks returned, and I was summoned from my chamber to
the evening feast in the hall. Passing the slaves at the doors
I was assailed by shouts and laughter, the clinking of goblets
and the clamour of conversation. The warriors scattered on
the cushions and rugs over the floor were in raucous good
spirits, their hair oiled – they had bathed after the day's
battle, then – and unburdened of helmets, breastplates and
shields. A strain of music broke through the barrage of
words. I glanced around and saw a bard seated on a stool
near the wall, singing with his face upturned and his eyes

roving the hall, though no one seemed to hear him. I moved closer to catch his song.

The Bebryces snatched up their clubs
and rushed upon the hero Hercules;
but the Greeks gathered round before him with pointed swords;
and Timiades struck upon the head a man attacking him –
his skull split in two over each shoulder.
Perses, Sthenelus' brother, slew two men:
one, he leapt upon and drove a blow to his chest
throwing him to the ground;
the other he struck beneath his lowering brows,
blinding him. Amycus, king of the Bebryces, now
thrust the bronze at Solois, grazing the skin as the blade
slipped beneath his belt; but he was not killed.

I turned away, sickened, wanting to hear no more, glad that Alcides was so occupied in talking with Theseus that he could not hear his own praises. The carcass of a deer hissed on the fire, and cupbearers were weaving in and out of the banqueters, pouring wine as each warrior held up his empty goblet. The shadows of the slaves slid over the white-plastered walls, and the flames threw the carved-wood pillars that supported the ceiling into high relief. As one of the slaves passed me, bowing, and offered me wine from the mixing-bowl, I shook my head.

'No, I thank you …' My voice drifted into silence as I pressed past him, then the servers holding baskets filled with bread, and the carver by the great spit over the hearth, towards Alcides. As I neared him I saw Theseus bend to whisper something in his ear, and Alcides let out a roar of laughter, spilling his wine so it splashed over the tiles.

'You have a jest to share?' I asked Theseus, approaching and settling myself on the woven rug beside Alcides.

'None that you would appreciate, daughter of Eurystheus,' he said, bowing, his eyes sliding sideways to Alcides, who laughed again.

'Then I would speak with Alcides a moment.'

'Alcides?' Theseus raised his eyebrows, his gaze not leaving mine as he took a draught from his goblet. 'And who, pray, is that? It is the hero Hercules I know.'

'Yes, well – him,' I said, my jaw tightening in irritation. Alcides was now running his hand over his hair and fussing at his sword-belt, his cheeks flushed at Theseus' open praise, or perhaps the wine and the heat of the fire. 'May we speak?'

'What is it?' Alcides asked, and his tone was short.

I waited until Theseus had begun to talk to Telemus.

'We are losing time,' I said, without preamble. 'Each day we linger here Alexander grows weaker. He may be worsening even now or . . .' I swallowed, unable to name the darkest of my fears. 'Please – I beg you – we must go on. Leave this battle. It is another man's war.'

He shook his head, his eyes over-bright. 'No. I gave Lycus my word of honour. And,' he gestured to the bard in the corner, 'it is a source of great glory for me. Zeus listens to the songs of the bards.'

I almost slapped my hand to the floor in frustration. 'There are more important things – this is not about your glory!' I said, trying with all my might to keep my self-control. 'We are on this quest because of my brother – because of me! I hope you do not forget that?'

'What does that mean?'

I let out a slow breath. 'I do not wish to quarrel with you, Alcides. The gods hate to see old friends at odds with one another. But you should remember, when next you name the crew of your ship and your companions on your voyage, that it was at my request that my father sent you on this task, and that we are here for my brother. My brother alone.'

He let out a crack of laughter that punctuated the tumult of the hall. 'Is that the source of your discontent? That I did not name you to Lycus?'

I felt my face grow hot. 'No, it is not. It is that you seem to have forgotten why you are on this quest and with whom.'

'What do you want, Admete? You wish me to proclaim your title and patronage to the king of the Mariandyni – here and now?'

'No,' I said, wresting the goblet from his grip so that his grin twisted into a childish scowl. 'And I am not jesting, Alcides. I wish you to put a stop to this war, and leave as soon as we may for the Amazons, so we may find a cure for my brother.'

I glared at him, as Theseus grabbed at the hand of a serving-girl as she walked past, and Telemus laughed and pulled her to sit beside them. For a moment Alcides and I glowered at each other, the shouting, the laughter and the twanging of the lyre ringing in our ears. Then—

'Oh, let us not dispute,' he said, and took the goblet back from me, his fingers brushing mine, his eyes softening. 'I am sorry for my words. I will speak with Lycus and, in any case, the Bebryces are almost vanquished.'

I let out a breath. 'I thank you,' I said, clasping his hand. 'I knew the old Alcides was in there somewhere.'

He said nothing, though I thought I saw the muscles of his jaw twitch at the name. Through the brief lull between us the bard's song floated across the chamber.

> *Theseus, bold son of Aegeus, seized his massive axe*
> *and plunged into the midst of the fray; with him*
> *charged Hercules, warlike Amphitryon's son, and with him*
> *cunning Telemus.*

I glanced at Alcides, but he was looking away and I could not see his expression. I knelt forwards and placed a hand on his shoulder to push myself to stand. At the last moment he turned to help me, his hand easily supporting my weight. 'Thank you,' I said again, and he gave me a half-smile.

'Off with you, then,' he said, making as if to push me from the hall. I laughed, feeling lighter than I had in days, now that I knew we would soon be on our voyage once more, and made my way back across the crowded room. I accepted some meat and bread from a slave and a little wine to take to my chambers, and when I passed the bard at his seat by the doors I heard again his song.

> *And so, like shepherds smoking bees from a rock,*
> *and they murmur with a low drone till at last*
> *they swarm away, ousted by the dark smoke;*
> *so the Bebryces fled . . .*

I decided to take it as an auspicious sign.

The War-Belt of Hippolyta

Ἀδμήτη

Admete

Amazons, Scythia

The Tenth Day of the Month
of the Harvest, 1265 BC

The journey seemed interminable, every new appearance of
the sun over the watery horizon bringing with it the fear
that we might be too late, that Alexander might not live for
our return. Yet now, weeks after our departure from Lycus'
court, I stood at the prow of the ship, leaning over the water
and straining my eyes, my heart pounding in my chest. Yes,
I was sure of it – there, on the horizon, to the east of the line
of surf where the river met the sea.

Flat grassland was coming into view under the rolling
clouds of the sky, the line of the river marked by dotted tufts
of trees, and as the drum beat, and the sailors rowed towards
the mouth of the channel, I thought I could begin to make
out peaked tents, scattered over the grass, and figures moving between them.

My breath caught in my throat.

I could hardly believe it. There – before me . . .

The Amazon camp.

'Take care you do not fall in. It would be a pity to see you fail at your quest now, after coming all this way.'

I turned to see Alcides pulling at the oar on the thwart closest to the prow. He was grinning, the sleeves of his tunic rolled up to his shoulders as he stroked the blade through the water.

'What do you think they will be like?' I asked, leaning on the beam of the ship's side.

'I hardly care,' Timiades answered, before Alcides could, seated one berth back. 'As long as they have fresh meat, and water to bathe in I, for one, shall be a happy man.'

'And you, Alcides? What do you expect of the Amazons?'

He paused for a moment. 'That they live up to their legends,' he said, then went back to his rowing.

I turned towards the shore, feeling the wind blowing into my face and the kiss of sea-spray. *And you, Admete?* I supplied.

A shiver flared up my spine and I closed my eyes, fingers gripping the carved wood of the prow. *Oh, gods, what am I doing here?* Forebodings crowded my mind one after another. *Perhaps these are not the Amazons. Or perhaps they will not have the cure for my brother's illness, and our voyage will have been in vain . . .*

Or perhaps my mother will spurn me, in front of everyone, tell me she did indeed depart Tiryns because of me . . .

Fear prickled my scalp, sickness rose in my belly, but I opened my eyes and forced myself to stare at the shore to keep the queasiness at bay, still clutching the prow. We were nearing the river's estuary now and the currents pulled and buffeted at the keel. The camp was set back a little from the shore but clearly visible. I could make out the tents properly now, covered with felt and animal-hide, horses wandering on every side, their coats shades of gold, chestnut and bay, the women chopping wood with bronze-bladed axes, flaying and preparing meat. My fingers flew to my mouth as I realized I knew their clothes: they were the same as my mother had worn. Cuffed boots, patterned trousers in vivid greens and blues, pointed caps, tunics bound with leather war-belts from which hung swords and battle-axes – though my mother's belt had always been bare.

And then I saw something that quite distracted me – a figure with hair unplaited. There, brushing down one of the horses . . . *A man?*

I stared. From all I had heard of the Amazons since my mother had left – morsels of information gleaned from conversations overheard and visiting bards at court – they were a fearsome tribe who shunned all relations with men, women who were truly the rivals of men and had no need of husbands or keepers.

Yet, now I think on it, my mother never told me it was so . . .

I felt pressure on my arm and blinked. Alcides was leaning forwards from his seat. 'It is natural to be afraid,' he said. 'You have waited many years for this.'

A rebuttal rose, then died in my throat.

I nodded, pressing my lips tight. 'What if they do not have the cure we are searching for?' I whispered, so quietly that only he could hear it, as I slid down inside the hull to sit on the planks by his thwart, my knees tucked into my chest. 'What if everything I knew about them is wrong?'

He said nothing. Moments passed, in which the prow dipped and broke into the waves, and I huddled against the ship's side as if to pretend I was back in Tiryns, seated in my chambers and waiting for my slave to fill the bath.

Alcides' voice broke into my thoughts. 'Admete, look,' he said.

We had entered the river now, slow-moving, quite unlike our darting Greek streams, and as I stood I saw the current swirling in eddies around the ship's hull. And then, with a thrill of fear and longing as real as physical pain, I glimpsed them ahead, along a bank and shaded by trees, some of the tribe, spears planted in the sand. A woman, tall with a hide cloak on slender shoulders, stepped forwards, a battle-axe at the gold-plated belt over her tunic. At once everything was forced from my mind, everything except this moment, as the steersman turned us to the bank and the keel ploughed into the sand. And I knew, as a bird, a yearling, flying to the south over winter knows its way, not because it thinks it, but because it feels it in every feather of its wings.

We had reached the Amazons.

𒀭𒂊𒉽𒀭𒅆𒈨𒌑

Hippolyta

Amazons, Land of the Saka

The Fortieth Day after the Day of Earth
in the Season of Apia, 1265 BC

I stood on the shore watching the ship sail towards us, my heart thrashing like a blue-thrush trapped in a net. It was a Greek ship, I knew it: I could have told it from the black-tarred keel to the square sheet and the deck astern with the steering oar pooling in the river. *Just as his was when he left me.* I could hear the sounds of their language floating towards me over the water: a long-forgotten music, which set the blood in my veins singing and made every nerve in my body thrum.

I tightened my grip around my spear and my knuckles whitened. Melanippe stood beside me on my left, Orithyia on my right. I knew Melanippe could sense the stiffness of my body, as easily as if I were a high-strung mare champing at the bit. But I refused to meet her eye.

I could look only towards the ship.

It was coming ever closer, its prow turning now towards the shore. Soon it would run aground and they would have to pull it up to land. I could see the faces of the rowers, began to make out their features, and I searched them as quickly as I could, eyes darting back and forth. I was not sure even what I wished to see, or whether I looked in hope – my heart pounding, searching . . . *The dark eyes, the flax-gold hair . . .*

It took me only a few moments to know that he was not there, and another to know by the drop in my shoulders and the hollow ache in my chest that I had hoped indeed. But then I thought, *Perhaps one of them may know where he is, or have some news of him*, and my breath caught in my throat once more, followed by the familiar pang of bitterness that I had allowed myself to be reduced to this, and the still-raw wound of his betrayal.

The first of the Greeks was leaping from the ship and wading through the water towards us: stocky, broad-shouldered and built like a bull, with a swagger to his stride as he crossed the sand towards me. As he knelt and our eyes met I saw a great emptiness in his gaze, a longing that would not easily be filled.

'My lady, *daimonié*,' he said, and I felt a surge of barbed joy at the sound of the word the other Greek had once used to say to me. 'I ask you as a traveller, in the name of Zeus who watches over guests and gives voyagers a roof above their heads. Have we come across the Amazons, or must we journey further?'

How like the Greeks to assume their language is spoken every-where, I thought. Melanippe's eyes were darting between me and the newcomer, and I heard Orithyia mutter, 'A foreigner, then! A barbarian!'

I stepped forwards and took him by the hand to raise him

to his feet. 'We are the Amazons indeed,' I said, feeling my tongue roll over the Greek again, unfamiliar as a kiss. 'And I am their queen, Hippolyta. What brings you here, stranger, and from so far?'

A moment's silence, then a whisper flew around the rest of the tribe, standing gathered behind me on the bank, ready to welcome my guests or join battle against them at my command.

'The queen speaks their language?' I heard my archer Aella murmur nearby.

'A strange tongue!'

'How can she have learnt it?'

'A foreign tongue!'

I turned towards them, frowning. The Amazons were wary of foreigners to a fault. We had been told by our mothers, and by their mothers before them, that – ever since Opoea, daughter of Targitaus, had founded the race of the Amazons with her consort-brother Colaxais – the gods had forbidden us to lie with others beyond our tribe, for fear of losing our warrior-spirit. Since I was a girl the women of the camp had spoken above all of Antimache, captured by a foreign tribe before I was born, still talked of as a traitor to our ways. She had lain with a foreigner – a *paralati* – a man of the earth, they said, and taught the outcasts our Amazon ways. We were a strong people, they said, and could not lose the ferocity that ran in our veins by befriending anyone beyond our borders, as Antimache had done. Any *paralati* was regarded with the utmost suspicion. The slanting glances they were giving the rowers on the ship now, and the way their fingers curled around the hilts of their swords, were proof enough of that.

We sisters had kept our secret well.

I gazed around at the Amazons, saw some of them lean back from whispering as my glance fell upon them, others – the councillors Thoreke and Iphito – hushing the younger warriors. I nodded this way and that, as if to say, *This is nothing but my duty as a queen* – and they seemed to settle, loosening their grip on their swords and shields once again.

Then I turned back to the stranger, and the Greeks gathered behind him. For a moment my breath snagged, like a thread on a hooked clasp. One of the Greek men behind him had turned his head, and for a moment, just a moment, I saw the face of another in his. *Those fathomless eyes that seem to scorn the world and everyone in it . . . the angle of the jaw . . .*

But then I blinked, and the resemblance was gone. This man was broader of chest, and surely years older than the Greek would have been, the hair at the edge of his temples streaked with grey.

I drew my gaze back to the stranger before me, who was now speaking, though my breath was coming fast and the collar of my cloak felt hot around my neck.

'My name is Hercules, son of Zeus,' he was saying, 'and these,' he gestured towards the band behind him, 'are my men, the finest warriors in all of Greece. We beg your hospitality, and . . .' his eyes flickered aside, then back to me '. . . that I might talk with you.'

I waited, taking the measure of him. 'You say you come in peace?' I glanced at the swords hanging at their waists, the spears and shields bundled on their backs. 'Why, then, do you bring so many arms to my land?'

He spread his hands. There was a smirk on his face, which

I did not quite like. 'We come in peace – if you will but speak with us.'

I matched my gaze with his. 'I see,' I said, running my finger over the looped plates that fronted my belt. 'Then we should talk, as you say.'

As he inclined his head, I noticed, for the first time, a woman standing behind him, among the crowd of warriors and slaves. My lips parted to utter an exclamation – for in everything but her dress, which was barbarously long-skirted and completely unfit for riding, she was an Amazon. Her dark hair was plaited long to one side, her cheekbones high, her eyes slim and sloping, and filled with bright, burning curiosity as she looked at me.

I turned my eyes back to the man who called himself Hercules. 'You are full of contradictions, stranger,' I said. 'You sail across the seas to the ends of the world merely to speak with us. You bring with you a woman who looks in every way an Amazon, yet wears Greek dress . . .'

And you are Greek, but you have not brought him with you.

He gestured to the woman. 'This voyage is a labour imposed on me by her father, the king of Tiryns. I must complete twelve tasks in his service. Admete requested that we journey to the Amazons.'

I smiled at the woman, and saw a swift response in her eyes.

'It is the law of the gods,' I said, raising my voice so all the Greeks might hear, 'that we take you into our homes, and offer you gifts to take back to your country when you leave so that all may know of the might of the Amazons. But first,' I gestured to the camp above the riverbank, 'let us sacrifice together to the goddess who creates all things, and eat and drink our fill. Then you will tell me whence and why you have come.'

He bowed his head. 'That would be welcome.'

'They come in peace,' I said, in our native tongue, and the tension in my clansmen's faces released, though Orithyia's scowl did not lessen.

'They are foreigners!' she hissed, coming close to my side. 'How can we trust them? They come laden with weapons, swords sharp at their belts – and still you invite them to our hearths?'

I turned and made my way towards the trees. 'It was my mother's command before me, and mine too, Orithyia, that we welcome all and every guest to our tribe. We must treat them as we would hope to be welcomed if we wandered far on the plain.'

As I glanced towards her, I saw the man who resembled my Greek across the shore, marshalling the drawing of the ship onto the sand. My eyes followed the turn of his head, watching the sunlight sew threads through his loose hair and letting his commands fill my ears.

Melanippe's voice cut across my thoughts. 'Have a care, sister,' she said, from behind me, and her voice, though low, sounded a warning.

Her words were like an awakening from a dream. I shivered and turned back, trying to gather myself as I trod the sand and the stranger's footsteps crunched beside me.

Remember who you are, Hippolyta, I commanded myself, biting my lip, and the voice that reprimanded me was my mother's, stern as a horse-whip: a queen who had always known her duty to her tribe and the customs of her people. *Remember your duty, as you did not when you were with the*

Greek before. The creeping sensation of guilt and shame, so familiar for so many years, laced its way through me and urged me on, as it always had.

You are the queen of the Amazons. You have to think of your people.

My fingers slipped to the eagle *tamga* at my belt, the cold bite of the iron against my skin like my mother's love, fierce and proud. I walked on, head high, towards the tents. And this time, I did not look back.

Ἀδμήτη

Admete

Amazons, Scythia

The Tenth Day of the Month of
the Harvest, 1265 BC

It was like a vision, yet better than a vision, because it was
real. Often I had to blink to remind myself that I was awake,
not dreaming. I had imagined the home of the Amazons so
many times. First it was my mother's whispered tales as she
rocked my cot in the summer evenings. I had seen her as I
closed my eyes and drifted to sleep, riding across the plains
with a hunting-eagle on her arm and the wind in her hair.
Then, with growing clarity, when I was older and had to fall
asleep alone without a mother's arms to hold me, I had
added to the scant details I had from her. Lying awake during the starless nights, I had made a world for myself, a
refuge of scree-covered mountains, tribes covered with furs
and women calling to each other, like falcons. And in the
midst of it all my mother rode.

But this sky, stretching like an arch overhead, the grass
without walls or boundary-markers, stirred only by the
wind – this was a vastness of which I could never have

dreamt. The camp was filled with the activity of daily life. There must have been at least a hundred Amazons, perhaps more, their tents clustered together, their lives interweaving as closely as those of their horses, which fed together at the troughs and slept huddled side by side for warmth. A pair of women seated on stools, one spinning wool, the other darning clothes, talked to each other in low voices while they worked; a group of men tanned hides in wooden vats by the camp's edge, where the breeze blew away the stench; several others tended their horses, filling the water-troughs and digging stones from hoofs with picks – and it was all so different from how I had thought it would be, yet so real, so alive, that I could feel my imagined world draining away, like water through cupped hands.

The queen, her riders and the Greeks, Alcides among them, had gone from the camp to hunt, and I was left behind, so filled with anticipation that here, after so many weeks at sea, we might find the long-sought herbs to deliver my brother that I hardly knew where to turn. And yet beneath my excitement, something else: that same fear prickling my skin, now that I had come, that she might not be here or, if she was, and did not want me . . . And so I distracted myself with seeking out the healer of the camp, trying not to look into the curious faces of the women who wandered past so that I could continue to think that somewhere, there, was my mother.

A day later and still I had not sighted her, and I had not had the courage to ask of her, though at times I thought – or perhaps imagined – I heard her name whispered as I passed. When I looked up, certainly, those whom I could have sworn had said her name were busy at their work, silent with their heads bowed. After some enquiry I had found the healer, an elderly woman, Ioxeia, with a scar gashed over a blinded eye, and she had agreed to take me through her stores of herbs when the sun was up.

At dawn, therefore, I rose filled with eagerness from the tent where they had given me a bed, along with some Amazon women of my age, Polemusa, Aella and Deianeira, who stared at my Greek clothes and my plaited hair and barely replied when I spoke to them in the Scythian tongue. The sky was streaked with pale pink clouds edged with gold as I hurried to the healer's tent, a cloak around my shoulders against the morning chill and dew on my sandals from the wet grass. Smoke was rising in a blue column as I drew back the tent-flap to see the healer holding a lamp and seated on a stool before a cauldron filled with the mare's-milk drink they called *koumiss* propped over the fire. Baskets of herbs were stacked against the hide walls. At once I smiled – I could not help it. The scents that greeted me were so familiar – meadowsweet, bright as honey, grass-like pennyroyal and powdered safflower – that, without thinking, I closed my eyes and drew a breath to take them in.

'A true healer, then,' Ioxeia said. She was regarding me with her good eye, head to one side and stirring the *koumiss* with a ladle as it simmered. 'But if you are half an Amazon, as you say, it is little wonder. We have always had a way with plants.'

My gaze wandered around the tent, taking in the bed of pelts, the dried plants hanging from the struts, then back to the herbs.

'Help yourself,' she said.

I stepped towards them across the rugs on the ground and held a basket of dried liquorice roots to my nose. 'I am seeking a cure for a particular ailment.'

'You have seen the disease yourself?'

I nodded, picking up a handful of elecampane.

'The signs?'

'Fever,' I said, replacing the elecampane and ticking off the symptoms on my fingers. Ioxeia had stood and moved over to me now, and as our gazes met, determined, absorbed, I felt the satisfaction of a language we shared, beyond Scythian, in our understanding of plants and their effects on the body. 'But not a fever such as I have ever seen. It cycles around and around, regular as the seasons, rising and falling, then rising again. Sweating. Chills. Weakness. Delirium.'

She pursed her lips, making the skin wrinkle. 'Fever,' she muttered, and moved past me to the baskets. I watched as she began to remove the herbs one after another, holding them to her nose to identify them, then naming them and their properties. '*Halinda* – but that increases warmth . . . Quince and black cumin seeds for digestion . . . Yellow pheasant's eye,' she took a handful of dried leaves and golden petals, 'you might try to slow the pulse.' She picked up a cloth pouch and dropped into it a couple of handfuls of the herb, then moved back to the stacked baskets, running her fingers across them. 'Hyssop, again, is warming, though it relieves sickness – is there sickness?' she asked, turning to me.

I nodded, and she took some for another pouch. 'Angelica induces sweat. Tarragon aids sleep. Carob for pain in the stomach . . .' She lifted another to her face, then turned to me. 'You might try yarrow,' she said, and she handed me a pouch of the dried leaves. I took it, feeling dispirited: I had used yarrow already, and to little effect, except to lower his fever somewhat. *Pray the gods she has more, or this voyage will truly have been for nothing.*

'You have tried feverfew?'

'Yes, and willow-bark,' I said, trying to keep the snap from my voice.

She returned the basket and moved back to sit before the fire, one hand on her back as she lowered herself to the stool. 'Then that is all I have.' She picked up the ladle and began to stir again. The tangy-sweet smell of milk curled into the air.

I pushed the pouches into my girdle and rounded on her, half desperate, half enraged. 'It cannot be. Please, I beg you. There must be more! My mother spoke of herbs such as we had never seen, of such potency that they might cure any ailment . . .'

She brought the ladle to rest and placed her hands one over the other on it, a look of resignation on her face, both eyes fixed on me. 'And who was your mother, child?'

I hesitated. 'Antimache,' I said.

Ioxeia grunted. 'I thought as much,' she said. She eyed me for a moment, then said, 'You have the look of her about you well enough.'

I started forwards, all thoughts of herbs forgotten, my heart leaping so hard in my throat I could barely breathe. 'Then – then you know her?'

'Oh, I knew her.' Her eye flicked up to me, and I thought I saw a shadow cross her expression. 'It was I who taught her to heal.'

'Then – but then –' I twisted my fingers together, hardly able to speak '– you must know where she is?'

She shook her head. Her grey hairs shimmered in the firelight. 'I'll say no more.'

'But—'

'No more.' Her voice was sharp. 'You must ask the queen.'

I took her in, her lower lip jutting forwards and her hands crossed before her. 'I will, then,' I said, 'I will go to her now. I thank you.'

'Daughter of Antimache,' she called after me, and I turned, slipping a little on the rug in my haste. 'If you still wish for a cure . . .'

'You have something else?'

The old woman shook her head and drew her stool closer to the cauldron. 'No. But if the disease is as potent as you say, I'll wager – for all you seem to depend on herbs – that it is a scourge sent by the gods, and only the gods will cure it. So, if you are to see the queen,' her blind eye gleamed milky-white, 'you might ask her of the golden apples.'

𒀭𒈾𒊏𒀭𒈾

Hippolyta

Amazons, Land of the Saka

The Forty-first Day after the Day of Earth
in the Season of Apia, 1265 BC

The Greeks, it transpired, had voyaged to our lands in
search of herbal lore. The king's daughter, who so resembled
an Amazon, had some fancy to cure her brother's illness
with plants, rather than the propitiation of the gods – there
was a bite in Hercules' voice as he told me – so they were
come in peace, that she might visit Ioxeia and learn her
trade. If the elders of my council murmured that it was
strange to have brought so many swords and spears in search
of knowledge, if the whisperings of my own caution told me
to be on my guard, then I was determined to ignore them. I
was resolute: I would trust their word, and their honour, as
my mother would have done, as a queen bound by the laws
of hospitality beneath the gods.

And so, as Ioxeia occupied herself with demonstrating her
knowledge of herbs, I spent the days leading the rest to the
plains. That morning we were to hunt together once more.
The Greeks seemed to enjoy the novelty of women who could

ride, and I took pleasure in demonstrating to them the skills of my tribe, our time-honoured customs and the beauty of a life spent beneath the sky, where men and women rode side by side, the wind flying through their hair and a quiver at their hip. I could hear my people gathering their horses in the camp outside my tent, the resounding *clop-clop* of hoofs on earth, the horses snuffling and whinnying. The hunting dogs were baying, and shouts in Greek and Saka mixed with the laughter of children, stirred up by the excitement of the hunt.

I straightened my tunic, embroidered at the edge and dyed in strips of purple and green, beneath my war-belt, checking the clasp at my side, the plates chinking beneath my fingers. My plait was twisted with a golden thread in honour of our guests, and pinned on my tunic I wore a brooch of a leaping stag – my mother's before me. I held up a bronze mirror, and in the reflection, proud and stern, I saw a queen, a leader of her people; her face pale, perhaps, but her jaw set and her eyes bright.

I raised my chin, set down the mirror and, with one thumb tucked into my war-belt, pushed my way out of the tent.

Theseus, prince of Athens, who so reminded me of that other Greek, was waiting outside amid the clamour of the gathering riders. His hand was on my horse's reins, and he looked well groomed with a careless grace about him. His hair was oiled back from his head, the beard dark on his chin and over his lip.

'My lady,' he said, taking my hand and bowing. 'You are as beautiful as Artemis before the hunt.'

I withdrew my fingers from his, disliking the intensity of his gaze on me. 'The Amazons do not usually address their queen so.'

He led Kati forwards. 'Then may I help you onto your horse?'

I moved around him. 'I am queen of the Amazons,' I said, taking Kati's mane in one hand and swinging myself up to her back. Kati sidled beneath me, whinnying. 'I have ridden since before I could walk. What do you think, prince of Athens?' I asked, looking down at him.

He bowed his head, saying nothing, a dull flush creeping beneath his beard.

'Melanippe?' I called, bringing Kati round to search through the milling crowds, the stamping horses and barking dogs. At last I saw her, and cantered over. She was mounted too, dressed for hunting, her quiver and bow at her waist and her wool tunic light-woven for the warmer spring weather.

She whistled to the dogs and the pack closed together. The rest of the Amazons – my band of fighters, Aella, Xanthippe, Asteria and the others, joined by some of the tent-holders who took pleasure in the hunt – leapt onto their steeds at my call, first in Saka, then in Greek. Hercules mounted Teuspa's horse, and the other Greeks followed suit, calling to each other, some complaining at the harsh-woven felt rugs we used for saddles, others adjusting their sword-belts and the spears fitted in the baldrics on their backs.

The air was scented with the promise of rain, that sweet-damp tang, and the sky was a rolling grey blotted here and there with dark stormclouds as I rode forwards. I took Kati's reins in one hand and brought her around to face the troop of Greeks and Amazons. Bright Amazon tunics and trousers mixed before me with the more sober Greek clothes, horses in all colours – black, bay, and tan, chestnut, dun and dark rich brown – and, weaving between them, Teres, Ainippe and Cayster, pulling at the horses' tails and laughing as they rolled on the grass with the hounds.

'To the hunt, then,' I called, drawing my bow from the case at my war-belt. The Greeks clamoured, the dogs bayed. Melanippe and Aella shook the wide-meshed hunting nets. I plucked at Kati's reins and, as always, mirroring my thought, she started into a trot, then a gallop towards the open plain. I heard hoofbeats behind me and saw Theseus at my rear. I tossed my head and spurred Kati on, rising and falling with her as if we were one, and Theseus fell behind.

'You cannot ride?' I threw at him over my shoulder.

'In Greece,' he called to me, 'women do not ride like this. Many would say it is improper.'

'In the land of the Amazons,' I replied, the wind whipping the words out of my mouth, 'women and men alike learn to ride, and it is often that a woman on horseback will be faster and better with a bow than a man.'

'If the women are so taken with riding and the arts of war,' he shouted back, 'then are they not mothers too? How is it, Queen, that you have so many children in your camp, if your women are always on horseback?' He laughed and hurled the next question forwards like a dart: 'Do women not also lie with men?'

I did not answer, for at that moment Xanthippe and Asteria galloped up beside me. In any case, my throat was dry, my heart pounding at what he had said. Was it mere chance that he had spoken so? Or did he know of the Greek? Had someone told him? And if he revealed . . . If the Amazons discovered . . .

My vision blurring with panic, I gestured blindly to the

121

outlines of a herd of deer grazing in the distance, and my women nodded, spurring their horses on. The dogs ran ahead, the rest of the hunt pressed forwards with cries and the thundering of hoofs, and I galloped on, feeling the wind whipping my cheeks and the familiar firm steadiness of Kati's back against my thighs. I tried to ignore the sensation that Theseus' eyes were on me, steady as a falcon on its prey.

A distant rumble filled the sky. Sudden as a thought, the dark clouds split into a pillar of lightning ahead, followed by a bellow of thunder. The deer started and sped over the open field, massing together in a fleeing herd. A second bolt arrowed down the sky before us, blinding white, then splitting into thunder so loud I felt it shiver through my ribs. Kati bucked and veered, tossing her head and galloping over the plain.

I cried out to her, pulling on one rein to bring her under control and gripping hard with my thighs to keep my seat. Now sleet was hissing down from the sky, and Kati's eyes were white with fear. I twisted around, shielding my face with my free hand, and saw other riders scattering across the plain, some attempting to calm their horses, others trying not to fall. And then the rain and sleet closed over everything in a silver-grey veil and I turned back, thinking only of clinging on, my trousers stuck tight to my legs and water filling my boots. I could see nothing but Kati's head before me as she galloped wildly and the pearls of rain sliding down her mane. I twisted the reins around my hands and ducked my head, calling soothing words to her, which were stolen from my lips and shot away behind me on the wind.

At last, the shrouded shapes of trees shimmered up before me. We must have reached the river's edge. Kati raced beneath the shelter of the canopy and then, abruptly, her whole body trembling, came to a halt. I slid from her back to the grass and ran to cradle her head in the crook of my arm, stroking her neck and muttering, 'It's all right, oh, it's all right,' as the rain spattered the leaves above us and the sky lit with sparks of white. I could feel her calming, her gaze growing steadier, responding to the firmness of my body and my voice. Her breath was warm on my sodden clothes and skin, and I smiled as I pressed my forehead to hers and inhaled her scent, of hay and smoke.

And then I started.

A second rider had approached us, and I knew at once that it was, must be, Theseus: the unpleasant tingle of apprehension on my skin told me so. He led his horse to me, then loosed the reins. I did not turn.

'You are not afraid?' he said, his voice soft, a thread of sound under the rain. A flash of lightning above made Kati's ears twitch. I stroked and soothed her, though my own heart was hammering at the thought of what he might know, and the presumption of his addressing me so.

'No,' I said quietly. 'The lot of a queen is to have no fear, except for her people.'

Silence fell between us.

Then he stepped closer, his hand gripping my wrist and the heat of his breath on my face. Fury welled in me, strong and sharp, like the flames beneath the breath of the bellows, and I thrust the heel of my hand against his face, feeling the nose break and split. As he reeled back, blood gushing, I drew my sword, swift as wind, and held the sharpened bronze at his throat. Drops of rain glanced off the blade, singing.

'How *dare* you?' I said, my voice low with threat. 'How dare you think to lay a hand on—'

He did not wait to hear me. Staggering, hands held up to his broken face, he reeled away and, slipping on the wet grass, crawled onto his horse's back. There was a moment, as he turned back to me, gushing blood, when our eyes met, and I felt the hatred of his gaze.

'Go!' I shouted, drawing myself up, my sword still outstretched, heat trembling through my veins as if my very skin was blazing with my fury. 'Do not – ever – dare to speak to me again.'

Without a word, he kicked his steed out into the storm and the darkness of the drenched plain.

Ἀδμήτη

Admete

Amazons, Scythia

The Twelfth Day of the Month
of the Harvest, 1265 BC

I did not go at once to the queen. A storm had broken overhead, and Ioxeia allowed me to shelter with her by the
warmth of her fire. When at last I decided to leave, seeing
that the rain would not abate, my spirit failed me as I crossed
the camp, water pouring down and pooling on the grass. I
felt the eyes of the Amazons glinting at me, heard their
whispered mutters in the Scythian they thought I could not
understand.

'But she looks like an Amazon!'

'She looks like Antimache!'

Thoughts chased themselves through my head –
presentiments as to why Ioxeia had refused to speak to me of
Antimache, why whispers of her name followed me. *Perhaps
she was disgraced. Perhaps she is dead. Perhaps she betrayed them
for the Greeks . . .*

I pulled the hood of my cloak over my head and walked

quickly, squinting against the rain. When I looked up, I had reached Alcides' tent.

And so I went to Alcides instead. 'I need to speak with you.'

I hung at the doorpost of the tent, taking in the felt walls covered with woven rugs, the fire sputtering in a brazier at the centre as drops of rain slid through the opening above. Alcides was sitting on a stool rubbing his hair with a cloth, and I realized that, though he had on a fresh tunic, his hair was drenched, and many of the others – the brothers Euneos, Solois and Thoas among them, Perses and Sthenelus, and Timiades of Argos – were warming themselves by the fire in sodden clothes. Theseus was there too, and his appearance, nose mangled, the bone at an odd angle, his face streaked with blood, shocked me – perhaps he had fallen from his horse, or come to blows with another of the Greeks. His face was as dark as the stormclouds overhead and a vein pulsed on his forehead as he allowed a slave to mop the blood from his skin. His eyes narrowed as he watched me pass.

I approached Alcides, moving past Timiades, who stood nearest, and knelt by him. 'The hunt?' I asked.

Alcides shook his head, spraying me with raindrops. 'We were forced to return,' he said, patting his jaw and neck with the cloth.

'Oh. I am sorry,' I said, reaching to brush his knee, wondering if they had come back because of the rain or Theseus' injury. 'But I am glad you are here. I would speak with you.'

Perhaps he heard the concern in my voice, or perhaps it showed in my eyes, for he ceased drying himself and leant forwards, elbows on his thighs, frowning at me – just as he had always done in years gone by when I had come to him with some worry or slight. My heart swelled at this sign of our old friendship.

'What is the matter?'

I bit my lip, glancing at Theseus, whose head was tilted back as the slave tended him, then at Timiades a few paces distant, warming his hands at the fire, but the rain was still hammering against the tent, and there was nowhere else to go.

'Did you find the cure?' His voice was low and eager as he leant closer to me, so quiet beneath the spitting of the flames that no one but I could hear him. 'Did you find the cure for Alexander?'

I shook my head, and his face fell. 'But I have a lead,' I added, and his expression lifted. 'I do not know if it amounts to anything but,' I swallowed my disbelief, for now was not the time to quell Alcides' enthusiasm, 'the healer told me of a garden of apples, belonging to the gods, which might cure my brother. She told me to ask the queen if she had heard tell . . . and also, of my mother . . .'

'Apples of gold?' he asked, frowning, and his voice rose over the licking flames.

Timiades turned towards us, his interest caught, and asked, 'Surely not the apples of the Hesperides?'

'You know of them?' I asked, taken aback. 'I had never heard . . .'

He shrugged. 'An old story,' he said, 'and not much repeated.'

'Well?'

He rubbed his forehead. 'There is said to be a garden, at the end of the earth, watched over by the Hesperides, the guardians of evening, daughters of Atlas. The apples of

127

gold – or so they say – were a gift from the earth to Zeus and Hera on their wedding day.'

'And – and these apples have healing properties?' *Perhaps there is more to Ioxeia's story than hearsay. If it has been told in Greece too, then perhaps it is more than a mere tale.*

He shrugged again, stretching his hands towards the fire. 'I heard it from my father's mother when I was a boy, so I do not remember it well. But I seem to recall – I may be wrong, mind – that they were said to bring immortality.'

I felt Alcides tense at the word. His eyes met mine, alight with exhilaration, his face burning, and I knew that he was remembering my father's words: *If the Amazons do not have the herbs you seek, then I pray Alcides seeks them out as the final labour of the twelve – whatever he has to do. You may say, Alcides, I gave the task to you before you left.*

And behind it, blazing in his mind, like a brand: *Immortality.*

'Gods, Admete,' Alcides said, and he placed his hands either side of my face, planting a kiss on my forehead and laughing, 'you should have been a man! How did Athena and Hephaestus fit so much cleverness within the narrow compass of a woman?'

Theseus, sitting the other side of the hearth, looked up at Alcides' cry, scowling. 'Cleverness in a woman?' he called, his expression twisted with scorn as he pushed aside the slave, his skin clean though his nose remained distorted. 'You might sooner persuade me that the river Achelous flows up to the peaks of the Pindus mountains.'

Alcides hesitated, a smile lingering. He caught my eye, and the merriment at Theseus' jest faded. Theseus snorted, then winced, bringing a hand to his face and his smarting eyes. 'But then,' Alcides said, 'we may press on with the battle for the war-belt at once! There is no longer any need for delay.'

Again, I heard impatience in his voice, and felt a twist of discomfort in the pit of my stomach. I had not considered what would happen when we found the cure we sought. The queen would not give up her war-belt without a struggle, and I had not thought that Alcides would quest for it in battle – that we would violate the laws of hospitality and rise up against those who had welcomed us. And now that I had come to know the Amazons – my own people – how could we turn against them?

'Alcides,' I began, 'you should hear me. Perhaps we should not fight—'

'Oh, for Zeus' sake, Hercules, that is enough!' Theseus had got to his feet and caught the corner of the table from which the slave was working, bearing a bowl filled with water and bandages, as he did so. The bowl fell, the water spilling over the ground, making the fire hiss. The slave dropped to his knees to clear it. Theseus' face was reddening across the fire and his voice was raised as he rounded on Alcides. I stared at him, unable to move from my position at Alcides' feet, sensing that something more had goaded the prince of Athens than my presence alone, though what I could not tell. 'How much longer will you continue to listen to the counsels of a woman?' he spat, over the slave's crouched back. 'We should have stripped the queen of her damned-to-Styx war-belt the moment we came ashore, as I advised you! First we are to delay so she,' he glared at me, 'may find herbs for the cooking-pot – and now she will dissuade you from your quest altogether, as if she knows anything of the ways of war! Gods!' He kicked at the overturned table beside him, and his slave cowered. 'Women are all the same – cowards one and all! How can you bring yourself to heed her, Hercules?'

I flinched, but anger was coming to my defence. 'Son of Aegeus,' I stood up and stared him full in the face in the dim half-light of the fire, 'I am the daughter of a king of Greece. You may not speak to me so! Alcides will not permit it!'

But Theseus went on, the words pouring from his mouth as if they had been pent up for weeks, and Alcides did nothing to stop him, though he shifted a little on his seat. Colour was creeping up his neck, beads of sweat visible on his skin in the firelight. 'You wished to know why he did not list you among the heroes at the court of Lycus?' Theseus pointed a finger at Alcides, spit flying from his mouth. 'It is because you are not one of us! He said it himself – ask, and he will tell you! You are not as strong or as courageous as a man, and you should not think otherwise – as if you and the son of Zeus are companions, blood-brothers who are the same.'

I turned to look at Alcides, and he glanced aside, avoiding my eye. 'You did not say that.' My voice was quiet, and the tent was hushed but for the beating of the rain against the felts, and the rustling of Theseus' slave on the floor. 'Tell me you did not say that.'

'I . . .' He hesitated. The red flush had reached his ears now. He glanced towards Theseus, then took a breath. 'You are a woman, Admete,' he said, and his eyes slid to mine, half defiant, half ashamed. 'It is as he said. You do not know the ways of war. War is the business of men.'

I thought I heard an exhalation of triumph from Theseus.

'The business of men?' I exclaimed, almost laughing as incredulity at what he had said swept through me. 'Do you not know where you stand? Have you not seen the Amazon warriors?'

But Alcides did not reply, looking past me. 'We take the war-belt, by force if need be, then journey to seek the golden apples. It is decided.'

A flutter of panic shivered through me, cold as the rain slanting through the opening above – *Gods, no, not a battle, not before I have found my mother* – and I dropped to my knees again beside him. 'At least one day, then,' I said, changing tack, like a ship with the wind, my words coming quickly in my fear. 'Grant me at least one day. I must speak with the queen!' I grasped his hand, and he wrenched his gaze towards me. 'She will tell us of the golden apples,' I said, holding him. 'Think of my brother, Alcides, and if not him, then think of your immortality. The apples of immortality.' I touched his chin, my fingers shaking. 'You must trust me – we need this. We are still friends, are we not?'

He did not answer, but neither did he shake me off. The air in the tent was thick with tension, and behind me I could sense Theseus watching Alcides, the eyes of Timiades and the others upon us. I could almost sense the quarrel within Alcides' heart: his burning ambition and desire to fight, his longing to be respected among men, princes above all; but, like a stone anchor thrown into the sea, the knotted cord of our friendship pulled at him still.

'Very well,' he said at last, not meeting my eyes as he stood and strode towards the tent entrance. 'But one day only, Admete.'

'Alcides!' I shouted after him, wounded into rage now as

131

he pulled aside the tent-flap. 'Alcides!' I struggled to my feet. 'Look at me! Come back!'

But the hides swung into place behind him and he did not return. When I ran after him, I could no longer make him out through the silver curtain of rain that splashed on my hair and ran down my cheeks.

Garden of the Hesperides

Scythia

An Amazon is creeping through the camp on the banks of the Tanais river, shrouded in darkness as the clouds swirl and gather overhead and the rain pours over her. From the way she keeps close to the tents scattered over the plain, her eyes darting this way and that, it is clear that she does not want to be seen. She wears woollen trousers covered with a soaking tunic, felt boots and cap, and a belt from which hangs a sword and battle-axe: everything a typical Amazon might wear, and nothing that could reveal her identity.

Yet she is no Amazon.

She is, in fact, the queen of the gods.

Hera ducks around a corner as a figure passes, running after two dim shapes retreating into the rain — a man she recognizes at once as the Greek Theseus, son of Aegeus and prince of Athens. He looks somewhat the worse for wear, she thinks, his nose twisted out of shape and a blue-black bruise blooming over one eye, his wet hair sticking to his forehead, yet he is still handsome, in that fearless, challenging way . . .

Her eyes linger on him as he disappears into the rain. Then she recalls herself, slips out of the shadows and moves towards the camp's edge. She has decided to search for Calliope in a mortal disguise, for there are only so many places that can be seen from

Olympus' heights, and a Muse might hide anywhere: beneath the fibrous branches of a forest, or within a tent at the edge of the Amazon wilderness. And she heard rumours from the wood-nymphs, as she climbed the slopes of the Carpathian Mountains, that Calliope had passed that way, heading east, so east she came, searching, searching always . . .

And then she stops short.

She has heard something from within a tent nearby, something that, if she were truly a mortal and not a god who lives for ever, would have made the blood within her veins freeze.

The voice continues – a woman's, hoarse with age, floating towards her from the tent ahead.

'. . . and I told her – the Greek girl, I mean, the one who looks like an Amazon – I told her that man, Hercules, as he calls himself, should ask Queen Hippolyta about the golden apples, for perhaps they may provide what she seeks.'

'Is it likely?' asks another voice.

But Hera does not hear the response. She stands there, and it is as if time has stopped its relentless march and the rain has ceased to fall as horror fills her. She has been so focused on Calliope that she forgot entirely about Hercules.

She almost stamps her foot in frustration and outrage. Hercules! Again! Always! Only he among mortals could be so arrogant as to try to take the apples from her. The bastard son of Zeus!

She snorts with fury. It is impossible – unthinkable!

And now she has two pretenders to the golden apples to deal with.

It takes all the self-control she possesses to prevent herself pursing her lips and blowing the Amazon camp into oblivion. For a moment she amuses herself by imagining the storm she would conjure: the howling winds plucking the tents from the earth, like frail-petalled flowers, the whirling vortex hurling them into the depths of the sea . . .

But then she scowls, remembering how irritatingly stern Zeus can be about the dictates of the Fates.

And it is not time for the Amazons to disappear from history. Not yet, anyway.

But there is another recourse left to her. She has a plan that will put a stop to Hercules once and for all, which she can – and will – implement on her return. For now, though, the apples – the symbol of her marriage, her queenship – must be safeguarded.

She closes her eyes and feels herself melt into the air, becoming one with the wind licking her skin until she is nothing but vapour, riding on the warm south wind, bringer of the storms of summer. She allows herself to be lifted up, up, until Hercules and the camp of the Amazons are dots on the grassy river-shore beside the delta, streaked with the slanting silver mist of the rain.

It is time for her to visit the Garden of the Hesperides.

She always enjoys the journey to the Garden, and, in spite of her fury at Hercules, Hera cannot help exulting in the feeling of flying light as a dandelion seed on the high winds. She passes over the wide flat plains of Scythia and Sarmatia, an undifferentiated expanse of green spotted with trees along the line of the Tanais. She heads further north and west over the tributary of the Borysthenes, its waters reflecting gold in the setting sun, and the land turns marsh-like in variegated colours of moss and emerald. Further north still, the winds are icy, snow crystals flying around her, and the earth is carpeted with white, punctuated with the bulging shapes of snow-covered firs. This is the land of Pterophoros, desolate and cursed with eternal winter. Ahead of her, as she coasts higher and higher, are the steep peaks of the bitter and *impassable Rhipaean Mountains, home of the north wind. She rests, letting the wind carry her over the highest ridge, marvelling at the sparkling snow and ice-furrowed glaciers beneath her.*

And now she is approaching the land of the Hyperboreans, the people who live beyond the north wind, where spring reigns all year and the Eridanus river threads through a wild, blossoming land. On towards the northern coast and the very edge of the world, where the unending Ocean begins. Here are the hinges on which the firmament turns and the constellations revolve; here mighty Atlas bears on his shoulders the sphere of the sky, inset with gleaming stars. The Garden lies ahead on an island covered with forest, pale beaches sliding into the sea, and even from here the tree with the golden apples – set at the island's very heart – shines blinding gold, mirroring the glow of the setting sun.

Hera lets herself sink, riding the current of air that is swirling towards the murky cloud-wrapped home of Night on the horizon ahead. The island draws nearer. Now she sees the marsh-grass at its coast and the tufted pines. Closer still, and a clearing in the forest becomes visible, jewel-bright with clover, crocus and saffron. She can see the three Hesperides, daughters of Atlas and the goddess Evening, wandering the field scattering droplets of water from bronze vessels, and in its centre, the tree – her tree – with its branches bowing beneath the apples of gold.

She lands beside Aigle, the eldest of the three sisters, and lets the wind slide off her back, like air from the feathers of a bird, and clothe her in her own white robes. Aigle looks up. Her eyes are the colour of honey, her hair tinted with red and gold, like all three of the daughters of Evening. She blinks at Hera, then gestures to the tree with a bow of her head.

'It is as you left it, my queen.'

Hera nods, lips pursed, and strides through the grass, the dew wetting her robes. Nothing can distract her from the tree spreading before her.

It fills her sight, with its copper-bronze bark, curling leaves and those apples dropping from the branches, like beads of amber, each in its place – except the three, of course, the three that were stolen so long ago. It is as if, for that moment, she is a young goddess again on her wedding day, standing hand-clasped with Zeus, as they watch the gift of Earth springing from the rock. She almost laughs – a bitter laugh – to think of what she had hoped then. How foolish the young are! How trusting! How full of hope!

But as she stretches her fingertips forwards to brush the bark of the tree's trunk, she realizes she is not done yet with hoping.

She turns away, commanding Aigle to double her guard, to bar anyone from approaching the island, whether god or man.

'He is just a mortal bastard,' Hera says to herself, and she feels a flicker of reassurance as she walks across the meadow, her eyes on the deathless nymphs who watch over it. 'He will never find them.'

Zeus peers down from the gathering-place of the gods on Mount Olympus where he stands with Hermes, holding a torch against the onset of night, looking through the gap in the clouds for his wife. He spots her at last – he would recognize her anywhere – and lets out a chuckle. 'Garden of the Hesperides,' he says. 'Oh, Hera.'

'She went there?' Hermes asks, swivelling to look north and squinting over the peaks of the Rhipaean Mountains. 'Why ever would she do that?'

Zeus considers for a moment. 'I suppose she heard that the daughter of Eurystheus has asked Hercules to seek the golden apples. It looks like . . .' he leans forwards, narrowing his eyes '. . . it looks *like she is checking the nymphs, the Hesperides, reassuring herself that her guards are safe.'*

Hermes grins. 'Elementary mistake.'

Zeus allows himself an indulgent smile. 'Yes, I'd say so.'

He turns to gaze east, towards the camp of the Amazons on the banks of the Tanais river, where smoke curls from the tents and mixes with the looming clouds. 'Now that Hera is gone . . .' His eyes meet Hermes' '. . . what would you say to a little interference?'

Hermes pretends to look shocked. 'But you said neither you nor Hera were allowed to intervene . . .'

'Well,' Zeus says, with a grin, as if he knows that what Hermes is about to say is far beyond the fine line between truth and lies, 'you're not me, are you?'

Hermes laughs aloud, throwing his head back. 'That's low, Zeus, even for you.'

'Are you saying you won't do it?'

Hermes holds up his hands. 'No! Of course I'll do it.'

'Good.' Zeus claps and turns on his heel, pacing as he thinks. 'Then what we need,' he says, and as he speaks Hermes' appearance begins to shift, transform, 'is a Greek – someone Hercules will respect, perhaps the one they call Timiades.'

At once it is no longer Hermes who stands before him but a man of the Greeks, thick-set, his hair gleaming with oil, a fine line of dark hair tracing his jawbone and a sword slung on a belt around his hips.

'You will join my son's tent,' Zeus says, his speech quickening as the ideas come. 'I will contrive to distract Timiades for a few days – I'll have him chase a deer over the plains and lose his way. And you,' he turns to Hermes, 'will ensure that there is no more delay in the capture of the war-belt, so that Hercules may succeed

in his labour and soon be on his way. Incite him to battle. Stir up his desire for glory. Tell him whatever you have to – tell him to think of his immortality. That should do it. They all want it.' He pauses. 'I believe Hera has a plan to foil Hercules in the Amazon camp. What it is,' he says, in response to Hermes' unspoken question, 'I do not know. But it would be best if he were gone with the war-belt before she returns.'

Hermes bows his head. 'It will not be easy,' he says. 'The Amazons will not give up their queen's prize without a fight. They are a people used to war, and hard to trick in battle.'

'Ah, but,' Zeus says, as Hermes prepares to leap into the air towards the darkening east, 'they have not met the trickster-god yet, have they?'

Antimache's Tale

𒀭𒌷𒋼𒀭𒀭𒈩𒈩

Hippolyta

Amazons, Land of the Saka

The Forty-first Day after the Day of Earth
in the Season of Apia, 1265 BC

I paced up and down my tent, my thoughts whirling. I slammed my hand into the tent-post in fury and shame at the memory of his fingers on my skin, the insolence of his thinking he might touch me. It was the Greek – the words, the way he looked, so similar to my own.

I dropped onto a stool by the fire, my head in my hands, listening to the rustling and spitting of the logs, my breathing coming short and fast. For a moment all was still, my vision dark where my palms covered my eyes.

And then, inevitably, as the surge of anger rose to such a pitch that I could bear it no longer, there was the tug of the memories . . .

I am younger. My mother Marpesia, queen of the Amazons, still lives. I am riding alone, chasing a white-spotted deer along the coast, delighting in my horse's speed and the strength of my arms. Further and further from the camp I ride, my only thought

145

to capture my prey, but she is fast and in the close-set woods my arrows go awry.

After many hours the daylight begins to fade, and I realize I have lost my way.

My palms fell from my face, my eyes slanted sideways to the fire, and the leaping bronze flames distracted me, lulled me, allowing the shadows from the past to lengthen around me, the tree-trunks slipping into darkness, and on every side the trackless wilderness, stretching as far as I could see.

I turn back, guiding myself north against the light of the sinking sun, telling myself that I will rest the night here and journey to the Tanais tomorrow. And then a band of men closes round me, raiders who scavenge the coast for prisoners to sell as slaves. I draw my sword and battle-axe to fight them, but I am alone, and there are many of them and but one of me. And so they drag me from my horse and truss me, struggling and screaming, but there is no one to hear me.

I gave a shuddering breath. *So long – so long since I have allowed myself to remember.*

I swallowed and allowed myself to slip back into the limpid pools of memory.

They load me onto their ship, and there they untie me and force me to row. It is aching work and my spirit almost breaks beneath the steersman's whip. But then, one night, after weeks of imprisonment, when the guards have fallen asleep at their post, I leap overboard and swim away. The sea is cold as my body hits the water, but I am strong and used to hardship, so I swim for many hours, my skin chilled as winter ice, praying all the while to Tar the storm-god to deliver me.

At last I come to an island – where, I hardly care. Coughing and choking I let the surf spew me onto the shore, and there I col-lapse from exhaustion.

I do not know how long I lie there, asleep to the world.

When I awake next I am in a bed, wearing a tunic and covered with blankets, my hair combed over a pillow. For days I sink into and out of a fever, and they care for me, wiping my sweating face with sodden cloths, forcing me to drink sips of honeyed wine.

When I emerge from my feverish state, I learn that I am on the isle of Skyros, far from my Amazon home, in the land of the Greeks. I am set on leaving at once, of course, my duty to my mother and my people foremost in my mind. Day after day I tie the laces of my boots, and I tell myself that this will be the morn-ing I will find a ship, set sail for the east; this will be the morning that I return home.

Yet something keeps me there.

The Greek is younger than I, barely a man yet, and hiding from the dangers of his warlike world. He comes upon me in the stables, bridling a horse to journey to the harbour, and he tells me of the twin horses his father has promised to give him when he comes to rule his kingdom. After that we spend almost all our days together. We leap from the cliffs to swim in the sea, and stand on each other's shoulders to pick ripe figs from the trees. He teaches me to play the lyre, and I show him how to ride without stirrups or saddle. We kiss in the wild grass of the valleys, and lie in each other's arms on the sandy shore. At length, one night, when the rest are celebrating a festival to the gods, he takes me apart from them, and there, simply, we lie together in love. Gradually, as the days pass and the months round the turning-post of the year, I learn his language and his ways. I change my boots for sandals, and wear my hair in loose curls as the Greeks do; I abandon the ways of war, and learn to love the sound of the wind blowing through the olive trees, the clanging of the goat bells, and the quiet rhythm of days spent weaving at the loom, waiting for him to call me out to ride. Slowly, the memory of the grass plains and the arching sky fades from my mind. I forget who I am.

I think that nothing can take away my happiness.

And then, one day, a ship sails into harbour, bearing Greeks — older than he, and equipped for war. They take him with them, telling us they need him, that he was born to fight, and that his hands are for holding the spear, not plucking the strings of the lyre. He is dazed by the glitter of the weapons and the stories they tell of immortal, never-dying glory; his mind is turned, and nothing I can say persuades him to stay. The worst of it is that I am a warrior too. I know he has to go. I know he has a duty. It is one that I have forsaken and forgotten, too long.

I do not tell him that I am with child.

And then it is too late, and he is gone.

Tears welled in my eyes and spilt down my cheeks as I remembered the raw, consuming pain of that loss, mixed with the bittersweetness of what he had left behind. I closed my eyes and let the tears come.

My courses stop; I watch my belly swell over many months; and then I bear his child alone on Skyros, knowing he will never see his son. I name the child Cayster, after a clear-flowing river that runs near the land of the Amazons.

The pain of guilt at what I have done and the pricking aware-ness that I have failed in every way in my duty to my people drive me home at last — despair propelling me to the responsibilities of my birthright, which happiness has allowed me to forget. I con-trive to board a trading ship bound for Troy. I travel back across the lands of the Hittites and the wilds of the Caucasus Mountains to my home, telling my people when I arrive that Cayster is a Saka foundling I came upon on my way by a nearby tribe. I give him to my sister Melanippe and her husband Teuspa to raise as their own. No one except Melanippe knows that Cayster is my own son. I will never be able to tell any other of my kin that he is mine – or where he comes from.

Then they tell me that my mother's spirit went to the gods while I was away.

And so, though I am the consort of a foreigner, the mother of a bastard child, and a liar to the people I am meant to rule with fairness and honesty, I am heralded queen; and for five years I reign, without once revealing my secret.

At once my mother's image swam before me, leading me out as a girl over the frost-tipped grass to ride, though I strained to return to the fireside in our tent. 'To be an Amazon,' she had said, striding ahead, her boots crunching a path for me, 'is to fight, whether man or woman, virgin or mother. You are destined to become a queen, so the fight to protect your people will be both your calling and your duty, and nothing, no man, no marriage, no child, shall come before it.'

I swallowed, my belly twisting with discomfort and bitter castigation, thinking of the flaxen-haired, dark-eyed child who played with the other children in the camp, and all the Amazons who watched him, thinking he was a foundling, knowing only that he was born to ride the plains of the Saka, like all the rest. I had given up my son, never allowed myself to breathe in the scent of him, to wrap him in my arms. I had been abandoned by his father, left like driftwood cast up on the shore, yet I had not allowed myself to give in to despair. I had tried, through it all, through all my errors and failings, to be the queen I knew I could be. Had I not done as my mother had told me? Had I not learnt?

I stared into the flames. Tears rimmed my eyes, and I blinked to free them.

To fight to protect my people.

I understood that now, as I had not when I first met the Greek.

I felt warmth in my belly, like the glow of the embers. *I know that I have to protect my people.*

And repeating those words in my thoughts, like a talisman, I sat watching the flames at the hearth flicker into nothingness, vowing to myself as the heat of certainty grew within me: *I will be – I am – the queen my people deserve.*

I have to be.

Ἀδμήτη

Admete

Amazons, Scythia

The Thirteenth Day of the Month of the Harvest, 1265 BC

I requested an audience at once with Queen Hippolyta, determined to take Alcides at his word, however reluctantly given. The next morning, as the sun broke through patches of cloud to dapple the Amazon camp in light and reflect from the pools of water on the grass, she agreed to speak with me.

Another of the Amazons – her sister, Melanippe, a quiet girl with dark eyes – led me to her tent. I could barely say my thanks, my throat was so constricted, but I bowed my head and hoped she understood. It was not simply anticipation at what Hippolyta might tell me, though that was occupying my mind: Alcides' words – *We take the war-belt, by force if need be* – were ringing in my head and I could not rid myself of them. How could I approach her when I knew the theft Alcides was planning? How could I keep from her what he intended? Guilt twisted in my stomach as Melanippe gestured me into the tent. I took a breath, then ducked beneath the folded hide and into the tent of the Amazon queen.

It was modestly decorated, not unlike the others I had seen. A blazing fire at the centre sent up smoke to a hole in the tent's canopy, the floor was covered with hides and rugs, scattered with low stools and cushions, and a fur-and-pelt bed was spread on its other side. Lamps were set on small tables, glowing dimly against the daylight pouring in behind me, and a ewer of water stood by the hearth. Her war-belt, I noticed, with a wrench, a strip of shining gold and leather straps from which hung all manner of weapons, axe and sword, lay slung over a table nearby, gleaming and reflecting the light of the flames.

The queen was seated cross-legged on the floor. Close to, she looked different from when I had first seen her on the river's shore. Her eyes were fiercer, brighter, and her mouth, which had been grave, now seemed set at the corners. She had drawn up the sleeves of her tunic in the heat of the fire, so that the black outline of the eagle pricked into her skin seemed to flit over her arm every time she moved. She beckoned to me, and I made my way towards her and onto a cushion when she gestured to one before her. Her eyes swept my face.

'What is it they call you?' she said in Greek, and at her accent – Greek mixed with Scythian, so like my mother's – I almost started.

'Admete,' I said, glancing down. 'I am the daughter of Eurystheus, king of Tiryns.'

'And yet,' she leant forwards, 'you have the look of an Amazon about you.'

I bit my lip, hesitating.

'It is that,' I said at last, in the Scythian tongue, and I saw her eyes widen, 'among other things, which I have come to ask of you.'

152

She arched her brows. 'Indeed. I hardly imagined you wished merely to make my acquaintance. But perhaps you should tell me more of yourself before you ask your question.'

'There is not much to tell, my queen.'

'A woman who has the look of an Amazon, travelling alone with a band of men to the ends of the world? I am sure there is a tale in there somewhere.'

'No tale,' I said, 'only a woman's search for a cure for her brother who suffers from a fever that will not abate. The legend that covers it is far greater. Alcides' quest to the Amazons will be remembered for ever, if he has any say in it.' I did not quite know why I was talking to her so freely, the words coming easily, except that she seemed familiar, and her gaze – sure and steady – seemed to invite confidence. 'I have been searching for cures, the herbs and healing of the Amazons, writing it all on my tablets, so that it may aid me in curing my brother when we return.'

'Then that explains why you have been occupying our healer Ioxeia.'

I could not tell if she was reprimanding me. 'I – I did not—'

'You are curious and quick-minded,' she said, and I was relieved to see she was smiling, 'and the gods do not punish curiosity.'

'I did not wish to do anything you would not like,' I said, eager to have her know that I, at least, meant the Amazons no harm. 'But I have longed for so many years to learn of your customs. The stories that are told in Greece! They say that you are all women, that you despise men and leave your sons to die. They say you slice off one of your breasts, so you can place an arrow to the bow while you ride.'

She snorted with laughter. 'How typical of the Greeks, who do not know the first thing about riding a horse or the proper handling of a bow, to imagine such a thing! And how would that aid us, pray?'

I shook my head. 'I have never used a bow.'

'So,' she said, after a while, her gaze thoughtful, 'you are searching for something.'

'And you?' I asked, unsure if I was overreaching myself, yet so at ease with this Greek-speaking Amazon that I felt I could not keep to the formalities. 'You are searching for something too?'

She considered me for a moment, and the dancing light in her eyes dimmed, as when wind flickers through a flame. 'Someone I lost,' she said.

I felt my heart leap at the words, so close to my own desire, and felt a bond of friendship, invisible as the thread of the Fates, twine itself between us at the longing and loss we had unknowingly shared. I leant forwards and took her hand in mine. 'I, too, am looking for someone I lost.'

Her eyes met mine, vulnerable, much younger, and I felt the question burst from me.

'My queen, I must ask. I have searched and found nothing. I have asked, but no one will tell me.' I took a breath. 'What do you know of Antimache, the Amazon?'

𒀸𒆠𒄿𒋾𒉌𒈾

Hippolyta

Amazons, Land of the Saka
The Forty-second Day after the Day of Earth in the Season of Apia, 1265 BC

'You ask of Antimache?' I leant back, surveying the girl. There was determination in the way she set her mouth and lifted her chin, yet also, I thought, something fragile in her eyes, the slight protective rounding of her shoulders. And the mark of our *tamga* was just visible on her forearm, branded into her skin. I could not deny that she intrigued me – not least because Antimache had been close to my own thoughts, for my own reasons, these past days. For a moment I gazed at her, gathering myself. 'Why would you know?' I asked at last.

She drew a breath, and her lip trembled. 'She was my mother.'

Her mother . . .

I let the words wash over me.

But it makes sense, I thought. *Her Amazon looks. Her Greek father.*

We had all considered Antimache lost, and when anyone had spoken of her it had been as a warning against breaking the customs of our tribe. She had become a myth, a byword for betrayal, and the figure of Antimache had girded my thoughts as I had left Skyros to return to my people; as only a few nights before I had vowed to myself again to protect them.

Admete leant towards me. 'Please,' she said, her voice shaking. 'Please, tell me what you know.'

I took her hand in mine and folded her cold fingers between my own. 'I will tell you, my daughter,' I said, and I saw a smile glimmer across her face at the word. 'But I do not know how much help I can be.'

She shook her head. 'It does not matter. All I wish is to know.'

I closed my eyes, trying to recall all my mother had told me. 'Antimache,' I said after a pause, 'was born a few years before my own mother, the queen.' I opened my eyes to find her hanging on my every word, her expression so eager it made my heart ache for what she had suffered. 'When she was just growing into womanhood, there was a raid on the camp by a group of Greeks who had lost their way sailing on the sea and were starved for food and drink. Though my grandmother, the queen, tried to offer it to them peacefully, they looted our stores, then captured Antimache and a few of the young girls. The others fought their way off the ship and returned. Antimache did not.'

Admete's jaw was jutting forwards, her teeth clenched as if she was determined not to allow tears, but her hands were trembling at her sides.

'Reports reached us from across the sea that Antimache had been taken to a Greek palace. They told us she had set-tled there – that she married a Greek, and forgot all her Amazon ways. From when I was a child her story was told

156

to me – to all of us – as an example of betrayal: to lie with a man beyond our tribe, and to conceive an infant with him in whose veins would run the blood of a foreigner. Yet how wrong they were!' I said, and I squeezed her hand, hoping to bring some cheer to her, for her mouth was drawn down as if weighted by sadness. 'I saw it from the moment you stepped ashore on our lands. You have all the looks and ways of a true Amazon.'

She looked up at me. 'You thought I was an Amazon?'

'Truly,' I said with a smile.

'And I suppose – she is not here, then?' I saw her grip the edge of her skirt and twist it in her fingers, clearly preparing herself for my reply.

'No,' I said, with a slight shudder. 'She is not. She tried to return, when I was younger. I saw nothing of her – I was barred by my mother for fear of her influence. They sent her to exile in punishment for having lain with a Greek.' I swallowed, my lips dry. 'I have heard nothing of her since.'

'She left us,' Admete said, her voice blank. 'When I was ten years of age, she left us, without explanation, without any word as to where she might have gone. I thought I might find her here.'

I shook my head. 'I am sorry.'

She took a breath, straightening her back. 'Then – well – that is done,' she said, her mouth tight. 'There are more important things.'

'You need not be so harsh on yourself,' I said, leaning towards her. 'You are grieving. It takes time – many years – to recover from the loss of someone you loved. I, above all, know that.'

She shook her head, and I saw single-mindedness in the

direct gaze of her eyes. 'No,' she said. 'There is more – there is something more important.'

Silence fell between us, broken only by the whinnying of horses beyond the tent and the drifting sound of conversation as some of my people passed us. I tilted my head to observe her – for, however much she said her grieving was past, I recognized in her apparent self-possession the yearning to be free from the weight of loss. 'Is there something you wished to ask of me?' I asked gently, feeling that this was a battle with which I could not help her. All Amazons, at one time or another, had to fight alone.

She nodded, fingering her plait. 'Yes,' she said. 'My brother in Tiryns suffers from a fever such as I have never seen. I am come in search of a cure.'

I leant forwards. 'What can I do to help you?'

She glanced at me, and I saw gratitude in her face that I had not tried to console her. Often I had found, as queen of my tribe, that the offer of assistance was more of a gift than a thousand words of comfort. *And, of course, poor girl, with no mother to care for her she cannot have had many people in whom to confide.* I sat still, waiting until she felt she could speak.

'I mean no disrespect to your healer,' she said at last, picking her words carefully, 'but I have searched Ioxeia's stores and found nothing similar to the treasures of herbal lore of which my mother spoke. I have found nothing here to cure his fever, nothing we do not already have in Greece, except . . .'

'What is it?' I urged her.

She bit her lip. 'Ioxeia mentioned a garden of golden apples, set far in the north, told of by traders who have come here from the Hyperboreans. She said,' her mouth puckered in doubt, 'that they are rumoured to bring immortality, to be the source of a powerful healing that induces life after death and can bring back the spirits of those who have already departed.'

I bowed my head. 'That is true. I have heard of them.'

She nodded, and her speech became quicker. 'And though I do not believe that the gods send diseases, I have nowhere else to turn, and my brother . . . Perhaps it is the only way . . .' Her voice quivered. 'I thought perhaps the apples – these golden apples – might be the cure-alls of which my mother told me.' She turned her face up to mine, her eyes filled with a quiet desperation. 'Do you know anything of them? Do you know where they might be found?'

I considered her. 'I have heard the legend,' I said, 'of the apples of gold that make men into gods. And it is true that the Hyperboreans with whom we trade have spoken of them. If it is as important to you to heal your brother as it seems to be, then I – like Ioxeia – would counsel you and your Greeks to seek these apples; for sometimes the only cures for our ills lie with the gods, no matter how much we wish it otherwise.'

She shrugged a shoulder, and said nothing.

'The Hyperboreans,' I went on, 'have spoken of them as far to the north, further even than their own kingdom. My outriders will be able to direct you towards the Hyperboreans from the borders of our lands. From them you can take more direction.'

A strange expression crossed her face – furtive, hesitant. 'You would do that?'

'Of course.' I smiled at her and clasped her hand in mine once more, enclosing the fingers with my own. 'I would do as much, and more, for any fellow Amazon.'

Ἀδμήτη

Admete

I could not sleep that night, tortured by the Amazon queen's words, her kindness to me, as the winds from the plain pummelled the tent and wolves howled. I wished more than anything to speak with Alcides, to dissuade him from the war-belt, to supplicate him by all the gods if I had to – but though I went to his tent and waited, and kept an oil-lamp burning by my side, I did not see a shadow move across the tent in all the long hours that the stars circled across the sky, and neither he nor Theseus returned.

I woke from a fitful doze to the pale yellow expanse of dawn through the tent's opening above me, and the sounds of raised voices. The tent was empty of all Greeks – Timiades, Euneos, Perses, all were gone, their fleeces and blankets pushed back in piles on the floor. Heart leaping in my throat, eyes stinging with fatigue, I threw a cloak over my under-tunic and wrapped a girdle around my waist, then clutched at my sandals and ran outside.

160

Alcides, Theseus and Timiades stood before the queen's tent, as I had feared, their way barred by two axe-wielding guards, and around them, buzzing like a hive of angry bees, Amazons were gathering, my tent-fellows Polemusa, Aella and Deianeira among them. I could hear Alcides shouting at the guards as I ran towards him, breath coming sharp. I could see Timiades gesticulating, and Theseus with his arms crossed over his chest. As I approached, the tent-flaps parted and the queen emerged, soothing the guards with a hand on their shoulders, her face pale as she drew a cloak over herself.

'What is the meaning of this?'

Her voice was quiet, but all talking ceased, leaving only the chattering of the birds swarming overhead.

'Your guards,' Alcides said roughly, 'refused to allow us entry.'

'We have come to demand of you a prize,' Timiades added, as I tried to push my way through the crowd of Amazons, palms sweating now with foreboding. 'Give it to us, and we will leave you unharmed. Refuse, and we will fight. You will know the pain of seeing your people die, like wheat cut beneath the scythe, before your eyes.'

I could just make out the queen through a gap in the bodies pressed before me, her dark brows arched, and beside her her guards, their battle-axes still raised, eyes narrowed.

'What is it you seek?'

There was a pause. Then Alcides said, his voice cutting the air like a blade, 'Your war-belt.'

A silence fell deep over the crowd, and I felt the Amazons around me tense, like hares about to spring. Fear welled in me, like a sickness, and all of a sudden I was aware of the sharpened swords hanging at belts all around me, the glint-ing points of the battle-axes. The air shuddered and seemed to thicken.

'That,' the queen said, with pride and menace in her voice, 'you may not have.'

It happened in a slash of bronze. Out of nowhere, a blade came swishing down, shrieking against the iron that blocked it. The guards closed ranks before the queen, and all around me there were heaving bodies, the flashing of metal and piercing cries.

I did not wait – I turned and, thanking the gods for my plaited hair and the Scythian tongue, I screamed to the Amazons, 'I am one of you! I am an Amazon!' Then, taking advantage of their confusion, I ran faster than I had ever done for the tents. My breath was tearing at my lungs, my senses white-blind with fear. Terror clutched at my heart for both the Amazons and the Greeks, for Alcides and Hip-polyta, as the splitting of metal on bone and shrieks followed on the wind. My panic overcame me so that I seemed to skim above the grass, the air curving around me.

And then I was at the healer's tent and flung myself inside.

'Oh, gods, Ioxeia, they are fighting! *They are fighting!*'

Battle for the War-Belt

Scythia

As a northerly wind rides over the camp, stretching its icy fingers across the land of the Saka, Hera drops to the ground and stands. Hidden behind a tent at the edge of the gathering-place, no one sees her arrive, and no one notices as yet another Amazon steps out to mingle in the fray.

She nods to see the screaming, heaving hordes of Amazons around her, the flashing of battle-axes.

She is just in time.

Hera draws a breath. In answer to her call, a fog begins to form, like mist over the sea, and rolls, swirling, snaking across the land towards the Amazon camp. Within moments the Greeks and Amazons are shrouded in an impenetrable, cloud-like mass, their figures shadows in the grey that covers all. She hears Hercules' cry, 'What enchantment is this?' then the Amazons shouting to each other, feels them fumbling their way past her in their panic.

She smiles and moves forwards through them.

Hippolyta has emerged from her tent, her war-belt over her tunic, and is turning this way and that, demanding to know what is happening. Hera wraps the fog around her like a swaddling-cloth, binding her, blinding her, and Hippolyta stumbles and falls to her knees at the side of the battle, unable to see and unseen by the rest of the screaming, swarming Amazons.

And now it is time to whip the Amazons into a frenzy of battle-fury, such as none has ever seen, such that the lives of the Greeks will be ripped from them, and none shall ever leave the camp again.

'The foreigners!' she screams, and her tongue – shifting shape with her disguise – speaks Scythian. 'They have taken the queen!'

The tremor of panic around her shifts to rage. 'The queen!' she cries, stirring them up, like wind whipping waves. The Amazons are echoing the refrain, eyes white with anger through the mist: 'The queen! They have captured the queen! Attack!'

She parts the fog, just enough to lead them back to where their horses are gathered, grazing the plain, and hears the Amazons, one after another, mounting their steeds, the clatter of quivers at war-belts and the screams of 'Oiorpata!' She runs to Orithyia and shouts to her, 'Treachery! Avenge your sister!' then watches as Orithyia, her face taut with fear and rage, cries, 'Oiorpata!' and brings the gathered battle-lines of the Amazons back to face the Greeks.

Caught in the fog and trapped between the tents, the Greeks are rushing to redouble their hold on their weapons and gather more, daggers scraping as they pull them from their scabbards. Hercules has his sword held before him in both hands, eyes darting this way and that through the mist; Theseus, Solois and Timiades gird him on either side, spears held trembling at their shoulders. The Amazons charge forwards, horses stamping, battle-axes swinging. First to join battle is Aella, her name given for her swiftness of speed, one of Hippolyta's chosen band. She rides screaming towards the Greek line, curving her battle-axe as if to cut through the mist that entraps the Greeks. Behind her rides another, but Hera cannot make out her face.

And then she shrugs. The fog has done what it was meant to do – and what god would miss the chance to see a battle?

Slowly, like a spinner teasing the wool into thread, Hera pulls the fog towards her, wraps it round and round her finger into a silver fibre until gradually it thins. Riders loom suddenly high out of the darkness, and the Greeks are caught by the Amazon onslaught, blinking into the light. Aella rides through the cowering Greeks, dealing death to right and left, shrieking the war-cry as her blade cuts down the enemy. Orithyia has leapt from her steed and fights hand to hand with Hercules – Hera watches, fascinated, as the sister of Hippolyta raises her axe, gritting her teeth, to block Hercules' blow, then draws her sword and, as Hercules prepares his next attack, strikes his blade with a shuddering stroke and brings it around, the hilt slipping from his fingers, the blade tumbling to the earth . . .

On Hera's right stand three sisters, and she turns to watch as they advance on a pair of Greeks, stabbing back and forth with their swords, goading the Greeks into following them. One Greek leaps forwards, and the Amazon takes her chance. Swiping with her sword she deals him a deathly blow, slamming the blade between his ribs, and he collapses beneath his brother's feet, his sandals staining with blood. Hera's eyes dart between Amazons and Greeks – three to one, now – as the Greek screams and rushes at the warrior-women, swinging his spear through the air.

There is Orithyia again, striking out at Thoas and Solois, battling both with a sword in each hand and a laugh on her lips. She dances with them, playing, tapping back and forth as the men battle her, their faces streaming sweat. Melanippe comes to join her, hair whirling as she battles Hercules, her sword slicing through the air with the deadly force of the wind itself. And then Hera hears a scream. Orithyia is poised with her swords outstretched, her mouth gaping in a vaunting laugh and a bloody gash ripping across her chest, tearing at her breasts. Timiades' spear, sent aslant, rips through her skin and falls to the ground, blade burying itself in the earth.

'Having fun, are we?'

Hera whirls around. A Greek stands beside her, thick-set and with oiled dark hair, yet there is something about the mischievous glimmer in his eye that not even the disguise can hide.

'Oh, no. Not you.'

'Oh, yes,' Hermes says. The battle-cries and sounds of clashing swords fade around them as the two gods speak. 'Glad to see you've been keeping busy.'

Hera's eyes are drawn back to the chaos surrounding her. 'It's only a minor skirmish,' she says. 'Not even a battle, really.'

'And I'm only a messenger,' Hermes says sardonically. 'But it's against the rules, and you know it. You and Zeus agreed, after the oracle: no interfering in Hercules' labours. If he succeeds or fails, it will be on his own merit.'

'Yes, yes, very well.' Hera waves him away impatiently. 'I know. There's no need to rub it in.'

'In any case,' Hermes says, 'I would have thought you had other matters to occupy yourself.'

'And what's that supposed to mean?' Hera snaps.

Hermes gives an innocent shrug of his shoulders. 'Nothing. But I did happen to see a certain Muse on my way here, getting awfully close to the Garden of the Hesperides . . .'

Hera swears under her breath. 'Can I not have one moment's rest?'

'When you want to rule the universe,' Hermes says, twiddling his thumbs and giving her a look of benevolent amusement, 'apparently not.'

Hera tears her gaze away from Orithyia as she slumps forward in death. 'Oh, all right,' she says. 'I'll leave.'

'Good.'

'But, Hermes,' she bites her lip as she prepares to go, 'don't stop the fighting, will you? I mean, it would count as interfering, after all.'

Hermes grins at her. 'Wouldn't stop it, even if I could,' he says. 'Not to worry.'

And so, as the queen of the gods departs, making with quick steps for the forests of the north, Hermes turns to watch the battle —

— and the full force of Zeus' favour swings towards the Greeks.

Leaving the Land of the Saka

𒀭𒉌𒊹𒉿𒀭𒈨𒐀

Hippolyta

Amazons, Land of the Saka

The Forty-third Day after the Day of Earth
in the Season of Apia, 1265 BC

I stumbled to my feet, shaking, my limbs filled with fear. Some terrible curse of the gods must have come upon me. All I remembered was darkness, like the yawning chasm of night, descending on me from the sea, and then I fell, blinded, as if dead.

And now the wind was whipping at my cheeks, bringing me back to my senses. My vision was clearing. My legs, though trembling, bore my weight once more. I looked around me, surveying the scene of chaos before me with a growing sense of horror. The gathering-place of the camp was a raging tumult of bodies – horses bucking and rearing, riders screaming battle-cries, sword clashing on sword, spears shivering through the air, darts hailing from every side, like rain from a clear sky. The tang of sweat and blood and death hit my nostrils and I leant forwards, trying to regain control of myself as the horror clamoured and battered against my senses. *My people . . . My people . . .*

How can this have happened?

But then, as I turned aside, I caught sight of one of the corpses littering the red-streaked grass, turned on her side, dark hair muddied and eyes white in death, the eagle *tamga* bared on her shoulder . . .

'Orithyia!' I shrieked, and without thought for anything except to reach my sister I leapt forwards, drawing my sword. Figures whirled before my dazed vision and I pushed them aside, thoughtless, my blade flashing, my thoughts screaming. And then a figure sprang into my path – and I recognized through the blur that it was Theseus, though his thigh was slashed and bleeding and his tunic was ripped off the shoulder.

'And here – the queen!' he snarled, hatred in his eyes. 'Shall I cut the war-belt from you, then?' He drew his sword, cutting and slashing, and I parried him with such swiftness that I saw the sneer on his face slide away, to be replaced by rage as I blocked him once, twice, streaking the air with the bite of metal—

'You dare to attack my people!' I shouted, as he raised his blade again, and I drew my battle-axe in my other hand and swung it, whirling round and round, then brought it down over his head with the force to split a horse's skull. 'You dare to offend the gods! You traitor, foe of all honour!'

'Honour!' he screamed, bringing his sword up against the axe-shaft so that my blow glanced aside, but the force sent his sword slipping from his hand. 'You have no honour – or if you do,' he said, grasping the sword from the soil and raising it to block me as I struck out at him again, his eyes savage, 'it is that of a barbarian.'

At that moment there was a scream from my right,

'*Oiorpata!*'. I turned to see Melanippe running through the fighting crowd towards us, her cheeks streaked with blood and dirt, her battle-axe raised, her eyes wide and horrified.

'Melanippe, *no!*'

She charged at Theseus, her plait swinging, her axe slicing like fire. I shifted my *sagaris*, ready to bring him down as he turned towards her, but another Greek blundered across my path, sword swinging. I wielded mine left-handed to deal with him – *slice, slice* – and it was done. Then, in my fury at their treachery and what they had done to Orithyia, I turned back to Theseus, the blood singing in my veins, ready to send him to the world of the dead with the rest of the Greeks, ready to destroy all he had for taking from me my sister, my—

And then I stopped, swaying.

The battle-axe had fallen from Melanippe's hands. Theseus was grasping her by the hair, panting hard, pulling her round to face me. Sweat shone on his face and forearms, and his teeth were white against his dirt-smeared skin as he bared a grin at me. He lifted his sword-blade to her throat, and Melanippe, though she struggled and kicked, could not free herself from the hand that was wrapped around her plait, pulling her head. My heart froze within me. *Not her. Not her as well.*

'What is it you choose, Queen Hippolyta?' he hurled at me, over the clashing of weapons and shrieks surrounding us. 'Your sister – or your war-belt?'

Melanippe's chest rose and fell as she called, 'No, Hippolyta!'

Theseus tore at her hair and she winced, biting her lip so she did not cry aloud.

'*Stop!*' I commanded him, my voice shrill, unable to see her captive, like an eagle caught in a hunter's net. 'You already have her prisoner!'

I lifted my sword so he could see it, then dropped it to the ground. I reached to my waist and started to fumble at the buckles of my belt, uncoiling it, then holding it out to him, fingers shaking so that the eagle amulet hanging on its strap shivered, as if it knew its own downfall. 'Please – let her go.'

His eyes glittered, and I knew that this humiliation was his vengeance for the hunt. He took the belt and tossed it to Hercules, who had pushed his way through from the fight nearby and slung it over his shoulder, as if it were nothing but a garment, not the most prized possession of the Amazon queens. 'For this alone?' Theseus said. 'You think that is sufficient payment?'

'What is it you want?' I asked, my voice trembling. *Not Melanippe. I cannot lose Melanippe too.* 'You may have anything. Gold cups, beads of glass, bracelets of silver and bronze – I will fetch them myself from our treasure-store.'

Theseus shook his head, and his eyes slid to where Hercules stood. Behind him Aella was fighting hand to hand with Timiades, making him dance over the blood-spattered grass, swinging the battle-axe back and forth to match the flicking of his sword-blade. 'I want you.'

The din of the battle around me seemed to grow hushed, as if I were muffled in fog once more.

Theseus' eyes grew harder. 'I want you as my captive,' he said. 'An Amazon queen for a hero of the Greeks: a fitting trophy. You give Hercules your war-belt, you give yourself to me, to return to Greece with me. Then your sister will go free.'

I clenched my jaw. 'And if not?'

'Then,' his lips thinned, almost into a smile, 'we will ravage this camp until there is no man, woman or child left alive to remember the name of the Amazons.'

'No! Hippolyta, you cannot – don't – remember—' Melanippe's words cut off as Theseus tugged harder at the hair wound around his fingers. Her dark eyes smarted, and I knew, as she blinked at me, that she was trying to warn me against the pain of another Greek, another rending from my homeland, another agony.

'Your captive, by the laws of the gods?'

He inclined his head, his eyes shadowed.

'You will obey the customs for a captive of royal blood, and take me as your wife?'

Again, he bowed.

'*No!*' Melanippe was kicking and struggling against his hold, shrieking my name, but I ignored her.

'You will treat me with the respect I deserve as a queen?'

He nodded. 'Oh, yes.'

I paused, staring at him, his dark eyes lingering on me, my freedom hanging on the wind.

'Then – I give myself up.'

To protect my people. That was what I had said, what I had sworn. I stood tall, my chin raised and my heart thundering, though my stomach twisted at the disgrace; and all the while, my mother's war-belt hung on Hercules, dangling before me on the shoulder of a *paralati*. Theseus grunted and freed Melanippe.

'What are you doing?' she cried, throwing herself to the ground before me and taking my knees in both her arms,

177

turning her face up towards me. 'You cannot, Hippolyta, you cannot go!'

I gazed down into her terrified eyes. 'I had no choice.'

'I would have died!' she screamed at me, her cheeks smeared with soil and blood and the tracks of her tears. 'I would have died, rather than see you sold to a Greek once more!'

I shook my head, my throat tight. 'I could not lose you, Melanippe,' I said, looking away. 'And I cannot put my people at risk. I have sworn to protect them.' I swallowed, shaking with emotion. 'There is no choice.'

The Greeks made their preparations to leave. All was a blur of colour and noise. I felt as if I were separated from my body, floating as if in sleep, and as I waded through the brown waters of the Silis and stepped up the rope-ladder onto Theseus' ship it was with a shiver distant from myself that I thought, *I will never see my home again.*

Melanippe, sobbing, had clung to me and sworn by all the gods that she would not let me go. I allowed myself to clasp Cayster once, near to breaking all self-control, almost allowing myself to clutch him to me, refusing to let him go. Yet to the world I looked strong as an Amazon queen, and for that – always for that – I could say nothing to my child. I had to unclasp my arms from him, turn and walk out of the tent, though every nerve in my body screamed at me to stay. Now my people stood on the banks – Aella, Xanthippe, Agar – watching, as I slipped away from them, their eyes filled with reproach, their sword-sheaths empty, for I had forbidden them to fight. My stomach turned as I slid onto the planks of the ship's hull and made my way to the stern, nearest the shore. I seemed to be taking quick breaths, my gaze darting over the tribe gathered on the sand, sliding away from me, to the outlines of the tents scattered over the plain, now the stage of death. Survivors picked their way among the bodies of the fallen, and the dark earth was churned up by the feet of the warriors, smearing the camp black.

Oh, gods, my people, my people.

Dread at what was to come flooded through me in a sickening wave – *how can I leave them?* – at the same time as the conviction, bold, bright, that I had had to do so for my people: the same tumult of emotions as before a battle. *Except that now you will never fight in battle again.*

I pushed the thought from my mind with the force of my will. As if by instinct, I reached to the *tamga* of the eagle hanging at my waist, searching for its comfort and certainty – and felt only the threads of my tunic. I looked down, thrown. And then, with a jolt of realization, it came over me again, the pain arrowing sharp through my side, like the blow of a pointed *sagaris*.

Of course. I have no war-belt.

I am a queen no more.

I repressed the ache of it, as if I were wounded in battle: one more parry, one more attack and slice and thrust, blind to the stinging pain, thinking always and only of my people. As the steering oar swung to turn the ship downstream, I looked to the river's mouth ahead, towards the sea – the one we called Temarunda, the Mother Sea. It opened vast before us, pooling over the world's edge in a mist of blue.

I swayed and clutched at the ship's side, knuckles whitening. And it was only thus, by digging my nails into the wood and driving my mind through the pain, that I could force myself to look ahead. Not to look back to the camp of the Amazons, knowing that I would never see my sisters, my tribe, again.

Knowing, I thought, my heart tearing within me, my eyes burning, *that I will never again see my son.*

Ἀδμήτη

Admete

Amazons, Scythia

The Sixteenth Day of the Month
of the Harvest, 1265 BC

It was like a nightmare: my dream of the Amazons had
turned, like a shifting shadow in the night, into a terrifying
vision. I had remained during the battle sheltered in Ioxeia's
tent, hidden by the herb stacks, holding my cloak over my
head like a shield, trying to drown the shrieks of the wounded
and the screaming clash of weapons that assailed me on all
sides. This was nothing like the battle of which the bard
had sung in the court of Lycus, with its measured lines of
duels, flashing bronze and great-hearted heroes. This was a
tumult, this was chaos, and there was no heroism to it but
only the rending screams of metal on flesh and a sweeping,
desperate fear.

I had spent the day of the battle and the next running
feverishly from tent to tent, ministering to Greeks and Amazons alike – the Amazons tried to push me away, but when I
spoke to them and showed them my *tamga* they let me care
for their wounded. My hands were sore from pounding herbs,

181

chopping cyclamen and a kind of sweet root I had found at the borders of the sea, mixing it with honey to fashion a poultice for skin wounds, making a paste of bitter wort for head-bruises, and a mixture of burnt resin, cassia, cinnamon and myrrh against inflammation. Then there was the care of the dead. The washing and anointing of a corpse, the closing of the eyes and mouth, the clothing of the body, the laying-out and lamentation, and the burning on the pyre till my linen skirt was black with ash, my hair filled with the smell of smoke, and my skin gleaming with the anointing oils.

While I cared for the living and the dead, and laid Solois to rest with shaking hands, Alcides, Theseus and the other Greeks prepared to depart. I watched with disgust as Alcides commandeered several horses at spear-point. The Amazons informed me that the queen – even as she left – had forbidden them to fight; and so they had to watch the source of their livelihood and their existence on the plains taken from them without protest. The silence between Amazons and Greeks was bitter, bred of fear and mistrust at the broken truce, and I worked quickly, keeping my head down. The other Greeks seemed to sense it too, carrying their weapons and looted supplies of food and mare's milk back to the ship: some were to set out ahead for Greece in an attempt to out-pace the autumn storms, and to return to kingdoms they had neglected. The Amazons watched them work with sullen expressions of hatred.

On the second morning after the battle, Alcides declared that it was time for us to leave, as Theseus' ship had already departed, along with the captive queen. I felt sickened by Hippolyta's surrender to Theseus, against which my every instinct revolted. That he should think to take her from her homeland! That he should force the queen of the Amazons into submission! It was worse than dishonourable: it was barbarous. And to have broken the truce, when Hippolyta had extended to us the hand of peace and welcomed us with such generosity into her home . . . It was more than I could bear, and I felt a twist of dread at the thought that the Amazon queen who had shown me such kindness might now hate me with the rest of the Greeks. And meanwhile, as we prepared to ride out on our stolen steeds, the Amazons skulked out of sight, restrained by Hippolyta's last order.

I stood in Alcides' tent, alone, dressing myself in Amazon clothes borrowed from Ioxeia, for how else would I ride on horseback? I slipped into the trousers she had given me, plucking out my tunic so it lay over my thighs, pulled on the boots, then twisted around, trying to see myself. The trouser-legs were over-wide, and my plain Greek under-tunic went oddly with the patterned material. But I would be comfortable, and that was all that mattered.

I looked around me, heartsick with sadness, taking in the tent-walls hung across with slivers of drying meat, the fleeces and cushions littered over the grass, the hearth at which Alcides, Solois, Euneos, Perses and I had shared meals – some with the Amazons, and some alone. I had not thought to leave like this, hidden, dragging with us our stolen prize, slouching away in the mists of morning instead of riding out with the cries and good wishes of the Amazons behind us on the wind.

As I stepped out, I saw that someone had led up a horse for me among the others that Alcides and the rest had chosen for themselves. He tossed his head against the slave's hand on the reins, his coat black and silken with a white mark on his forehead, and I recognized the steed of Mela-nippe, sister of Hippolyta.

'This is not right,' I said, walking up to Alcides where he stood among the gathered Greeks speaking with Telemus, placing my hand on the horse's nose, feeling the warmth and softness as he nuzzled against my palm. Hippolyta's war-belt was slung around Alcides' waist, and a wave of nausea over-took me, at the remembrance of what it had cost, of the queen who had worn it so proudly. 'This horse belongs to the queen's sister.'

Alcides ignored me and continued his conversation with Telemus, as if there had been no interruption. Indeed, he and I had not spoken since the battle: he had been busy with preparations for departure, and I ministering to the sick and the dead.

I bit my lip. 'I do not want this horse,' I said, more loudly.

Alcides broke off and turned to me. 'Gods,' he exclaimed, lowering his eyes from my trousers to my boots, 'who did that to you?'

'I did,' I said, my voice shaking, but I steadied myself. 'And I do not wish to ride a stolen horse.'

He stared at me, then gave a half-glance to Telemus beside him, who made a curt nod.

'You will ride it,' Alcides said, puffing out his chest and making sure that all of the Greeks gathered nearby could hear him, 'whether you like it or no. I have had enough of your insurrection.' He placed his hands around my waist and almost threw me onto the horse's back. I clutched at its mane to stop myself falling and gripped with my thighs, pulling myself to sit.

'What?' I rounded on him.

But Alcides gave a slap to the horse's hindquarters and it bolted. I snatched at the mane and pinned my eyes to the horizon as the camp flashed past me, then the long grass.

'Follow her!' I heard Alcides shout, and as I twisted my head, I saw the Greeks trotting out of the camp, their mounts weighed down with leather panniers. The tents of the camp already looked small, the earth-brown felt and fleeces dull against the endless grass, and I felt a hollow ache of anger at Alcides and pain in my chest that this was how I would say farewell to the Amazons, of whom I had so often dreamt. I had come with such hope, and now . . .

I tried to tug at the reins to slow my horse, but he was tossing his head and kicking at the earth beneath him like an animal possessed, his dark-lashed eyes wide. Instead I tightened my grip, and tried to lose myself – as my mother must once have done – in the rise and fall of the beast beneath me and the air on my cheeks.

And ahead the plains stretched endlessly towards the north.

𒀭𒉌𒈾𒊩𒈠𒉌

Hippolyta

River Silis, Land of the Saka

The Forty-fifth Day after the Day of Earth in the Season of Apia, 1265 BC

A southerly wind blew strong over the next days, filling the sail and sending me further and further from the land of the Saka. I passed the hours gazing into the waves, watching one after another form and break against the hull, my eyes trained away from the coast, from the camps of other Saka tribes I knew were scattered along the shore of Temarunda – people with whom I had traded as a queen, ridden out with against the Budini in armed force, and shared the marriages of our young.

We put in for the night at a spur of land that pointed, like a finger, out into the water, shallow with sandy beaches where the Greeks could drive the ship's keel ashore. There Theseus had the slaves build a fire, and, as the sun blazed golden towards the sea in the west, he pronounced that we would be joined in marriage – so that he could proclaim to the world that he had taken his captive Amazon bride.

I stood by his side, wearing only my tunic, my hair loose

over my shoulders as Theseus had ordered. No Amazons attended me. There was none of the singing to Tabiti, the scattering of rose petals, the horse-sacrifice by the priest and the incense poured over the sacred fire. And yet I said nothing: for what small price was this to pay for Melanippe's life? For the lives of my people?

Theseus beside me had his hands raised in prayer before the burning fire. The eldest of the Greeks, Thoas, performed the ceremony, while his brother stood to one side, his mouth twitching at the farce of the marriage. I bore it with all the dignity I could, my lips drawn together in determination.

Before us, Thoas raised his dagger and slit the throat of the young deer they had caught for the sacrifice. The blood spurted from the victim's throat and spattered my flaxen tunic with bright scarlet drops.

'A good sign,' Thoas said. 'The goddess Hera has blessed the marriage.'

I composed my face, and tried not to wonder which gods delighted in a blood-covered bride. *But these are not the gods of the plains of the Saka.*

The fire spat and hissed as the ritual continued, preparing the meat for the spit. Theseus' hand in mine was slipping with sweat, the air around me becoming stiflingly warm, and I felt the orange of the flames, the scarlet dripping meat, the earth-red blood melt into one mirage of colour, the scene whirling before me, like a dream. Was I in Greece or the land of the Saka? Was I a queen or a slave? The ground beneath me seemed to tilt and darkness began to swallow my vision.

And then I felt a hand behind me, propping me. I blinked,

the swirling figure of Thoas before me and the leaping flames coming back into focus. Thoas' brother was holding me upright, the palm of his hand steady on my shoulder, and I nodded to him – 'My thanks to you; I am well' – and he stepped back, his face grim, all trace of a smile gone now. Thoas had not ceased his chanting. Theseus had hardly glanced my way. I felt a sudden wave of sickness overtake me – *The heat and the stench of the roasting meat, probably*, I thought, trying to calm myself. But I could not quench the flutter of panic, which was making beads of sweat stream down my forehead and setting my hands shaking at my sides. The Greek words, smooth as oil, bore down on my ears. The girdle at my waist was unbearably light without my war-belt to cover it. My legs felt naked with no trousers to cover them, my hair unbound.

I will never again ride as an Amazon. This was the sign and seal of my fate, from now on: to be a Greek woman, a Greek wife. *Yet I have to do it. I have to.*

There was no other way.

I had sworn to be a good queen to my people, to protect them above all others. I had already seen how far the mercy of the Greeks extended. If I went back on my word, the exchange of my freedom for theirs – if I attempted to escape, or fought my way from Theseus – then, I would have laid my mother's honour on it, Theseus would not cease until he had unleashed bitter strife on all my people. No, it was unthinkable.

I shuddered and bit my lip, steeling myself against the flickering of the fire and the Greek incantations. *There is no other way.*

The words droned on, washing over me, like the waves on the shore.

And perhaps, another voice whispered, quiet as the beat of a bird's wings on the air, *perhaps – if I go to Greece – I may see him again.*

I may see the Greek once more.

And so it was that, holding this thought to me, I was married to Theseus, prince of Athens.

I sat alone on the shore, apart from the Greeks, knees tucked into my chest, feet bare on the sand. The sun was setting in a blaze of gold, lining the clouds with purple and blue and streaking the sky with a veil of light. As the stars began to shine overhead and the circle of Tabiti's moon rose into the sky, I heard footsteps. Then a hand rested on my arm.

I did not turn.

'You sleep with me tonight,' Theseus said. 'Remember, we are man and wife now.'

Heat bloomed in my cheeks as he walked around and crouched before me, taking me in as if I were a deer caught in the hunt and spread before him for spearing on the spit, not a living, feeling queen. I felt his gaze rest on me, taking in my lips, my throat, my breasts, barely visible beneath my tunic. I nodded stiffly, feeling my throat constrict at his insolence. 'As you wish.'

His fingers closed around my wrist, as if he would draw me to him. 'I have captured you,' he said. 'A wild Amazon, tamed like a falconer's bird to fly to me at my call. You were meant to belong to a Greek, I think. You need a man to guide you.'

He drew me to stand and led me along the shore, not talking, the only sound the lapping of the waves and the sand crunching beneath our feet. At last he turned to me.

'My Amazon,' he said, running his fingers through my loose hair, his expression shadowed against the bright moon behind him. I turned my face up to him, jaw clenched, shuddering at the touch of his hands. 'My captive eagle.'

He bent to me and kissed me full on the mouth, his tongue rude, exploring. As he pressed himself into me and I felt the tautness of his body, a sudden thrill of desperate fear shot through me.

I broke apart from him, panting, a sob caught in my throat. 'Theseus – please—'

But he pushed me down onto the sand and, with a single thrust, drove himself into me so that I almost cried out with the pain. I bit my lip to stop myself shouting at the soreness in my hips, the ache in my belly, and lay on my back staring up at the stars as he thrust himself into my body again and again, invasive as the blow of a battle-axe. As he pushed harder and the pain mounted I felt my eyes fill, then tears rolling down my cheeks. And then, feeling more alone than I had ever done, I was crying in the darkness, as Theseus made one final thrust, and all was done.

GREEK

*Hippolyta broke the laws of the Amazons, lying with
Theseus and following him from her home to Athens,
living with him there as his wife . . .*

Isocrates, *Speeches* 12.193

To the Ends of the Earth

Admete

We rode north-west for two days with the god-wind Eurus
at our backs, guiding our path by the sun. All I knew of the
Hyperboreans was what the queen had told me – that they
lay north of the Tanais, beyond the Scythian lands – for
after the battle the Amazons had refused to help us. We
passed bands of nomads, living much as the Amazons had
in tents and spending most of their day on horseback, and as
we did not attempt to attack they let us be. On the second
day we passed into the territory of a settled people, who
farmed the dark soil for cabbage, vetch, flax and a type of
thick-stemmed wheat. The plain stretched on endlessly
around the neat plots and timber-framed huts, and, as I rode
at the back of our pack, relishing the solitude and the wind
blowing on my cheeks, I thought it strange now to find the
horses stabled, instead of roaming through the grassland.

That night we were forced to stop and ask for the hospitality of the Skoloti – for that was the name these people

gave themselves. Alcides had suffered a wound to his thigh at the hand of an Amazon, and the cut was deep, the flesh now swollen, filled with pus. He was sweating and his skin was pale. I had a few of the Greeks support him into one of the huts and lay him, muttering my thanks to the inhabitants, on their cot. Quick as I could to prevent the spread of the contamination, I cleansed the wound with yarrow, applied an ointment of comfrey I had brought and some arnica to stop the swelling, then gave him an infusion of yarrow and elderberry to drink – there was a river nearby where I could fetch fresh water – to reduce his fever. Soon he had fallen into a doze, his eyes rolling beneath the lids. I left him to sleep off the illness. The Skoloti had prepared some food for us in another hut, and I sat in silence beside the other Greeks as we partook of a boiled stew of vetch and edible roots, a fish they called *pelamys*, and buttered bread.

I returned to Alcides before retiring to the bed the Skoloti had provided for me. He was awake and sitting up, eating a bowl of stew, his face still pale in the lamplight but with a tinge of colour to the cheeks, his eyes not as over-bright as they had been. He had tossed away the blankets and his leg was stretched over the straw pallet, the bandage still neat and unstained. My jaw clenched as I saw that he had laid the war-belt of Hippolyta over the stool beside him, so that the gold plates glowed in the low light.

'Admete.' He swallowed the spoonful of stew and spread his hands wide. 'You are a miracle-worker. I am quite restored.'

I said nothing, but walked over to him and placed my hand to his forehead and bent to look in his eyes.

'You are not speaking to me now?' He caught my gaze,

then my wrist, as I straightened and turned away to fetch more water. 'You are still angry with me?'

The family of the hut – grandmother, two sons and their wives – were sharing *koumiss* by the fire, now that the children had been put to sleep in their cots, and were talking in low voices. The light of the flames glimmered over the coloured tapestries that hung on the walls and cast leaping shadows.

I shook him off. 'No.'

'It was a jest, Admete – nothing more!'

'If you mean the rude manner in which you sent me from the Amazon camp, then I am not angered at that.'

'Then what?' he asked. He leant forwards and pulled me to sit on the pallet beside him; I allowed him to draw me. Had he not always been my closest friend – my only friend, if truth be told, the only one to whom I had been able to confide my fears about my mother? 'I cannot stand it when you speak in slanted words. Tell me what you mean and be done with it.'

I bit my lip, feeling a spasm of irritation flare up. 'The battle!' I hissed at him. 'At the camp.' I shuddered as the images rolled before my eyes, and I glanced towards the embers of the fire, trying to forget them, trying to ignore the swell of nausea in my belly. 'How could you? Girls who were barely entering womanhood and mothers of children! You cut them down, without mercy – I saw it!' My voice broke as I remembered the fury of his blade flashing this way and that, the horror of the rage in his eyes, and the bleeding, suppurating wounds of both Amazons and Greeks. 'I came to the land of the Scythians expecting to find barbarians. I did not know I would find them within you.'

He let out a spluttered oath. 'You think I took pleasure in it?' he asked, his face flushing. 'I hate it as much as you do! But I had no choice – I had to capture the war-belt, at whatever cost!' He grasped my hand. 'You wish to see your mother, do you not?'

I looked aside. I had not told him of my conversation with Hippolyta.

'Well,' he went on, not waiting for my response, 'this is the price I must pay to have what I wish for – to have my glory!'

'And what price will you not pay?' I asked him, my voice rising. The family glanced at us from the hearth and shifted on their stools. 'What more will you ask? Can you not see how terrible it is? Is the immortality of one man really worth the freedom of the queen of the Amazons, the deaths of so many innocent people?'

'Yes,' he said, crossing his arms over his chest and setting his jaw. 'It is. It has to be.'

I recoiled from him. 'You do not mean that.'

He thumped his fist against his hand, and I felt the heat rise in him. 'Do not attempt to tell me what I mean!' His eyes were blazing, the muscles along his neck tensed though his wounded leg was stretched before him, a bizarre spectacle of impotence. 'I have no choice, I tell you! This is how it has to be!'

I got to my feet, looking him up and down, fingers trembling at my sides. 'If you think you have no choice, then you are not the man I knew. The man I knew was kind, and loyal, and courageous, and would have spat on the kind of outrage you committed yesterday. He would not have listened to dog-hearted cowards like Theseus, who whisper only arrogance

198

and privilege. He would have known to be the man you are –
instead of the man you think you have to be.'

It happened within a moment. He raised his hand and
slapped me full across the face, with such a *crack* that the
blow resounded through my skull, setting my ears singing.
Tears smarted at my eyes as I pressed my fingers to my
cheek.

'What by Hera do you think you are doing?' I shouted at
him. 'You – you—' I stammered for the words, and all the
while my face burnt with pain. 'I hope your wound pains you
tonight, Alcides,' I cried, strode to the wicker door and
slammed it behind me.

'Hercules!' he screamed after me. 'My name is Hercules!'

I ran out under the stars, swept across the sky like a thousand glimmering lamps, with his cries ringing in my ears. I
brushed the tears from my eyes and winced as I grazed the
bruise on my cheek, then turned back towards my hut across
the village, shoulders hunched against the cold, my feet
chilled on the wet grass.

I knew then that my friend Alcides was truly gone.

Hippolyta

Athens, Greece

The Twenty-second Day before the Day of Fire
in the Season of Tabiti, 1265 BC

The rock of Athens shimmered before me, white in the afternoon heat, sparse ridged stone towering to the sky, topped by walls made of slabs large as a man and crenellated, a gateway sitting squat above us like a sentinel. I squinted up at it, my eyes smarting against the bright sun and sweat. Never, with my broken remembrances of the pine groves and wildflowers of Skyros, could I have imagined something like this – so bare, so lifeless, only a few shrub-like olives clinging to the rock, as if all life had withered beneath the beating sun. And the air was scented not with pine but with smoke and mule-dung from the dwellings shambling around the lower slopes. A breath of sweat washed over me as the Athenian townsmen passed us on the road, bowing to their lord, bearing pots filled with grains threshed from the fields or netted fish, or dragging mule-carts loaded with wood. I did not see any women among them. The rock above me seemed almost prison-like, its

200

precipice falling down either side, the walls shielding the palace from view – as much for keeping captives in as guarding against enemies from without.

'Do you like it?' Theseus asked me, turning back with one foot on the lower step of the stairs that were carved into the rock, leading up to the gate. The back of his neck was browned from the days at the oar, his hair slicked with sweat. His eyes narrowed, as if reading my hesitation.

I said nothing. I might have been brought low. I might have no recourse to freedom. But I would not let him play with me. Neither would he make me admit I was there for anything other than the safeguarding of my people. The hair was sticking to the back of my neck, and I pushed away my longing for the cooling breezes that swept the plains.

I held his gaze, defiant, and for a moment I thought his hand twitched at his side, as if he would strike me. But then he began to climb the steps. I lifted the hair from the nape of my neck and, gritting my teeth – *This is how it has to be* – I followed Theseus.

The voyage across the seas to Athens had taken many weeks, though the steersman had told me that the sailing was fair. We had journeyed out onto the open sea, and for days we had sailed without sight of anything but the water stretching from side to side. I had sat alone near the prow, my knees tucked into my chest. I stared at the waves breaking against the keel and tried not to see Orithyia's eyes staring at me in death, to accept the overwhelming, terrifying certainty that I – a queen who had been raised by her mother, who had loved and lived with her sisters as her dearest companions – had lost both Melanippe and Orithyia: one to protect my people, the other – the fiercest warrior

I had ever known – to the land of the dead, from which none ever returned. At night we had nowhere to go to shore, so the sailors threw down the anchor and we floated mid-sea beneath the stars. Those were the worst moments: for then Theseus would come to me and, though all the other Greeks lay in their blankets on the rowing-benches near us, he would take me pinned against one of the thwarts without a thought for my shame before the men who lay silent and unmoving nearby. I submitted to him every night as I had that first time on the shore in the land of the Saka. Every time I gasped with silent pain, as he thrust his body upon mine, and tried not to inhale the bitter tang of his sweat, I knew that my spirit was broken a little more, like a horse from the wilds being tamed to the bit and bridle. Often his force left me bruised in the hips and unable to sit, my skin mottled green and blue-black (thank the gods my tunic was long enough to cover it). I tried to hide it from the rest as best I could.

Yet now that we had sailed through the islands, which were scattered like stones across the sea, and had landed in Athens, I hoped – with the fading hope of a traveller on the dark plains as her torch sputters its last flame – that things might be different. Perhaps Theseus had been eager to return to his home. He might have been a different man at sea, fatigued from the oar and the swelling sickness of the waves. Perhaps now that we were back on land he would treat me with more respect: the respect that the gods demanded be afforded to a queen, even in captivity. Perhaps even – when he was assured that I would not risk my people's lives by running from him – we might journey to Thessaly. Perhaps then – I felt contempt for myself, yet

I had not the strength, here, in Greece, to curb it – I might see my Greek once more.

We reached the gateway and entered, spear-bearing soldiers bowing their lord through, to a courtyard. It was scattered here and there with colonnaded buildings and, to my left, a columned sprawling structure that must have been the palace, two or three times larger than that on Skyros. My heart tightened to see it: the stone foundations bore the weight of several floors, rising one above the other to the sky; the columns and the roof-beams were painted blood-red, with a frieze of yellow-blue around the high roof, so dazzling against the sun I could barely make it out. And there, again, planted by the path as we walked, were the olive trees, their roots so gnarled and twisted that they seemed to suck water from the rock by mere force. Slaves were tending the trees, pruning the branches and raking away dead leaves. They looked up as we passed, and their eyes fell on me, and I thought how strange I must seem, wearing only an unbelted tunic, not a Greek dress with skirts, and with my Saka cheekbones and browned skin.

We passed through an open arch into a smaller court-yard, bounded at one end by two more columns fringed at the top with leaves carved in stone. Theseus snapped his fingers, and a woman emerged from between the columns ahead in red and blue skirts, her hair long and ringleted.

'Theia,' he said, as she approached, her hem sweeping the floor behind her. She bowed to him, and I saw – memories of Skyros flooding back to me, half painful, half dreamlike – that her eyes were outlined with black, her lips and cheeks reddened, her skin pale as if she had never seen the sun: the complexion of a Greek noblewoman. 'Theia is of my mother's family, and serves here in the women's quarters,' he continued, as she smiled at me, her eyes warm and welcoming. 'She will find you what you need. Theia,' he said, waving in my direction, 'this is,' he considered me, 'Antiope – a good Greek name, do you not think? Not one of those barbarous horse-taming names from the east. She is to stay here in the palace.'

I felt the smile stiffen on my face, as if he had slapped me. *A Greek name.* My insides twisted as every fibre of my body revolted against it. In the land of the Saka our names were a thread that connected us to our tribe, like leather straps to a war-belt, to the land, the earth: Melanippe was Black Horse, for her mount; Orithyia – an arrow of pain darted through me as I thought of my brave, wilful sister – Mountain Raging, for her spirit, and I, Hippolyta, Releaser of Horses, as our swiftest rider. How could I lose that? How could he think of taking that from me?

And yet, I thought, as the slaves marched past bearing sacks from the ship, and my fingers brushed the swelling bruises girding my hips, *he has already taken much. Why should his arrogance not lead him to take my name, too?*

And no mention of our marriage. I opened my mouth to speak, but he had turned away.

'Gods,' he said, 'I need a bath – Eurydamas!' he called, his voice echoing down the corridors, and I heard the hurried patter of footsteps.

'Come,' Theia said, drawing me by the arm.

'Wait,' Theseus called, turning back as I crossed the court with Theia. 'I forgot.' I blinked back at him, eyes fixed on his, hope bubbling inside me, taking in again his dark gaze and the curling beard now covering his chin after the long sea-voyage. *Now he will say it. Now he will tell them that I am a queen chosen by the gods, that he has not meant to treat me as he has, that – though I am his captive – he will afford me the respect to which I have a right, as he swore to me in the land of the Saka.*

'I will be leaving for Sparta tomorrow.' His eyes narrowed, sweeping over my tunic, my dark hair plaited over my shoulder, then to Theia, 'When I return, I expect her to look like a civilized Greek, not a savage.'

He strode off into the shadows.

Blazing with mixed anger and shame, feeling more powerless than I had ever done without my war-belt and a blade at my hip to defend myself, I allowed Theia to lead me through a hall and into a suite of chambers – dressing room, a room for bathing with a clay tub inset into the floor surrounded by tiles coloured white and blue, then a bedchamber. Guards stood posted at every door, two each side, armed with long-swords chosen, I was sure, for my benefit: Theseus had no doubt measured, and rightly, that an unarmed woman – even an Amazon – would not overpower four heavy-armed soldiers. The thought did nothing to cheer me.

The coverlets on the bed of my chamber were folded, decorated with a sprig of lavender, and sage had been scattered over the floor, sending up its scent in the cool dark rooms. I marked that the closets were filled already with women's clothes – perhaps Theseus had sent word ahead that I was accompanying him – the pots on the dressing-table filled with cosmetics and scented oils, golden earrings and gold filigree hairpins laid out on a cloth.

Theia led me to the bathing chamber to see a train of slaves tipping cauldrons of hot water and throwing pale rose petals into the tub, steam billowing up to the ceiling and bringing with it the scent of rosemary and olive oil. She waited until the last of the slaves had left, then helped me out of my tunic, saying nothing at the green-blue bruises blossoming over my skin, and into the bath, where the spirals painted on its inside glimmered like waves on the sea. I eased myself into the water, letting the warmth flood my bones, the thick pink petals skimming the surface protecting my shame. We had no baths in my home, only steam-tents heated by vapour over red-hot stones where we sweated the dirt from our skin and covered ourselves in pastes of cypress, cedar and frankincense. I had not bathed like this since Skyros. A sigh escaped my lips, and the steam from the water swirled around my neck and face.

'Theia?'

'Yes, my lady?'

'You may,' I said, opening my eyes and gesturing to her to sit on the stool nearby, 'call me Hippolyta.'

She hesitated. 'My lord has given the order,' she said, her gaze flicking aside to the guards. 'You are Antiope now.'

I felt a swoop of anger that she would refuse my request, that she would observe this ungodly breach of all honour – *But you are a queen no longer.* 'Then call me nothing,' I said at last, my chest rising and falling, 'for I am not, and will never be, Antiope.'

She lapsed into silence and leant forwards, sweeping my hair back from my neck so that it draped over the bath's edge. It was a caring gesture. *And yet perhaps*, I thought, my anger slackening a little, *in spite of her deference to Theseus, she might be a friend to me. She is commanded by him, after all, as much as I.*

I paused, and the question rose to my lips. 'Has Theseus taken a wife before?'

Her eyes softened. 'He has had many women,' she said, leaning down to pick up a clay bowl filled with honey and oil. Her speech was rapid as she went on, as if she had had to answer this many times before: 'Ariadne – he carried her from Crete and abandoned her on the isle of Naxos on his return. Phaedra – Ariadne's sister, whom he brought here – she still lives in the dwellings of the lower town. He goes to take his pleasure with her when he wishes. Periboea, Phereboea, Iope, daughter of Iphicles . . .'

I felt a chill, in spite of the water's heat, which raised the hairs on my skin as the names went on. *What if I am but another on his list of conquests? What if he never meant to be bound by the laws of royal conquest and marriage, as he swore before the gods, but merely to keep me as his slave?*

The muscles of my legs tightened, as if I would run – but where? Where could I go, on the world's other edge from my people and my home, with no weapon to protect me and no steed to ride upon?

And yet, another voice within me said, attempting to bring back reason, *he wedded you, did he not? He brought you back to Athens. He could have left you stranded on an island, as he did with that other.*

A mercy to be grateful for, indeed, I thought, my mouth twisting.

'You are blessed to be his now,' I heard Theia saying, her fingers gentle on my skin as she pressed the honey-paste to my temples and my cheeks. 'He is wealthy and powerful, the lord of all Attica, which he has united beneath his rule. You should enjoy his favour while it lasts.'

'I was a queen, you know,' I said, my voice unsteady. 'I ruled my own people. I fought as a warrior on horseback and could ride more swiftly and aim an arrow further than any of my tribe.'

She picked up an oil jar, poured it onto her palms and rubbed them together, then drew her fingers through my hair, massaging the scalp. The scent of lavender filled my nostrils and I closed my eyes again. It was hard to be fearful with these soft, soothing strokes, and I felt like a steed being calmed by its rider. 'You are a Greek now,' she said simply. 'And a word of warning, if I may, Antiope – my lady.' I gritted my teeth, but did not reprimand her. 'Theseus does not take disobedience. If you try to escape, he will have his guards run you through with their swords, without mercy, and no matter how skilled you are with a bow, you will have little chance against them unarmed, and you a woman.'

A lump of fear rose again in my throat, my fingers quivering at my sides as if longing to snatch up the *sagaris* from the war-belt I had given up. There was no escape and, like a hawk that hops into a cage after a mouse, I had trapped myself, tied myself to the falconer's gauntlet.

I am trapped.

That night, I lay alone in my chamber. I told myself that it was not too different from my tent: when I closed my eyes I could hear the wind rustling the leaves outside the window, but the mattress was stiff on its roped cords and I missed the feel of wolf-skins against my cheeks, the woodsmoke scent of the fire. Theia had remained by my side all through the dinner-feast and had talked to me pleasantly enough of the court, while Theseus sat on the hearth's other side reacquainting himself with the Athenian nobles, drinking deep of his goblet and wreathed in smiles. He had not glanced once at me.

The door to my chamber creaked open. I sat up, heart pulsing at my throat, clutching at my side for my sword and dagger before I remembered where I was.

'Who – who is there?' I asked into the darkness, and heard my voice tremble. What if Theseus had tired of me already – if he had sent one of his guards to dispose of me, quick and clean in the night? *What an Amazon queen you are now.* I clutched my blankets to my chin. Footsteps came towards me, sounding over the tiled floor, then the smell of a man's sweat, and in a moment hands were clasping around my back and a mouth was bearing down on me, pressing me down so I could barely breathe.

'Theseus!' I gasped, coming up for air. I saw him move back, saw his eyes glitter in the moonlight raking through the slat-covered windows. 'It is you, is it not?'

He let out a throaty chuckle. 'You are cautious tonight, my eagle?'

I let out a breath and sank onto the bed. 'No, only – I was not sure it was you. That is all.'

'And who else would it be?'

I smoothed the linen of the white under-tunic I wore, embroidered with fine-stitched laurel leaves at the hem. 'No one,' I said. 'You only startled me.'

A sudden spark of light: he had lit a lamp with a flint and taper. The flame flared and glowed dimly in the deserted chamber, the dressing-table in the corner with a mirror laid upon it, the cupboard and chests with all his other

women's clothes, the chair on which I had draped the tat-
tered, salt-stained tunic I had worn on the journey.

'Unplait your hair,' he commanded, running a hand over
my head and down my back. 'I do not like it when you look
like a barbarian.'

Obediently, I swung my plait around and unknotted the
ribbon holding it, then teased apart the strands with my fingers. He was standing very close to me, and it struck me
again how much older he was than my Greek had been.
From here I could see the wisps of white in his beard and the
soft skin of the pouches beneath his eyes. He was staring at
me, his expression hungry, unsmiling.

'Take it off.' He gestured to my under-tunic.

Confusion sent a rush of heat to my cheeks. 'I – my lord—'
I slid my hand protectively across my breasts. Not even the
Greek had seen me naked, and with Theseus the act had
always been done quickly and sharply in the dark, with my
tunic pushed up around my waist.

'Take it off,' he repeated. 'I command it.'

Slowly, shame burning on my face, I raised myself to my
feet and undid the tunic where it fastened at the shoulders,
my fingers fumbling.

'Faster,' he said, his breath coming quickly. He pulled at
the ribbons and tugged at the tunic. It rippled off my shoulders, catching a little at my hips, then fell to the floor, a pool
of white in the moonlight from the window.

I stood before him, utterly humiliated, the lamp's flame
lighting the contours of my skin, probing, and I longed to
hug my arms to me and cover my shame. *I am the queen of the
Amazons*, I thought, and at once a sob caught in my throat.

See how the gods have thrown me down. Watch my despair, Theseus. Does it please you? Does my humiliation give you pleasure?

He was panting now, his eyes darting over my body, lingering on my breasts, the hard muscles of my belly and the dark warmth of my thighs.

'So this is what an Amazon looks like,' he said. He lifted me and threw me back onto the bed. I tried to twist away, to hold my legs together in a last desperate attempt, but he forced them apart and then he thrust himself into me. I squeezed my eyes shut, but still I could see the flames of the oil-lamp burning on my eyelids as he pushed, feel the pain shoot through my belly, and I could staunch the tears no longer. Silent as a river on a windless summer night, they ran down my cheeks and into the bolster beneath my head. My lip was bleeding where I was biting into it to stop myself crying aloud – I could taste the iron tang of it in my mouth mixed with salt.

And round and round my head went the mocking refrain: *So this is what an Amazon looks like.*

Ἀδμήτη

Admete

Pine needles scraped at my legs and forearms. The air was
thick with the scent of damp and moss, and overhead I could
barely make out the grey sky, shielded by the webbed branches
of the spruces. My eyelids were heavy, my legs rubbed raw,
my hips and back aching so that it took all my strength
simply to remain seated on my mount.

'Can we not rest?' I called to Alcides, where he led the
train of Greeks pushing through the woodland. At the edge
of the territory of the Skoloti the plain had given way to a
dense forest of pine – spiny red-trunked trees bending over
us and barring our way, brown ferns brushing the horses'
hoofs, and an interminable darkness barely parted by the
sun's rays even in the middle of the day.

Alcides did not answer, looking forwards as he rode, but
I knew from the stillness of his head that he had heard me.

I let out a breath and looked about, searching for something,

212

anything, to break the dominion of needle-bearing trees. There had been barely any plants to record since we had left the land of the Skoloti, except a few mosses and grey curling lichens. My frustration at not finding herbs for Alexander, as I had hoped, and my growing fear that we might return too late, even if we found what we sought, hardly diminished the discomfort of the ride. I had never felt so far from Tiryns, from my father and brothers, and the comforts of the herb-garden; at this time of year the figs would be ripening, dark purple on the tree in the courtyard.

My stomach rumbled. Our meals of wood-mushrooms, roots and berries were less than satisfying, and my memory wandered to the figs, the sensation of the small sharp seeds in my mouth, the sweet flesh . . .

The cracked cry of a buzzard seared the air, bringing me to my senses. The train ahead had halted, the horses standing nose to tail, tossing their manes and snorting. I kicked forwards to the head of the party, drawing level with Alcides, his horse drawn up side by side with Telemus', stamping and snorting in the damp air.

I saw at once why they had halted.

The forest tumbled abruptly into water edged with grass and reeds, a wide river with slow-moving blue-grey waters that eddied in currents, ducks swimming or diving into the water for fish. On the opposite bank there was a clearing of flooded marsh, brown water dotted with wet-grass, and at the marsh's edge a gathering of tents, sheltered by the forest, which stretched on behind them.

'The furthest river,' I said. I would not look at Alcides, not after he had struck me, even after all these weeks, so I turned

to Timiades. 'It is, is it not? *Danu Apara* – the furthest
river – that's what the leader of the Skoloti said? And
beyond it . . .'

My voice trailed away. Beyond the river lay the Sarmatians, whom the Skoloti had told us would know how to
reach the Hyperborean land. My stomach clenched and I
felt my thighs tighten around my horse's back. *And perhaps
then I may find the apples, the cure for Alexander's fever, and we
may return to Tiryns, and all will be as it once was.* My chest
lightened at the thought.

I glanced over at Alcides. Perhaps I had been too harsh
with him. Perhaps he had not meant to strike me in anger.
Perhaps I should apologize for what I had said – for I, too,
had wounded him with my words.

He was testing the water with a branch, trying to find
the shallowest place to cross. I would speak with him later, I
decided, that night, when we made camp. I watched as he
leant over the bank, up to his shoulder in the water, feeling
for the swimming reeds of the riverbed. At last, after much
walking up and down the banks, he and Timiades called to
us that they had found a shallow ford. As I rode towards it,
I could see the water bouncing and bubbling around rocks,
creating disturbances in the river's surface. We crossed on
horseback, slowly so as not to slip, our feet dangling in the
cold water, the current tugging at our steeds' tails.

When I came to the other shore, wet and shivering, I
could make out more clearly some tents I had seen from the
other side, clustered together beneath the shade of the trees
where the forest opened out into marsh. The people of the
tribe were crowded before their dwellings, holding hoes and
buckets of water, watching us. They had no swords at their

belts and wore the same dark-dyed cloaks as the Skoloti, which had led Perses to refer to them lightly as the *Melanch-laeni*, the Black Cloaks; somehow the name had stuck.

Perses had seen them too. His horse sidled over to Alcides, and I heard him say, 'These?'

Sthenelus called from his mount, 'Yes, indeed, Alcides – they are easy prey.'

Timiades drew his spear from his baldric and weighed it in his hand. 'Gods, what I would not give for a hunt and a chase after such slow riding.'

I kicked my horse towards Alcides, where his steed curvetted over the needles of the forest floor. 'What is this?'

He avoided my eye. 'Nothing with which you should concern yourself.'

'Men's work,' Telemus said, riding up behind me. 'Merely some sport.'

'The men are becoming restless,' Alcides said, in a low voice, still looking away.

'And this is your sport? Stealing from unarmed tribespeople who have done nothing to provoke you?'

Perses had drawn his sword and was cutting and thrusting through the air. 'It is not stealing if you win the prize.'

'And you should not speak to the son of Zeus so,' Telemus said. 'It is not your place.'

'My place?' I exclaimed, heat rising in me at the sneer, at the hatred and scorn of these men that had borne down upon me these past weeks. 'I am the daughter of Eurystheus! It is at my command, and the command of my father the king, that this expedition occurs!' I turned to Alcides, glad to see Telemus' face fall, and leant across to place my hand on his rein. 'I know you can see this is unjust,' I said. 'I know

215

you.' I covered his hand with my own. 'You do not have to do this, Alcides.'

'Hercules,' he muttered, his mouth turning down. 'They call me Hercules.'

'But you said—'

'Yes,' he said, withdrawing his hand from mine and flicking the reins so that his horse side-stepped past me, 'but I am nearly done with my labours, and it is as you said. There can be no room for doubt.' His eyes were glinting, hard. 'I will be enough, I have to be, and that begins with making sure you call me by my name.'

Confusion and irritation rose within me. 'I never said you should not doubt,' I said, 'only that you should trust yourself. Those are very different things.'

A dull red was creeping over Alcides' cheeks, and I knew that he, like me, was aware of the stares of the other Greeks upon us. 'Enough!' he said loudly, for the others to hear. Perses laughed and Telemus nodded at the snap in his voice. 'I will not allow you to speak to me so.' He raised his chin. 'Stay here and keep your opinions to yourself, as befits a woman. I will not have you contradict me.'

He kicked his steed towards the tribe, throwing up clods of earth and sitting stiff, the others bringing their mounts around to follow, leaving me open-mouthed and fuming behind them.

Storm

Scythia

As Hercules gathers his troops, Hera, too, is travelling north. A cloak flung over her shoulder and still in her Amazon guise, she is galloping through the forests of Scythia, her eyes fixed ahead, searching through the trees for a pale ankle or the flash of a robe – any sign of that damned-to-Hades Muse Calliope. She knows – she can sense it – that she is getting closer, and it is her anger at Calliope's theft that drives her on through the pitch-dark nights and the driving rain, across sodden marshes and through these interminable forests. For Hera has surmised that a Muse, who knows what it is to look upon the earth from a god's-eye view, will have chosen a hiding-place that cannot be seen from above.

And then, downstream, along the river she has just crossed, Hera catches sight of a few figures who – her eyes widen, and she halts her horse – look remarkably like . . . Greeks.

Her breathing comes short and rapid as she tries to make them out. Yes – there at the head, that must be Hercules, and behind him, seated on her mount and dressed as an Amazon, shouting imprecations that are whipped to her on the wind, that must be Admete.

She curses aloud, and a wood-pigeon nearby flutters, startled, from its nest.

'Zeus be damned!' she says, and kicks her horse forwards,

whipping at it with the reins. How by Styx did they survive her attack on the Amazon camp? How did the Amazons – some of the most famed warriors in the world of mortals – fail to dispose of them? It is enough to make her spit with rage.

Trees fall away into frail skeletons of ash either side of her as she purses her lips and blows. Just as it had at the banks of the Tanais, a cloud forms, mist-like, around her. She raises one hand to the skies as she rides, tossing the fog up till it swirls around on itself and becomes a dark, rumbling stormcloud. She whips it up further, till it is a tumbling mass, spreading, like a curse, over the land of the Sarmatians. Winds slash across the forest, howling and tearing, bending the spruces and sending pine needles flying arrow-sharp through the air, and birds are hurled against tree-trunks, tossed like fish in a sea-storm. As she hawks and spits, the rains start to fall – not soft summer rains but a torrent of plunging water, falling hard as darts – enough to prevent any mortal travelling on. Enough to keep them far from the apples – until she has dealt with the Muse and can unleash her anger on the son of Zeus.

Hera squints and sees the Greek horses stumble, some rearing in fright, others slipping on the wet carpet of moss and needles, and the Greeks are staring skywards, their panicked shouts ringing in her ears as they recall the dread mist of the Amazon camp, and know the wrath of the gods.

She smiles to herself and urges her horse on.

Not a hundred miles away, Calliope looks up into the storm, clutching the cedarwood chest to her soaking robes, and knows that Hera has almost found her.

Becoming Greek

𒐊𒉌𒌋𒁲𒌋𒈨𒐊

Hippolyta

Athens, Greece

The Fourteenth Day before the Day of Fire
in the Season of Tabiti, 1265 BC

'Hold the mirror for me,' I ordered Theia, my fingers trembling as I brushed threads from my skirts. This was the first time since Skyros that I had dressed as a Greek – Greek gold hanging at my ears and neck, Greek cosmetics painted on my lips and cheeks, and the full skirts that Greek women wore cascading from my hips, my breasts pushing uncomfortably against my bodice. *How will it be to see myself like this again?*

Theia picked up the bronze hand-mirror and held it back so I could see my reflection.

My skin paled visibly in the shimmering likeness before me, what colour I had left draining from my cheeks. The transformation was well done – Theia had done her job with skill – but, as I gazed into my dark, frightened eyes, I saw a wild horse that had been broken and dressed, its mane knotted with ribbons, till it looked like a performing animal, not a proud creature of the plains. My face had been powdered, disguising the nut-brown colour of my skin; my lips were tinted red, my cheeks pinched till they blushed, my eyes seductive with their dark lampblack rims. My hair had been oiled till it was glossy and shining, then piled on my head, a few curls escaping down my back; heavy earrings shimmered at my lobes, and a golden necklace with a pendant of a lily hung between my breasts.

'You would not even know I was an Amazon,' I said to Theia, trying to keep my voice steady, and as I did so I saw the reflection before me falter, the forehead crease. I tried to pull my lips up into a smile.

I shook myself to banish the remorse I felt at the thought of what Melanippe would say if she saw me as I was now.

Yet I am a Greek so that there may still be Amazons. What small sacrifice is that?

I stood straighter as Theia put the finishing touches to my dress, tying a girdle tight round my waist, dabbing a little more perfume at my wrists and behind my ears.

'There,' she said, stepping back, her eyes skimming over me. 'Theseus will find you a vision well worth returning from Sparta for, my lady.'

I heard him before I saw him: the deep boom of his laughter echoed down the corridors as I stepped out of my quarters and made my way towards his. I quickened my step past the guards, my sandals slapping against the flagstones, brushed a curl away from my face, wetted my lips with the tip of my tongue; then took a deep breath as I rounded the corner into the court before his quarters—

And halted at once.

Theseus was bent over, laughing, twirling a wooden hoop

around the grey-leafed olive tree that stood at the courtyard's centre. Behind him ran a girl, her blonde hair in
disarray and her teeth showing as she let out a peal of laughter. She could be no more than ten years of age, with clear
skin and eyes that sparkled in the sunlight; her hair was
tossed in ringlets over her head that still showed the softness
of childhood, and she wore a simple tunic belted at the
waist. I drew in a breath. She was perfect, delicate as a carved
marble statue. No, that was too rigid: like a downy swan's
wing. I had always longed for a daughter. When I had been
in the land of the Saka, I had wanted to teach her to ride, to
be a queen like me, and to pass the sacred war-belt of the
queens of old to her. *The war-belt I have lost*, I thought with
another pang.

'Theseus,' I said, making my way to him. He stood up,
shielding his eyes against the sunlight, the hoop caught in
one hand. The girl ran to him and started to leap for it, trying to snatch it from him. He laughed and tossed it across
the court, his eyes trailing her as she ran after it.

'Theseus?'

His gaze lingered on her for a moment longer, and then,
at last, he looked at me. 'Antiope. What is it?' he asked,
irritation in his voice.

At the name, a spasm of anger darted through me, but I
collected myself almost at once. 'I merely wished to welcome
you from Sparta.'

I swallowed as the silence lengthened, broken only by the
thrumming of the cicadas in the olive branches, the girl's
laughter and the clatter of the hoop and stick. Still he made
no remark.

'You did not tell me you had a daughter,' I said, following

his gaze, which was back again on the figure playing at the court's other end, the sun shining on her hair and turning it into a cloud of gold. 'I shall be glad to be a mother to her.'

He snorted, and a flash of annoyance crossed his features. 'She is not my daughter,' he said.

I frowned. 'But then,' I said, 'who is she?'

His eyes darkened, and I saw a muscle in his cheek begin to pulse. 'Her name is Helen,' he said, not looking at me, 'Helen of Sparta, and she is my guest here for as long as I choose. You would do well not to question me again, woman.'

He walked away. I watched his retreating back, his cloak stretched tight across his shoulders, and longed to shout after him, to demand that he return and explain himself, but knew better than to do so.

Instead, with as much dignity as I could, I left the court, not caring that my hair was falling from its style, or that my curls were losing their shape in the heat. I paced the corridors towards my quarters, steps quickening, crossed the courtyard and the great hall, then threw open the doors to my chamber, not waiting for the guards to do so for me.

'Theia!'

She straightened from the chest, a pile of folded clothes in her arms. She took in my expression at once – I must have looked half wild, torn between anger and the deepest shame, my cheeks flaming hot – and laid the clothes on a chair. 'Yes, my lady Antiope?'

Her eyes were all too knowing for my liking.

'Theia,' I repeated, trying to calm my voice, though it was leaping with emotion. 'Do you know who that girl is? Did you know that she was come?'

She bowed her head, her eyelashes sweeping her cheeks. 'Yes, my lady.'

'And why is she here?'

Silence.

'Why is she here?' I repeated, slamming my hand on the dressing-table so that the pot of lampblack tottered and spilt, spreading dark dust, like ashes, over the wood. 'Never mind that,' I said, as she moved to clear it. 'You will answer my question, Theia. You are in my service as well as his.'

She nodded. 'It will bring you no happiness,' she said.

'I have little of that in any case,' I said. I balled my hands into fists, digging the nails into my palms, trying with all my might to maintain what little dignity I had left. I raised my chin and met her stare. 'I wish to know.'

For a moment I thought I saw my own despair mirrored in her face – the sagging of the skin beneath the eyes, the downturn of the lips, and realized I had been harsh to think she bore no cost in all of this. 'Her name is Helen,' she said, plucking the pot of lampblack to set it right, her finger smudging through the dust. 'My cousin tells me he stole her from Sparta while she ran, alone, by the banks of the Eurotas river. It seems he has become so accustomed to having what he wants that he thinks nothing of it now to seize a girl – not even a woman yet – and take her for his own.'

My fists were at my sides, my stomach clenched. 'And his purpose with her?' I asked, through gritted teeth.

The look of pity and scorn she threw me was enough to tell me everything.

I felt my knees weaken as if a sword had sliced through the tendons, and at once Theia's hand was at my elbow. She guided me to a chair and set me down in it. 'It is an offence against the gods,' I said. My teeth were chattering and my palms clammy with sweat, though the room was warm and filled with sunlight. 'He will bring the stain and the curse of his offence upon this city – upon us all. Upon me.'

She said nothing.

'What am I to do, Theia?' The words escaped through dry lips, and I looked up at her, trembling. 'What am I to do?'

She shook her head, her mouth set in a thin line. 'There is nothing you can do,' she said, 'but wait. He will tire of her soon enough, as he has done with the others.'

'But,' I whispered, 'what if he tires of me? What then?'

She glanced back at the guards standing at the door, immovable, their hands on the hilts of their long-swords, and began placing the clothes in the chest, layering them with lavender posies, avoiding my eye. And in the silence of that moment, I knew, as perhaps I had done for many days, without acknowledging it.

He had tired of me already.

I was trapped like a falconer's hawk tied by a leather jess to the glove, unable to escape, bound by my oath to the gods and my fierce love of my people.

And the worst of it was that he knew it.

Ἀδμήτη

Admete

Sarmatia

The Twenty-fourth Day of the Month of Threshing Wheat, 1265 BC

And then, after six days more of hard riding through rain and sleet, with thunder crashing over our heads and an endless sky of rolling grey, we came upon the Sarmatians. I held my breath as we rode up to them, peering through the thick veil of rain that had settled over the land ever since we had left the land of the Melanchlaeni. Here the trees seemed to have thinned to reveal a plain, and a brown river moved slowly to my right hand, its surface pitted with water-drops. Gathered across the fog-ridden meadow were scores of wagons, some four-wheeled, some six, covered with felt and with steps to the doors. People in green and blue trousers and tunics trudged through the mud, holding their cloaks over their heads against the storm. Others peered from the shelter of wagons, while sheep and oxen snorted, damp mist pouring from their nostrils.

My fingers tightened on my reins, and my horse – a new

steed stolen from the Black Cloaks, which I had tried and failed to refuse – tossed its head, feeling the pull at the bit.

Not far now. It cannot be far now.

The Sarmatians welcomed us, leading us to a steam-tent to bathe and wagons in which to sleep. When I climbed inside one, I found it was heated by an iron brazier, the walls lined with colourful patterned cloths, and the beds, with carved wooden frames, were heaped with patchwork rugs. That night we ate together, huddled in blankets, before a fire, sheltered by a canopy held on birch branches, the moon hidden by rolling clouds, and the howls of wolves echoing behind the patter of rain. The sheep, oxen and horses had been gathered into a pen and were guarded by men who sat before it, drinking *koumiss* from a leather pouch and sharpening their sword-blades, seemingly oblivious to the storm. The boiled horse's hock, lifted from the cauldron and served with bread, was tough and without flavour, but I ate without complaint. After roots, berries and mushrooms, it was as welcome as a feast of ox-chine and sweet wine.

As we ate and warmed our hands, I talked with our Sarmatian hosts, glad to break the silence of the past days – for I had refused to speak with Alcides, and none of the Greeks had seen fit to converse with me in the wake of my rebuke of Telemus. Having passed so many weeks without hearing a word of Scythian, I found that the Sarmatians' language was similar to the dialect spoken by the Amazons; indeed, the tribesmen with whom I spoke told me that the Sarmatians claimed descent from a union of Amazon women and the men of a Scythian tribe, who had moved north to found a clan of their own. Alcides was still irritable and did not take notice of me, applying himself to gnawing the meat from the bone. When he finished it and tossed it onto the grass, his eyes wandered towards one of the younger Sarmatian girls, smooth-skinned with youth, who sat on the other side of the fire. I had just turned from watching him to engage the Sarmatian tribesman again, when I caught sight of a woman standing behind him. She was tall, conversing and laughing with someone I could not see, her hair edged with grey, face drenched in light by the flames of the fire, shoulders thrown back, sharp nose and cheekbones silhouetted in the light against the silver rain behind.

I felt a wave of dizziness engulf me as the world shook and tilted. I groped blindly to steady myself, fingers clutching at the blades of grass.

It is impossible. It cannot be. And yet—

It was her.

It was my mother.

Hippolyta

Athens, Greece

The Eighth Day before the Day of Fire
in the Season of Tabiti, 1265 BC

Darkness had fallen over the rock of Athens, sweeping across the sky in a swathe of deepening blue above the Great Hall from the east. The evening meal was done, the pine-torches in their brackets on the walls were lit. Theia was watching over the slaves in clearing the hall, the nobles had departed for their dwellings below the palace, and Theseus had left for the store-rooms with his chief steward to review the accounts of the estate. Helen was lying belly-down on a pair of cushions, absent-mindedly rolling a toy horse of wood back and forth, its wheels creaking over the tiles, her eyelids drooping.

'Come,' I said, clapping my hands, and she glanced up at me. My heart twisted at her pale face, the faint pleading in her eyes that said quite plainly: *Will you take me home now?* All thoughts of my own plight faded, and I picked her up, relishing the warm weight of her body and the way she wound her hands around my neck.

'Let us move to my quarters,' I said. 'They will be more

232

comfortable than this draught-ridden old hall. Theia,' I nodded to her, 'make up the fire in the queen's hall, and provide us with some sweetmeats. We will retire there. What would you say to a handful of honey-dipped almonds, Helen?'

The girl tilted her face to mine, then cast her eyes down as if she would chastise herself for her eagerness. 'I do like them, if it pleases you, my lady.'

'You may call me Hippolyta,' I said, and, though I saw her mouth open and then close, Theia said nothing at my resistance to Theseus' orders. Helen glanced up at me and smiled, her long blonde lashes sweeping her cheeks as she tucked her horse under her arm. *By the gods, she is a beautiful child*, I thought, swallowing the fear that seemed to rise to the surface so easily, these days. I longed for nothing more than to gather her to me and cling to her, for pity at what her beauty might bring her. *What it has already brought.*

'Has Theseus been kind to you?' I asked, shifting her around so she sat on my hip-bone. Her grasp tightened on my neck, and I felt her fingers close around my under-tunic at the collar. I said nothing more, and set out across the darkened hall, treading carefully to avoid scattered cushions and wine-goblets, the remnants of the feast, my skirts gathering crumbs and my sandals slipping on the morsels of gristle and the discarded bones that the slaves were sweeping up. I held Helen to me, laying my cheek on her head and taking in the scent of her curls, as sweet as Cayster's when he was a babe.

If only that was what we were – a family – not the captive slave of the lord of Athens and his new plaything.

The hearth was only just lit when we arrived in my quarters, and the hall – smaller than Theseus' – was cool, now that an evening breeze was blowing through the opening in the

rafters. I sent Theia for blankets, and we sat before the leaping blue flames, huddled together for warmth. I pulled a
gold ringlet back from Helen's forehead and tucked it behind
her ear, watching the flames play over her pale skin as if her
face were alight and burning.

'You did not answer me before,' I said to her, when Theia
had set a bowl of almonds before us and an oiled bronze pan
on a rack over the flames. I tossed a nut into the pan and it
sizzled, sending up a warm, rich scent. 'Has Theseus been
good to you?'

She shrugged. 'I suppose so,' she said. 'He lets me eat figs
from the kitchens whenever I wish it. But I miss my home.'

'And he has not ... ?' My voice trailed away into the
crackling of the flames and the spitting oil. I could not bring
myself to finish.

Her blue-grey eyes widened. 'Not what?' She stared up at
me, sucking the almond, her lips sticky with honey, and her
expression so unknowing that I could tell he had not.

I let out a breath. 'Well, that is something, at least,' I said to
myself, then went on, 'He has not taken you to the lower city?
I hear there are many different villages spread beneath the
rock, which he has undertaken to bring together into Athens.'

She shook her head, and her ringlets bounced. 'No,' she
said. 'I have not been allowed outside the palace.'

You and I both, I thought, feeling a flutter of panic in my
chest, which was overtaken at once by the sight of her sloping shoulders and the downturned corners of her mouth.

She was silent for a moment, watching the nuts as they
leapt and danced on the bronze pan. Then she looked up at
me and, as easily as if it meant nothing, she asked the question I had been dreading: 'Why am I here?'

I hesitated, and she picked at a nut but did not eat it, peeling the browned outer layer with the thumbnail. I saw her lip quiver. 'I – I want to go home. I want to go home to Sparta.'

The strength drained from me. I heard my sharp intake of breath, felt myself lighten and drift, as if I were somehow outside myself, looking down at the strange pair of captives in their prison: a Spartan princess and an Amazon queen, cowering together in the shadows of the stone-walled garrison of Athens.

'Oh, my love,' I said, drawing her close to me, biting back tears. She curled up in the crook of my arm, and a terrible sadness engulfed me, an itch of powerlessness so strong that I wanted to scream aloud, to Theseus, to the gods, to all the masters of our fate: *Is this what you have done to me? To this poor, innocent child? Have you not had enough from us?*

I longed more than ever for my weapons and my war-belt, the smooth shaft of a *sagaris* in my right hand and a sword-hilt in my left, a bow and quiver at my hip. I longed to have more with which to protect her than my embrace alone. 'I cannot tell you why you are here,' I said, closing my eyes and cursing myself silently. *It is in your power to tell her, but you do not want to. You do not want to tell Helen the terrible reason for which she was brought here. You do not want to admit to her that you are a captive, as powerless as she – you, who were once a queen.*

But the pain of it . . . I clutched her to my breast and tried to ignore the aching hole that seemed to have opened there, gnawing as a puncture wound.

And the gods and the ancestors, Scythian and Greek, looked down on us from the stars above – and did nothing.

Ἀδμήτη

Admete

Sarmatia

The Twenty-fourth Day of the Month
of Threshing Wheat, 1265 BC

I tried to loosen my hands, which had clenched, fingernails digging into the palms, to breathe, to command my gaze, which was flicking to right and left, but it was no use. My pulse was dancing and I could not staunch the fluttering in my stomach, in spite of the cold that was making my skin clammy and my bones ache. I got to my feet, legs shaking. The firelit scene around me seemed to dim and sway, figures growing larger and receding, like looming shadows. I forced myself to walk, though my legs were heavy and there was a humming in my ears; and all the while my gaze was fixed on her, the figure standing at the hearth's other side.

It seemed to take a long time to cross the crowded space, and all around me Sarmatians and Greeks talked and ate, as if nothing was happening, as if my life were not changing – as if it were not my mother there, laughing just as I remembered her. I could not tear my gaze from her face – as familiar to me as the contours of the hills around Tiryns, though it was older now, the eyes sunken and creased with lines, the skin darker, red in the cheeks from days in the sun and wind. She wore the tunic and patterned trousers of the rest of the tribe, a war-belt with a pointed dagger at her waist, and a baldric across her chest and shoulders. It suited her, in a way that Greek skirts and bodices never had.

As I neared her, close enough to see the wisps of grey threading through her plait, close enough to reach out and brush her with my fingertips, I felt a sickening swell of fear, and also a rush of anger, prickling along my skin, like heat. What daughter should have to approach her mother after she had been abandoned, left to grow into a woman alone? What daughter should have to fear to face the woman who bore her? I had done nothing – nothing! – to deserve abandonment, yet here, on the very edge of the world, my mother hid, having deserted the daughter who had needed her.

Heat flooded my face, my heart was hammering against my ribs, and in the moment of silence before I called her and she saw me, I realized that perhaps it was not my fault she had gone, as I had thought so long ago. Perhaps it had been her error, her weakness – not mine.

I took a deep, shaking breath.

'Mother.'

She turned. The colour had drained from her face, making her seem haggard and old. She swayed and I moved to hold her, but she gripped my shoulders, fingers digging painfully into my flesh, her eyes wide, staring into my face.

'Say it again,' she said. She shook me, and I gasped aloud. 'Say it again!'

'Mother,' I repeated, my voice breaking, my eyes filling with tears. I searched her face. 'It is, isn't it?'

She let out a strangled sob. 'Admete!' In one movement she pulled me to her and embraced me so that I could barely breathe, stroking my hair and saying my name over and over again. I had never been so full of emotion as I was in that moment, like a goblet of wine full to the brim and spilling over, and my tears and hers mingled into our robes.

At last we broke apart. I brushed my face with my sleeve, and she gestured to a stool near the fire. Most of the others seemed to have finished their meal and returned to their wagons for the night. I sank onto it, feeling as if the strength had drained from my legs and longing for sleep, though my mind was feverish with questions. It was she who spoke first.

'How is it that you are here?' She leant towards the fire, which was now a glowing pile of embers casting her face bronze-red. Her eyes were raw, and I noticed again – almost with pity – how much older she looked.

'Alexander,' I said, breathless. 'He has a terrible fever, the like of which I have never seen.'

Her face sagged. 'My boy?' She rested her head in her hands, then looked up at me, running her fingers through her hair. 'Oh, gods, what must you think of me?'

I bit my lip. What truthful answer could I give? *I think you left me for your own selfish reasons, because you had made a mistake in coming to Greece, and you could not hold to it. I think I remember a courageous, wilful woman, yet the one I see before me is old, uncertain and afraid.*

'Why did you leave?' I said, and cursed my voice for faltering. I did not look at her, fearing the regret I might see in her eyes.

'Greece was never my home.'

I let out a breath, and she cowered at the burning look

I gave her, forgetting at once my resolution to look away. 'You chose to make it your home when you wedded my father,' I said, 'and when you bore me. You had a duty to your family. Did you care nothing for that?'

I was becoming angry, I could feel the heat creeping up my neck.

'I do not say that what I did was right, Admete. I am explaining why I did it,' she said.

'I know why you did it,' I said. 'You left because you longed for the wind of the plain in your hair, to ride once more with the Amazons. Is that enough of a reason for you to throw your marriage vows to the winds, to desert your daughter . . .' I glanced aside, my eyes filling with tears again and my throat obstructed '. . . and leave her to find her way to womanhood alone, always wondering if she might have done something more to keep you with her?'

She opened her mouth, her eyes wounded and afraid. 'Admete,' she said, stretching out her fingers to brush my arm.

I stood, knocking over the stool. 'I do not want to hear it,' I said, bitterness coursing through me. 'I was a fool to think I would be spared any pain in finding you.'

And with that I ran from the tent into the storm, my tears mixing with the rain, my hand rubbing at the terrible gnawing pain in my chest, more alone than I had ever been in my life.

The Amazons Attack

Ἀδμήτη

Admete

Sarmatia
The Twenty-fifth Day of the Month
of Threshing Wheat, 1265 BC

'I wish to speak with you.'

'I have nothing to say.'

'But I do – there is so much I would tell you.'

'Then I do not wish to hear it.'

I was seated on a stool in the wagon the Sarmatians had offered us, the rain pouring on the roof, like the gods' tears. Outside the door, an arm's reach away, stood my mother, her voice brittle against the howling rain and wind. Alcides and the rest of the Greeks had been gone all day with the Sarmatians and were now, no doubt, partaking of the evening meal together. I had remained here by the brazier, unable to bring myself to speak with Alcides, shunned by the rest of the Greeks, and furious with my mother. Emotion pounded through me, like the storm, and I narrowed my eyes, staring at the flames that blurred to streaks of red and orange with my tears as I thought of her betrayal.

Why did she never come back?

Why was she content to stay here, safe, when I yearned for so many years to see her?

'Admete, please—'

A fresh bout of wind pummelled the wagon, making it rock to and fro.

A pause, then: 'I am soaked to my skin.'

I let out a breath through my teeth, thinking of all the days I had wandered over the hills of Tiryns calling her, wearing my sandals through, tearing my tunic and cutting my shins on the brambles. As the silence outside lengthened, I gritted my teeth, stood and walked to the door, undoing the latch and pulling it open.

She did not fling herself into my arms. She nodded, trembling, shivering, her trousers wet through, then passed by me to the brazier, water dripping from the end of her plait and her clothes. I shut the door and resumed my position.

'You are angry with me,' she said, crouching before the brazier and looking across the flames at me. My heart twisted at her gaze on me, her eyes clear in the firelight as I remembered.

I turned away, forcing myself to trace the dancing shadows over the wagon walls rather than look at her.

'You have more than enough cause for anger,' she went on, her voice trembling. 'But, daughter,' the word was like a pain in my stomach, 'you must hear me.'

I bit the inside of my cheek, staring fixedly at the wall. 'Why? Why must I hear you? Why do I owe you anything when you took everything from me?'

Her voice broke as she said, 'You must allow me to explain.'

Silence fell between us, but for the clattering of rain on

the roof and the wind through the cracks in the wagon's sides. The fire in the brazier sputtered.

'Very well,' I said at last. 'Say what you have to. I have not come this far to return without answers.' I turned to her, keeping my gaze cold, though anger and fear beat through my veins. 'Why did you leave? I would know,' I said, 'so that my father and brothers and I may be free of the pain you brought us, not to have you return.'

'I told you,' she whispered. 'I was no Greek.'

I opened my mouth to retort, but she held up a hand to forestall me. 'Please.'

I fell silent, watching her – her skin still gleaming with rain-water, her eyes searching back and forth, her brow creased as she remembered. 'It came over many years, as you grew from an infant and your looks came to be more and more like mine – and for a while I was proud. I gave you our *tamga*. I plaited your hair and dressed you in the tunic and trousers I wore. I raised an Amazon as I had always wanted to, and you laughed with me as we spoke of riding the plain. But as you grew older, the nobles of the court began to see you, and what had started as the fanciful play of the foreign queen became a threat to their ways, to their line. What if I turned Alexander into a barbarian, too? What if the next king after Eurystheus – renowned for his justice, his fairness as a ruler – was a savage?'

I found I was staring at her, drinking in her words, in spite of my resolve to feign indifference. My hands were clammy in my lap, my lips parted.

'There were many incidents – small, at first, harmless. A Spartan noble visiting the court who refused to bow to you when you were presented to him, and who spat on my boots.

Cries that I was a barbarian, an enchantress, a witch, as I tried to tend the sick in the dwellings of the city. Accusations. Whispers. Condemnation. Rumours that I had seduced the king of Tiryns with herbs and spawned a witch-daughter. Demands that the cursed Amazon women, you and I together, should be tied to the rocks, left to have our innards pecked out by eagles.'

As she spoke, memories flooded me, unbidden: faint, half-forgotten thoughts, pointing fingers, cries, doors slammed in my face . . . children of the court pulling my plait and chanting, *Amazon, Amazon*, as they danced around me . . .

Her eyes shone with tears as she looked at me. 'I realized what I had done to you – the legacy I had left you, unthinking, selfish, to be different, to be stared at, to be distrusted always. Many times I tried to persuade your father to let me leave, for your sake – for the sake of all the children. Often we argued. He restrained me, saying it would pass, that the people would become accustomed to it. And then there came a day,' she swallowed, blinking, 'when I happened upon you in your chambers, and the slaves were tying your hair in ribbons, and you were laughing and spinning before the mirror in your Greek dress, smiling in the sunlight – and something within me broke. My guilt and fear tore me apart as I thought of the life you might have lived without me. I knew that I was holding you back, preventing you from being all you could, free from doubt and prejudice and the scorn of a people among whom, if I stayed, you would never belong. And so,' she pressed her eyes closed, tears rolling down her weathered cheeks, 'I left, though it broke my heart – I left you with your people, and I went to mine.'

I felt a tightening in my chest, a stinging in the corners of my eyes.

'Believe me,' she said, her voice low, and her hands extended to me, trembling, around the flames. 'You have to believe me. I would never have done anything to hurt you.'

The pressure in my chest was building, rising to my throat. Our fingers touched, and a sob emerged from my lips.

'Believe me,' she said again, in Greek.

And then I was nodding, and tears were wet on my cheeks, and I was in my mother's arms as the dam of my fears broke, sweeping through me like the first torrents of melting snow in spring, and the flames crackled beside us.

Dawn stole through the rain, like a silver veil, lightening the sky. From what I could hear above the soughing of the wind through the trees, the birds were beginning to herald the dawn. I took a cape from a hook on the wagon's wall, undid the latch and pushed open the door, my sandals slipping on the wet wooden steps.

I crept across the still-shadowed camp, my way lit by the dull grey of dawn reflecting off the slanting rain. I knocked three times on the red-painted door of the wagon where my mother slept.

She opened it, a lamp in one hand and a blanket thrown over her shoulders. Her eyes, bleary with sleep, widened at the sight of me and she smiled, shedding the years that had passed so that she looked like the woman I remembered. 'Come,' she whispered, gesturing to me, the blanket slipping as she did so. 'Come in.'

I slid past her. The air in the wagon was thick with sleep and scented with smoke from the brazier. I could make out several figures huddled on the beds beneath the piles of patchwork blankets. I crept to her bed and drew the blankets around us both, leaning my head on her shoulder. For a long time we sat together, her arms around me, as the logs in the brazier sputtered and the rain hissed overhead. I found I did not want to speak; the contentment I found in her presence, her embrace, was enough.

At last I looked up at her. 'I have decided to stay,' I said, my eyes searching hers.

Her hand dropped from my shoulder. 'Admete . . .'

'No, no, you misunderstand me – I return to Greece,' I said, reading her hesitation. 'For Alexander, before all else. Alcides is set to voyage on for the apples of gold in Hyperborea. I thought perhaps . . . I thought I might remain here, with you, till he returns. He hardly needs my help and, truth be told, I am weary of his company and that of his men. Perhaps,' I twisted my fingers in my lap, 'we might spend time together – you might show me your store of herbs. I might tell you more of Alexander's disease, and – perhaps – we might work together to find a cure.'

She laid a hand on my fingers and prised them apart. I glanced up at her, feeling my cheeks redden. 'Of course,' I went on, stumbling, 'of course, if you do not wish it . . .'

'I could think of nothing I would wish for more,' she said, her eyes burning into mine, and as she clasped me to her I closed my eyes and prayed that this moment would never end.

Hippolyta

Athens, Greece

The Thirty-seventh Day after the Day of Fire in the Season of Tabiti, 1265 BC

The moon had waxed and waned twice since I had arrived in Athens, and as I stumbled through the corridors towards Theseus' court, my ankles and wrists jangling, I knew, in the way that a foal tied and bound for sacrifice knows, terror-struck and powerless, that I had reached my lowest ebb. On Theseus' orders I had been stripped of my linen blouse so that my breasts were bare in my bodice, and Theia – her eyes averted – had knotted clanging cymbals of bronze on red ribbons to my wrists and bare ankles. Now she led me across the forecourt, an oil-lamp in one hand glowing on the columns, and gestured to the doors of the hall, through which the noise of raucous laughter and the scent of sizzling fat drifted, and where the guards stood dark-eyed and glinting with weapons.

'I am sorry,' she said in a whisper, her eyes downturned. 'Truly I am. He would not do this if he were not deep in his cups – believe me.'

I shook my head. 'It is not your doing,' I said. 'You are his captive as much as I am, though I thank the gods he treats you better than he does me.'

She took a sharp sip of breath, as if in pain, then, not looking at me, she fled, leaving only her retreating shadow.

As she left my stomach clenched as if I were withholding a silent scream. *Is this what I am reduced to?* I wanted to cry aloud. *Breasts bared like a whore? Clattering with cymbals like a market performer? Are you laughing, Tabiti?*

But as I had done so many times these past days, I bit back my pain. This was simply another battle, another enemy to be faced. Though I had no weapons and my war-belt was lost, I could still stand on the field and say I fought, my eyes level with my foe. I raised my chin higher and tugged the bodice across my chest. Then, jaw set, I stepped past the guards, through the doors and into the hall.

The stench of male sweat, wine and meat-grease assaulted me so that I almost reeled back. The room was thick with smoke and so close that I felt my temples break into a sweat. There was barely any light but from the fire that smouldered in the hearth. A few oil-lamps hung from stands around the men who lay on the floor, some on cushions and some sprawled on the tiles, playing a drinking-game and laughing so that my head ached with the echoing sound.

Theseus looked up as I drew nearer, his cheeks flushed. His dark eyes, dull and hooded in the shadows, met mine. I shook my head and tried to implore him across the hall, my arms pressed across my breasts, the air before me shimmering as if it would dissolve into mist. *Please. Do not make me do this.*

Theseus' smile broadened, and I wondered, my breath

catching in my throat, for one brief moment, whether he might grant me a reprieve. *Please . . . I will do anything . . .*

'Friends, Athenians,' he said, clearing his throat, swaying as he pushed himself to stand. His skin was covered with a sheen of sweat. 'Behold my Amazon captive.'

All eyes turned to me across the smoke-filled hall. He lumbered towards me and kissed me, hard, his tongue exploring my mouth and filling me with the musty taste of wine.

'Please,' I whispered, as he broke apart from me, meeting his eyes. 'Please, spare me this.'

He tilted his head and laughed. 'The prisoner thinks to make terms of her own!' he roared. He grabbed my hair in his hand – my eyes smarted – and drew me close to him. 'You do not ask anything – *anything* – of me. Do you understand that?'

I stayed very still, trying not to move my head, as if he would tear the scalp from me.

'Now,' he said, thrusting me away so that I stumbled, tripped on my skirt, then fell forwards, breasts tumbling from my bodice and pressing against the floor. I pushed myself to stand, trying to close my ears to the howls of laughter and the jeering of the Greeks. 'Now, Antiope – dance!'

I turned, about to fall to the floor and clasp him in supplication, but as I lowered myself he landed me a blow across the jaw, which sent a shock through my skull, my eyes rolling with the force of it. I stumbled sideways, clutching my face.

I fought against the darkness that was threatening to engulf me until the hall stopped spinning and came back into focus: the dim colours of the painted walls, the glow of the fire and the grinning dark-eyed faces, like a pack of wolves in the night.

'Dance!' Theseus bellowed again.

And so I danced. My breasts ached as I leapt and whirled, clicking my wrists together and lifting my skirts to stamp the floor with my feet as we had used to do on the plains, but the pain was almost welcome. It gave me something on which to focus other than the dark despair that hung over me and would consume me entirely if I stopped. One of the men launched himself to his feet, drawing his sword unsteadily from its sheath, and poked and prodded me with the tip, jeering as I swayed and darted away from it. Once, when I had had my war-belt and my *sagaris*, I would have knocked the sword from him, like a toy from a child. But I lacked my weapons and my strength, sapped like a young oak that withers wasted. Theseus slapped my breasts as I danced past him, and the others followed suit, pinching all over my body till my skin stung and my face was red with shame. And still I swayed and jingled, whirling round and around, and the clattering of the cymbals and the howls of the men dinned in my ears, sweat poured from my skin in the heat and my limbs ached, until I could move no more.

My legs collapsed beneath me, and I was enveloped in darkness before I hit the tiles.

Ἀδμήτη

Admete

Sarmatia

The Seventh Day of the Month
of Ploughing, 1265 BC

It was by tacit agreement – hardly spoken, for it seemed it
had come to that between us – that Alcides left with his
band of warriors for Hyperborea, and I remained with the
Sarmatians, with my mother. I had told her at once of Alexander's fever, the curious nature of its rising and falling every
few days, and we worked long into the nights in the wagon
where she kept the herbs, while the oil-lamps flickered and
our eyes ached, speaking of yarrow and elecampane, willow-
bark and feverfew, sorting through herbs and testing
tinctures and draughts. Though I basked in relaying to my
mother all that had happened since she had left, and there
was companionship in working together at the herbs, I felt a
growing impatience and frustration as still we failed to find
a cure. The days lengthened to weeks, and Alcides had not
returned – with or without the golden apples, in which my
trust was daily waning.

It was late in the day, the shadows already slipping into

night, and we sat together in the herb-store in near-silence, working through the pouches, bottles and sprigs hanging from the rafters. My mother, seated at a trestle table set by the brazier, brought a handful of leaves to her face, holding them close to her red-rimmed eyes so she could examine them in the dim light.

'You might try sweet wormwood,' she said, with a half-sigh, her voice carrying across the darkened wagon, hoarse from lack of use. 'I use it against rashes, but as it counters heat, it might have the effect of reducing warmth somewhat if my son's illness is indeed a disease of fire, as it seems.'

We had said this before, over and over again – *a disease of fire requires a herb to counter heat; a herb whose properties are soothing, calming, a balance to his excess* – but I recognized in her desperation my own desire, so I took the pouch of dried leaves she handed me without reproach, and sniffed them. There was less bitterness to the scent than I was used to. *A different type of wormwood, then.* Wormwood, as I knew it – a grey-green plant of feathery leaves – stimulated digestion, in which case it would be of no use at all. I took it from her, pressing her fingers lightly in thanks, though feeling dispirited. Alexander had no rash, no lesions on the skin. *Pray the gods we find something more.*

I added the sweet wormwood to my collection and continued to work through the stores in silence, handling the herbs and taking records on my tablets, noting those I had not seen before and marking where in the store-room I had found them. I came across a strange type of moss, which still clung to the bark from which it had been gathered, growing in yellow, leathery tufts. Sweet-smelling husked seeds and dried stems stood in sacks on the floor, and there were many pots holding collections of needle-like leaves gathered from the forests.

One by one I took down their properties – all the indications of a healing herb, from scent to size to the parts of the plant gathered – and let my thoughts wander as my hands worked. *Even now, Alcides might have the golden apples. He might come soon from Hyperborea – and then, at last, I may return to Tiryns, tend Alexander again, and I will have my brother.*

And yet . . . Doubt gnawed as I reached for my stylus. I had always held to my belief that diseases of the body could be healed by herbs and herbs alone. I had scorned the priest-healers in Tiryns when they made sacrifices to the gods, and whispered prayers, or attempted to withdraw the evil spirit with enchanting words. What if, after all this – even if Alcides was able to retrieve the golden apples – the cure I had been hoping for did not exist? What if Alcides succeeded in his task, and the cure was as we had hoped, but our quest had taken too long and Alexander had—

No, I thought, with a shiver, *I cannot allow myself to think that*. I turned aside and drew a vessel towards me, just as another troubling thought rose to the surface.

And if Alcides does indeed complete the task, he will be done with his labours.

I sat back on the stool before the table, contemplating it, watching the light of the lamps dance over the wood. Strange – I had expected to feel sadness. I had expected regret that Alcides would no longer peer into the herbary, that I would no longer look forward to his return, to walking together in the herb-garden. A few years ago I had dreaded his leaving the palace, loved the life and laughter he brought to us. He had been the only one to whom I could speak freely about my mother, the only one who truly understood what it was to feel abandoned, to feel alone. But now I felt – nothing much. Wistfulness, perhaps, for what was gone.

Yet is it so surprising? These past months since we had left Tiryns we had done nothing but quarrel. The voyage had made it clear, as it had not been in Tiryns, how different we were, how different the things we wanted. The ending of his labours would be simply the next step on the path he had chosen for himself – along which, for some part of the way, there had been our friendship. *It is a friendship I am glad to have had*, I thought, crossing my hands on my lap before me and gazing across the room at my mother. She looked up at me briefly, and gave me a swift smile, then returned to her work. And yet it had the feel of something that, like a child outgrowing its infant swaddling, I no longer needed.

'I think I have done all I can for tonight,' I said. I stood and took the lamp from the table, the light sliding up the wooden walls in orange and gold. The pleasant smell of chamomile wafted from my hands into the air as I walked over to my mother and pressed a kiss to her forehead. She reached up and patted my cheek. I closed the door behind me and, for a moment, leant against it, eyes closed, breathing in the clear night air.

I know where I am going.

𒀭𒌋𒈾 𒅆𒌋𒈨𒌋

Hippolyta

Athens, Greece

The Thirty-seventh Day after the Day of Fire in the Season of Tabiti, 1265 BC

I blinked. My eyes felt as if they were rimmed and weighted with lead. I blinked again. Slowly, the hall swam into view around me. The fire had gone out and it was dark but for a few low-glowing lamps. I was lying on the floor.

I tried to sit, and tasted blood on my lip. I turned my head, feeling the tender swelling of a bruise, and saw only cushions, some stained with wine, platters and goblets dropped here and there. The hall was deserted.

I winced and pushed myself to sit, beginning to remember. *The dance* . . . I glanced at my wrists and shook off the cymbals still tied there, my breasts hanging bare and pricked with cold. I shuddered, a wave of nausea pulsing through me. The memories were crowding in on me now, faster and faster: *whirling and spinning, wrists and ankles jangling.*

The air seemed to close in around me, snatching the breath from my chest. I stumbled to my feet, trying to ignore the numbness in my legs, the swaying of the walls around me, unsteady.

And then I halted. I had heard something – something so familiar that it called to me, like the shriek of an eagle to its brood, nesting hidden in the long grass.

But it cannot be . . .

My breathing was sharp and fast. I must have knocked my head when I had hit the floor. How could it be? It was a dream, an echo from my fevered mind.

And then, clearly, so clearly that I could not doubt it, I heard the cry again: '*Oiorpata! Oiorpata Amazones – oiorpata!*'

It was as if I had awoken from a dream, as if I had been living these past months in a trance. For a moment I hesitated, taking in my cage: the pools of red wine staining the floor; the blue and red painted walls splashed with faint light from the oil-lamps. Was it my longing for my home that had made me hear their call?

I heard the cry again. I had to find out what was happening. I had to see for myself if it was true, or merely the whisper of my disordered mind. I gathered my skirts in one hand and ran to my chambers, heart clattering, mouth dry. Theia was standing by the shutters, which were thrown open. She was panting and pale in the moonlight, wearing only her under-tunic. Now that I was on this side of the palace I could hear war-trumpets, ripping through the night, and again, the shrieking cries of '*Oiorpata! Oiorpata Amazones!*' But the courtyard beyond the window was still and silent, the sand undisturbed and milky-white.

'Theia!' I gasped, and she turned, her eyes wide. 'What is it? What has happened?'

Her lips parted. 'The Amazons have come,' she whispered,

her voice hoarse. 'They are attacking the city.' She gripped the windowsill, face taut with terror, and I realized – I almost laughed aloud at the strangeness of it – that she was afraid of me, though I stood there half undressed, with the discs she had tied clattering at my wrists.

'You need not fear me,' I said, striding towards her and gripping her by the shoulders. She flinched. 'But you must tell me – now – what is happening.'

'The Amazons have come, I tell you. My lord Theseus received a messenger from their camp demanding your return. He refused, so they are attacking.' Her voice was rising in pitch, her fingers now kneading her tunic. 'I saw them from the tower on the battlements, raging like the Furies, slaying our men with sharpened axes and—' She swallowed, closing her eyes.

I swayed on the spot, darkness tugging at the edge of my consciousness. It was too much to take in. And yet the cries I had heard – and Theia had seen our *sagaris*.

I felt a glimmer of warmth in my belly, like a single ember that burns through the night, though the fire has been banked down.

I am an Amazon still.

I pushed myself to stand, my whole body alive as it had not been for days, certainty flooding me. It was as if I had lived in darkness, not knowing who or where I was, wandering through the last weeks as in a labyrinth, blindfolded. Now I was awake, my vision cleared, and I knew, in every part of myself, what I wanted to do. What I had to do. What I should have done, from the very first moment Theseus had mistreated me, and I had felt myself less than an Amazon.

'Theia,' I said, turning to her, my voice sharp with determination. 'You have to come with me.'

The group of outlying buildings by the gate that formed the palace stables were filled with commotion. The doors hung open, and slaves rushed out leading horses, their hoofs sounding over the paving-stones and clashing with the ringing of bronze on bronze, the shrieks and cries from the valley below. I slipped inside, my hood over my head. I had run at once to Helen's rooms, wrapped her in a cape and told her we were going away. Now I led her by the hand over the straw that littered the stable floors, her eyes creased with tiredness. Theia hurried behind me. None of the slaves so much as glanced at us as they ran by, sweating and shouting for more horses, more weapons.

'We have to act quickly,' I said, and the joy of giving commands again, of having authority over what was done rather than being ordered this way and that, filled me like a bird stretching its wings in the open sky. 'Theia – can you ride?'

She nodded, her eyes wide with fear. 'But, my lady—'

'Helen,' I said, bending to her, 'Theia will take you back to Sparta. I want you to ride with her, and be good on the journey home. Soon you will see your parents again. Yes?'

I took her head in both my hands and planted a kiss on her curls. 'Here,' I said, moving to a stall at the back of the stables where we were sheltered from the view of the slaves, and unknotting the reins of a bay mare from its post. It snorted and whinnied, and I smelt the familiar scent of hay, horse-sweat and leather as I helped first Theia, then Helen to mount.

'Take the gate to the east, and circle the battle,' I said,

keeping my eyes on the figures at the stables' entrance. They were gathering spears from a stockpile near the door, passing them one to another in a chain. 'I do not know the way to Sparta, so you must ask at the villages if you lose the path, but speak to no one till you have ridden a day or more from here, and if you come across the Amazons then say Queen Hippolyta,' I felt a thrill to say my name once more, 'has granted you safe passage. They will know me by the sign of the eagle, the *tamga* of our tribe.' I pulled a ring from my finger, gold shaped into an eagle with encircling wings, and dropped it into Helen's hand. Theia's arms were wrapped around the child. I could see her pale little face shrouded by Theia's embrace. 'You have not a moment to lose. Leave here at speed. They will not challenge you if you keep your hood up and say you are riding in aid of Theseus. And, Helen,' I said, reaching out to stroke her cheek with my finger, 'hide yourself in Theia's cloak. It will not do if you are seen.'

Theia reached down to take my hand. 'How can we ever thank—'

'Go!'

She nodded then, wheeled the horse around in the stall and, with a final glance, raised her hood over her hair and cantered out of the stables. I heard the men by the door crying out as she knocked through the pile of spears – 'What – hey!' – and Theia's shouted reply: 'I ride for Theseus!'

I crept to the next stall where a black stallion flicked his dark eyes warily over me. I stepped nearer to him, soothing him with words in my own tongue and stroking his nose. He calmed, quietening at the closeness of my body, allowing me to slip the bridle on him and throw a rug on his back. Silent and quick, I leapt up to mount, taking the reins into my fingers, feeling the leather rub at my thumbs. A swell of exhilaration – to be mounted again, to be free – surged in me, and a smile, the first in many days, broke across my face.

'Come, *ippa*,' I said, digging my heels into the horse's sides, then turning towards the doors that opened onto the palace forecourt and the boundless night beyond, where the slaves had run out to follow Theia, crying and waving their arms. I took a deep breath.

'We're going home.'

The Battle for Athens

Mount Olympus

If you were to journey back across the night-darkened Sarmatian plains, cross the ridges of the Carpathian Mountains and traverse the wilds of Thrace into Thessaly, if you were to climb the seven folds of Mount Olympus with a flaring torch in your hand, scrambling through pine-forests and rocky scree to the highest peak, you would find almost all of the gods of Olympus gathered there to watch the battle for Athens.

The assembly-place is crowded as the gods jostle for the best view south towards the city. Zeus, Poseidon, Athena and Ares are seated, each leaning forwards to gaze eagerly at their contenders. Athena is for the Greeks, of course – Athens is hers, recently founded and raised from the rock, the olive trees still young and shallow-rooted. She hardly wants to see it ransacked and burnt by an invading barbarian horde. Zeus is feigning neutrality, though in truth both he and Poseidon – having vested interests in the Greeks by way of sons – are more than a little partisan, and Zeus' thoughts are, in any case, far away with Hermes as he tails Hera through the wilds of the north. Ares, for his part, is shouting for the Amazons: for it was he who had given the war-belt to Hippolyta's mother, Marpesia, and he cannot help but admire their skill.

Ares peers through the darkness. The Amazon general Melanippe decided – against his attempts to direct her otherwise – to launch an offensive against the Athenians at night; and, he thinks, rubbing his chin, it seems to be working. The Amazons' allies, the Scythian tribe of Sagylus whose help they had enlisted on their journey to Greece, are ravaging the countryside of Attica, torching villages and isolated farms which burn like fireflies over the landscape. The Amazons themselves have breached the walls of Athens and set up camp on one of the western hills. Their army is ranged in a line to the Pnyx, and though the Athenians are galloping down into the valley from the Hill of the Muses and blasting their trumpets, they will be no match for the Amazons.

Ares, a connoisseur of war, has to admire the sheer extent of their prowess in battle. Take Melanippe. She rides her dappled grey stallion as if they were of one body, one mind; her sickle-shaped shield seems to be but an extension of her left arm. Galloping up and down the Amazon ranks, calling her orders and summoning them by name, she brings them round in a pincer movement to entrap the Athenian troops, who, unused to fighting at close quarters without the serried ranks of the army lines and the warriors' shields locked side by side, stumble and break apart. The narrow valley becomes a vicious killing-ground, as Melanippe and her Amazons descend on the encircled Greeks and deal their blows, swiping left and right, some leaping from their mounts to fight hand to hand, others trampling the Athenians beneath their horses' hoofs. The clanging of bronze, the screams and cries and the blaring of trumpets drift to Olympus on the breeze, like the chirruping of cicadas, and from time to time a sword-blade catches the moonlight and reflects a beam of silver towards the watching gods.

And then Ares blinks.

He hears Athena beside him splutter, and he knows that she, too, has seen.

266

A figure is charging on horseback down the rock of the palace hill, slaves running after her and throwing spears that hurtle far from the mark, her hair flying loose in the wind behind, weight effortlessly balanced as the horse stumbles over the rocks. She is screaming the war-cry, and even the way she rides – hips moving seamlessly with her mount, chin held high – it is clear she is a queen. The Amazons hear her shout and turn to see her as she gallops through the clustering pine trees of the valley, up over the boulders and through the dark-flowering shrubs, beating their spears on their shields and shrieking till Olympus shudders with the clamour. Queen Hippolyta bows her head and smiles. She reins her horse in, stamping and snorting mist into the night air, and catches the battle-axe that Melanippe throws her from her steed at the army's head.

Then, together, side by side, grim with determination, the sisters turn to battle.

Some gods, however, are not watching the battle as it rages over Athens.

Calliope, disguised as a Hyperborean, is pacing up and down a colonnade of the palace of the king of the Hyperboreans, Abaris, at the world's other edge. Her sand-coloured robes swirl out behind her, her hair furling in the wind that whips inland from the storm at sea. She can barely hear her own thoughts over the thundering and crashing of the waves and the rumbling of Hera's storm, which has followed Hercules all the way from Sarmatia, pouring on him the displeasure of the queen of the gods. Calliope glances out at the sky, but the moon is swaddled in clouds and she cannot tell what time it is. She checks the colonnade again for the two goddesses she has summoned, but it is empty, the benches unoccupied, the pine torches flickering in their brackets.

She tightens her grip around the coffer she is holding, and begins to pace again.

'Calliope!'

She whirls around. There, seated by an arch, as if they have been there all the time, are Aphrodite and Iris. They are disguised as Hyperboreans too, as she bade them, with their robes knotted across their breasts, their sleeves slipping down their shoulders and laurel leaves in their hair – yet nothing could mask the voluptuousness of Aphrodite's silken curves, or Iris's sharp, knowing look.

'So you have been hiding here,' Aphrodite says, getting to her feet and kissing Calliope on one cheek. She holds her hands and stands back, appraising her. 'The Hyperborean dress suits you,' she says, tilting her head to one side and taking in Calliope's loose hair falling over her shoulders. 'I cannot stand to see you in the plain poet's robes you usually wear.'

Iris stands too, crossing her arms over her chest. 'Let us get to the point. Why have you brought us here, Calliope?'

Calliope sucks in a breath through her teeth. She hates having to do this, but what choice does she have? Hera is almost onto her: she can feel the presence of the queen of the gods nearby, just as a farmer looks at the skies and senses the chill onset of winter.

She looses her hands from Aphrodite's grip and pulls the casket from beneath her arm. 'It has to do with the golden apples.'

As the goddesses watch, she slides a fingernail beneath the clasp and opens it. There, again, are the three sockets, engraved with gold. One is empty, but the other two are filled with the perfect gleaming apples. She feels her chest constrict with the burden of it. If her gamble doesn't work . . . But it has to.

Iris's eyes dart to her face and back to the chest. Aphrodite lets out a snort of laughter, which she attempts to stifle behind her hand. 'So it is true! I thought Hera made it up . . . You know, to make Zeus pay her a bit more attention. But you did, did you?'

Iris's face has taken on a look of grudging admiration, and her eyes narrow as she scans Calliope's. 'How, by the waters of the blessed Styx, did you manage it?'

'Never mind that,' Calliope says. 'We do not have much time.'

'What happened to that one?' Iris is pointing at the empty socket, where an apple once lay.

'You have to listen,' Calliope says. The truth will be told soon, but not yet. 'Time is short.' She gestures to the bench, and Aphrodite moves with a swishing of robes and sinks down on the cushions, gazing at Calliope with a curious smile. After a moment or so, Iris follows suit.

'I have three apples – how I came by them is no concern of yours,' she says, stifling Iris with a look. A gust of wind from the shore blasts through the colonnade and the torches sputter and spit. Another rumble of thunder rolls in from the sea. She feels her throat tighten. Hera is very close now. 'All you need know is that Hera is after them, and knows I have them. I had to hide to be close to the mortals, to bestow it on one when the time was right yet keep them from her. I have done so for the first. The others I can no longer protect. She has almost found me – I cannot hide for ever. I need you to safeguard them for me.'

Iris raises an eyebrow, and a wave tumbles onto the shore with a resounding crash. 'Why would we do that?'

Calliope ignores her and carries on, pacing up and down before them. She will tell them everything in due course – that is part of her plan – but it has to come at the crisis-point, and not a moment sooner. 'I have already given one to the mortal Hercules – you will know why soon, do not ask me now, I beg you – and the other two I give to you, to guard until I tell you that the time is right.'

269

'Hercules?' Aphrodite asks, sitting up a little taller. 'Son of Zeus?'

Calliope nods impatiently. 'He was ready, the labours were complete. I diverted his ship, sent him to an island north of the Hesperides. If he were to land at the Garden, the daughters of Atlas would have alerted Hera at once. He thinks he has the apple for his labours. He need never know otherwise.'

'But,' Iris says, frowning and leaning forwards, 'supposing we do accept the apples, what are we to do with them then?'

Calliope stops pacing. 'Is that a yes, daughter of Thaumas?'

Iris scowls. 'Perhaps.'

'Oh, come on,' Aphrodite says, and stretches out her hands. Calliope prises an apple from its slot and places it, with the care of a mother handing her newborn to the wet-nurse, in Aphrodite's palms.

'Look how beautiful it is!' Aphrodite holds the apple by its stalk and sends it spinning with one finger, so the torchlight glints off it and out into the darkness beyond the arches of the colonnade, like the beam of a beacon to a stranded ship.

'Don't do that!' Calliope snaps. She snatches the apple and clamps her hands around it. 'Don't you understand? We have to hide them from Hera until the appropriate time! You cannot flash it about as if it were . . . oh, I don't know! Some bauble fashioned for you by Hephaestus!'

There is a moment of silence, punctuated only by the storm pounding the shoreline and the hissing of the waves, as Aphrodite pouts and Iris runs a finger over her lips, thinking.

'And this is directly calculated to put out Hera?' Iris asks at last.

Calliope pauses, and Aphrodite takes advantage of her distraction to snatch the apple back and bury it in the folds of her robes.

The Muse rubs her eyes. She anticipated a problem here. Iris is Hera's messenger, after all, bound to her by the ties of loyalty and service, but she had not been able to think of any goddess as cunningly greedy as Aphrodite, or as clever as Iris, with whom she could trust her secret.

'Yes,' she begins, 'and I know you are Hera's messenger, and—'

'I'll do it,' Iris says, holding out a hand.

Calliope stares at her. 'Really?'

Iris snaps her fingers. 'Yes.'

Calliope fumbles at the final apple and lifts it out, handing it to Iris, who pockets it with the swiftness of a practised thief. Calliope looks down at the chest in her hands, feeling as bereft and empty as the open sockets – but she knows she has done the right thing. She sets it down and takes Aphrodite and Iris's hands in hers.

'You have my gratitude, and the gratitude of all the gods,' she says.

Iris stands, and Aphrodite follows suit beside her. 'And we are to keep them hidden until . . .?'

Calliope bows her head as she leads them to the opening in the colonnade and down the steps into the hammering rain, and they prepare to transform themselves into the birds in whose shape they flew here from Greece. 'As I said,' she watches the robes slither off Aphrodite's back into the soft plumage of a dove, and Iris's nose lengthen into the down-curved beak of the falcon, 'I shall tell you when the time is right.'

Final Encounter

𒀸𒋾𒎏𒌷𒈨𒌍

Hippolyta

Athens, Greece

The Thirty-eighth Day after the Day of Fire
in the Season of Tabiti, 1265 BC

I saw the battle from my vantage-point on the hill, like a
bird swooping over the moonlit plain. Our left wing, stretching to the right upon the Pnyx . . . The Greeks plunging into
the valley ahead from the Muses' Hill . . .

I charged, shrieking the battle-cry. Melanippe echoed it at
my side, and behind me my troops clashed their battle-axes
on their shields. I felt the war-fury rip through me, turning
the scene ahead into a smudge of opal moonlight, bronze and
the black silhouettes of trees. Anger and a fierce, pounding
joy to be riding as an Amazon once more hammered in my
chest as I galloped down the western slope of the hill, yelling, whirling the *sagaris* around my head, like a demon sent
by Tar the storm-god. I wheeled at our right-hand flank,
then charged the full length of our battle-line – archers
arranged on the steep overhang of the hill, bows taut, arrow-
tips shimmering, riders on their mounts with me in the valley

below, teeth gleaming in the darkness, screaming back to me the battle-cry as I whipped past them.

Through the clustered trees ahead I saw the shapes of the Greeks emerging, heard the thundering of their hoofs over the dry earth and smelt the pine-needles they threw up beneath them. I pulled my horse around at the furthest left of our line, where the hill I had ridden from dropped into a narrow valley, edged on the other side by the white-shining rock of Athens. The Greeks had taken my bait: they were charging towards me, dust like mist behind them, and as I cried '*Oiorpata!*' my warriors circled in, tighter and tighter, like a net, driving the plunging horses of the Greeks into the chasm between the two hills.

Galloping into the fray, I twisted right and left, my battle-axe meeting skulls, cracking shoulder-blades, felling warriors, like a scythe to long grass. Ahead of me, cut into the rock, I saw a shrine Theseus had once told me of – a worship-place to the Furies, goddesses of vengeance, a bowl still standing on the altar filled with fruit and grain – and thought that we were, indeed, the Furies of whom Theia had spoken, come to bring revenge on Theseus for his crimes against the gods.

I moved as if in a dream, possessed by my fury, my vision streaked red with blood, slicing and plunging. Time seemed to stand still as I worked.

It was an eerie orange glow burning at the back of my eyes that awoke me. I peered upwards, craning towards the source of the light, aware now of my ragged breathing, the sweat dripping down my neck and between my thighs. I registered flames – sparks leaping into the air above, pillars of red-orange fire – then smelt the acrid scent of smoke. It was the smoke – sharp, in the back of my throat, making me retch and my eyes water – that brought me back to myself.

'Melanippe!' I shouted, clutching at her as she cantered by me.

'Sister?'

I pointed up to the burning flame on the rock above. 'What—' But I could not finish. Visions were shimmering before my eyes. Slaves trapped in the palace kitchens, rushing screaming through the burning chambers, their hair alight, arms clutched around their children ... A convulsion of pain shuddered through me.

'They were innocent,' I gasped. 'The slaves were innocent. The palace should never have been touched.'

Horror spread through me. I saw the scene before me as if for the first time: the Greek dead lying sprawled over the earth, arms flung out, trampled and mangled by horses' hoofs, their armour, crafted of fine bronze, dented, their spear shafts broken. The helmet of one of the soldiers before me had rolled away as he fell, and I saw his face – white with youth, his black hair tousled, the same age as my own Greek had been when we had lain together beneath the pines. An Amazon lay beside him – I recognized her at once as Arga, daughter of Iphito – her legs curled into her body and a thin, shining slash across her pale cheek, her limp arms stretched out to the Greek youth as if to embrace him. It was as if I were looking down at myself and the Greek, embracing in death. Sickness welled in my belly and threatened to overtake me, bitter-tasting in my mouth.

'This is not godly,' I said, my voice shaking. 'We have done what you came for. We must go.'

'Go?'

'We must leave!' I shouted at her. 'You came for me, did you not? We have dealt vengeance on the Greeks. You have me and now – it is my order – we must *leave*!'

The light from the flames of the torched palace washed the battleground in streaks of orange as I turned my horse around. A fanfare rent the air, trumpets, coming from the west – and painted red in fire I saw more Greeks charging from around the flank of the palace rock, eyes glinting darkly through their helmets, spear-blades shimmering scarlet.

'Melanippe,' I shouted, 'gather the troops,' and I galloped off, calling to my Amazons and shouting the retreat, through duelling warriors fighting hand to hand, ducking spears and arrows and parrying the swords raised against me, blood and iron scenting the air.

I swore then, my heart singing with pain – my vision blurring as I forced myself to gaze on the flames of the blaze that consumed the palace where he had done me wrong – that I would never, in all my life, trust another Greek.

Ἀδμήτη

Admete

Sarmatia

The Eighth Day of the Month of Ploughing, 1265 BC

I started awake. The door to the wagon in which I slept had flown open, rebounding against the wall with a crack. My vision was blurred, and for a moment I could not recall where I was. *Tiryns, with the fire lit by my father's slaves? Or is it the hides of the Amazon tents flapping in the wind?*

I blinked to see the outline of Alcides, framed against the sparkling light of dawn. I pushed myself to sit, rubbing my eyes, taking a breath to greet him.

But he was holding out a golden apple, and the words faltered in my throat.

Even in the half-darkness, lit only by the smouldering embers of the brazier, it made me gasp. I had never, in all my life, seen anything so perfect. Was it the shimmering skin that shattered the light into a thousand golden stars, or its fullness that drew my eyes so? As I gazed at it, it seemed to tease together all my desires, then bring them to life: visions spun in gold-thread filaments flashing before my eyes until I could barely see, and sparks spun bronze around my head, like the constellations turning in the heavens. And the letters inscribed across the skin in a fine, slanting hand: ΤΩΙ ΑΘΑΝΑΤΩΙ – *For the Immortal* – seemed to dance before me.

I swallowed, blinked. The scene around me resolved itself into reality. Alcides held out the apple. Cracks of light filtered through the wooden shutters at the windows, barely illuminating the patchwork covers on my bed, and the brazier hissed as a gust of wind blew over it.

I gathered the blankets up around my chest. 'How did you come by it?'

He stepped forwards, tossing the apple into his other hand, and as he did so I heard Timiades, Perses and some of the others out in the clearing, talking and laughing, their horses whinnying. 'We landed on the island of the Hesperides in the midst of a storm, a terrible storm,' he said, spreading his hands wide, as a poet would tell the lay of a great hero. 'I found it beneath a tree. The apples of the Hesperides were not so well guarded after all! But . . .' he took my hands and pulled me to stand, his face taking on an expression of beatific joy '. . . that is not what matters. I have finished, Admete! I have completed my labours! All mortals will know of my greatness, and I will be accepted by Zeus among the gods!'

I shuddered at the darting whiteness of his eyes. 'Alcides,' I began, but he went on, rambling, half raving. 'Alcides!'

He ceased muttering his own praises, and I saw his eyes focus on me, as if he had quite forgotten I was there.

'Do you not find it strange,' I said, keeping my voice low and wrapping a blanket tight around my shoulders, 'that the apple was so easily found? And that there was only one? What if you did not find the Garden of the Hesperides at all?'

He frowned in the half-light. 'Why would you say such a thing?'

I let out a breath. 'Because all reason suggests it! A garden, Alcides – Timiades said it was a garden, and guarded by the daughters of Atlas! Why would the king and queen of the gods leave an apple there unprotected—'

He gave an incredulous laugh, and dropped my hand. 'You are envious!' he said, stepping back from me. 'Envious of my glory!'

Now it was my turn to laugh. 'Envious?' I exclaimed. 'When have I ever been a peacock-headed fool prancing around before others to earn their praise? But you, Alcides—'

'You are calling me a fool?' His voice was rising, and the Greeks in the yard beyond quietened.

'I am merely saying that you would do well to be cautious!' I snapped back. 'Why would the gods allow you to find the apple with so little difficulty? Surely even you must see that it is worthy of suspicion.'

'It was hardly simple!' he roared, spit flying from his lips. 'The truth is, Admete, you never wished me to succeed. You wished to have me always to yourself, as it was when we were in Tiryns, and now that I have proven myself an equal of the gods and will be famed among mortals I have piqued your vanity!'

I tightened the blanket around my shoulders and returned to my bed, shifting so that my back was turned to him. When I spoke it was to the wall. 'The trouble with you, Alcides, is that you think always of your glory, and when you are distracted by fame and immortality you fail, always, to use your head.'

I heard nothing more from him, until a slam of the door and a shuddering of the wagon told me he was gone.

The next morning, as we were breaking our fast with the Sarmatians seated on the grass by the open fire at the centre of the enclosure, eating bread and cheese and drinking mare's milk, Alcides came to me. Many of the Greeks had already finished, and my mother was occupied with the Sarmatians, so we were alone. I did not look up from my dish, and focused my gaze instead on the fire before me, feeling the breeze fresh on my face.

'What?' I asked.

He said nothing, but settled on the stool beside me. He took a breath to say something; then, unable to speak and for want of anything better to do, he pushed a morsel of bread into his mouth.

He has come to apologize, then, I thought, as the birds chattered in the trees nearby and the sheep bleated in their pen. My anger with him softened.

I opened my mouth to say something, but it was he who spoke first.

'You know what this means?'

I wiped my bread around my bowl, catching the crumbs and frowning. 'What?'

'Finishing the labours,' he said. 'Completing my tasks.'

'Immortality?' I asked. 'Eternal glory?'

'Yes,' he said. He was pushing the clay plate back and forth over his lap. 'But – I do not know if you ever knew . . .' He cleared his throat, evidently at a loss for words.

I turned to stare at him. 'I have not seen you so incapable of speech since we sat in the apple orchard all those years ago and I first told you of my mother.'

Instead of laughing, as he would usually have done, his face reddened. 'Yes – well—' He swallowed, his jaw working. 'I asked your father Eurystheus for your hand, but he said he could not allow it until my labours were complete – if you agreed. Well – now they are. I will be remembered across the ages. I will become a god.' He turned his face to me at last, his eyes challenging. 'What do you think, Admete?'

My mouth was dry. 'What do I think – of what?'

'Becoming my wife, of course. Is it not obvious?'

I let out a laugh. I could not help it. After the quarrel we had had the night before, he was asking me, here, in the land where I had found my mother . . . 'Alcides, surely you cannot be serious!'

The flash of anger and hurt in his eyes was enough to tell me that he was. *Oh, gods. Hera, defend me.* I leant forwards to catch his hand as he made to push back his stool. 'No – no, don't go,' I said. He was frowning at me, brows lowering, and his cheeks were flushed, but he allowed me to pull him back to his seat.

I took a breath to steady myself, my mind working quickly as I gathered the words. 'I am honoured by your request,' I said. 'Truly I am. Had you asked me before we left Tiryns, I believe I would have accepted. But,' I pressed his hand between my own, leaning down to catch his gaze, 'surely you must have noticed that things are broken between us?'

He did not reply.

'We have done nothing but quarrel these past months,' I went on. 'We are too different, you and I. We long for

283

different things. Your heart is set on immortality, and I . . .'
I smiled a little and squeezed his fingers '. . . I would wish
for someone whose heart was mine alone. I would want a man
with whom I could spend my life in Tiryns, in my father's
home, and, when life is done, pass quietly together to the
Underworld. Eternity would be lonely, I think, without someone to share it with. I do not long for Olympus. But you do,
Hercules.'

He looked up at the name, and though his face was
creased with hurt, I saw the old longing, bright in his eyes.

'You do. And I would not wish it otherwise. This is your
calling, as I have mine.'

A long silence passed between us.

'This is your choice?' he said at last, and his voice was
bitter, and he avoided my gaze.

I bowed my head, my heart pounding. 'It is.'

He withdrew his hand from mine and stood, his broad
frame casting me in shade.

'Hercules,' I called as he moved away, and he turned back.
'I wish you to know. I will always be proud to have been your
friend.'

A faint smile flickered over his face as his eyes rested on
me, and beside him the fire spat and wood-pigeons called
from the branches.

'And I yours, daughter of Eurystheus.'

The Voyage Home

𒀭𒌑𒋼𒀸𒌷𒈦𒐏

Hippolyta

Attica, Greece

The Thirty-ninth Day after the Day of Fire
in the Season of Tabiti, 1265 BC

I rode a day from Athens to reach the Saka allies who had
accompanied Melanippe, a tribe I later learnt she had come
across as they traversed the Danastris, who claimed a distant
kinship to our clan. After a disagreement between Melanippe and their leader, Panasagoras, they had chosen to
pitch camp and to raid and burn the homesteads of the Attic
fields rather than aid the Amazons in their attack on Athens. Neither Melanippe nor any of the others attempted to
speak with me as we rode. It was as if they were giving me
time to come to terms with what had happened; as if they
knew that, when I was ready, I would come to them. For
that I was grateful, and for long stretches of time I would
lose myself in the sway of the horse beneath me, the cries of
the kestrels and chattering swifts skittering overhead and
the grey-green line of the horizon. I let my mind catch
on inconsequential details, like a fisherman's net snagging

rocks: the play of the evening light on the silted sands of the Cephissus river; the rutting of a track where it had been passed over by chariot wheels; the bracken that lined the path, darkened by our allies who had burnt the crops of this fertile land. I felt that if I allowed myself to think at all – of the shame I had brought on my people, how I had failed as a queen, failed my sisters, my mother and all my tribe – I would be unable to go any further for the prickling goad of my humiliation. All I could do was to ignore it, to pretend I did not feel the creeping sense of failure in the pit of my stomach, to act as if I did not know that all the Amazons' eyes were on my back as I rode before them, whispering between each other at my foolishness, pointing to their wounds and muttering of all I had cost them.

And so I rode on, trying, as I had always done, to keep my back straight and my chin lifted, as though I were a queen still in more than name.

Melanippe cantered ahead, her plait swinging behind her, to approach the allies with whom we would return north. I hung back, picking at the stitching on my reins, trying not to think how much better a leader my sister would have been than I. The Saka had taken over a Greek farmhouse and its outbuildings, a whitewashed stone dwelling surrounded by a low wall, a couple of barns for the hay, a pigsty and stables. Their horses were scattered over the hill behind, cropping the feathery grass, and most of the Saka ducked in and out of tents they had erected over the farmland, trampling the stalks of wheat and sending the dry scent of chaff onto the evening air. Melanippe guided one of the Saka towards me, a man with deep-socketed eyes and long hair tied back. I slid from my mount to greet him.

'This is Panasagoras,' Melanippe said. 'He is the son of Sagylus, and pledged his support to us.'

Panasagoras gave a forced bow, his nostrils flared. 'What your sister means,' he said, 'is that we were not informed when we joined her cause that you went with the Greeks in exchange for the freedom of your people. It is hardly an unlawful capture if the captive gives herself up willingly so that her people may be spared, is it – my queen?' This last he added with a sneer.

The insult cut me like a dagger against the skin. I turned aside to recover myself, running my fingers over the war-belt Melanippe had given me: less fine than my own had been, but fitted with hooks enough for a couple of *sagaris* and a quiver. *You have nothing to be ashamed of*, I told myself, trying to force myself into belief. *It was not your offence but Theseus's that led to this.*

'The prince of Athens did not keep his oath,' I said at last, looking up at him, keeping my gaze steady. 'Though by all the laws of fair conduct in war he should have respected me as a captive queen, he treated me in every manner as a slave. Though he swore to take me as his wife, he broke my trust and abused his rights as a husband. I do not claim that Melanippe foresaw this, only that she had right on her side to come after me. And,' I forestalled him, holding up my hand, 'do you truly think I had a choice in the matter, when the Greeks threatened to raze the camp of the Amazons if I did not accompany them – having already caused much slaughter and destruction to our people? Having already,' I swallowed, 'slain my beloved sister?' I held his gaze as his horse shifted beside him, sensing his discomfort. 'Would you have acted any differently, son of Sagylus?'

He snorted, a line appearing between his brows.

'And if the Greek lord comes after us to take you back? Why should I risk my people for that?'

I shook my head. 'I assure you he will not. I know him: his pride will be hurt by his defeat in open battle. He will not try again for fear of failure in the eyes of the Greeks. And,' I thought of the other women of whom Theia had spoken, and the vengeful look in his eyes as he had gazed at me that last night at the feast, 'he is not so attached to me. Come,' I said, extending my hand to him. He hesitated, then, at last, he took it, his grip firm. 'Let us ride together, as kinsmen.'

He gave a half-nod and turned aside. 'We ride tomorrow, then,' he said. 'We have raided all the horses we can, in any case, for they are scarce to be found, and kept guarded in stables.'

He strode off, and I turned to Melanippe, who was watching me, her eyes shining with tears. 'Oh, sister,' she said. She caught me and pressed me to her. Together we sobbed and wept and laughed, the blue sky whirling above us. 'Sister,' she said, over and over again, 'sister.'

At last our tears subsided, and we broke apart. I lifted my cloak and dried her cheeks, then my own. She tried to smile but her mouth wavered. 'I thought I had lost you.'

I grasped her hand in mine, feeling the flesh that was mine, too, tracing the blue veins beneath her skin that carried the same blood. 'You will never lose me again,' I said fiercely, interlacing our fingers so that we were woven together, her knuckles turning pale as we gripped each other. 'Never, do you hear me? I will never leave you, or Cayster, or any of you again.'

Ἀδμήτη

Admete

Sarmatia

The Fourteenth Day of the Month
of Ploughing, 1265 BC

Five days after Alcides' return, as the morning broke and
the tips of the trees nearby were fringed with gold, I came to
my mother's wagon. She opened the door, and her mouth
tightened as she took in my expression.

'So,' she said. 'You are going to leave.' It was not a
question.

'Do you have your belongings?' I asked, in a soft voice, as
she beckoned me in, latched the door and turned, the lamp
flaring in my face. 'From Greece,' I added.

She sighed, her breath warm on my face, and nodded. 'I
knew it would come to this.' She reached a hand to my
shoulder and curled the end of my plait around her fingers,
her eyes over-bright. 'I am proud of you, my daughter.'

Kneeling on the rug beside her bed, she reached beneath
and, with a scraping sound, brought out a wooden box. She
handed it to me, and I slid back the lid. They were all there,
laid carefully on coloured squares of felt: the bone comb

I remembered her using to dress her hair, a flask of scented oil that had hung on a cord from her girdle, the delicate gold chain she wore around her neck. I looked up at her. 'Will you – will you help me?' I asked her, and I knew from the flicker in her eyes that she understood what I meant.

It is time.

It is time I chose to which of my two worlds I belong.

It is time I became a Greek, at last.

I sat on the edge of her bed, the blankets sinking beneath me and sending a waft of her scent over me, and started to unplait my hair. She hesitated, and I wondered for a moment whether she would refuse to do it. She set the lamp down, and I saw the shadows shift and change. And then, in utter silence, with nothing but the wind about us, the rise and fall of the breathing of the Sarmatians in the wagon as they slept, she started to comb my hair. I closed my eyes, feeling the comb scrape against my scalp, the brush of her hand. There was an intimacy to it, sadness, too – an echo of the days we had missed together. I felt her breath upon my neck as she bent to tuck a strand of hair into the ribbon, felt her deft fingers knotting and twisting till my scalp prickled. I winced as she pulled at my lobes to fasten the earrings.

At last, as a sliver of light was creeping beneath the wagon's door and my feet were numb with cold, I stood to face her. I could not see myself, but the brightness of her eyes as she took me in told me that I looked every part her daughter.

I moved towards the door, and lifted the latch to let in the cold grey light of dawn. Then I turned back.

'Thank you,' I whispered. 'I will cure Alexander for you – for all of us. I do not know how yet – but I will.'

Her lips – cracked and dry – parted for a moment in a smile, and she nodded, though her eyes were filled with tears. For a moment she pressed her lips to my forehead, and I shut my eyes, relishing her closeness.

'You know,' she said, her voice unsteady as we broke apart, 'that I wish I had acted differently. I am not proud of it.'

I nodded. 'I know.' I took her hand in mine, holding her in my gaze a last time, trying to convey in my faltering smile how much I would miss her, even though I knew I had to go on. Then, summoning my resolve and lifting my cape over my head, I stepped out into the open air, towards the horses gathered for our departure back to Tiryns.

I never saw her again.

𒃻𒋾𒂊𒀭𒈬

Hippolyta

Amazons, Land of the Saka
The Thirty-fourth Day before the Day of Storms in the Season of Tar, 1265 BC

No words could describe how it felt to ride along the shores of Temarunda, cross the Silis at its shallowest fording point, and see my people again, just as they had been when I had left them. The crowding tents flapped in the wind, moved further upstream now towards the source of the Silis where the grass was more plentiful. The horses grazed over the plain. The Amazons – my people – were drying and salting horse-meat for the winter, as we had always done when the Season of Tar began. It was a bittersweet happiness, a pain, like a sword-blade, beneath the ribs, a sob swelling in my throat that was also a cry of joy to be home. The sense of my past repeating itself – the memory of a time when I had ridden into camp many years before, younger then with an infant at the breast – almost overwhelmed me, so that I could hardly tell which of myself I was: the young Amazon, wilful, broken by love, fleeing Skyros with her bastard child, or the queen who had been captured and scorned by a

Greek a second time, rescued by the people she was meant
to rule.

The clouds scudded overhead, grey and sea-blue, as I
spurred my horse, pangs of love and guilt riddling me as the
Amazons in the camp distinguished me at the head of the
train and cried out, their cheers rending the air even as they
were whipped away by the wind. I laughed, and Melanippe
galloped up beside me, letting out a whoop of joy and our
battle-cry, '*Oiorpata!*' Soon the sky was ringing with shouts
of '*Oiorpata!*', the stamping of feet, the clapping of hands,
the whoops and cries. I could see Ainippe and Teres jump-
ing up and down in the camp, waving coloured ribbons over
their heads, and Toxis rattling her spear against her crescent
shield, Thraso beside her giving a piercing whistle, like
an eagle's call. At the clamour even the horses raised their
heads from grazing, whinnying, and my steed snorted in
reply. It was with a hollow pang that I realized I was searching for Orithyia among them, and that, though I was
returned to our Amazon home, I would never see her again.
My vision blurred as I rode into the camp, feeling hands
grasping at me, hearing a cacophony of voices welcoming
me. I slid from my horse's back into their midst and felt the
grass of the Saka plain beneath my feet again. Everyone
seemed to want to touch me, to grasp at my hair, my cloak,
my arms, as if they feared I was some dread apparition sent
by Tar. I laughed and greeted them one by one, embracing
them, clasping to me the children, the warriors, the mothers
and tent-holders, inhaling the scent of horse, leather and
smoke – *my home* – as tears of happiness poured down my
cheeks.

I could not tell how long I stood there, hand-clasped with

my people, reacquainting myself with them, hearing their news, smiling, laughing and reassuring them that I was well, that I was returned. Yet as full as my heart was to see my people again, it was nothing to the moment when I saw Cayster standing beside me, tugging at my trouser-leg and reaching a hand up to me.

I knelt beside him, the blades of grass brushing my arms, and gathered him into me, stroking his head, his hair, his arms.

'Cayster,' I said, over and over again, 'Cayster.'

I did not know how long I knelt there with my son in my arms, feeling the warmth of him, the softness of his curling hair. When at last I let him go, he ran back to Melanippe and, as our eyes met, I knew what I had to do.

I vaulted onto my horse so that I might see them all, sidling left and right as I surveyed my people. There was Ainippe, looking up at me from her mother's waist, her thumb in her mouth; and there Ioxeia, her blind eye shining milk-white. There was Teuspa, and beside him Agar, talking with Toxis. With a singing of metal I drew the sword from my sheath and raised it glittering to the wide arch of the sky.

It took some time to quiet the gathered crowd of Amazons, many of whom were rejoicing at the return of their loved ones as well as their queen. At last the chatter died away.

I slid the blade back into my war-belt, my heart thudding in the silence, and their gazes upturned to me, hopeful, joyful.

Yet I can hold it from them no longer. If I am to be their queen, then I must be truthful with them.

And if they do not accept me – at least I will know I have told them all. At least I will no longer have this fear, this guilt.

'My people,' I said, swallowing as my mouth dried, 'by all the gods, I am so glad to be returned to you.'

They raised a cheer so loud that my horse shimmied nervously beneath me and tossed his head, but I raised my hand to silence them.

'There will be time for festivities later,' I said. 'What I have to say concerns my right to be queen, and as such I feel you should know it – you should have known it for many years – so that you may accept me now or . . .' My voice wavered. I could not say it. 'So that you may be ruled by one whom you deserve.'

I gazed over at Melanippe, smiling, though my lips shook. *Have courage*, I thought, and my smile grew as I realized my mother's voice was speaking within me; that, though I might have lost the war-belt, I had not lost her. *Have courage, Hippolyta. They will accept you for who you are.*

I felt the strength rise in me.

'You all know that this is not the first time I have returned here from the Greek lands. You know the tale of my capture in my youth. You know that I leapt from the ship in which I was held and swam to the lands of the Greeks, and that at last I made my way back to our home.'

I took a deep breath, trying to steady myself.

'What you do not know is that I lay with a Greek man while I was there; that I had a child with him. This child.'

I gestured, my hand shaking, towards Cayster.

I had expected an outbreak of muttering, curses, oaths, perhaps even cries of *'Paralati!'* But the Amazons stood there, watching me, their eyes not moving from me except, once or twice, to glance towards Cayster, who stood at Melanippe's side, clutching her trouser-leg.

'I did not wish to be any less than the queen you expected, the queen you had known my mother to be,' I said, my words rushing one after another. 'But I know, now, that I was wrong to keep it from you, for the queen you deserve is also one who speaks with you the truth, who opens herself to you with honesty. I submit myself to your judgement. I have told you the truth, before the gods.'

I was twisting my hands in my lap. *Oh, gods, they hate me. They have nothing to say to me. Please, Tabiti, let them give their sentence, and this torture be done.*

And then, at last, someone spoke.

'You are our queen.'

It was Ioxeia. She had not spoken loudly, yet the words were as clear as a wolf's howl over the plain.

'You are the eldest of Queen Marpesia's daughters,' she said. 'The blood of Opoea, daughter of Targitaus, runs in your veins. You are the rightful queen, chosen by the gods, sworn in by the sacred stone. There can be no other.'

I swallowed. 'But Melanippe—'

Melanippe had stepped forwards. 'You are the queen,' she said, her dark eyes warm and bright. 'We rode to the ends of the earth to find you. We are lost without you. You are our queen.'

The Amazons were talking, the sound rising to a great swell, and then, all at once, they were shouting together, waving their *sagaris* in the air. 'The queen! The queen! *Oiorpata!*' Teres and Ainippe were swirling their ribbons again. Yet still uncertainty lingered. *Surely they cannot have understood. Surely they must not have heard.*

'But I—'

My words were lost as they surged towards me. Hands pulled me down from my mount and pressed me to my people, everyone shouting, 'The queen! Our queen!' and from somewhere Melanippe appeared with Cayster and lifted him into my arms.

'Cayster,' I said, holding him to me so tightly that I almost knocked the air from him, my voice breaking. 'Oh, gods, Cayster, my love, can you forgive me?'

He said nothing but clasped his hands over my shoulder and bit his thumb. 'You are my mother?' he asked at last, amid the tumult of the Amazons dancing and shouting around us.

I nodded, my throat tight, unable to speak.

He waited a moment more. Then: 'I am glad you are home,' he said shyly.

I laughed aloud, tears running down my cheeks, and gathered him to me, and felt my joy overflow.

Ἀδμήτη

Admete

Somehow – though I knew not how – we made our way
back, following the course of the Borysthenes south to the
sea, then tracing the desolate coast, past the mountains of
Thrace and down to Greece. Alcides and I spoke but little
on the journey, both involved with our own thoughts. For
my own part, the fear of returning to find Alexander deathly
ill – or worse – goaded me on as we neared home. I was
barely conscious of the chattering of my teeth and the fatigue
that threatened to engulf me. All that mattered was Alexander. The men were tired, sweating in the driving rain that
poured down on us from the heavens as winter neared, and
the horses' flanks foamed with sweat as we urged them
towards Greece.

The night we returned to Tiryns I did not spare a moment
to find my father, I was so anxious to see Alexander – and so
I did not witness the cheering and feasting that greeted
Alcides' return, or his pronouncement of the end of his

labours to the gathered crowds who thronged to the throne room of the palace of Tiryns. My hair was lank, my lips and fingers dried out by the cold winds, my legs trembling after many days spent riding in the snow, but I ran through the corridors towards my brother's chamber, a torch flaring in my hand, without any thought but one.

He has to be alive. He has to be . . . The words drummed in my mind, driving my feet on, on, up the steps, through the archways and over the court beyond, hardly registering the heat of the open hearth that burnt in the hall creeping over my skin, the chatter and the colour and the warmth all blurring into a single slash of light, when all that mattered was Alexander, that he was still alive . . .

I blinked. I was at the doors to his chambers, the guards standing either side with their spears planted on the tiled floor.

'Alive?' I gasped, trying to ignore the stitch burning in my side.

One nodded, though his slight hesitation told me all I needed to know. I pushed my way past them through the doors, and the sickly stench of death and firesmoke filled my nostrils.

'Oh, gods . . .'

Alexander lay ahead, a limp form, flesh clinging to bone, spread on his sheets, surrounded by slaves whose figures glowed in the low light. I ran to the bed, panic filling me, thrusting the torch into the hands of one of the slaves. 'Oh, my brother, my brother . . .' His skin was pale and translucent as papyrus, his lips dry and his hair soaked with sweat. As I thrust a hand to his head, my heart pounding, I felt his flesh burning beneath my touch.

301

'Admete – oh, thank the gods you are returned.'

My father strode across the room and gathered me into his arms, pressing his face into my hair.

'He is so weak!' I exclaimed, breaking apart from him to look at Alexander, and shuddering as I saw how thin he had become, the bones of his wrists and collarbones protruding from the skin. I turned to Elais, who stood beside me, her eyes hollow and dark in the torchlight. 'What have you given him?'

'Feverfew and willow-bark, as you said,' she replied, her voice breaking, 'but he has only worsened. It is a miracle you are come, Admete, for truly I think he is but a few days from death.'

I gritted my teeth. 'No. No. We do not say that until it happens. There is always some recourse.'

I sank to the stool beside his bed, sweeping the hair from Alexander's face, though it was covered with a sheen of sweat and his eyes rolled from side to side beneath the lids.

'I am here,' I said, 'I am here, brother.' I fumbled in the pouch at my girdle for the golden apple, almost dropping it in my haste, my fingers numb and my eyes blurred with tears.

'Here,' I said, ignoring the streak of sound with which the slaves in the room greeted the gorgeous gold, holding it to his mouth, which was hanging open and smeared with spittle. 'Bite, Alexander, please – you must bite. It is the apple of immortality. It will cure you.'

I held his head cradled in one hand, my arm straining under its weight. He tried to move his jaw, but his lips were swollen and he could not manage it: his mouth kept slipping over the skin.

My fingers shaking, I lifted the apple to my own lips, holding it tight between finger and thumb, and tried to bite, but it was as solid as a lump of granite on a riverbed, and my teeth scraped over the skin.

'What?' I cried, trying again, but again my teeth slid from it. I attempted to open it, twisting it with my hands, feeling all over in case there was a catch I had missed that might open, but there was nothing, and even as I held Alexander in my arms I could feel the strength draining from him. *Oh, gods, what will we do if we lose him?* 'It's the apple – the golden apple of immortality. How can it give immortality if it can't be eaten? Oh, this is no *use*—' and I let the apple fall from my fingers, sobbing now, the gasps snagging on my throat and coming out in high-pitched moans. I clung to Alexander as he hung limply in my arms, his breath shallow and faint. 'What am I meant to do? What by all the gods am I meant to do?'

His head lolled in my hands, and though he was still breathing his pulse was shuddering.

He is about to die. I knew it – I could sense it in the chill that was creeping across his flesh and the floundering of his heart. Terror gripped me, and I gasped for breath, gulping at the stifling air as tears streamed down my cheeks. What else could I do? I had tried the apple, our last hope, the very last, and it had been as useful as if I had attempted to cure dropsy with the root of the mandrake, which everyone knew was only good for . . .

For . . .

And then I realized.

My heart pounded painfully against my ribs and my fingers slipped on the cords of the pouch tied to my girdle as I tried to tug it open. *Of course!* I thought. *Of course!* How could I have forgotten – the wormwood our mother had given me. It was the faintest, the very faintest of hopes, but still, there was nothing I would not try.

'Oh, come *on*,' I shouted, tugging harder at the pouch, the knotted thongs biting into my fingers. At last it gave way, snapping open, and the contents tipped onto my lap. 'Sweet wormwood, sweet wormwood,' I muttered to myself, and though there was not enough light to see well in the dim-lit chamber, I knew what the leaves I was searching for should feel like. I had written it myself in my records. '"It has a leaf like bitter wormwood,"' I quoted beneath my breath, blessing the gods as I did so for the gift of memory, '"but a brighter green, and yellow flowers and a sweeter scent. They use it for rashes and lesions, and in general to counter diseases of heat, which they conceive of as a fire in the body. It is administered in a draught mixed with vinegar, or an infusion which is drunk, and in treating a rash they make a plaster of it." Hah!'

A spark flew from the hearth, golden-red, at the same time as my fingers snagged on the wormwood my mother had given me, the leaves coarse beneath my touch and folded in on themselves. Pulse racing, I tore them as fast as my fumbling fingers would move and, wincing at the bitter taste, ground it to a paste between my teeth. I spat it onto my hand, took up the goblet from Alexander's bedside, which bore an infusion of willow-bark, tipped in the paste, stirred it and forced his head up so that he could drink. Much of the liquid slopped down his face, but I hardly cared. I had forced at least some of it into his throat, and – pray the gods – that should be enough.

Then all I could do, holding my breath and digging my nails into my palms, was wait.

After that I administered the wormwood every day, cold-pressed with vinegar and some of the Amazon *halinda*. I did not know which of the slaves or priest-healers stood there with me, or how many hours passed as I worked. My senses were filled with the aromatic scent of the sweet wormwood as I chopped and pounded it in the mortar, the tang of the vinegar as I stirred it in and tried to force a little down Alexander's throat. My eyes could take in nothing but the pallor of his cheeks and the shallow rise and fall of the linen covers over his chest – the last sign of the fraying thread of his life. I lost my awareness of time, and though the light splashed across the wall before me, then faded again, I did not eat or sleep, but continued to tend him, bathing his hot face and hands, pouring out measures of the wormwood tincture and tipping it into his mouth, till my eyes were dry with exhaustion and my hands shook.

And then, at last – so faint I might not have heard it had not my every nerve been straining for the sound – Alexander's swollen lips parted, and he gave a gasp.

My eyes flew to his face. I saw the lashes strain, then pull apart – and though his eyes were red-rimmed and bruised with fatigue it was him, and he was alive. I let out a strangled cry, and my hand fell to my side, letting the pestle I was holding drop to the floor with a clatter.

'Alexander!' I said, my voice trembling, but I hardly cared. My heart was racing, and I stretched my hand towards his cheek, felt the flushed skin beneath the backs of my fingers. 'Alexander – can you speak? Oh, gods – Elais, fetch my father!'

Alexander pressed his eyes shut and swallowed. Then he opened them, blinked, his mouth dry and moving soundlessly.

'Hush,' I said, bending forwards to push the hair off his face. 'Hush. Do not try any more now. It is enough that you are alive.' I leant forwards and pressed a kiss to his forehead, my eyes closed against his hair.

'I thought you had died,' I whispered. 'I thought you had left us. But you are here. You are here!'

I heard footsteps thundering down the hall and the doors to the chamber burst open. I saw my father and behind him my brothers – Iphimedon, Eurybius, Mentor and Perimedes – stumbling past the guards.

'He is awake?' my father gasped, his face taut. I nodded, smiling, my lips pressed together and my eyes aching, and he came towards the bed, collapsing on his knees at Alexander's side. Alexander opened his eyes and looked at him. For a moment, as the king wept and Alexander blinked, there passed between them a silent word of comfort. Then my father looked over to me, mouthing his thanks through his tears, and Alexander's gaze slid towards me. I could hear the words they wanted to say, both of them: because they were mine, too. I took Alexander's hand, and my father placed his on the crown of my head, where I had woven the smallest plait among my loose hair – a memory of my mother, whose cure had, at the very last, rescued her son.

My brother and the kingdom of Tiryns are saved.

The battle is won.

On Fate

Mount Olympus

Calliope tries to loosen the manacles cutting into her wrists and shifts on her knees in the snow. Hera has led her here, from Tiryns to the peak of Mount Olympus, to be tried before all the gods. The memories flash before her, vivid as thought. The realization — enough to make her doubt herself as a Muse — that she had made a mistake in giving the apple to Hercules; that it was not to be him, after all. The decision to risk everything by coming out into the open in Greece to get it back. Slipping into the disguise of a slave and entering the chamber of the prince of Tiryns. Bending to the floor to catch the golden apple as Admete, despairing of a cure, let it fall from her hand. And then Hera, coming upon her and snaring her, like a hare in a net, as she prepared to go into hiding in the valleys of Parnassus until the true owner of the apple was ready to take it. Hera, snatching the apple from her, binding her and dragging her to Olympus, and now holding her prize clasped in her hand.

The assembly-place is lit by a circle of torches that illuminate the snow falling in soft flurries of glittering white and the serried ranks of the thrones, like a stone-carved army. She gazes at the gods seated there: Aphrodite, Athena, pale-skinned beside Ares; Poseidon and Hephaestus, Hermes and Apollo, Artemis and Iris; and there, far at the back — always given second place to the

Olympian gods, she thinks – her sisters, the Muses. She can see dark-haired Euterpe, Terpsichore, her legs crossed before her, and Thalia talking with Urania; Polyhymnia, Clio, Erato and Melpomene huddled together and speaking in whispers.

Hera circles around her, a snow-queen, a queen of ice with frost crystals in her hair like pearls, robes glowing palely. Calliope grits her teeth at the triumph in Hera's face, barely concealed, the light of revenge smouldering behind her eyes. And then Zeus enters the council, a cloak draped over his shoulders, and takes his seat beside Hera's empty throne. He looks up, searching for his wife, and for the first time his gaze meets Calliope's.

His expression of irritable fatigue vanishes. It is replaced first by recognition and then, as he takes in the manacles binding her, a creeping fear, which makes his mouth sag.

He knows, Calliope thinks, and she feels a surge of satisfaction even though she is kneeling and bound in the snow, shamed before all the gods.

He knows that I am going to give up his secret; guesses, perhaps, that I planned it all along, ever since I stole the apples from the tree.

He knows that I will tell them all. And then how will the king of the gods fare?

She raises her chin and stares back at him, defiant, a smile on her lips, until he turns away.

And then Hera starts to speak, and Calliope knows that it has begun. That, perhaps, it has always already begun, and that they are all engaged in a dance around eternity, spinning and circling over and again to the same unending tune.

'Gods,' Hera calls, prowling beside Calliope. 'Sons and daughters of Cronus. Fellow immortals. I have summoned you here to witness the charges I bring against the eldest of the Muses,

Calliope,' her tone hardens as she speaks the name, 'who stole from me what was rightfully mine. She took three of the golden apples from the tree that you yourselves, gods, witnessed given to me and to Zeus as a gift of Earth on our wedding-day. I bring you here to judge her case and to determine whether, as I think is fit,' her eyes turn to Calliope, dark as opals, 'she should be cast in punishment from the company of the gods, and live out her days as a mortal upon the black earth.'

Athena rises to her feet. 'May I speak?'

Calliope sees Hera's grimace, and knows that, for all her speech of fair judgement, Hera longs for nothing more than to thrust Zeus' daughter from the steepest precipices of Olympus for daring to spoil her triumph – a triumph that is all the more precious because she failed, at the very last hurdle, to prevent Hercules completing his labours. Hera lets out an impatient breath. 'I hardly think it necessary—'

But Athena's mouth is drawn. 'As god of wisdom, I believe I have earned a say.'

Hera says nothing. Choosing to take her silence for assent, Athena speaks: 'Calliope deserves the chance to defend herself,' she says, and around her the gods murmur agreement. Calliope can see her sisters nodding, and Clio is urging Athena on, standing and gesturing, fingers outstretched, for her to continue. She feels a surge of affection for them. They, like she, alone of all the immortals, know the power for which she fights, for which she has always fought, that goes beyond the strength of any god. 'You speak of charges against her, Hera. Surely it behoves the Muse to rebut them, if she can.'

Hera draws a breath through her teeth. 'Very well,' she says, turning to Calliope and drawing her cloak with her so it raises a flurry of snowflakes in her face, but the Muse does not flinch. 'Tell *us, then. What excuse do you have for your thievery?' Her nostrils are flared and her breath forms clouds of steam on the winter air as she holds up the golden apple, written over in Calliope's own hand with the words: For the Immortal.*

Calliope casts a glance at Zeus, who is leaning forwards, lips parted, his arm outstretched as if he would halt his wife. 'You will regret asking me to tell it, Hera.'

Hera laughs aloud, without mirth. 'You are always the same, you Muses! You think you are so cunning, so clever, with your wiles and your woven plots! See, Athena – she is afraid to defend herself, so she makes us think she knows something we do not! But you will not escape so easily. Come, tell us,' she sweeps a hand towards the gods, her eyes narrowing to slits, her voice deepening with the hint of a threat, 'tell us your excuse for your crime! The only person who will regret it if you speak, Calliope, is you.'

'Hera.' Zeus has got to his feet, his eyes darting from Calliope to his wife. 'You should not—'

Hera rounds on him. 'You do not command me!'

Zeus slaps his thigh in impatience. 'Wife, this is no time for—'

But Calliope interrupts him, and though her voice is quiet, it cuts through Zeus' words. 'What I have to say regards the Fates.'

At once the gods are silent. The Muses sit straight in their seats, straining to hear. Even the gale howling through the pines on Olympus' slopes, whipping the sea below into a heaving frenzy, seems to quiet itself to listen.

Calliope takes a deep breath, relishing the moment: the silence on the air before the word is spoken and takes wing.

'They do not exist.'

There is no murmur of outrage from the gods, merely a shocked emptiness, a blankness on their faces as, one by one, they turn to Zeus. The king of the gods lets out a low whistle through pursed lips and sinks into his throne, hands over his eyes, snowflakes settling in his beard.

Hera's chest is puffed with rage as she spits, 'What?'

'The Fates do not exist,' Calliope repeats, without taking her eyes from Zeus, watching with satisfaction as he slides lower and lower in his throne, his shoulders sagging. 'The Hall of the Fates is an invention. There are no three crones seated in Hades, spinning the lives of mortals, portioning out their lot. We receive no scrolls from the Underworld. The nightingales we send out ourselves, and they return to us our own papyrus. The oracle at Delphi speaks our words, not the words of any other god or Fate – why else do you think she speaks in poetry? It is we – the Muses – who inspire the stories of the mortals, for we are the poets, the story-makers, and it is by the power of stories that the world is driven.' Her eye catches that of her sister Erato, and she knows they are both wearing the same rapt, shining expression that only poetry can bring.

'Do not speak in riddles,' Hera snaps. 'I see little difference between inspiring the mortals and setting them to their fates – it is merely a game of words, and I cannot abide twisted words.'

Calliope shakes her head. 'That is where you are wrong. There is all the difference in the world! To inspire a story is to set it off, to spark it, like a fire catching – yet the flames themselves may burn as brightly and for as long as they desire. But Fate – Fate is like a slave who decides that the day is done and throws earth on the flames to put them out, because it has been determined that it shall be so.' Hera opens her mouth to object, but Calliope presses on: 'The golden apples,' her gaze moves to the orb in Hera's hand, 'are intended to inspire the three greatest epics ever known. These are tales,' she looks up at Hera, whose face is shadowed, 'which will last a thousand years and more, told by the mortals and told

313

again till they make those of whom they sing immortal in their song – and us too. We shall be remembered for ever in their lines. Immortal glory, for us all,' she says, tasting the words on her lips, like nectar.

'We are immortal already,' Ares calls across the assembly-place. 'What need is there for more?'

A smile spreads over Calliope's face. 'We may be immortal,' she says, looking over the gathered gods one by one, raising her chin high, though she kneels in the freezing snow and her hands are bound, 'but the mortals are not. Their memory slips with every generation that crumbles to ash. Their worship falters. In years to come they may not even remember our names, let alone send up the smoke of sacrifice that is our due. But we can be remembered.' She pauses, letting the words hang on the air. 'We can preserve our memory among the men that walk the earth. And the golden apples are the way.'

There is silence as her words flow over the gods, spell-like. Iris is leaning forwards, her eyes gleaming. Aphrodite's face is radiant, and Calliope knows she has been caught, like a silver fish on a hook. Even Hermes is frowning.

At last Hera speaks.

'If the Fates are an invention,' she says, her voice trembling with fury, 'then who, pray, made them up?'

Calliope's eyes slide towards Zeus.

'Zeus?' Hera's tone is icy enough to freeze the Alpheios river.

His fingers part over his eyes, and, with a sigh that shivers through the white mounds of the trees on Olympus' slopes, he gets to his feet, pushing one hand to his knee as he stands.

'Oh, yes, very well, very well,' he says, not looking at his wife. He is mumbling into his beard as he brushes the snowflakes from his cloak. 'I invented them.'

'You invented them,' she repeats, her voice biting, eyes flashing sparks, and Zeus scuffs at the snow with his toe, like a child found pillaging the larder. 'You invented them?' Her voice rises to a shriek that sends a blast of wind howling from the mountain, blowing a flurry of snow over the plain below.

'There is no need to shout,' Zeus says, wincing. 'Everybody heard me.' The stillness is so complete now that, if they cared to listen, the gods could have heard the fox that pads over the ice in search of a mouse on Olympus' lower slopes. 'I came up with the idea when I came to rule Olympus, you know, after – my father . . . well, anyway. It seemed a good notion at the time. And it's not such a crime, is it? After all,' Zeus says, turning towards the gods, and his voice takes on a pleading tone, 'the mortals invented us. Why should I not invent a higher power, too, to keep the gods in check?'

'So,' Apollo says, rubbing his forehead and frowning, as if he has been told that all the nymphs have gone away to Hyperborea, 'there is no such thing as Fate?'

Zeus shakes his head, and a whirl of snowflakes bursts from his beard. 'Ah, well, strictly speaking, ah – no,' he says. 'Only inspiration – you know, that sort of thing . . .' He stammers into silence.

'And where do the gods fit into this?' Athena calls, drumming her fingers on the stone arm of her throne.

'Oh, well,' Zeus says, his expression lightening at the interruption, 'that's quite easy, really. It's the inspiration of the Muses that ensures the mortals' song-making and thus our immortality, just as Calliope said. As long as we're told of in song, we never die. Our names go on for ever, as long as we are remembered by the mortals who created us. And there's the added benefit,' he says, quite jovial now, 'of overseeing the stories of the mortals. After

all, though the Muses start it off,' he tips his head in a bow to Calliope, 'a tale can go many different ways – and we can give the
mortals a nudge, you know, in the right direction, or take sides if
we want. Much better than being restricted by the Fates, really,
if you think about it.'

The gods do think about it. Athena considers. Apollo ponders.
At last Hermes gets to his feet.

'It seems to me,' he says, shifting his weight from foot to foot,
'that, all things considered, it's considerably less of a headache just
to believe in Fate.'

The gathered gods, one by one, begin to nod, like pines bent
over with snow, and a murmur of assent flows between them.

'Yes,' Apollo says, 'definitely much easier.'

'Don't understand all that story stuff,' Ares puts in.

'Best left to the Muses,' Hephaestus agrees.

Zeus relaxes visibly, his shoulders slumping from his ears and
his mouth easing into a smile. He moves towards his throne, rubbing his hands together. 'Well, that's that, then. We're all agreed
to keep pretending the Fates exist.'

But Hera holds out an arm to stop him. 'No, it is not all,' she
snaps. 'Have you forgotten my apples? Since you won with
those – those labours,' she swallows, apparently unable to say
Hercules' name, 'I should be allowed some retribution on this
score, at least.'

Zeus sighs. 'Oh, let it go, Hera,' he says, taking a seat again,
accepting the goblet of nectar Hermes hands him. 'Hades knows
we need a good story. And it isn't as if Calliope took them for her
own gain – we'll all get immortality from these epic things too,
won't we?'

He glances over at Calliope, and she nods. Her eyes flick back
to the apple clutched in Hera's hand, her whole body tensed with

anticipation. Come on, she thinks. Come on, just give me the apple . . . Give it to me . . .

'Give it to her, Hera,' Athena calls. 'What have you to lose?'

'You have many more in the Garden of the Hesperides!'

The rest of the gods join the chorus: 'Give it to her! Give her the apple!'

Calliope's entire being is fixed on the golden orb, purpose burning within her. Give it to me. Just give me the apple. Give me the apple so I can begin the epic that I thought was meant for Hercules but now, I know, belongs to someone else . . .

And at last, Hera's fingers trembling, she extends the apple towards Calliope, then drops it, tumbling and flashing, to the snow before her, so that it lands like a drop of amber.

And Calliope feels the manacles fall from her hands to the ground, and she reaches out, barely breathing, to pluck the apple to her.

The three greatest epics the world has ever seen are about to begin.

Fourteen years later – the blink of an eye, for the gods – Calliope stands before Aphrodite's chambers, inhaling the scent of musk rose and myrtle floating through the door. She smiles, relishing again the sensation of standing on the brink of a story, a kind of heightened awareness that makes the moments dance by, discrete as coloured butterflies: another tale to be told, another great epic unfolding, like a scroll unfurling.

And then she pushes open the door.

Aphrodite is lying on her bed at the centre of the circular chamber, her eyes closed in pleasure as the cupids flutter around her combing her hair. She is wearing nothing but a gauzy robe and her feet are bare, dangling over the bed's side. Calliope hesitates, wondering if she should make her presence known. Then she starts forwards, treading on rose petals scattered over the floor, their scent drifting up to her as they crush beneath her feet. A breeze blows from the sea and parts one of the white gossamer veils at the windows lining the walls, to reveal the Aegean Sea below, sparkling over the rocks, blue as Aphrodite's eyes. Doves coo in the rafters, the rustling of their feathers like the wind over the waves, and the walls glimmer, set with broken sea-shells gleaming pink and pearl-blue. Calliope cannot help but think that her own romantic experience – thus far limited purely to the imagination – could not but be aided by such a sensuous chamber as Aphrodite's, billowing with the heady scent of roses.

And then she shakes herself, remembering why she is here, and what she has to do. The tense anticipation of the beginning of the story – like the silence before the singer takes up his tune – fills her again.

'Aphrodite.'

The goddess of love opens her eyes, and a smile spreads across her face. 'Calliope,' she says. 'I didn't hear you come in.'

She rolls over onto her front. The cupids drape her hair across her back and flutter away to her dressing-table for perfumes and oils. She props her head on her hands, rosy and gorgeous as the sunrise.

Calliope takes a deep breath. 'It is time.'

Aphrodite blinks once, twice, then her lips draw together in a silent exclamation. She sits up, gathering her gauzy robes over her shoulders.

'You have it still?' Calliope asks.

At the word, two of the cupids – giggling among themselves – flit to a rosewood chest, then return clutching the golden apple. They drop it into Aphrodite's lap.

On Fate

She lifts it. 'Here.'

Calliope holds out her hand and, with a thrill of pleasure, feels the skin of the apple in her fingers once more. She walks to one of the windows, examining it, turning it over and over in the light with a critical eye, but it is unblemished, as perfect as it was when she gave it to Aphrodite many years before on the shores of Hyperborea.

Oh, yes, she thinks, as she gazes out towards the islands that scatter the Aegean, like pebbles on a pond. Of course the mortals will say it happened at the wedding of Peleus and Thetis. It is a story she herself will seed among them – when the snake-haired, bat-breathed goddess Discord wreaked her revenge on the gods for not inviting her to the marriage-feast, and rolled an apple in their midst, inscribed with the fatal words that would set a war raging across the world of mortals . . .

But she and Aphrodite alone know that it is happening now, here, quietly and deliberately, in the chamber of the goddess of love as the peach light of dawn streaks the horizon to the east and the swallows chatter on the warm summer air.

She turns back towards Aphrodite, who is watching her with a faint look of curiosity.

'What is your plan?'

Calliope does not answer. Instead she draws a stylus from where it is tucked into her girdle and – just as Iris did many years before – she inserts the tip into the apple's flesh, gouging into it two words: ΤΗΙ ΚΑΛΛΙΣΤΗΙ.

'For the Most Beautiful,' Aphrodite reads aloud. She moistens her lips with the tip of her tongue. 'So. It is time for my epic.'

Calliope bows her head.

'And?' Aphrodite asks. 'After the voyage of Jason and the Argonauts to the ends of the earth – well, what next?'

319

For the Immortal

'A war,' Calliope whispers, her breathing ragged in her excitement. 'A war that will be waged from east to west and will give birth to the greatest heroes Greece has ever known – fought over a beautiful woman.'

She hands the apple to Aphrodite, who holds it to her bosom, caressing it, tracing the letters inscribed there with her fingertip. 'I see,' she says. 'And you want me to—'

'Yes,' Calliope says, as their eyes meet and they exchange a look between them. 'Exactly.'

A moment's silence, broken only by the cooing of doves and the breaking of waves against the rocks below.

Then Aphrodite slips from the bed to her feet. The cupids flutter to her and drape a shawl of shimmering gold around her shoulders that catches the early-morning light, like dew on a spider's web. 'Well, then,' she says. 'I suppose I should fetch Hera and Athena.'

'Yes,' Calliope says. 'I suppose you should.'

A moment more, as they smile at each other in acknowledgement of a job well done, a contract completed. Then Aphrodite turns towards the door, slips through it with a swift nod back to Calliope, and is gone.

Calliope listens to the fall of her feet over the marble corridors beyond. Then, when she is sure Aphrodite is gone, she slides her fingers into the fold in her robes and draws out the last of the three apples, her own, the one Hera was forced to give to her in the council when everything changed, when the Muses gained their victory and the Olympians were forced to concede defeat. She holds it up to the pale light, watching the surface sparkle, her eyes darting over the words she wrote there, when she thought it was an epic of Hercules: ΤΩΙ ΑΘΑΝΑΤΩΙ – For the Immortal.

But she knows now that it is not Hercules this apple is meant for.

On Fate

Her gaze moves past the apple towards the eastern horizon, now a blaze of golden light threading the clouds into yellow ribbons, then to the sea, sparkling white-gold beneath the sky, and beyond, the vast grasslands ridden by the horse-taming Scythians.

A slow smile spreads over her face.

The very last epic is yet to come.

IMMORTAL

One year later,
at the time of the Trojan War

The Amazons did not cease to disregard danger – though their
camp was attacked by Hercules, and later they sacked Athens;
no – still, they went to Troy, and fought with all of Greece.

Pausanias, *Description of Greece* 1.15.2

To Troy

Hippolyta

Amazons, Land of the Saka

The Twenty-third Day after the Day of Fire
in the Season of Tabiti, 1250 BC

Night was spreading her dark veil over the plains as I settled myself on a cushion by the fire, folding my legs beneath me and surveying the council gathered in my tent with quiet contentment. These were moments I treasured: the whispering of the flames and the low murmur of talk, the passing of the *koumiss* pouch between us, the councillors of our tribe gathered together in peace. Fifteen years had passed since we had ridden out together to sack the citadel of Athens – of the elders only Sitalkes and Iphito now remained, and my band of twelve warriors was studded with younger fighters, as well as my son Cayster, who had grown tall and sturdy in my care as a shoot in fertile ground grows into a sapling. These had been years of plenty, in which we had measured time by the rhythm of the seasons, changing pasture over the plains in summer, making camp by the river's banks as the colder months approached. I had negotiated a truce with the Budini, and raids had been few. All was well.

Yet we were Amazons still, and still, after all these years, our talk turned, inevitably, inexorably, to war.

'Any news of the conflict?' Sitalkes asked, once the *koumiss* had made its rounds and I had placed it on its stand.

I saw Cayster and Thermodosa, one of the youngest warriors in my band, exchange a smile. Sitalkes was more than three times their age and wire-muscled with the years, his cheeks sunken, yet he had the battle-spirit of a warhorse.

'None, since I spoke with the leader of the Hialeans last,' I said, taking up a poker to stir the fire, watching the embers spark. 'Thus far the reports are all the same. The city of Troy remains besieged by the Greeks. Battles are waged back and forth, but as yet there is no decisive victory.'

'Is there no end to the Greeks' lust for blood?' asked another of the elders. 'Must they now sail the waters of the seas to seek it out?'

'It seems so,' I replied. 'Yet if the tales we hear are true, it was Paris, son of Priam, who was at fault for capturing Menelaus of Mycenae's wife.'

'You know that is not the reason,' Melanippe said, from beside me. 'You know no one would go to war on such a pretext. For one man's marriage! I wager rather it is the greed of the kings of Greece.'

'Or perhaps,' Sitalkes said, 'it is the storm-god Tar and his consort Tabiti who stir up these battles. A war to shake the very foundations of the earth – is that not what the Hialeans told us?'

I bowed my head. 'Rumours, Sitalkes, these are but rumours.'

'May I speak?'

Cayster was leaning across the hearth, and I had to repress a smile as my eyes met his. His flaxen hair, pale like my

Greek's in his youth, had darkened with age, and a beard was growing on his chin, but his eyes were the same – that dark passion, intensity, like a black flame.

I gestured to him to continue. 'Cayster. Of course.'

He clambered to his feet, lithe and agile. 'Are we not age-old allies of Troy? Did not your own mother the queen, my grandmother, do battle with Priam, fighting with the Trojans side by side as sworn friends?'

I let out a sigh that made the flames before me shiver and send smoke curling into the air. 'Speak on.'

'We should go to Troy!' The words gushed from his lips, like water bubbling from a spring, and his eyes shone. 'We should join the Trojans and fight the Greeks!' He hesitated, then, almost imploring, said, 'It will be the greatest battle the world has ever seen!'

The council was quiet, waiting for my answer. Only the spitting of the fire and the whinnying of the horses on the plain broke the silence. I wondered how to respond, what I could say that would curb my son's enthusiasm – for, though he truly longed for battle with the warrior spirit of an Amazon, I also guessed his desire. Had it not been mine also, when I had left for Athens? Had I not hoped, when I was younger – as he was now – to see the Greek again?

Cayster's gaze burnt as I lifted my eyes to meet it. My lips parted, though what I was to say I did not know.

'I say we let the Trojans deal with their own disputes,' Iphito said, breaking the tension. She drew the dagger from her war-belt and poked at the fire with the iron tip. A shadow crossed her face. I knew she was thinking of Arga, her daughter, fresh and pale as an apple-blossom, who had fallen beneath the sword of the Greeks in the battle for Athens so

329

many years ago. *But how*, I thought, *how can we make the young understand what we lost in those long-gone battles?*

The tent-flap billowed open, and the evening air blew across us. Polemusa, daughter of Toxis, was standing in the entrance, breathing hard, sweat shining at the base of her neck.

'Polemusa!' I exclaimed. 'You interrupt the gathering of the council!'

'My apologies, my queen,' she panted. 'But there is an emissary arrived from the Trojans, and he demanded to see you at once. I could not prevent him.'

A man with the haggard look of one who had not slept in many days pushed past Polemusa.

'What is this?' I stood, my hand on the hilt of the sword at my belt, and around me the council did the same. Cayster drew his blade. 'What has happened?'

'I am Idaeus, herald of King Priam of Troy, your friend and ally,' he said, in stilted Saka. He, too, was short of breath. 'I have grave news of the war in Troy.'

'What news?' I asked sharply.

'Prince Hector is dead,' he said, and his voice broke as he spoke the words. 'The defender of our city has been killed before our walls, and even now the Greeks rampage over the plain. If we do not summon help soon, all will be lost.' He straightened himself, and I shuddered at the look in his eyes – the cold desperation of one who had seen death and wished to see no more. 'I beg you, Queen Hippolyta. I am here as King Priam himself could not be, to clasp your knees as he would,' he dropped to the floor and wrapped his arms around me, his face tilted up, creased with pain. 'I beg you, in the name of your mother Queen Marpesia, who rode out with King Priam in the famed battle against the Phrygians, and swore to him a lasting alliance, I beg you to come to our aid, you and your Amazons – not merely for ourselves, but for the protection of all the peoples of Anatolia and the Saka tribes, against whom the Greeks will surely come, if the gates of Troy fall. You are the last hope for our city – the very last.'

I bent forwards, took his hand and raised him to stand. 'You need not kneel to me,' I said gently, moved beyond words by the emotion with which he spoke. 'I hear your plea.'

And how easily the gods change our fortunes with a single word. My hand fell from my sword-hilt and my fingers brushed my war-belt – crafted for me after my return from Greece, leather and studded with gold, a beautiful thing. And yet it was not – it never could be – the same as my mother's. I remembered every embellishment pricked on those gold plates by the craftsmen, every dent hammered into them in battle, as if my mother's belt had been a tale, like those the bards sang, each hollow telling its own story. I felt a surge of certainty in my heart. I knew what she would have done, faced with this herald, with this choice. Better, far better, I knew that it was not my bitterness at the Greeks that drove me to it, but my kinship to the Trojans, and my determination to protect my people, my Amazons. All that enmity against the Greeks, that sense of betrayal, that longing – it had subsided now into nothing but a dull memory. My lips twisted into a smile. Perhaps, at forty years of age and ripe in my womanhood, I had become a queen at last.

'We will send our troops to your aid,' I said, and the old man trembled. 'Melanippe,' I said, turning to my sister, 'how many can we spare?'

Melanippe stepped forward, and I thought how much

older she looked, her dark hair threaded with grey – how much older we all were than when we last rode to battle against the Greeks. 'How many do you need?' she replied, addressing herself to the herald Idaeus.

He wiped his face on the sleeve of his tunic. 'I have brought ships, a fleet, anchored out on the open sea,' he said. 'We rode to the Bosphorus and took ship from there, as the harbour of Troy is no longer safe. It is fastest this way – the passage south through the Hittites' lands will take too long, and the gods know that every day we delay more Trojan lives are lost. We came first to you, as our oldest allies and the most famed fighters. We intend to sail the coast supplicating the other Saka tribes.'

'And the number of your ships?'

'Enough to take a few hundred troops. Steeds we can supply from the Trojan plain.'

'A hundred troops—' Melanippe glanced at me.

'We send you forty of our fighters willingly,' I said, cutting across her. 'I will apply at once to the tribes of the Saka and King Panasagoras to join us. And I will join the expedition myself, with my twelve finest warriors, a band of fearsome Amazons to guard your city, my lord, and your king.' I laid a hand on his shoulder. 'The lady Tabiti knows I do not go to battle with joy in my heart,' I said, and my gaze went to Cayster, whose face was alight with anticipation. 'But when we ride out to restore peace and to drive the warmongers from our lands, this I do gladly. It is my duty as your ally sworn by my mother's blood, and,' I said, the corners of my mouth lifting in a smile, 'my calling as an Amazon queen.'

Ἀδμήτη

Admete

I shivered – some prescience of the hand of the gods playing over me, perhaps – as the ship rounded the tip of Lesbos, and the city of Troy came into view, perched on its headland, like a coronet ring slipped onto a finger. The memory of so many years before overwhelmed me: when, bound for the Amazons, our ship had slid through the waters of the Hellespont, and Alcides and I had climbed from the harbour to enjoy King Priam's hospitality in his halls. For a few moments I had to close my eyes, inhaling the salt-scented sea air, to remind myself how many years had passed since then – how many things had changed.

I smiled as I thought of my daughter, Lysippe: a gift to me and my husband Proetus to bless our marriage. Whether it was a gift of the gods or the work of the chaste-tree berries, which I had found to aid in quickening a child in the womb, I was content not to ask. She was grown now almost to a woman, her hair dark as her grandmother's had been.

Alexander had come to the throne of Tiryns, healthful and full of vigour, and we lived there in peace under his rule, I with the noble Proetus, and my brothers with their wives, laughing in the court as we watched our children play together. Those were sun-filled days of much joy in which Lysippe and I tended the herb-garden together, and sat in the evenings by the hearth in our home as I recorded by the lamplight on my tablets the herbs I had found.

And then the call had come to war.

It was Agamemnon, king of Mycenae, who summoned us. Bound by ties of kinship and loyalty, Iphimedon and Eurybius had led the troops of Tiryns out to battle. Alexander, remaining behind to rule the city, sent our eight black war-ships and our finest warriors – Proetus among them – with the contingent of Diomedes of Argos. As spring wore into summer I had watched Lysippe grow and tried to seem as if my only business was with herbs, but when a messenger was announced from Troy I picked up my skirts and ran to the throne-room to hear his news.

'No news of Proetus,' the herald had said, when I asked. 'But, my lady, it is with you, not the king, I have come to speak.'

I frowned, listening as his story unfolded. Patroclus, comrade of Achilles, had been killed. Without his skill with herbs, and only two healers left to attend to the army, Nestor, lord of Pylos, had sent for me. My reputation as a healer had spread throughout Greece after Alexander's cure, and I had devoted many years to herbal lore, healing many who had been said to be past the help of the gods. Yet I was hesitant to leave Lysippe. Only when the messenger invoked the names of my husband, my brothers and other Greeks, who would be in peril if I left them to die of their wounds, had I agreed – at last – to go.

334

I opened my eyes again, recalling myself. The ship Alexander had given to convey me was a broad-bottomed merchant ship, which the slaves of the palace had filled with pickled olives and salted meat from our stores, weapons, and as many of the plants, bandages and linens from the herbary as I could bring. The oars cut into the sea and sent white fountains of spray into the air, while ahead of me the leaping dolphin of the prow seemed to cavort over the waves. The wind blew against my back, sending my hair flying forwards in a mass of curls. Before us, the headland that protected Troy's harbour stuck out into the gushing waters of the Hellespont. As we rounded it, the steersman pulling on the oar to guide us into the bay, I saw again the city, sitting atop its hill with the lower town spilling beneath it, towers rising against the sky, and beneath it, across the Scamandrian plain, a cloud of dust swirled thick as fog. Nearing the beach, I could make out black-hulled ships ploughed into the shore, a makeshift rampart circling a camp of tents erected from sailcloth and wooden huts, some in sore need of repair, with holes smashed through their roofs, and littered around with debris. Soldiers called to us as our fleet approached, and a herald ran towards us, beckoning us ashore. I felt a thrill of anticipation – not excitement but some strange sense of unreality, as if I, the camp unfolding before me and the billowing cloud of war-dust were already legend, and that the battle here took place outside time, outside history.

The prow shuddered before me as we made land, and I climbed after the ship's captain down the rope-ladder that was thrown to shore.

'We bring supplies and reinforcements from Alexander, king of Tiryns, son of Eurystheus,' I said to the herald come to greet us. I gestured to the ship, which was being drawn onto its props, looking fresh-painted and sturdy beside the rest of the Greek fleet, some of which were blackened and charred as if from fire.

'And you, my lady?' His eyes swept my dress, which, though creased and stained from weeks on the sea, showed my status as a noble born and bred, then the gold pendants hanging at my ears, and my husband's seal-ring on my finger. A group of warriors clattered past, carrying breastplates and spear-blades in sacks on their shoulders, and it was a while before the herald spoke. When he did so, his voice was curt above the crashing of the waves and the soldiers' talk. 'This is no place for a woman. The fighting has resumed after the truce for Hector's funeral. We are at war, my lady. You would do best to return home at once with our thanks to your lord.'

'I thank you for your concern,' I said, 'but I am here at the request of Nestor of Pylos, as a healer to the Greeks.'

His expression faltered. I looked back at him, unwavering, as behind me the slaves unloaded the herbs from the ship.

'Very well,' he said at last. 'I will lead you to my lord Nestor, then, if it is he who has summoned you here.'

The sand crunched beneath my sandals as I walked behind him, trying to avoid the broken arrow shafts that were scattered everywhere, vestiges of battles past, and holding my breath against the foul sweet stink of the rotting corpses of men and horses felled in the fight, then left out for the crows. I found I was searching for the faces of Proetus, Iphimedon and Eurybius among them, and shuddered at the thought, but when I started forwards to ask the herald of my husband and brothers, he told me – *gods be thanked* – that they were alive and well. *I will see them soon*, I thought, trudging after the herald. *But first I must fulfil what I was summoned here to do.*

At last we came to a square hut, built from the trunks of pines stripped, thrust into the sand and roofed with reeds, slaves milling about it and a couple of warriors seated before it on upturned helmets playing at dice. The herald pushed the door and we were engulfed in darkness, my senses assailed at once by the close air laden with sweat and smoke.

'My lord Nestor,' the herald said, 'and my lord Ajax. This woman claims she is here at your command.'

As the smoke before me cleared I saw a grey-haired man with the sword-belt of a noble, standing by another, broad-shouldered and hunched forwards – though he would be tall when he straightened, taller than most – seated on a stool, a slave trying to apply a poultice to a deep wound slashed across his shoulder, ragged at the edges and oozing dark blood. Ajax – for it could only be Ajax, kin of Achilles and bulwark of the Achaeans – gritted his teeth and the slave's hand slipped. The poultice fell to the earth, and Ajax cursed.

'I will do that,' I said, starting forwards. I picked up the fallen cloth and lifted it to my nose. I flinched. 'Comfrey?' The slave nodded. 'But comfrey is injurious to an open wound ... Herald,' I twisted around to him from where I knelt, 'have you a herbary?'

He nodded.

'Then bring me yarrow and fresh bandages,' I said, tossing the comfrey poultice onto the hearth, where the flames licked at it. 'Water?'

The slave ran forwards with a pitcher, and I ripped a strip of linen from my skirt and dipped it in.

'Who is this?' Ajax asked, looking over my shoulder as I set about washing the wound.

'I am the sister of Alexander, king of Tiryns,' I said, answering for myself, 'and wife of Proetus.'

'You are well versed in the art of healing?'

'Well enough to know that comfrey will surely poison that wound if it has not knitted first. Please, my lord, be still,' I added, as Ajax shifted on his seat and the water I was wringing over the wound dripped down his arm.

'And you are here . . . ?'

'At my summons,' Nestor laid a hand on Ajax's good shoulder, 'and you, for one, shall not complain of it.'

'I have come with supplies from my brother Alexander,' I said, taking the yarrow leaves his slave handed me and applying them over the skin, 'and to aid Machaon and Podalirius in healing.'

I wound the clean bandage around his shoulder and knotted it twice, then brushed my hands on my skirt and got to my feet. 'There,' I said. I turned to Nestor, whose eyes were upon me. 'Will you host me, my lord, while I am here? I bring a gift from my brother, with his thanks – a fine dagger with a hilt of gold, wrought by Daedalus of Sicily.'

But he waved me away. 'You have earned your keep,' he said. 'I am glad you are come, daughter of Eurystheus. The sons of Greece will thank you for your work, and the gods know there is much to be done. Talthybius here will find you a cloak and pelts to make up a bed of your own. Your husband resides in the tents with the soldiers. It would not do for you to sleep there.'

I nodded my thanks, turning to leave. 'Then I will return to partake of the evening meal with you, if I may.'

As the brilliant white sky opened above me and the clear breeze blew in from the sea, I took a breath, gazing at the tents and huts studding the shore, the warriors milling here and there. The sound of bronze ringing against bronze drifted to me from the plain, and gulls screeched overhead.

And so, I thought, clenching my fists at my side and readying myself for the struggles to come, *to the Trojan War.*

⟨⟨𒌍 ⟨𒈬⟩𒈦

Hippolyta

The Ocean

The Twenty-ninth Day after the Day of Fire in the Season of Tabiti, 1250 BC

We left as soon as we could after the messenger arrived. I led our horses, stumbling and tossing their heads, up the gangplanks onto the ships, loaded *sagaris* and *pelta*-shields, swords and spears through the night, guided only by torch-light. I sacrificed a mare at the sanctuary of the gods before an iron blade stuck into the earth, letting blood and metal mix in the black soil. Derinoe, my fastest rider, had galloped to ask the many tribes of the Saka for their allegiance against the Greeks. They, too, had spent the days in preparation and, as the morning mist rose over the banks of the Silis, an army forded the shallows of the river, pennants flying, and came to march for Priam, sworn ally of the Saka.

I leant against the ship's side where I sat astride the thwart. The oars were banked and all but the captain at the steering-oar were sitting at their ease. The gods were blessing our voyage with a fair wind, and our fleet skimmed the waters, like a flock of dark-feathered birds. The wind brushed my face, and I thought how strange it was that this same wind, this same air, had shaped itself to the mould of my face three times now: once when I was young and fresh as a virgin maid, again as a mother and wife, and now as a queen going to war. I wondered, passing my fingertips over my face with a faint smile, whether the wind-god knew me still.

'Sister.' Melanippe stood before me, stray wisps of hair flying in the breeze, her figure silhouetted against the blazing sun, which was burning itself into the sea to the west, beyond the prow. 'May I?'

I gestured to her to sit, and she settled beside me, one booted foot drawn up onto the bench, her arms clasped around a knee. It was such a familiar gesture that I smiled to see her.

'How does Cayster fare?' I asked. I had been unable, for all my efforts, to force my son to remain behind, to protect him from the war. He possessed all my own spirit and fire – *and*, I added as an afterthought, *that of the Greek, too.*

She tossed her head and smiled. 'He enjoys every moment,' she said. 'He is eager to help the ship's captain in any way he can, tightening the ropes, keeping watch from the mast. He is all strength and vigour. You remember,' her eyes slid sideways to me, 'what it was to be young.'

'It is his second voyage on this sea,' I mused, gazing out to the setting sun, blazing into pinks and purples on the horizon and turning the water a dusky, rippling rose.

'Hippolyta,' she said, and her voice was very low. I turned to her, my heartbeat quickening as our eyes met and I caught the seriousness of their expression. I knew what she was about to ask me.

'Yes?'

'Have you thought ... Have you thought what might happen, if the Greek from Skyros fights in the battle around Troy?'

I wetted my lips with the tip of my tongue. We had not spoken of it – none of us had – and made as if Cayster had always been accepted as my son, his care shared between Melanippe and myself.

'I have,' I said, my mouth barely moving.

'And? If you meet him in battle? What will you do then?'

'You are assuming I will recognize him at once.'

Her look was enough to tell me she knew, as well as I, that I would.

'Very well,' I said. 'But he may have died, Melanippe, far off in his own land. He may have been carried to the land of the dead by illness, or killed in battle. It was long ago – so very long ago.'

'But if he is there?' she pressed on. 'If he is living, and fighting at Troy?'

'Then I have determined I will spare him my sword.'

She let out a long breath through her teeth. 'After what he did to you? After the pain you bore for so many years?'

I nodded. 'Indeed, sister, believe me. It has taken me many years but I bear him no resentment. And it would be a great wrong to harm the father of my child.'

'Then why embark on this voyage?' she hissed, her eyes shadowed in the deepening night. 'Why sail at all?'

'I have sworn my allegiance to Priam and the Trojans,' I say. 'I am my mother's daughter, the queen of my people. As a woman, as a mother, I will spare him and him alone. But to the rest of the Greeks I will show no mercy, in defence of my allies and my homeland.'

Her expression softened somewhat. 'Then I am satisfied,' she said. 'I care for you, sister, but I care for our people also. I would not have you risk them.'

'Do not doubt me,' I said, rising to my feet and turning aside. A group of Saka allies were moving towards the mast-box as the yardarm was lowered. At the stern, several young men lifted the anchor, a stone drilled with a hole and knotted to a rope, and with a splash dropped it into the sea. I placed my hands on Melanippe's shoulders and leant down to look into her eyes, putting all my weight into my words. 'I will not fail you.'

The Epic Begins

𒀭𒌅𒆠𒈾𒌅 𒌅

Hippolyta

Troy, Anatolia

The Thirty-fourth Day after the Day of Fire
in the Season of Tabiti, 1250 BC

The days of our journey to Troy passed in quick succession with a fair wind, and soon the Bosphorus was in sight. We pushed on, through the swirling currents and across the Propontis, until we reached a bay cut into the Hellespont just north of Troy where Idaeus had said we should disembark. Trojan envoys waited there, with a herd of horses in a holding pen, kicking up dust with their hoofs and sweating in the heat. We left the army there to pitch camp and prepare for tomorrow's battle while the herald, Melanippe, Cayster, my twelve maiden warriors and I cantered south to enter the city alone.

We followed Idaeus, circling to the east of Troy and keeping to the cover of the forests until the city was within sight, its walls rosy in the light of the setting sun, like a beacon shining out to sea. I felt my blood rise at the sight of its thick, fortified walls, the torches already flaming on the ramparts, and the thought of the war that would be waged beneath them tomorrow. I turned to Melanippe, and she nodded at me, her chest rising and falling. Beyond her, Cayster's eyes were shining as he gazed over the city, the warden of its plain.

Idaeus turned to me. 'You are ready?'

I bowed my head. 'I am.'

He dismounted and struck a flint, holding a taper to it till it flared. He took it to the torch he had brought with him, waiting for the resin to catch. After a while I caught the acrid smell of burning pitch, then the flame leapt into the air, dancing and shimmering pale in the sunset. He walked to the edge of the trees and held it high, waving the flame back and forth, trailing sparks, like a star shooting across the heavens.

And soon we saw them: a mounted guard of Trojans, galloping over the plain, their hoofbeats muffled by the wind. Idaeus dropped to one knee as they approached, cloaks swirling behind them, and the others did the same. I alone remained standing, my hand on the hilt of my sword and my chin raised in greeting.

'I am glad to see you, sons of Troy,' I said, as they leapt from their mounts and came towards me.

One, a prince to judge from his purple tunic threaded and edged with gold, stepped forwards and bowed low. 'Queen Hippolyta,' he said, and his voice was just on the verge of manhood, his face pale at the meeting. 'I am Deiphobus, eldest son of King Priam.' His bearing heightened as he said it, and I had the shrewd feeling that someone, at least, was not mourning the death of Hector. 'I am come on my father's orders to lead you and your retinue to Troy, so that you may partake of food and drink with us in our halls and rest before tomorrow's battle.'

'We would welcome your father's hospitality,' I said, gesturing to him to mount his horse once more. 'We have travelled far and without rest along the voyage.'

The prince knelt, hands held towards my boot, as if to help me mount. I suppressed a laugh and swung myself onto my horse as easily as a bird taking wing. Behind me my Amazons did the same. He rose from the ground, a red flush creeping up his neck, and climbed unsteadily onto his steed.

'They must indeed be mourning the loss of Hector,' Cayster whispered to me, from the corner of his mouth, as he urged his horse forwards, guiding the reins with a flick of his finger, 'if they are left with such a prince.'

I did not reply, not wishing to be disloyal to his father the king, but I could only exult in the practised swiftness of my Amazons as we galloped over the plain, and savour the thought of our troops riding out to battle tomorrow, shining like the goddess Tabiti, and smooth-sinewed as the horses we rode so well.

The gates of Troy swung back as we approached, opening to Deiphobus' call, and we cantered into the city up the stone-paved street, past plastered houses where Trojan women hung from their doors to watch us, through a market-place empty of stalls and towards the stables, where slaves were waiting to brush down our horses. Idaeus led us to the palace, and as the doors of the Great Hall swung open, I caught sight of the pillars around the hearth and smelt the mixed stench of fire-smoke, sweat and roasting meat, torches flaming on the walls and patterned rugs covering the floor. As I took a breath, a shadow fell across me, and I turned to see the figure of the king.

I reeled back in shock at the man before me. My mother

had described King Priam of the Trojans to me from the days of the battle they had fought together. She had told me of a well-mannered ruler, with dark curling hair and an easy smile. But the man before me stank of death. It hung around his hair, grey and lank at his ears, and in the white, haunted expression of his eyes, as if he were watching the spirits of the dead process through his halls. I glanced at Melanippe and Cayster, my warriors Harmothoe, Derinoe and Thermodosa to see if they had noticed, but their faces registered only interest as they gazed around the arch-ceilinged hall. Perhaps, I thought, no one but another ruler who had felt the death blows of each and every one of their own people like a strike to their own soul, as I had, could have seen it. It was worse than the grief of a father for his son – *if,* I thought, *there can be anything worse than that.* It was the grief of every Trojan father for every Trojan son, burdened on the sagging shoulders of this one king, this one man.

My heart went out to him as he held out his hand to me.

'Hippolyta,' he said, drawing me to him and pressing a kiss to my forehead with a tenderness that quite over-whelmed me, as if he was my own father, and I his daughter returned home from a far country. He took me by the shoulders, his hands gripping my tunic, and spoke in my ear. 'You and your troops are most timely. You find us here in Troy in dire need of your help. I would not admit it easily,' his voice quavered, 'but if you do not aid us, I do not dare think what will become of us.' His hands slid to his sides and hung there.

'My lord,' I said, leaning close to him, 'I will do anything – anything – to help you to the victory that is and shall be yours. My sword-arm and the arms of all my people, the finest warriors on all the black earth,' his eyes darted towards the band of warriors behind me, 'are yours to command. And with the Amazons fighting by your side you will win this war, my lord. I know it.'

He nodded to me and clasped my hand. 'May your words be an omen of good fortune to us, Queen Hippolyta.'

Then he drew back and announced to the room at large, 'Let us feast tonight, and toast to our victory tomorrow in battle over the Greeks!'

My Amazons drew their swords and battle-axes and shook them to the ceiling, glinting like bronze lightning-bolts, and the Trojan nobles, gathered around the hearth on stools and cushions, raised their goblets and echoed the refrain. These were a people in need of hope. *Perhaps*, I thought, *we have brought them some this night*.

Priam took me by the hand and led me towards the stone-carved thrones where he and the queen sat. At his direction I knelt at his feet as he took a two-handled golden goblet from the cupbearer and raised it to the heavens.

'Lord Zayu,' he said, into the silence that had fallen, 'may the Amazons' safe passage here be further proof of your favour to the Trojans. Gird their hearts and arms for battle on the plain, and grant them victory, Storm-bringer, as we grant you the fat of this sacrifice and the wine of this cup.'

I felt the wine splash the tiles before me, tasted the richness on my lips as the drops spattered my robes.

'And to you, Amazons,' Priam said, reaching for my hand and drawing me to my feet, 'I offer many gifts.' He snapped his fingers, and a line of slaves moved from the shadows towards me, bowing to the floor and laying costly tapestries, robes iridescent as the stars, plates of gold and thick ropes of jewels over the tiles. 'I pledge many more, if you bring us the victory over the Greeks that we desire.'

He turned then, as talk subsumed the hall once more, to introduce me to his family, who surrounded him, naming them one by one: Deiphobus, the pale youth who had fetched us, and Aeneas his brother; Hecuba, his queen; Andromache, widow of Hector, clutching their son Astyanax, her complexion dulled by grief, her eyes red, crouched on her stool.

'My son Paris,' Priam said, as he swept his long tunic beneath him to sit, and gestured to me to do the same, 'is not here. He seems to prefer the company of Helen of Sparta in his chambers, of whom, I do not doubt, you have heard much.'

Helen of Sparta. 'Helen.' I stared at him, the image of the young girl with the golden ringlets from Theseus' palace shimmering before me. 'Helen of Sparta? She is here?'

And then I realized: *The wife of Menelaus of Mycenae.*

'Indeed.' Priam inclined his head, his brow creasing. 'She is a guest here in the palace.'

His voice was composed, though Andromache's hissed intake of breath and Hecuba's swift reach for her hand, clutching at her robes, told me that not all of Priam's family were so forgiving. Helen lived, then. She had reached Sparta. And now she was here, in Troy, prey to another man, another captor – or perhaps, this time, she had loved him. I felt myself fill with pity for her, for the frightened child whom I had once comforted by the hearth of Theseus' palace. Perhaps, this time – I hoped it was so – she had left of her own accord.

My mind wandered along the winding corridors of the

palace to Paris's perfumed chambers, the bed where, even now, perhaps, the two lovers lay together in tangled sheets, their eyes dark in the lamplight, Helen's fingers tracing the hardness of his belly, his hands caressing her hair. Another pair of lovers, one Greek, one from the lands of the east. Another ship stealing into a foreign shore, heated glances, murmured words, the brief touch of a hand; another fumbled escape. Could I blame her? Would I have acted differently? Was I not Helen, too, by another name?

My thoughts were interrupted by a slave who bowed before me, offering a platter of bread and meat, a goblet of wine. I took them and returned to the conversation around me. Andromache and Hecuba were talking in low voices, fussing over the child; Priam was speaking with his sons of the war.

'. . . the ships,' Priam was saying. 'I have great hopes that, with the Amazon forces, we may break into the camp once more and torch the ships of the Greeks. If we take from them their means of escape . . .'

His eyes alighted on me with a question, and I answered it. 'My king, I swear to you, I will cast the brands on the ships and see them burn to the sky, if it will protect our people,' I said, my voice rising as the visions appeared before me. *Amazons riding out to battle, standards flying, roaring the war-cry and flattening the invading foreigners, like wild grass trampled beneath our hoofs.* 'This I promise: to lay low even the greatest of the Greeks, and to smite the wide host of the Argive men. I will bring back to you their stained battle-armour as your prize, and return to you your kingdom as reward for your loyalty and friendship to my mother and my people.'

Priam's eyes kindled bright with the flame of war, and now, as he sat on his throne, I saw again the warlord my mother had spoken of. Andromache, however, leant forwards to me across the body of her child. 'You are not half the warrior my husband was.' She spat the words at me like venom, and I recoiled at the look in her eyes – proud and broken and filled with horror.

'I did not claim to be so.'

'Then why boast that you would achieve the deeds he did not?' she cried. 'You insult his memory, you insult his family and his people, when you suggest that he was slain because he did not . . . that he could not . . .' Her voice faltered.

'You are not in your right mind to speak such words to one who would be your friend.' She leant back, her spine stiffening. 'But you should know this: I do not seek to defame your husband's reputation, only to finish the war he fought to defend his home – yours and mine both.'

'You will die,' she hissed. A frisson went around the circle of royal persons at the unlucky words, spoken like a prophecy, like a curse. Hecuba got to her feet, attempting to take Andromache's hand and draw her from the hall. But I waved a hand, and the queen stalled.

'You do not frighten me,' I said, holding Andromache's gaze, and her lip trembled. 'You are grieving, and you loved your husband. Both are to your credit. But I am an Amazon, born to rule, taught from my very earliest days to ride the swift horses of the plain, to put my trust in the strength of my sword-arm. I am here to aid you as a warrior and to ally with you as a queen. In neither of those, I think, would Prince Hector have opposed me.'

I pushed back my stool and stood, glad to have an excuse

to leave Andromache's forebodings and the stifling heat of the hall. 'My lord Priam,' I said, bowing to him, and I saw his eyes crinkle in return as he rose, buoyed by my self-assurance. 'My Amazons and I would gladly bathe and rest after our journey in preparation for tomorrow's battle.'

Ἀδμήτη

Admete

Troy, Anatolia

The Fourth Day of the Month of Ploughing, 1250 BC

I was pushed into a chair in Agamemnon's tent, nursing my hands, which were raw from pounding herbs, and glaring at Machaon, another healer of the Greeks, whose bloodshot eyes danced back at me in the lamplight.

'I would prefer—'

'Even the gods take rest,' he said. 'You have been of great service to us, daughter of Eurystheus, but now it is time for wine and good cheer. The sick and the wounded can wait until the morrow.'

He reeled away in search of drink, pushing past the lords who were crowded into the tent, leaning back on the carved chairs or reclining on cushions, raising their goblets to victory and shouting about their exploits in that day's battle, pulling up their tunics to display fresh wounds and taunting Thersites, a rat-faced man who stank of stale urine, for his cowardice.

I tried to get to my feet, choking on the stench of old

blood, unwashed bodies and putrid wine, blinking in the low light of the lamps and the embers of the fire where the carcass of what had once been a deer hung skeletal on a spit. This was not the battle I had thought it would be: heroes fighting hand to hand in glorious combat, bronze-shining warriors, tall and godlike, whose stories would be told down the ages. This was a mess of death, and there was no glory in the healers' hut where the soldiers groaned as they clutched at their wounds and cried for their wives and mothers. Agamemnon might host a feast to celebrate that day's battle. The men the Greeks now called heroes – Achilles, dousing himself in a pouch of wine till his hair dripped red, Diomedes and Ajax, laughing and duelling with their goblets over a half-naked slave girl, Odysseus, Nestor, Menelaus – might spend their strength there, wallowing in drink like pigs in a sty; but I would not be a part of it.

'I like it as little as you do.'

I turned. A young man had been standing in the shadows behind me, unnoticed, a lyre hanging from a strap at his side, his arms crossed over his chest. He stepped forwards and leant towards me. 'But you should hide your distaste. This is not a court that tolerates criticism of its ways.'

'And you know this . . . ?' I began.

He shrugged, his face slanted with shadows, and I noticed that his eyes were blind, filmed with white. 'I am but an itinerant bard, and a young one at that,' he said. 'I heard your protest against Machaon,' he explained, 'though I'd wager your expression is as good as a poem.'

'A bard? A singer of tales?' I glanced at him. 'But you do not sing tonight?'

357

'Not tonight,' he said. 'No warrior wishes to hear a story when he is busy telling his own, and it is the first duty of a poet to know his audience.'

I laughed for the first time in days.

'And why are you here, a woman?' he asked, shifting his weight on one leg. 'You know the craft of song, too?'

'Not song, no,' I said, reaching forwards to strum at the strings of the lyre at his side. They sounded with a sweet ring, barely audible over the shouts and laughs of the drunken lords. 'I am a healer, here to remedy the warriors' wounds as I can. I learnt the ways of plants in the court of my father Eurystheus, king of –'

'– Tiryns,' he finished for me. 'The names of the kings of Greece and their forebears have been my study since the Greeks came to Troy. You would marvel at how it enchants them to hear stories of their own people – as if they are transported in their minds and thoughts to Greece, though here they are so far from home.'

My gaze flicked to Menelaus, red-faced and sweating, his hair tied back. He was attempting to toss his goblet across the tent to Odysseus, and Diomedes launched himself over the table to catch it, knocking aside chairs and breaking a stool, roaring with laughter as he landed in a heap on the rugs. The smile faded from my lips.

'It is strange, do you not think,' I mused, my thoughts returning to those many years ago at the court of Lycus, when the bard had sung of Alcides' deeds, 'that warriors all want immortality – they long for it more than anything, saying it drives them to glorious deeds and death-dealing battle – yet when they have summoned the bard to sing their praises they ignore the poetry that would grant it to them,

358

that hands their names down the ages and allows them to live beyond the grave?'

A moment passed before he replied. 'Yes,' he said. 'Yes, it is strange. But perhaps,' he leant closer to me, 'they fear it too. I think they fear they might hear their own deaths told in song. It is a great gift, immortal glory,' he sighed, his expression distant as if he were seeing something I could not, 'but they know the cost of it, better than any other. There is no glory on the battlefield, when the edge of a sword is singing through the air and you hear the sigh of the river Styx in your ears. It is a poet's task to make it seem as if there is.'

And with that he walked away, leaving me looking after him, my mind filled with thoughts and my fingers playing with the stylus hanging at my girdle.

꧁ꠁꠅꠇꠊ꠵

Hippolyta

Troy, Anatolia

The Thirty-fifth Day after the Day of Fire in the Season of Tabiti, 1250 BC

I awoke the next day as rose light tinged the sky outside the window of the chamber in which the handmaids had laid my couch. Cayster, Melanippe and my warriors were placed in other rooms. I preferred to sleep alone, as I had always done; and that morning, of all mornings, I was glad to awake to my own thoughts.

For I had dreamt of my mother.

I had not dreamt of her in years. Yet last night, as the stars rolled in the heavens above me, she had appeared to me as clearly as if she had been standing there, as if I could have reached out and touched her. I tugged the covers to my chin as I sat up, the fleeces and blankets shifting beneath me, and gazed outside, such joy blazing through me that I could not help but smile.

She had urged me to defend my people. She had told me to fight fearlessly face to face with the Greeks. I had done

360

her bidding, by coming here. I had done right by her and my people.

I threw off the rug and leapt to my feet, feeling the polished wood cool beneath me, the chamber bathed in pale pink light. I moved to the chest on which I had placed my weapons and armour, gifts of Priam, eager to fit myself for battle. I slid the rich-patterned tunic over my arms, then bent on one knee to fit my boots and the greaves of hammered gold. I slipped on the breastplate and tied the buckles at my sides, then fastened my sword-belt beneath it with my trusted *sagaris* and dagger. The sword – another gift, set in a scabbard of ivory and silver, shining like the moon – I slung over my shoulder, and the helmet, with its shuddering crest of horsehair, I slotted onto my head, the metal enveloping my face soft as a caress. Last of all I caught up my shield, sickle-shaped, and two javelins, and in my right hand I took my bow. I turned towards the rising sun, now a glowing golden orb, and knelt, my head bowed, spears planted.

'Goddess,' I said, my voice low, speaking to the sun, 'grant me victory in battle today. Strengthen my sword-arm if it grows weak, and let me lay the Greeks low in defence of my people. Mother, watch over me with the ancestors, and give me your favour.'

I raised my bow to my lips and kissed it, eyes closed, tasting the beeswax polish sweet on my mouth.

A tap on the door caused me to start to my feet.

'Yes?'

The door was pushed ajar. A herald stood there, younger than Idaeus, his hair burnished auburn in the sunrise, his tunic ill-fitting and hanging loose on his sloping shoulders.

'My queen.' He knelt to the floor, his eyes downcast as if he could not look at me, shining gold in the sunlight. 'You are the very image of the war-goddess, no mortal woman, clad in such armour.'

'What news do you bring?' I asked him, gesturing to him to rise, and he stood, though still he spoke to his feet.

'No news, my lady,' he said, 'only a gift. A further token from King Priam of his gratitude that you fight with us, for Troy, and that we can count your sword-arm among our own.'

He fumbled in his tunic and then, from the folds, drew something that flashed golden, so bright I could barely look at it. I took it from him and moved towards the shade. At once its form materialized: an apple, pure gold, the skin stretched taut, and fine gold filaments for a stem – a work of such craftsmanship, such detail that I held my breath, wondering that such a thing could have been made by the hands of man. And then, as I turned it over in my fingers, I saw writing curling across its surface. Three words.

For the Immortal.

I laughed aloud, my spirits rising at this further portent of glory. The herald glanced up, and for a moment I thought I saw a laugh gleam across his face too.

'It is most beautiful,' I said to him, tossing the apple into my other hand, drawing open the thong of the leather pouch at my sword-belt and slipping it in. 'A lavish gift, and an oracle of the battle that is to come. Give my thanks to your lord, and my oath,' I raised my head, the crest on my helmet shaking as I smiled, 'that I shall not fail him this day.'

I left the palace with Cayster, Melanippe and my war-band as the sun's rays poured through the lower colonnades of the palace and the sky burnt blue. Deiphobus and his Trojan forces were gathered at the Scaean Gate to meet us, and the Amazon troops would join us on the plain. We left as a small guard, mounted on our horses, with Priam's prayers for our victory ringing in our ears. As I trotted forwards from the stables, my horse's hoofs sliding on the paving stones on the road towards the lower city, I felt a hand grip my reins and looked down.

Andromache was standing there, her feet bare, her arms empty of her son. She wore only her under-tunic, and her hair was dishevelled, as if she had run from her chambers, but in her hand she carried a dagger, unsheathed and sharp-tipped.

'Take me with you.'

Her voice was low, urgent. I glanced over at Melanippe, nodded, and signalled to the rest to go on. The sound of their hoofs clattered away as I slid from my mount.

'Andromache . . .'

'Take me with you,' she sobbed, her voice dry, cracked. 'I wish to come. I wish to fight. I need to do something.'

I bent forwards and rested my javelins and spear against a bush of boxwood growing in the palace gardens, then took her by the shoulders. 'Andromache, look at me.'

'No, you look at me!' she cried, and she raised her face to mine. I took in the red-rimmed eyes, aching with lack of sleep, the sagging mouth, the tears gathering on her lips and dripping from her chin. 'What have I left? I have borne every sorrow known to woman, my father killed, my brothers killed, and now my husband.' She took a great gasp of breath. 'I have lost my husband, who was father and mother and brother to me at once.' Her voice shook, and the tears quivered on her face. 'You are a woman, and you fight – why not I? Better by far to die in battle now than to watch my city and my husband's grave burn, and be taken as a slave to Greece.'

'I shall tell you why not,' I said. 'I have been taught to wield a weapon since before I could walk, and you have never once raised a blade against another in your life. And,' I said, gripping harder, my eyes boring into hers, 'you have an infant son who is helpless, who cannot defend himself, for whom you care more than anyone in this world, and you *will not* leave him behind.'

She wavered. Then she dropped to her knees, the blade clattering from her hand, her face in her palms, weeping and gasping, spit pouring from her mouth.

I moved to retrieve my weapons, and she flung her arms around my knees, her head tilted upwards.

'Avenge him, then,' she gasped. 'Avenge my husband for me, as I cannot.'

I bent forwards, took her head in my hands and kissed her forehead, overwhelmed with emotion. 'I will,' I said, clenching my jaw. 'I will protect all the people of the Trojan plain and beyond, if I can. I will do you justice on the battlefield.'

I joined the Amazon guard at the gates, cantering down the street towards the mass of Trojan troops gathered by the walls, bronze breastplates gleaming, their voices and stamping feet a low hum of noise against the chattering of the birds. I nodded to Melanippe that all was well and brought up my steed beside Cayster. He was bent forwards, checking the quiver that was slung over his horse's withers.

'Cayster,' I said, in a low voice. He looked well in his war-dress, there was no denying it, his hair covered with a glittering helmet, the eyes visible as narrow slits beside the nosepiece, his broad shoulders and well-muscled arms accentuated by the fitted breastplate. My heart wrenched within me, as it always did, to see my boy – the boy who, all those long years ago, had told me that he was glad I was returned from Greece – clothed in the raiments of war. My mouth was dry of a sudden, my throat swollen, and I found I could hardly speak.

'I cannot prevent you from fighting,' I said at last, 'neither as a queen, as an Amazon, nor as a mother.' I swallowed. 'But I beg you, Cayster, have a care on the battlefield, for my sake. Can you swear it to me?' My voice shook, and I reached a hand to brush his where it lay on the reins of his horse. 'Will you swear to keep yourself safe?'

'I swear to do as any Amazon does,' he said, his horse sidling beneath him, sensing his impatience, 'to fight with honour, to fell as many of the enemy as I can, and never to fail in strength or courage. I cannot promise more.'

I bowed my head, pressing his fingers between mine, the apprehension that still twisted in my stomach like a knot loosening somewhat. 'That is enough, then,' I said. 'I know I cannot ask more.'

I kicked my steed forwards to Melanippe and Deiphobus, the crowds of infantry parting before me with a clatter of spears and shields.

'All well?' I asked them, tightening my grip on the reins as my horse tossed its head.

Deiphobus bowed. 'We are ready to fight, my lady, if you are.'

I thought of my dream, my mother clothed in war urging me to fight, the portent of immortality brought to me by the herald that morning, and righteous battle-fury surged through me. I drew my sword from its sheath over my shoulders and held it glinting to the sky. My horse reared, pawing at the air, and the sunlight flashed from my blade. For a moment, all was quiet but for the swishing of bronze.

'Then let us ride!' I shouted, and sound came back to the world with a roar from the gathered troops and the creaking of the gates as they were hauled open. The war-trumpets sounded shrill, and the commanders were shouting orders to their troops. My eyes were on the plain that was opening up before us, an expanse of dust ploughed by the feet of a thousand warriors, and beyond it, just visible against the line of the sea, a rampart of wood and the beaks of ships.

The sense of destiny's hand at my back set me galloping, and I cried to my Amazons, *'Oiorpata!'*, and the guard followed me first out of the gates of Troy and onto the plain, hoofs pounding: Thermodosa to my left, Melanippe to my right, behind me Polemusa and Derinoe, then Cayster and Evandre, all urging their horses faster. And above all – above the pounding of my heart, the screaming of the war-cry and the thudding of my horse's hoofs over the hard earth – I heard Andromache's words ringing in my ears. *Avenge him. Avenge my husband . . .*

I saw, streaming from the coast, like a back-flowing river, the Amazon and Saka forces joining the Trojans behind us. Ahead, the warriors of the Greeks issued from the open gates of their camp, shields locked side by side in a wall of bronze.

I gritted my teeth. *'Oiorpata!'* I cried, and raised my sword, charging forwards, my horse's mane streaming, my vision white and clear.

And then the battle began.

My blade whirled over my head. Men were streaming around my horse's flanks, and I was slicing and cutting, holding the blade two-handed, felling warriors. At a pause in the onslaught, I drew my bow and aimed an arrow at a warrior charging towards one of my Amazons, then whirled around, brought my battle-axe from my belt and crashed it onto an infantryman's skull as he tried to swipe his sword at my horse. Moments seemed to slow to ages, as if I were truly immortal, as Príam's gift had proclaimed me, and, like a god invulnerable, I swept through the battle. *Parry with my shield, knock aside the blow of a spear – thrust my javelin into a Greek's shoulder, pushing down till the collarbones crack – turn, knock aside the sword of my attacker and plunge my blade between his ribs—*

The blood pounded in my ears, sweat trickled down my nose. To my left, I saw Clonie slay a son of Greece—

Slice with the sword-blade as I ride – draw the battle-axe and bring it down on the shield of the one who hides beneath it—

Time slid out of focus, hours passing with each breath. I could taste dust in my mouth, dry, and the iron tang of blood mixed with the stench of death. Derinoe was fighting a Greek, swords sparking as they clashed, her plait whirling behind her. She slipped, wrong-footed, and the Greek took up his spear and drove it hard between her hips. She shuddered at the impact of the blow, her mouth open, gasping. I screamed and hurled my spear at her attacker, catching his arm and sending him tumbling to the ground. I whirled around, searching for Cayster—

Recover the spear, cut with the sword, stab, ploughing down men beneath your horse's hoofs till no Greek dares come near you—

With a shudder of relief I caught sight of my son, side by side with Evandre and Thermodosa, their steeds plunging, their battle-axes swiping the air and cutting a swathe before them, like a ship's prow. Behind them the Trojans and their allies were pressing the Greeks back, piling corpses on the earth, and the Greeks were stumbling, some flinging their armour to the earth and fleeing, others sheltering on the ground beneath their shields. Horses were breaking free from chariots, snapping their reins and careering loose, eyes wide with terror as they darted through the battle, trampling the fallen Greeks. Men screamed with agony.

The wood ramparts of the Greek camp were close now, and as the Greeks stampeded to safety the gate was thick with warriors pushing to get through, some falling as arrows hailed down, others tripping and drowning beneath the mass of fighting bodies. I urged my horse forwards, blazing with war-fury and shouting, 'To the ships! Burn the ships!', and I heard the thunder of Amazon hoofs behind me.

And then I pulled up hard, my mount bucking and tossing his head.

I had seen five of my finest warriors – Antandre, Polemusa, Antibrote, Hippothoe, Harmothoe – fighting by the ramparts twenty paces distant, the battle clearing around them as they attacked and parried, their axes flashing. They circled a figure, a man, unhelmeted, his breastplate gleaming gold and his sword whirling among them, so quick I could barely see the blade, his fair hair whirling around his head. Though they outnumbered him, I watched as one after another he slew them, slicing till their lifeblood poured out onto the earth and they collapsed like dark poppies, bowing their heads in the rain.

I let out a cry, and he turned and saw me, seated high on my mount above the Trojan warriors.

Time stopped.

I could not breathe.

I could not move.

I could hear no sounds, though I was dimly aware of the screams and clamour of battle around me. I could see nothing, though I knew that figures ran before me, swords raised, parrying and blocking and thrusting, and horses cantered and shrieked, their manes swinging.

There were only his eyes – his black eyes, staring at me across the corpses littered between us – his flaxen hair, the stubble on his chin, no longer fair after all these years . . . Even the way he held himself, his chin set, his eyes narrowed, just the same . . .

'Achilles,' I whispered, half sobbing. It felt strange to say the name, after so long. *So long.* 'Achilles.'

It was the Greek.

I raised my hand, trembling, to lift my helmet.

And then I saw him raise his great ashen spear, and I gasped, 'No! *No!*'

And then a whistling through the air, and the spinning point of bronze arrowing towards me, and an explosion of pain above my right breast, so agonizing that all the breath gulped from my lungs and I arched back, my fingers loosening on the reins, my mind reeling at the shock that was lacing outwards from my shoulder. My vision blurred, and I had a dim sensation of wetness drenching my tunic. When I raised my hand to my shoulder it was dark with blood. Strength was draining from me: I could not hold my sword and felt it slip from my fingers, like the life that was leaking from me with my blood.

I could hear his voice dimly above the humming that was

filling my ears, shouting, vaunting as he ran towards me: 'And so the mighty warrior is slain! You thought you would see your home again, Trojan?'

My thighs could no longer grip the horse's sides, my hands would not move. I felt myself slide sideways, tumbling through the air, and then, with a shuddering jolt that drove the spear-point deeper into my ribs, I collapsed to the earth, gasping, my breathing shallow, tears pouring down my helmet into the dust.

Through the numbness, I felt pressure on the sides of my head, then blinked as the vault of the sky opened bright above me. Someone had removed my helmet. I saw, as if through a veil of mist, Achilles' face above me, his eyes locked on mine.

I heard his cry, felt it pierce my bones as his spear had done.

'Hippolyta.'

My name. He had said my name. I tried to speak his, as if it were a contract between us of all that we had done, and all that we had failed to do. But my lips were covered with spittle and my tongue would not move.

And then a tearing agony as he drew the spear from me and I felt myself lifted. I felt his arms around me, and I closed my eyes, letting the tears leak into his skin as he gathered me to him and the pain overtook me, so exquisite that it was almost more than my body could bear, stabbing and rending and tearing at my flesh as my weakening heart thudded the last moments of my life's blood.

'Hippolyta,' he whispered, and I saw his eyes dark above me through a haze, felt his tears mingle with mine on my face, 'Hippolyta.'

He was walking now, each step sending a jolt of pain

through my ribs, and I was dimly aware of the soldiers parting in the battle to allow Achilles and Hippolyta, the Greek and the Amazon, to pass. I shuddered a breath, felt the air tear through me, tried to move my lips again, but I could not. And then I smelt him: the scent of his sweat, branded on my mind, and a flood of memories overtook me with a force and vividness such as I had never dreamt.

His hand in mine, pulling me under the waves, laughing as the blue salt spray splashes us.

The heat of the sun searing my skin as he guides my hand on the lyre, the wind blowing from the east through my hair, and the sense of his skin as our fingertips touch on the string.

My back against the pine-bark, his body pressed against mine and the moon red above us.

And with that last rush of life I looked into his eyes and opened my mouth, and I said his name, and the name of our son.

And then I knew no more.

Ἀδμήτη

Admete

Troy, Anatolia

The Fifth Day of the Month of Ploughing, 1250 BC

I sank down on the ramparts where I had run to watch the battle, my hands clutching at my breast, nails digging into the skin, unable to believe what I had just seen.

Hippolyta.

Queen Hippolyta of the Amazons, who welcomed us to her camp so many years ago.

Hippolyta, who summoned me to her tent and called me her daughter, and told me of my mother, lying dead in the arms of Achilles.

I let out a low moan and closed my eyes, willing away the memory of Achilles' spear throw, the way the shaft had spun and then, with deadly accuracy, slashed through her. The way her body had shuddered, and her hands gripped at the reins; as if, even in dying, she would remain seated upright on her mount, a queen to the last.

I groaned again, shivers prickling my arms. With the impatience of one who longs more than anything to be proved wrong, I turned back towards the plain, taking hold of the wooden posts of the rampart and pulling myself to stand. *It cannot be true*. Perhaps my mind, feverish with the excitement of the battle, had taken another woman for Hippolyta – another woman who sat astride her horse with the assurance of a queen, who wielded a sword that flashed like fire, who led the Amazon warriors into battle with a proud war-cry on her lips . . .

And though in my heart I knew it could be no other, I forced myself to watch, to hope, until I had no other choice but to believe it.

The fighting had come to a standstill. Everyone, as I, was transfixed by the figure of Achilles walking across the battlefield towards the Greek camp with the dead Amazon queen in his arms, his breastplate stained with her blood. As he approached the gates the warriors stepped back to make a path for them, and I turned to see him pass beneath me, closer now, his head bowed over her and his face dark, though whether with fury or sorrow I could not tell. And then I caught sight of her face against his shoulder, and I gasped, and closed my eyes and opened them, like a child, hoping it was gone: because it was her, of course it was.

She looked beautiful in death, gorgeous as a goddess sleeping. Her brow, though stained with blood, was uncreased, and there was the faintest smile upon her lips as she seemed, still, to gaze upon Achilles. One arm was draped over Achilles' shoulder, and I saw a bracelet circling her wrist, knotted and tied at the back. Had she thought, when she tied it absent-mindedly, that she would never undo it? That when she pulled on those boots that morning she would never take them off? That her breastplate, dented by the impact of Achilles' spear, would be dragged off her limp body and taken as spoil?

I half thought, then, to run after her, into the midst of the warriors, and to take her body myself, though where I did not know. But even as the impulse spread through me I saw a man, the coward Thersites, accosting Achilles. I could not hear his words, though from his tone it seemed to be a kind of taunt. Achilles' roar of rage echoed over the camp, and then the *smack* as his fist met Thersites' jaw, dashing the teeth from his skull. I gasped aloud as he rolled forwards upon his face on the earth, a torrent of blood gushing from his face, moaning and shuddering.

And then I saw, just visible among the crowd of Greeks now swarming around Achilles and his charge, a man run through the gate carrying the glittering sceptre of a herald – a Trojan – no doubt soliciting Hippolyta's body for burial. I gripped my fists so tightly that the knuckles whitened, praying with all the strength I possessed that they would grant her this last, most important honour.

And yet, I thought, *would Achilles return such a prize?*

I was too far to hear more than raised voices and to see the gestures made by others in the crowd. I waited, breath held, watching as they conversed, the Greek lords gesticulating to each other, Achilles saying nothing as he listened to what the herald had to say.

And then, at last, he turned and sent one of his slaves running, returning with a two-horsed chariot. Achilles laid the body of Hippolyta in the chariot himself, and removed his own cloak, covering her with it. The Trojan herald leapt onto the chariot board and whipped the horses out of the gates and on to Troy.

I let out a breath and slid to the planks, my hand pressed to my forehead, my breathing fast.

'They did it,' I whispered. 'They released her to the Trojans. She will have a proper burial.' The words began to make sense as I said them. 'She will have that, at least.'

I stayed, unable to move, resounding with sorrow and shock. I had not expected so much of Achilles, whose terrible anger with Agamemnon had sent so many souls to their deaths. I watched, long after the crowd of Greeks had dispersed to drag back their dead and tend their wounded, as Achilles stood alone, gazing after the chariot, now nothing but a dustcloud halfway to Troy.

Then he turned back towards his hut, making his way over the sand to where a woman stood, her white tunic billowing in the breeze, by the doorpost, watching him. They did not exchange any words as he bent beneath the lintel and went inside.

Days passed before I could summon the courage to attend a feast in King Agamemnon's tent and hear him boast of Achilles' defeat of the Amazons, so it was with relief that I saw, as I entered the tent, the bard I had conversed with before, sitting in his same corner upon a stool. He was holding his lyre still on his lap, and his head was tilted towards the noble lords, gathered around a game of dice between Achilles and Ajax, laying bets, swigging wine from drinking-horns and clapping each other on the back. I moved towards him.

'You are not playing,' I said, drawing up a stool beside him, its legs catching on the rug.

He bowed his head. 'I am not. All I can play these past days is a lament to the fallen Amazon, and there is none here who would wish to hear it.'

My answer came at once. 'I would.'

He gave me a veiled smile. 'You are kind, daughter of Eurystheus, but I shall uproot myself and my lyre to Troy. The Trojans will have more need of me now, in their grief, than the Greeks in their victory.'

'But I have not yet heard you sing!'

He considered me. Then he said, 'The lament for the Amazon, then?'

I nodded.

He leant towards me, his fingers just brushing the strings, his voice a breath of sound as he played his song for me alone.

> *When early dawn appeared, rosy-fingered,*
> *the people gathered round the pyre of far-famed Hector.*
> *And taking the bones they placed them in a golden casket*
> *covered with downy purple robes,*
> *laying it in a hollow grave and piling*
> *stones over it, close-set;*
> *heaping up the tomb-mound thus they went back*
> *to feast in the halls of god-born Priam.*
> *And so they buried Hector; and then came the Amazon,*
> *the daughter of Ares, the great-hearted man-slayer . . .*

He stopped, and I felt the echo of the haunting notes resounding within me. His eyes downcast, he set the lyre across his lap. 'I cannot. Forgive me, daughter of Eurystheus, but my heart is sore grieved for the Trojans.'

I laid a hand over his. 'Then you should return to them,' I said. 'But it is a most beautiful song. It is sad that none other will have the pleasure of hearing it.'

'The nature of song,' he said, reaching into the shadows

for his pouch, which lay beside him, 'as of life: it is but fleeting.'

It is but fleeting . . .

Yet if only there were a way of capturing it.

And then, suddenly, it came to me. He had straightened and was turning aside, the lyre slung over his shoulder, when I placed a hand on his arm. 'Wait.'

I stood, my breath coming fast. 'Have you ever considered . . .' I took a breath, then started again. 'Have you ever written them?'

A crease appeared between his brows. 'Written what?'

'Your songs!'

The crease deepened. 'I am a singer, my lady. I do not write. My task is to sing the lays of legends past and the stories of our ancestors, to bring pleasure to those who listen. The scratching of the stylus,' he said, making as if to push past me towards the lords, gathered near the entrance to the tent, 'is for scribes, for the records of palaces, not the deeds of heroes. Each song is different from the next, for a new audience, a new occasion. They cannot be set down, like a list of bushels of wheat.'

'But it need not be so!' I barred his way, willing him to listen to me. 'I am trained in the art of writing for the recording of herbs. Here.' I turned, looking around me for something on which to write. When nothing presented itself, I bent to the stool he had been sitting on, untied my stylus from my girdle and scratched there a few words, in a stilted script.

'*And so,*' I read aloud, '*they buried Hector; and then came the Amazon, the daughter of Ares, the great-hearted man-slayer . . .*'

I looked at him, the words hanging on the air, waiting for him to complete them.

His expression was unreadable – between suspicion and disbelief. 'The words I sang to you – they are written there, for all to read?'

I nodded, and took his hand in mine, feeling the imprint of the lyre-strings on his fingers, tracing them over the lines scratched into the wood.

'Young man – I do not even know your name,' I laughed. 'I beg of you . . .' I looked at him more solemnly, the lamp-light casting his face and milky eyes in a strange glow. 'You are as grieved as I at the fate of the Amazon Hippolyta. I am the daughter of an Amazon, and I knew the Amazon queen once, many years ago. You are a bard, and I a scribe. Together we may make a story, a tale of heroes that will be told down the generations. Will you sing your lament, so that I may write it? So that I may take it back to Greece with me and share your song with my people?' I saw him waver, and added, 'So that the tale of the Amazon queen and the Trojans who fought by her side will never die?'

He hesitated. 'Song – in writing?'

'Our words,' I said. 'Only our words.'

And so it was that, several days later, on the shores of Troy in the camp of the Greeks, a Trojan bard and a daughter of Greece sat together on the sand, the sea-foam lapping at their feet, writing the tale of the Trojan War and Hippolyta, queen of the Amazons.

She would be immortal after all.

Epilogue

Calliope leans back with a smile, wondering. What comes next in Hippolyta's tale? What comes after immortality?

She pauses, still watching the bard on the Trojan shore, vaguely aware of the humming of the cicadas beyond the colonnade and the scent of the pines on the autumn breeze. Then she gets to her feet and moves away from the portico, her robes sweeping the marble floor.

At that moment a couple runs into the Hall of the Fates, the door clattering behind them, laughing and breathless. They are hanging on each other's arms, her hair disordered and her robe slipping from her shoulder, his wreath lopsided on his head from when he bent to kiss her, for all the world like a young couple newly wed.

Calliope smiles and walks across the hall to welcome them. 'You seem to have resolved your differences, then.'

Hera laughs and tilts her face up to Zeus, who plants a kiss full on her mouth. 'What, that?' she asks, giggling. 'Oh, we made up ages ago, didn't we, Zeus?'

He chuckles and pulls her closer to him. 'Around the time you seduced me on the slopes of Mount Ida to get Achilles back into the war, I'd say.'

She slaps his chest. 'You know that wasn't the only reason.'

'I didn't say I was complaining.' He turns aside to Calliope and says, in a mock whisper, 'She's been in such a good mood since Hector's death that we've barely had time to watch the war.'

Hera nudges him in the ribs. 'Zeus!'

'So,' Zeus says, striding over to the colonnade where Calliope was seated a few moments earlier, 'how is the epic coming along?'

The vault of the sky is blue, endless blue, as the three gods stand at the colonnade's edge, the rock of Olympus dropping away beneath them, high as eagles perched in their nest, gazing out towards Troy. Calliope shrugs her shoulders. 'You'll have to ask the bards. Although,' her glance shifts towards the Greek camp, 'it may not be they who make the stories for much longer.'

As she watches, she notices a ship ploughing the sea from the Trojan harbour, heading west through the jaws of the Hellespont. Admete returns, then, to Tiryns. It was the ending Calliope had hoped for. A smile creeps across her face, and hope, an unquenchable joy, as she thinks of the bard plucking the song to the hollow lyre and Admete inscribing it on her tablets, now stored in the ship's hold and winging their way back to Greece. Her imagination stretches to the years to come: scribes brushing on papyrus, copyists aching over their manuscripts in the guttering candlelight, and ink-fingered printers setting the type as they send the poems further and further over the land of the mortals, across time even, a never-ending song of glory to the gods . . .

'An epic of Hercules,' Hera says, her mouth twisting in distaste. 'I cannot say I am overjoyed.'

'Oh, no.' Calliope stretches out a hand to reassure her. 'Not Hercules – did I not tell you?'

'Not Hercules?' Hera asks. 'What do you mean?'

Epilogue

Calliope shakes her head. 'I thought it would be Hercules. But it turned out it was Hippolyta it was meant for, after all.'

Hera gleams a smile at her. 'Well – I'm glad to hear it.'

The couple wander off, arm in arm, to stroll around the garden of the Muses and – perhaps – to find one of its more private corners. Calliope stands alone a little longer, her hands clasped behind her back. How strange, she thinks, that she stood here, fifteen years ago – or was it a day? – at the dawn of the age of heroes, thinking she would take refuge from Hera in the forests of the earth's edge, that she would wait until the moment was right to tell the tale of Hercules. And in the end it was Hippolyta to whom she had given the apple of gold, disguising herself as a Trojan herald on the morning of that fateful battle. Hippolyta, whose name would go down the ages, in the words of Admete.

Her eyes are caught by a spiral of blue smoke curling to heaven from Troy. Hippolyta's burial, of course. The Trojans have built a funeral pyre outside the city walls. The queen is laid upon it, still wearing her battle-armour but helmetless now, her dark hair plaited over one shoulder, her hands resting on her chest holding the hilt of her sword, her eyes closed as if in sleep. Golden shields, ashwood spears, vases of beaten silver – all are placed around her, in tribute to her royal birth. But they do not know the greatest treasure of all, kept in the pouch that still hangs at Hippolyta's belt.

Calliope lets out a sigh and closes her eyes, inhaling the scent of perfumed oil and incense from the flames as they lick higher. And as she turns away, with a strange hollowness in her chest and an ache in her throat, unable to watch more, she thinks that at least, at the very least, she can ensure that mortals all over the dark-soiled earth will tell the tales of the immortal heroes through the ages . . .

. . . and also, the heroines.

Author's Note

This book differs from the first two in the Golden Apple trilogy, *For the Most Beautiful* and *For the Winner*, in that it has its origins in an epic poem which has not survived to the present day. Many people are not aware that the two most famous archaic Greek epics – the *Iliad*, the tale of the Trojan War, and the *Odyssey*, the story of Odysseus' return – were not, in fact, the only epics circulating at the time. The *Iliad* and the *Odyssey* were two of many epic poems, known collectively as the Epic Cycle, which are now lost to us. We know some of their titles, and a little of their subject matter, from a late Roman scholar known as Proclus who recorded the titles and a brief summary for us.

Among these is the *Aethiopis*, the 'sequel' to Homer's *Iliad* and supposedly composed by Arctinus of Miletus. Picking up from the end of the *Iliad* with Hector's burial, Proclus tells us that it began by describing how 'the Amazon Penthesilea, daughter of Ares, arrives to fight as an ally with the Trojans . . . And Achilles kills her as she excels in the fight, and the Trojans bury her'.[1] Even more suggestively,

---

[1] All translations are my own.

one eleventh-century CE manuscript of Homer's *Iliad*, now held at the British Library, contains a comment written in the margins suggesting that the first line of the *Aethiopis* – the arrival of the Amazons at Troy – actually continued directly after the last of the *Iliad*:[2]

> And so they buried Hector; and then came the Amazon,
> the daughter of Ares, the great-hearted man-slayer . . .[3]

This idea of continuation, a sort of 'call-and-response' between the epics of archaic Greece, points to another important feature of early Greek epic in which I am particularly interested: orality. My research as a classicist focuses in part on the history of the early Greek epics – the recent discovery of features of oral tale-telling embedded in the Homeric poems, pointing to a long history of retelling and re-performance by singing bards, long before they were written down.

This, then, suggests a much more complicated picture of archaic Greek epic than that to which most of us are accustomed. Instead of thinking of the two mammoth (and fixed) Homeric epics, the *Iliad* and the *Odyssey*, we need instead to think of a complex interweaving of spoken stories, some picking up from where the others left off, exchanging ideas, phrases, tropes and motifs, all told orally over many generations until – at some point – two of the tales were recorded in writing and survived for us to read.

So, this book is as much a search for a lost epic as anything

---

[2] Burney MS 86, known as the Townley Homer.
[3] Arctinus, *Aethiopis* fr. 2; scholiast on *Iliad* 24.804, Schol. (T) Il. 24.804a.

else. Rather than following (and responding to) a literary text, it is based on a conglomeration of different myths from all sorts of sources, from the poems of Homer in the eighth century BCE, to the retelling of the story of Penthesilea by Quintus of Smyrna (late fourth century CE), to the scholarship of the Byzantine grammarian John Tzetzes in the twelfth century CE, to recent discoveries of Scythian graves in modern-day Ukraine and Russia – all in an attempt to re-envisage the lost epics of archaic Greece, and the *Aethiopis* in particular, the opening line of which has been so tantalizingly preserved for us.

As such, given the huge variety of the sources drawn on here and their likely general unfamiliarity, I will go into greater length here to describe the historical background of *For the Immortal*. (See also Suggestions for Further Reading, pages 392–4.)

To begin with the Amazons. From a Greek perspective (and, as a classicist, this is where I always begin), the Amazons first appear in Greek literature in Homer's *Iliad*, where they are described as *antianeirai* – a difficult word, which (depending on your interpretative slant) can mean either 'opponents of men' or 'equivalents of men'. The Amazons continue to appear in Greek history, myth and art from then on, as a kind of counterfactual to the Greeks – an all-female, martial, 'barbaric' society in counterpoint to which Greek men could define themselves. One of our most important literary sources is the Greek historian Herodotus (writing in the fifth century BCE), who devotes a section of his *Histories* to an ethnography of the Scythians; Diodorus of Sicily, Strabo, Pliny the Elder, Justin and Orosius all provide additional helpful accounts.[4] The Greeks envisaged the Amazons as a band of women fighters, living at the mythical eastern edge of the world, who rode on horseback and fought with bows and arrows. They were said to live without men, and (so it was said) had sex purely for the purposes of procreation, exposing any male children to die. Amazons also appear on vase paintings in archaic and classical Greece, depicted in their trademark outfit of patterned trousers, tunic and felt cap.

Throughout these Greek accounts, the stories of three Amazon queens – and sisters – emerge particularly vividly, each focused around their interactions with a different Greek hero. Their names: Hippolyta, Antiope, and Penthesilea. Hippolyta was said to be queen of the Amazons, and it was her war-belt that Hercules was sent to claim as one of his labours. Antiope, her sister, was captured by Theseus, king of Athens, during Hercules' raid on the Amazon camp and was taken to Athens, to be rescued by the Amazons in a battle that formed one of the early myths of the city. And Penthesilea led the Amazon troops to Troy against the Greeks, and was struck and killed by Achilles, who – so it was said – fell in love with her at the moment their eyes met. (A later Byzantine tradition, which I have followed here, has

---

[4] Other ancient sources referred to in this book include: Aeschylus, *Eumenides*; Apollodorus, *Bibliotheca* and *Epitome*; Apollonius, *Argonautica*; Arctinus, *Aethiopis*; Dictys Cretensis, *Chronicles*; Diodorus Siculus, *Bibliotheca Historica*; Euripides, *Hercules Furens*; Hellanikos, FGrH 4 F 149; Herodotus, *Histories*; Hippocrates, *De Aeribus Aquis Locis* and *De Morbis Popularibus*; Homer, *Iliad* and *Odyssey*; Hyginus, *Fabulae*; Justin, *Epitome*; Nonnus, *Dionysiaca*; Orosius, *Historiae*; Ovid, *Heroides*; Pausanias, Description of Greece; Pliny, *Historia Naturalis*; Pindar, *Carmina*; Plutarch, *Vita Thesei*; Polyaenus, *Strategmata*; Proclus, *Chrestomathia*; Propertius, *Elegiae*; Quintus Smyrnaeus, *Posthomerica*; Statius, *Achilleid*; Strabo, *Geographica*; Theophrastus, *Historia Plantarum*; John Tzetzes, *Scholia in Lycophronem*, *Chiliades*, and *Posthomerica*.

Achilles and Penthesilea meeting before the Trojan War
and having a son together, Cayster.)

As with Briseis and Chryseis in the post-Homeric tradition, however, their names were often confused. To give the
most well-known example, Shakespeare in *A Midsummer
Night's Dream* (1595/6) has Hippolyta, instead of Antiope, as
Theseus' wife.[5] Even in antiquity, however, there was confusion over the names and identities of the Amazon sisters.
The historian Plutarch cites Simonides and Clidemus, who
apparently named Hippolyta as Theseus' wife; the Byzantine
scholar John Tzetzes is emphatic in asserting that it was
Antiope, not Hippolyta, who was stolen by Theseus. To me,
this is a signal of not only the importance, but also the flexi-
bility and interpenetrability of these myths – and led me to
merge the figures of the three sisters into one, Hippolyta,
who, through Shakespeare, became the best-known Amazon
in the post-classical tradition. The three sections of the
novel – *Amazon*, *Greek* and *Immortal* – can thus also be read
as the stories of the three Amazon sisters: Hippolyta in *Amazon*; Antiope in *Greek*; and Penthesilea in *Immortal*.

So much for the literary tradition of the Amazons. But I
was also keen to make my Amazons as historically accurate
as possible, and that meant delving into the archaeological

---

[5] This is probably derived from William Painter's 'Novel of the Amazones,'
which begins Book 2 of *The Palace of Pleasure* (1575): 'but Theseus for no offer
that she coulde make, woulde he deliver Hippolyta, with whom he was so
farre in love, that he carried her home with him, and afterward toke her to
wyfe, of whom hee had a sonne calle Hipolitus' (*The Palace of Pleasure* 2.163).
It is perhaps also traceable to Plutarch's *Vita Thesei* 27, which Shakespeare
would have read in North's translation (Plutarch, *The Lives of the Noble Gre-
cians and Romanes*, trans. Thomas North (1579): *The Tudor Translations*,
2 vols. (1895; rpt., New York, 1967), vol. 1, p. 116).

evidence. Adrienne Mayor's outstanding book, *The Amazons: Lives and Legends of Warrior Women across the Ancient World* (Princeton: Princeton University Press, 2014), was my constant companion and guide in this respect, as was the catalogue to the British Museum's recent acclaimed *Scythians* exhibition (Hippolyta's war-belt, as well as other artefacts, are based on Scythian finds displayed there). Mayor describes how recent archaeological excavations across the Eurasian steppe have shed light on ancient cultures that seem to correspond to the Amazons. Skeletons have been excavated from *kurgans* (burial mounds) across the steppes, buried with weapons, armour, and sometimes even horses – and analysis with modern bio-archaeological techniques has demonstrated that, in Mayor's words, 'armed females represent as many as 37 percent of the burials' (Mayor 2014: 63). This is extraordinary evidence of a nomadic, horse-riding culture to the north and east of the Black Sea where women could fight as well as men – and provides an insight into both the truths and the prejudices revealed by the Greek myth of the Amazons. My depiction of the world of the Amazons in this book is as close to the world of the Scythian nomadic tribes discovered in archaeological excavations and described in Mayor as I could make it, combined with the ethnographic descriptions of the Scythians in Herodotus: from the armour and weapons they used, to the clothes they wore, the food they ate, their customs, religion, language and names. (For more information on the Amazons' names, see the Glossary of Characters, pages 397–407.)

A brief word on the Scythian language. The symbols that precede Hippolyta's scenes in this book are something of an anachronism as there is no evidence for a written Scythian language. The few words we do know – and which are included in this book – come mostly from Herodotus, quoted and transliterated in Greek, from which we can assume that Scythian was an ancient north Iranian language. (A useful example is Herodotus' explication of the word *oiorpata*, used here as a battle-cry: 'the Scythians call the Amazons *Oiorpata*, which could be translated in Greek as "man-killers"; for *oior* means "man" and *pata* "to kill"', Hdt. 4.110.) In a nod to this heritage, I have used the cuneiform script of old Persian – one of two attested Old Iranian languages to have left inscriptional evidence, though from a much later period than the Bronze Age treated in this book – to transliterate Hippolyta's name (the cuneiform literally reads *ha-i-pa-la-u-ta-a*, which is closest to the Greek *Hippolutē*). Throughout the novel I have kept both Greek and Scythian terms where both are attested: thus, for example, Hippolyta calls the Scythians *Saka*, a word attested in the Persian Behistun Inscription, while Admete uses the Greek Scythian or *Skythos*. You will find both terms included in the Glossary of Characters (pages 397–407) and Places (pages 408–15). On the subject of names, readers will notice that I have chosen to use the Latinized version of Hercules' name (Greek: *Herakles*) (as well as the patronymic Alcides, which Apollodorus tells us was Hercules' name before he completed his labours). This is consistent with the spellings I have used elsewhere in the trilogy – for example, Latin *Achilles* instead of Greek *Achilleus*, Latin *Hecuba* instead of Greek *Hekabe* and so on.

As for Admete and the voyage for the war-belt of Hippolyta: the evidence for Admete's request for the war-belt and her accompaniment of Hercules come from two different sources, the first or second century CE mythographer Apollodorus, and the Byzantine scholar John Tzetzes, who suggests that 'Admete, daughter of Eurystheus, wanted to have Hippolyta's war-belt; and she voyaged in a ship with Hercules, Theseus and the rest' to retrieve it. The additional story of Admete's mother as an Amazon is my invention, though suggested to me by the record of Eurystheus' wife's name as Antimache (' fighter-against'), an attested Amazon name. The ancient sources claim that Admete wanted the war-belt as a source of power – but this seemed to me a typically 'masculine' interpretation. When I delved into the myth, the theme of motherhood clearly resonates around the war-belt, which was a gift from Hippolyta's mother – and thus a symbol both of motherhood, lineage/heredity, and the paradox (from a Greek point of view) of a female fighter. It was from this starting-point that I began to imagine Admete's search for her mother and her identity as an Amazon, and a woman, within a very male world.

The story of Hercules' labours, and the jealousy of Hera after Zeus' affair with the mortal Alcmene, is one of the best-known legends of ancient Greece and hardly needs introduction. Hercules, son of a god and destined for immortality, stood in the ancient world for everything that was masculine, larger-than-life, heroic – and so it was his lesser-known relationship with Admete that intrigued me, hinted at in Apollodorus' and Tzetzes' story of her voyage with him to the Amazons, bringing out as it does a different side to Hercules' character and his relationship with the king of Tiryns who set his labours. Moreover, the question of how – and why – a woman in Bronze Age Greece would have been allowed to give one of the tasks to the archetypal male hero, let alone accompany him, was, I felt, one that needed to be addressed, and provides a fascinating new perspective on the possible roles of women in the Bronze Age Aegean. My description of Admete's journey with Hercules to the Amazons is based almost entirely on Apollodorus' description of Hercules' labour in his *Bibliotheca*, although some of the scenes – for example, the battle with the Bebryces – are adapted from another similar voyage, the journey of Jason and the Argonauts as given in Apollonius' *Argonautica*. The tradition of Hercules receiving an oracle at Delphi, telling him that he would be granted immortality if he completed his labours, comes from Apollodorus and Diodorus Siculus.

There is little evidence for the practice of medicine and healing in the Bronze Age Aegean, so in order to describe Admete's work as a healer I drew on both recent pathological evidence from excavations in Greece, the evidence of Linear B tablets, votive prophylactic offerings left at the sanctuaries of the gods, later classical works such as Theophrastus' *Enquiry into Plants* (the earliest known and most important systematic botanical work to have survived from classical antiquity) and the Hippocratic corpus, and a cross-referencing of herbal cures (using Andrew Chevallier's comprehensive *Encyclopedia of Herbal Medicine*) with plants native to Greece. Some of the more interesting examples include yarrow, whose Latin name *Achillea millefolium* reveals its (supposed) use by Achilles in the Trojan War; saffron (*ko-ro-ki-no*), which is listed on a Linear B tablet from Knossos, Crete; and elecampane or *Inula helenium*, which was said to be the plant Helen of Sparta held in her hand as she left with Paris for Troy.

If you are interested in finding out more about the world of Admete, Hercules and the Amazons, take a look at the suggestions for further reading (pages 392–4), and visit my website, www.emilyhauser.com.

Suggestions for Further Reading

Arnott, Robert. 1996. 'Healing and medicine in the Aegean Bronze Age.' *Journal of the Royal Society of Medicine* 89: 265–70.

Ascherson, Neal. 1995. *Black Sea*. London: Jonathan Cape.

Cope, Tim. 2013. *On the Trail of Genghis Khan: An Epic Journey through the Land of the Nomads*. London: Bloomsbury.

Davies, Malcolm. 2016. *The Aethiopis: Neo-Neoanalysis Reanalyzed*. Hellenic Studies, 71. Washington, DC: Center for Hellenic Studies.

Diker, Selahi. 1999. 'Scythians and their Language.' In *And the Whole Earth was of One Language: Decipherment of Lost Languages including Etruscan, Scythian, Phrygian, Lycian, Hittite, Hurrian, Urartian, Sumerian, Achaemenid Aramaic & Elamite, Parthian*. 2nd ed. Izmir: S. Diker, 155–88.

Graziosi, Barbara. 2002. *Inventing Homer: The Early Reception of Epic*. Cambridge: Cambridge University Press.

Grmek, M. D. 1994. 'Malaria in the eastern Mediterranean in prehistory and antiquity.' *Parasitologia* 36 (1–2): 1–6.

Hall, Edith. 2004. *Inventing the Barbarian: Greek Self-Definition through Tragedy*. Oxford: Clarendon Press.

Hartog, François. 1988. *The Mirror of Herodotus: The Representation of the Other in the Writing of History*. Transl. Janet Lloyd. Berkeley, Los Angeles, London: University of California Press.

Hughes, Bettany. 2005. *Helen of Troy: Goddess, Princess, Whore*. London: Jonathan Cape.

Jensen, Minna Skafte. 2011. *Writing Homer: A Study Based on Results from Modern Fieldwork*. Copenhagen: The Royal Danish Academy of Sciences and Letters.

Lord, Albert. 2000. *The Singer of Tales*. Edited by Stephen Mitchell and Gregory Nagy. 2nd ed. Cambridge, MA: Harvard University Press.

Man, John. 2017. *Amazons: The Real Warrior Women of the Ancient World*. London: Transworld.

Mayor, Adrienne. 2014. *The Amazons: Lives and Legends of Warrior Women across the Ancient World*. Princeton: Princeton University Press.

— 2016. 'Warrior Women: The Archaeology of the Amazons.' In S. L. Budin and J. M. Turfa (eds.), *Women in Antiquity: Real Women across the Ancient World*, 969–85. London: Routledge.

Minns, E. H. 1913. *Scythians and Greeks*. Cambridge: Cambridge University Press.

Nagy, Gregory. 1996. *Poetry as Performance: Homer and Beyond*. Cambridge: Cambridge University Press.

Rolle, Renate. 1989. *The World of the Scythians*. Berkeley: University of California Press.

Romm, J. 1992. *The Edges of the Earth in Ancient Thought: Geography, Exploration and Fiction*. Princeton: Princeton University Press.

Rostovtzeff, Michael. 1922. *Iranians and Greeks in South Russia*. Oxford: Oxford University Press.

Sallares, R., A. Bouwman, and C. Anderung. 2004. 'The Spread of Malaria to Southern Europe in Antiquity: New Approaches to Old Problems.' *Medical History* 48(3): 311–328.

Simpson, S.J., and S. Pankova, eds. 2017. *Scythians: Warriors of Ancient Siberia*. London: Thames and Hudson.

Skjaervo, P. Oktor. 2002. *An Introduction to Old Persian*. 2nd ed. Online resource http://sites.fas.harvard.edu/~iranian/OldPersion/opcomplete.pdf.

Smith, William. 1854. *Dictionary of Greek and Roman Geography*. London: Walton and Maberly.

Talbert, R. J. (ed.) 2000. *The Barrington Atlas of the Greek and Roman World*. Princeton: Princeton University Press.

Warren, C. P. W. 1970. 'Some aspects of medicine in the Greek Bronze Age.' *Medical History* 14 (4): 364–77.

West, M. L. 2011. *The Making of the Iliad: Disquisition and Analytical Commentary*. Oxford: Oxford University Press.

West, Stephanie. 2002. 'Scythians.' In E. J. Bakker, I. Jong and H. Wees (eds.), *Brill's Companion to Herodotus*. Leiden: Brill, 437–56.

Willekes, Carolyn. 2016. *The Horse in the Ancient World: From Bucephalus to the Hippodrome*. Library of Classical Studies, 10. London: I. B. Tauris.

Bronze Age Calendar

The evidence from ancient Mycenaean Greek tablets for the calendar is fragmentary and difficult to piece together, but various different words have been found that seem to apply to months of the year. Thus we have *wodewijo* – the 'month of roses'; *emesijo* – the 'month of wheat'; *metuwo newo* – the 'month of new wine'; *ploistos* – the 'sailing month'; and so on. Although we have no further clues as to which months these referred to, by matching them to the farming calendar in Hesiod's *Works and Days*, as well as the seasonal growth of plants and crops in Greece, I have amassed the following Bronze Age calendar, which is followed throughout the text:

dios	The Month of Zeus	January
metuwo newo	The Month of New Wine	February
deukijo	The Month of Sweet Wine	March
ploistos	The Month of Sailing	April
amakoto(s)	The Month of the Harvest	May
wodewijo	The Month of Roses	June
emesijo	The Month of Threshing Wheat	July

amakoto(s)	The Month of the Grape Harvest	August
...	The Month of Ploughing	September
lapatos	The Month of Rains	October
karaerijo	...	November
diwijo	The Month of the Goddess	December

As for the Scythians, no evidence survives regarding their calendar, although Herodotus' description of the Scythians' certainty that no more or less than a thousand years had passed from the reign of their first king to the arrival of Darius in 513 BC (*Histories* 4.7.1) suggests that they did have a means of measuring and dating the passage of years. According to the seasonal movements of Scythian nomads described in Adrienne Mayor's *The Amazons* (2014: 130), I have accordingly split the calendar year into three seasons – spring, summer and winter – and attributed to each a presiding Scythian god: Apia, goddess of earth, for the fertile season of spring; Tabiti, goddess of fire, for the hot seasons of summer and autumn; and Tar, god of sky and weather, for the cold and stormy winter months. Within each season, I have placed a mid-winter/mid-summer/mid-spring festival at the mid-way point of the season (see below), each named 'The Day of Earth' (spring), 'The Day of Fire' (summer), and 'The Day of Storms' (winter) after their respective gods. Dates are then counted either towards or away from the mid-point of the season.

The Season of Apia	1 Feb–31 May	(mid: 1 Apr; 'Day of Earth')	Spring
The Season of Tabiti	1 June–30 Sept	(mid: 1 Aug; 'Day of Fire')	Summer
The Season of Tar	1 Oct–31 Jan	(mid: 1 Dec; 'Day of Storms')	Winter

Glossary of Characters

Most of the characters in this book come from the real myths, legends and literature of the ancient Greeks; names of the Amazons are either from classical sources (mostly Greek) or are attested Scythian names. Mortals are indicated in **bold**, and immortals in ***bold italics***. Characters I have invented for the purposes of this story are marked with a star (*).

Achilles – The son of Thetis and Peleus, Achilles is the greatest warrior to fight on the Greek side against Troy in the Trojan War. His mother, Thetis, fearing his death in the war, attempted to hide him when he was young on the island of Skyros, but he was discovered by Odysseus and went to Troy.

Admete – Daughter of Eurystheus, king of Tiryns, and Antimache. The name means 'unwedded, unbroken' in Greek.

Aella – One of Hippolyta's band of fighters. Attested Amazon name (in Greek); means 'whirlwind'.

Agamemnon – King of the Greeks and ruler of Mycenae, Agamemnon leads the expedition against Troy with his brother Menelaus.

*Agar – Amazon councillor. Attested Scythian name.

Aigle – The eldest of the Hesperides, guardians of the golden apples. The name means 'light, radiance'.

Ajax – One of the Greek warriors and lord of Salamis.

Alcides – The name of Hercules before he was granted the title for completing his labours; it is a patronymic (derived from his father's name), in this case from his grandfather Alcaeus, through his step-father Amphitryon.

Alcmene – Wife of Amphitryon of Thebes and mother of Hercules by Zeus, who appeared to her in the guise of her husband.

Alexander – Son and heir of Eurystheus, king of Tiryns, and eldest brother of Admete; the names of Eurystheus' sons are attested in Apollodorus.

Amphitryon – Step-father of Hercules and husband of Alcmene, Hercules' mother.

Amycus – King of the Bebryces and adversary of Lycus, king of the Mariandyni.

Andromache – Princess of Thebe and daughter of King Eëtion, later wife of Hector. After the fall of Troy, she is taken prisoner by the Greeks and becomes a concubine of Achilles' son, Neoptolemus.

Antandre – One of the band of twelve Amazons to accompany Hippolyta to Troy. Attested Amazon name (in Greek); means 'instead of/against men'.

Antibrote – One of the band of twelve Amazons to accompany Hippolyta to Troy. Attested Amazon name (in Greek); means 'instead of/against men'.

Antimache – Wife of King Eurystheus of Tiryns and mother of Admete; her name is given in Apollodorus.

Aphrodite – Goddess of love and sex, and winner of the golden apple in the Judgment of Paris.

Apia – Scythian goddess of Earth (equivalent to Greek *Gaia*), given in Herodotus.

Apollo – God of archery, medicine and healing, the sun, prophecy and poetry. *Paeon* was an epithet given to Apollo to describe him in his role as god of healing.

Ares – The god of war.

*Arga** – Daughter of Iphito. Attested Scythian name.

Artemis – Goddess of hunting, the moon, childbirth and virginity; twin sister of Apollo.

Asteria – One of Hippolyta's band of fighters. Attested Amazon name (in Greek); means 'star'.

Athena – Goddess of wisdom and war; founder and patron goddess of Athens.

Atlas – Leader of the Titan gods, who bore the sky on his shoulders; father of the Hesperides.

Budini, the – An ancient Scythian tribe located by Herodotus north and east of the Tanais river (Scyth. Silis, modern Don), said to be a powerful nation characterized by their red hair and blue eyes.

Calliope – Muse of epic.

Cassandra – Daughter of King Priam and Queen Hecuba of Troy.

Cayster – Son of Hippolyta and Achilles; traditionally the son of Penthesilea.

Clio – Muse of history.

Clonie – One of the band of twelve Amazons to accompany Hippolyta to Troy. Attested Amazon name (in Greek).

Deianeira – One of Hippolyta's band of fighters. Attested Amazon name (in Greek); means 'man-destroyer'.

Deiphobus – The second of King Priam's sons, and husband of Helen after Paris dies.

Derinoe – One of the band of twelve Amazons to accompany Hippolyta to Troy. Attested Amazon name (in Greek).

Diomedes – One of the Greek heroes and lord of Argos.

*****Elais** – Greek priest-healer. Attested Greek name.

Erato – Muse of love poetry.

Euneos – Brother of Solois and Thoas of Athens. Companion of Hercules on the voyage for the war-belt of Hippolyta.

Eurybius – Son of Eurystheus, king of Tiryns, and brother of Admete; the names of Eurystheus' sons are attested in Apollodorus.

Eurystheus – King of Tiryns and father of Admete; sets the twelve labours for Hercules.

Euterpe – Muse of song and lyric poetry.

Evandre – One of the band of twelve Amazons to accompany Hippolyta to Troy. Attested Amazon name (in Greek); means 'brave, prosperous'.

Fates, the – Three goddesses whose task was to spin the thread of human life.

Harmothoe – One of the band of twelve Amazons to accompany Hippolyta to Troy. Attested Amazon name (in Greek).

Hector – Eldest son of King Priam of Troy and husband of Andromache.

Hecuba – Wife of King Priam of Troy and mother of Hector, Deiphobus, Aeneas, Paris, Troilus and Cassandra.

Helen – Daughter of Zeus and Leda; her step-father is Tyndareus of Sparta. Originally Helen of Sparta, she becomes Helen of Troy after she departs for Troy with Paris, prince of Troy, thus setting in motion the events of the Trojan War.

Hephaestus – The lame craftsman god and husband of Aphrodite.

Hera – Queen of the gods and wife of Zeus, Hera is angered with Hercules as Zeus' son by the mortal woman Alcmene. Goddess of marriage and childbirth.

Hercules – Son of Zeus and Alcmene, and hero of the twelve labours; his step-father is Amphitryon of Thebes. The name (Heracles) means 'glory of Hera' in Greek.

Hermes – The son of Zeus and Maia, Hermes is the messenger god and god of tricks and thievery.

Hesperides, the – Daughters of Atlas and Evening (Hesperis), these three nymphs dwell in their garden at the edge of the world tending the mythical golden apples.

Hialeans, the – *see* Glossary of Places s.v. **Hylaea**

Hippolyta – Queen of the Amazons, daughter of Marpesia and sister of Orithyia and Melanippe. The name means ' horse-releaser' in Greek.

Hippothoe – One of the band of twelve Amazons to accompany Hippolyta to Troy. Attested Amazon name (in Greek); means 'swift horse'.

Idaeus – Trojan herald of Priam.

*Ioxeia – Amazon healer and councillor. Attested Amazon name (in Greek).

Iphimedon – Son of Eurystheus, king of Tiryns, and brother of Admete; the names of Eurystheus' sons are attested in Apollodorus.

*Iphito – Amazon councillor. Attested Scythian name.

Iris – Messenger goddess for Hera and goddess of the rainbow; daughter of the sea god Thaumas and the nymph Electra.

*Laodamas – Greek priest-healer. Attested Greek name.

Lycus – King of Mysia, at whose court (according to Apollodorus) Hercules stopped on his way to the war-belt of Hippolyta.

*Lysippe – Daughter of Admete and Proetus. Attested Amazon name (in Greek); it means 'horse-releaser', the same as 'Hippolyta'.

Machaon – Healer of the Greeks in the Trojan War.

Marpesia – Mother of Hippolyta, Melanippe and Orithyia. The name is taken from one of the early Amazon queens, given in Justin; her daughters are traditionally Orithyia and Antiope.

Melanchlaeni – *see* Glossary of Places s.v. **Melanchlaeni, Land of the**

Melanippe – Sister of Hippolyta. The name means 'black horse' in Greek.

Melpomene – Muse of tragedy.

Menelaus – Lord of Sparta and brother of King Agamemnon of Mycenae. Menelaus was originally married to Helen before she left for Troy with Paris, and sails back to Sparta with Helen after the capture of Troy.

Mentor – Son of Eurystheus, king of Tiryns, and brother of Admete; the names of Eurystheus' sons are attested in Apollodorus.

Muses, the – The nine goddesses of poetry and song, daughters of Zeus and the goddess Memory.

Nestor – A Greek noble and lord of Pylos.

Odysseus – Lord of Ithaca and husband of Penelope, known for his cunning. He discovers Achilles hiding on the island of Skyros and persuades him to fight in the Trojan War.

Orithyia – Sister of Hippolyta.

Panasagoras – Son of Sagylus and leader of the Saka tribes in alliance with Melanippe; the name is given in Diodorus and Justin.

Paris – A son of King Priam and Queen Hecuba, Paris was chosen by Zeus to judge the beauty contest over the golden apple. He was sent soon after on the embassy to Lord Menelaus of Sparta, along with his elder brother, Hector, where he stole Menelaus' wife Helen and took her back to Troy with him.

Perimedes – Son of Eurystheus, king of Tiryns, and brother of Admete; the names of Eurystheus' sons are attested in Apollodorus.

*Perses – Brother of Sthenelus of Paros. Companion of Hercules on the voyage for the war-belt of Hippolyta. Although Perses is not listed among the companions of Hercules, he was reputedly (according to Herodotus and Apollodorus) the founder of the Persians.

Podalirius – Healer of the Greeks in the Trojan War.

Polemusa – Daughter of Toxis; one of the band of twelve Amazons to accompany Hippolyta to Troy. Attested Amazon name (in Greek); means 'warlike'.

Polyhymnia – Muse of hymns.

Poseidon – God of the ocean and brother of Zeus.

Priam – The king of Troy, husband of Hecuba and father of Hector, Deiphobus, Aeneas, Paris, Troilus and Cassandra.

*Proetus – Husband of Admete; the name is taken from the legendary king of Tiryns.

Pythia – The oracle of Delphi.

Royal Scythians, the – *see* Glossary of Places s.v. **Royal Scythians, Land of the**

Sagylus – Father of Panasagoras, who leads the Saka tribes in alliance with Melanippe; the name is given in Diodorus and Justin.

Saka, the – *see* Glossary of Places s.v. **Saka, Land of the**

Sarmatians, the – *see* Glossary of Places s.v. **Sarmatia**

Scythians, the – *see* Glossary of Places s.v. **Scythia**

*Sitalkes – Amazon councillor. Attested Scythian name (Herodotus).

Skoloti, the – *see* Glossary of Places s.v. **Skoloti, Land of the**

Solois – Brother of Thoas and Euneos of Athens. Companion of Hercules on the voyage for the war-belt of Hippolyta.

Sthenelus – Brother of Perses of Paros. Companion of Hercules on the voyage for the war-belt of Hippolyta.

Tabiti – Scythian goddess of fire (equivalent to Greek *Hestia*), given in Herodotus.

Talthybius – One of the heralds of King Agamemnon.

Tar – Scythian god of storms and war (equivalent to Greek *Zeus, Ares*), given in Herodotus.

*Telemus** – Son of Aeacus of Salamis. Companion of Hercules on the voyage for the war-belt of Hippolyta (name adjusted from the Greek Telamon).

Terpsichore – Muse of dance.

*Teuspa** – Husband of Melanippe. Attested Scythian name.

Thalia – Muse of comedy.

*Theia** – Cousin and handmaid of Theseus.

Thermodosa – One of the band of twelve Amazons to accompany Hippolyta to Troy. Attested Amazon name (in Greek).

Theseus – Son of Aegeus and king of Athens; companion of Hercules on the voyage for the war-belt of Hippolyta. One of the Argonauts; also famous for defeating the Minotaur in Crete with the help of Ariadne.

Thoas – Brother of Solois and Euneos of Athens. Companion of Hercules on the voyage for the war-belt of Hippolyta.

*Thraso** – Amazon councillor. Attested Amazon name (in Greek).

*Timiades – Son of Pheidon of Argos. Companion of Hercules on the voyage for the war-belt of Hippolyta.

*Toxis – Amazon warrior. Attested Amazon name (in Greek).

Urania – Muse of astronomy.

*Xanthippe – Amazon warrior. Attested Amazon name (in Greek); means 'pale horse'.

Zeus – King of the gods, Zeus is the god of thunder and husband of Hera.

Glossary of Places

Aegean (Sea), the – The part of the Mediterranean Sea that separates the mainland of Greece from what is now the mainland of Turkey.

Anatolia – The region later known as Asia Minor, encompassing all of modern Turkey and some of modern Syria and Iraq, bordered on the west by the Aegean Sea and to the east by the Euphrates river, to the north by the Black Sea and to the south by the Mediterranean. It was peopled in the thirteenth century BCE (late Bronze Age) by a number of different groups, from the Masians and Kaskaeans in the north to the vast Hittite Empire that spread across the Anatolian Plateau, to the Trojans, Mysians, Maeonians and Lycians on the western and south-western coast of the Aegean.

Argolid, the – The area around the ancient city of Argos.

Argos – A city state on the north-east of the Peloponnese in Greece, ruled by Diomedes. The ruins of Argos can still be visited today.

Athens – The major city of Attica, a city state on the Attic peninsula; settled in the Bronze Age and legendary home of Theseus, but not the centre of democracy until the fifth century BCE.

Attica – The area around the ancient city of Athens.

Borysthenes, the – The ancient Greek name for the modern Dnieper river (Scythian: *Danu Apara*), which flows through Russia, Belarus and Ukraine into the Black Sea; *see also* **Danu Apara**

Bosphorus, the – The strait lying between the Propontis and the Black Sea, separating the kingdom of Thrace to the west and Anatolia to the east.

Carpathian Mountains, the – A range of mountains crossing central and eastern Europe.

Caucasus Mountains, the – The great mountain system that spans the Black Sea and the Caspian Sea.

Crete – The largest of the Greek islands and home to a flourishing Bronze Age Greek culture, most famously at Knossos (the site of which was excavated by Sir Arthur Evans; impressive, if vastly reconstructed, ruins can still be visited today). Crete was also said to be the location of the wedding of Zeus and Hera, where the gift of the golden apples was given by Earth.

Danastris, the – The Scythian name for the modern Dniester river (Greek: *Tyras*), which flows through Ukraine and Moldova into the Black Sea; the name possibly means 'near river' in Scythian.

Danu Apara – The Scythian name for the modern Dnieper river (Greek: *Borysthenes*), which flows through Russia, Belarus and Ukraine into the Black Sea; the name possibly means 'far river' in Scythian. *See also* **Borysthenes**

Delphi – Said by the Greeks to be the 'belly button of the world' and the home of the oracle, who was thought to relay the words of Apollo to mortals, Delphi is still an imposing and beautiful site.

Egypt – One of the most powerful ancient civilizations of the Mediterranean, builders of the famous Pyramids and a key player in Bronze Age politics and trade, the Egyptian pharaohs exported grain, paper, gold and linen around the Mediterranean.

Garden of the Hesperides, the – Mythical garden in which the golden apples, a wedding gift to Zeus and Hera, were guarded by the Hesperides. Two different traditions in antiquity place them either in the far west of the Greek world, around Libya (Pliny, Virgil, Pomponius Mela), or to the far north beyond the Hyperboreans (Aeschylus, Apollodorus), which is the tradition I have followed.

Greece – Homeland of the Greeks, comprising the city states of Argos, Ithaca, Mycenae, Phthia, Pylos and Sparta, among others.

Hades – Both the god of the Underworld and the name of the Underworld itself, where the ancients believed that the spirits of the dead went to spend eternity. It was reached by crossing the river Styx in a boat ferried by a man called Charon. There were several different parts to the Underworld:

Tartarus, where the wicked were punished, the Elysian Fields, where the heroes went, and the Isles of the Blessed, the ultimate destination and eternal paradise.

Hellespont, the – The narrow strait opposite the ancient city of Troy, now called the Dardanelles.

Hialea – Location of an ancient Scythian tribe (Greek: *Hylaea*), probably on the modern Crimean peninsula.

Hittites, Land of the – One of the largest empires of the Bronze Age, the Hittite Empire reached its zenith in the mid-fourteenth century BCE. It endured until its sudden collapse around 1200 BCE, about the same time as the destruction of the Bronze Age kingdoms in Greece and the fall of Troy. Its capital was at Ḫattuša (modern Boğazköy in Turkey).

Hylaea – Location of an ancient Scythian tribe (Scythian: *Hialea*), probably on the modern Crimean peninsula.

Hyperborea – Mythical land at the extreme far north of the world, beyond the home of the north wind in the Rhipaean Mountains; blessed with eternal spring, fertile land, and sacred to Apollo.

Ida, Mount – The largest mountain on the Trojan plain and the home of the gods.

Ithaca – A rocky island to the west of mainland Greece ruled by Odysseus.

Maeotis, Lake – The ancient Greek name for the modern Sea of Azov (Scythian: *Temarunda*), at the far north-east of the Black Sea. *See also* **Temarunda**

Melanchlaeni, Land of the – An ancient Scythian tribe located by Herodotus north of the Royal Scythians (Scyth. *Skoloti*); the name means 'black cloaks' in Greek.

Mycenae – A city in the Peloponnese, one of the largest in the ancient Greek Bronze Age world. It was ruled by King Agamemnon and was rediscovered by Heinrich Schliemann in 1876. The ruins of the impressive palace can be seen today. Mycenae was famous for its gold: Homer calls it 'rich in gold'.

Mysia – A region to the east of the Troad.

Ocean – The ancient Greeks believed that the ocean encircled the whole world like a river around a flat disc of land. The sun and moon were thought to rise and set from the waters of the ocean.

Olympus, Mount – A mountain in northern Greece and the home of the Olympian gods.

Parnassus, Mount – The mountain above Delphi, said to be home of the Muses.

Phthia – A city state in the north of Greece, in the southernmost part of Thessaly, and home to Peleus and Achilles.

Pnyx, the – A hill to the west of the Acropolis in Athens, later used as the assembly-place during Athenian democracy.

Propontis, the – The ancient Greek name for the Sea of Marmara, the inland sea that connects the Aegean to the west and the Black Sea to the east. The strait to its south-western end was called the Hellespont (modern Dardanelles), and to the north-east, the Bosphorus.

Glossary of Places

Pterophoros – Mentioned in Pliny and Herodotus as a dark land of endless snowfall and cold winds to the far north; the name means 'wing-bearing' or 'feather-bearing' in Greek.

Pylos – The ancient kingdom of Nestor in the south-west of the Peloponnese; impressive ruins of a Bronze Age palace were discovered nearby, at modern Ano Englianos, and you can still visit them today.

Rhipaean Mountains – Mythical mountains to the far north, beyond the land of Pterophoros and bordering the south of Hyperborea; home of the north wind, which gives them their name, from the Greek *rhipai*, 'hurricanes'.

Royal Scythians, Land of the – An ancient Scythian tribe located by Herodotus east of the modern Molochna river, extending to the river Don (Greek: *Tanais*; Scythian: *Silis*), said to be the largest and bravest of the Scythian tribes. *See also* **Skoloti, Land of the**

Saka, Land of the – Known in Greek as Scythia, a large portion of central Eurasia stretching east over the Black Sea from Ukraine into Russia, occupied in antiquity by many different nomadic tribes. The name *Saka* is the later Persian word, which is adopted here. *See also* **Scythia**

Sarmatia – An ancient nomadic tribe closely related to the Scythians, placed in various locations; I follow Strabo in locating them north of the Scythians.

Scythia – A large portion of central Eurasia stretching east over the Black Sea from Ukraine into Russia, occupied in antiquity by many different nomadic tribes. *See also* **Saka, Land of the**

Silis, the – The Scythian name for the modern Don river (Greek: *Tanais*), which flows through Russia into the Sea of Azov; its Scythian name is given in Pliny. *See also* **Tanais, the**

Skoloti, Land of the – An ancient Scythian tribe located by Herodotus east of the modern Molochna river, extending to the Don river (Greek: *Tanais*; Scythian: *Silis*), said to be the largest and bravest of the Scythian tribes. The name comes from Herodotus, who says that this is what the Royal Scythians called themselves. *See also* **Royal Scythians, Land of the**

Skyros – A Greek island in the centre of the Aegean, where Achilles' mother Thetis was said to have attempted to hide him from the Trojan War.

Sparta – A city in the south of Greece ruled by Tyndareus, father of Helen of Sparta (later Helen of Troy).

Styx, the – The river that formed the boundary between Earth and the Underworld; to enter the Underworld the ferryman Charon had to be paid to take the dead across. It was seen as sacred by the gods: they would often swear oaths by the Styx. Its waters were thought to confer immortality, and it is into the Styx that Thetis dips her son Achilles in the hope of making him immortal.

Tanais, the – The Greek name for the modern Don river (Scythian: *Silis*), which flows through Russia into the Sea of Azov; its Scythian name is given in Pliny. *See also* **Silis, the**

Temarunda – The Scythian name for the modern Sea of Azov (Greek: *Lake Maeotis*), at the far north-east of the

Black Sea. The Scythian name, meaning 'mother of the sea', is given in Pliny. *See also* **Maeotis, Lake**

Thebes – A city of Boeotia, north of Athens, where Alcmene and Amphitryon (parents of Hercules) took refuge.

Thessaly – A large region to the north of Greece, incorporating Mount Olympus, Mount Ossa and Mount Pelion, as well as the cities of Pagasae and Iolcos.

Thrace – The mountainous region to the north of Thessaly in Greece.

Tiryns – The city of Eurystheus in the Argolid; Tiryns has one of the best-preserved Bronze Age palaces, which can still be visited today, and archaeological artefacts including the stone throne of Tiryns' king can be seen in the National Archaeological Museum of Athens.

Troy – The ancient city of King Priam, which was besieged by the Greek forces of King Agamemnon around the twelfth century BCE. It was rediscovered by Heinrich Schliemann in 1871 on the hill of Hisarlık in north-western Turkey. Its ruins can be visited today.

Underworld, the – Also called Hades, this was where the ancients believed that the spirits of the dead went to spend eternity. It was reached by crossing the river Styx in a boat ferried by Charon. There were several different parts to the Underworld: Tartarus, where the wicked were punished, the Elysian Fields, where the heroes went, and the Isles of the Blessed, the eternal paradise.

Glossary of Scythian Terms

halinda	a type of wild cabbage, which is said to grow along the banks of the Tanais (modern Don, Scythian *Silis*) River
ippa	horse
koumiss	a fermented drink of mare's milk
Oiorpata	Amazon; man-slayer/man-lord
paralati	common people, non-warriors (here extended to mean 'foreigner')
pelamys	a fish (probably a kind of tuna) found at the mouth of the Borysthenes (modern Dnieper, Scythian *Danu Apara*) River, according to Herodotus
pelta	sickle-shape shield
sagaris	battle-axe
Saka	Scythian(s)
tamga	sign, seal
uran	battle-cry